BACK TO REALITY

MARK STAY
MARK OLIVER

THE BESTSELLER EXPERIMENT

CONTENTS

Back to Reality: A Novel
by Mark Stay & Mark Oliver

"*Back to Reality* is everything the world loves about British Comedy. For those who wished Simon Pegg wrote novels, you now have the Two Marks. Destined for the big screen."
Shannon Mayer, USA Today bestselling author

"Like if Nick Hornby wrote a time travel, body swap adventure!"
Mimi Strong, New York Times bestselling author

"I LOVE IT! Brilliant stuff - engaging, pacy, smart and funny. It's *Back to the Future* meets *Freaky Friday*."
Lucy Vine, author of Hot Mess

"Like a book version of *Hot Tub Time Machine* with fabulous female characters and great music, *Back to Reality* keeps you hooked to the very last note."
Kate Harrison, author of the bestselling 5:2 books

"Written with an authentic touch and plenty of good humour, this is a tough book to put down."
Mark Dawson, USA Today bestselling author of the John Milton series

"I laughed, I cried, I hummed along... *Back to Reality* crackles with all the addictive energy of a pop hit, and the heart of a soul classic. Feel-good fantasy with a pulsing beat of sharply observed urban reality!"
Samantha King, author of The Choice

"If you love time travel and rock and roll, you'll love this book!"
Julie Cohen, author of *Together* and the Richard & Judy Book-club title *Dear Thing*

"*Sliding Doors* meets *Back to the Future* in a story to make you sing with joy." **Karen Ball, Speckled Pen**

"What a magnificent book! Loved every page. Beautifully written..."
Callan McAuliffe, actor *The Walking Dead*

For Jenni & Claire

PROLOGUE: I DROVE ALL NIGHT

Yohanna had a choice. Go east to Vegas, or north to Big Sur.

She had to get away. She needed time and space to clear her mind. Time to think. Space to take in the insanity of a life she'd dreamed of since she was a child, singing along to Top of the Pops with a hairbrush microphone.

There was nothing but a whole lot of desert between L.A. and Vegas, but she had always wanted to see where the Pacific met the rocks of Big Sur, so she chose north.

The vintage double-decker bus was designed for sightseeing around London, not toying with winding bends around two hundred foot drops. She gripped the over-sized steering wheel, turning it with all her might. The bus lurched as the front tyre teetered like a tightrope walker along the cliff edge of the Pacific Coast Highway.

The bus had been Lawrie's idea. A publicity stunt. 'You want to be remembered forever, darlin'? Well, this big Red Riding Hood is about to announce to the world that you've arrived.'

He had it on loan from Rand, who had more money than he knew what to do with, and had started collecting buses as a hobby. She hadn't asked why. Out here, stuff like this was normal.

L.A., recording studios, top session musicians, gigs at the Troubadour, Hollywood stars who collect buses. This was Yohanna's new normal, and it had arrived just a little too fast for her liking.

The back of the bus screeched and whipped like a snake as she pushed harder on the stiff brake pedal.

After tomorrow, the press conference, the launch, her life would never be the same.

All she needed was a moment to take it all in and be sure that this was what she really wanted. Lawrie had joked how these old buses had no keys, and would be so easy to steal. He had even showed her how to start the thing, so when the anxiety dreams woke her, it seemed only natural to jump in and drive.

The cell phone rattling about in the footwell beeped again. The fifth call in as many minutes. She knew who it was without having to look at it. She glanced in the rear view mirror, looking for flashing lights, wondering if he would set the cops on her. Instead, she caught sight of her own eyes, wide with fright.

The road took a sharp right and the bus careened forwards, the front wheel parting ways with the tarmac, sliding on the loose gravel by the side of the road. The double-decker hurtled over the edge of the cliff.

Okay, this wasn't part of the plan.

The end-of-life slow motion kicked in, just like her teenage dreams of death.

Ronnie's voice came to her, 'Relax. Breathe deeply. You can do this better than anyone I know. Just let it happen.'

As the bus began to plummet headfirst towards the jagged rocks, Yohanna let go of the steering wheel.

'Oh, poppet, stop being so silly.' Another voice. One she hadn't heard for over twenty years until tonight's bad dream. 'Time to let go.'

Yohanna closed her eyes, rested her hands on her knees and with just one deep breath she connected to the familiar inner silence. A feeling of serenity washed over her. Yohanna's mind disconnected from the moment, a heartbeat before the bright red bus became a bright red fireball.

Yohanna had a choice. She chose to live.

EMPTY ORCHESTRA

Jo was only on her second gin, but it made ignoring her
husband so much easier.

Not that he was here, of course - he was at home. But
today, of all days, Joanna Adams just wanted to forget who
she was, and so she agreed to celebrate payday with her work friends
and a few drinks.

Her phone buzzed. Nick.

Can't get a table. Overbooked. Not my fault. How about I cook?

SHE TURNED the phone face down and sipped her gin.

Jo and her colleagues in Mayer Marketing's accounts department
had descended on Friends - a past-its-prime bar tucked down a side
alley near London Bridge. Above the door was a trademark-
infringing logo of the old TV show in flaky paint. And it was karaoke
night.

The place was buzzing and Jo was hemmed in by a dozen of her colleagues in a corner booth, while on the makeshift stage a tormented soul was murdering Neil Diamond's *Sweet Caroline.*

'Bloody hell, that's Pete,' Jo said, astonished to find the normally timid man from work bestriding the stage in an open shirt, his lips pursed against the microphone like a Koi carp gasping for bread, as he turned Neil Diamond's celebration of love into a dirge of bitterness and regret.

'So good, so good, so good,' he wailed, throwing his arms to the ceiling.

'Wank it off, mate!' came a cry from the crowd. This opinion was a popular one, buoyed by a wave of cheers.

'His wife left him,' Michela, the hub of all office gossip, told Jo as Pete ended the song to a smattering of sympathetic applause, drowned out by unsympathetic boos. Pete raised a defiant middle finger to the crowd, then brought it down on the karaoke touch-screen's replay button, starting the song again and generating more jeering than Prime Minister's Questions.

'Left him a few weeks ago for a Junior Doctor. Apparently, she did a spreadsheet with all the pros and cons of living with Pete or this doctor, and poor Pete lost out because of his credit rating and pension prospects.'

'Ooh, that's cold.'

'Sweeeeeeeeet Caroliiiiiine!' Pete howled from the stage.

'She was called Caroline,' Michela whispered, like this was some kind of revelation.

'Course she was.'

Jo's phone vibrated on the table. Another text from Nick. The tenth in an hour by her reckoning. She scooped up the phone, tucked it away in her bag, and took another sip of gin and tonic to help numb her guilt.

'*Grease* medley next? You and me?' Michela nudged Jo's elbow.

'Me? Karaoke?' Jo shook her head. 'No. No way.'

'Oh, c'mon, it'll be a laugh,' Michela said.

'No, it'll be excruciating,' Jo said. 'Long story short, I have a genuine fear of singing.'

'Is that a thing?'

'It is for me.'

'C'mon, just one.'

'Not gonna happen.'

'You can't be any worse than Pete,' Michela said, as their colleague ripped off his shirt and tossed it into the crowd. He was rubbing his hands across his belly as he wailed the chorus. 'We'll sound like Pavarotti after him. C'mon, just one?'

'Michela, no,' Jo said. 'Why would anyone put themselves through that? It's the worst kind of humiliation.'

'If you haven't done it, how would you know? Eh? Eh?' Michela grinned at her own cleverness.

'I *have* done it.' Jo shivered at the memory. 'And I have no intention of repeating the experience, thank you very much. Oh, look, they're all filming him. Poor Pete's going to be a bloody Facebook meme. Someone should stop him.'

One of the bar staff shuffled closer to Pete with her palms facing forward, like a zookeeper approaching a dangerous animal.

'Come on, mate,' she said. 'Let someone else have a go, eh?'

'SO GOOD!' Pete screeched at the woman, who backed away rapidly, falling back into the braying crowd.

'He's gonna get thumped in a minute,' Jo said.

'Your phone's ringing.' Michela nodded to Jo's bag, where the silent phone glowed with an incoming call.

Jo zipped the bag shut. 'Isn't anyone going to help him?'

'Why?' Michela asked. 'He won't remember any of this anyway. Let him get it out of his system.'

Someone threw a can and it rebounded off Pete's head. He staggered back, but continued regardless.

'He's really going to get hurt,' Jo said, but Michela was busy emptying the remains of a wine bottle into her glass.

Pete was crying now, his body shaking with sobs as he sang. Jo looked at her colleagues. Those who weren't wallowing in his humiliation were either looking at their phones or engaging in inebriated conversation.

'Sod it.' Jo necked the rest of her gin and got to her feet, using the table to steady herself. 'Whoa.'

'You all right?' Michela looked up from her brimming wine glass.

'I may be just a teeny bit tipsy.' Jo's head felt light, and the room banked at an angle like a ship lurching in rough seas. 'Look after my bag, will you? I'm going to reel him in.'

'You're what?' Michela asked, but Jo clambered over her colleagues, moving away from their table, doing her best to look as upright and un-drunk as possible. 'Jo?'

Jo weaved her way through the crowd and positioned herself in the front of the little stage in Pete's line of sight. She remained firmly on the pub floor.

'Pete, come on, mate. Enough's enough.'

Pete was singing into empty space. His eyes were bloodshot, glistening, and his lips were trembling. Jo waved and hopped, but either he was ignoring her, or was so out of it that he didn't see her.

She would have to get on the stage.

It wasn't even a stage. Just a black wooden box edged and dotted with white tape. It wasn't particularly high, so Jo told herself it was just a bit of wood, took a breath and stepped up.

It felt a lot higher up once she was on it, and she was greeted by a few appreciative whoops and whistles.

Jo was on a stage. She was actually on a stage. She felt an unexpected rush of adrenaline course through her body.

People had expectations of anyone who got on a stage. They wanted to be entertained. She was on a stage, yes, but she told herself that in just a few seconds she would be off again.

Pete gripped the mic like an Olympic relay baton as he sang. Jo gently placed her hand around his, trying to move the mic away from his mouth.

'Pete? Can I...?'

'No,' he pouted, shaking his head like a toddler refusing broccoli. 'No, no, no!'

Jo smiled and leaned towards the mic, miming along with his singing. This reassured Pete that she wasn't trying to steal the mic from him, and he resumed caterwauling. Mercifully, the song soon came to an end, and Jo was able to take the mic from his grip.

'You were brilliant,' Jo said without hesitation. 'Bloody brilliant. We were all in tears. Seriously. Let's hear it for Pete, everyone.'

Jo called to the crowd with pleading eyes that said, *If we give this poor sod a round of applause he might just leave the stage.* Some of them took the cue and began cheering. It was fairly pathetic, but enough to bring a smile to Pete's face, and he finally teetered off the stage.

That got a bigger cheer.

Jo was about to follow Pete off the stage, when a man in the crowd yelled, 'Go on, love, you can't be any worse than him!' generating a ripple of laughter.

'No. No way,' Jo declared through the PA. 'There is no way on God's green earth I'm singing.' This drew boos, then cheers, then rhythmic clapping from the masses. If she left the stage there was a chance Pete might clamber back on again. They wanted her to sing.

The cheering and the applause triggered something in Jo. A shiver of excitement rippled through her as she realised she was standing on a stage with a microphone for the first time in over twenty years.

Her mind flashed back to the last time, and the horror and humiliation. It wasn't karaoke then. It was the moment she'd been working towards all her life. The buzz of anticipation. Looking out into the crowd, the many eyes of the major labels staring back at her. The sound of the song starting. That first line going over and over in her head. Her mouth opening, and then... nothing. No words. Panic. Tears. Throwing the microphone down and fleeing offstage, never to return.

Until now.

Another song began to play, bringing Jo back to reality. It was the one Pete had cued-up next. Much slower. A restrained upright bass, a gentle guitar and piano intertwining, a trilling ride cymbal. Jo knew this one. More than that, she *loved* this one. The Roberta Flack song *The First Time Ever I Saw Your Face.*

As the karaoke display finished the countdown from the intro into the first verse, Jo, invigorated by the gin coursing through her veins, thought *What the hell*, took a breath, and sang.

The song started quietly, and it took her a moment to recall the phrasing. She found the notes easily and just let it happen. People in the pub returned to their drinks and chatter, relieved that Pete's reign of terror was over. Jo closed her eyes and continued to sing about the sun rising in someone else's eyes, and the moon and the stars being gifts, the Earth moving in her hand, and so on.

It wasn't long before something else happened. It began in her belly, flushed through her heart, and pushed against her eyes, forcing little tears to come out. It was a moment of pure, blissful rapture, and Jo remembered why she loved singing. It filled her with joy. A joy she hadn't realised she'd missed. It was like discovering a lost piece to a puzzle, and now everything could finally click into place. As her voice soared she revelled in the feeling, bringing the song to its tender conclusion.

Jo smiled and opened her eyes.

To find everyone in the bar staring at her in astonishment with open mouths.

Oh god, was it that bad? she thought, and the dread of public humiliation consumed her. *Here we go again.*

Jo was about to apologise when the entire room got to its feet, applauding, whooping and punching the air. The noise hit her like a blast wave. Across the bar, she could see Michela, Pete, and the others from work bouncing like pogo punks, pausing only to tell everyone around them they knew the woman on stage, they were best friends, and they always knew she was special.

'Thank you very much,' Jo said into the mic, taking a little bow.

'More!' people began to shout. The synchronised clapping returned, and before long people were stomping on the bar's wooden floor in unison.

'Oh, crikey, okay.' Jo turned to the karaoke machine and began tapping on the touchscreen. 'Er, maybe something a little more upbeat, eh?'

Most people who dare to venture on a karaoke night with work colleagues will recognise that sinking feeling, when the most tone deaf one in the group grabs the microphone and refuses to let go, singing with misguided enthusiasm, completely unaware of their bum notes. And all this after spending the first half of the night saying they would *never* join in. A lucky few might know that pleasant feeling when they discover a colleague actually has a good set of pipes and can hold a tune.

Few, however, would understand what it was like that evening when Joanna Adams let rip in the Friends bar near London Bridge. She continued with a couple of Atlantic soul classics, belting out *I Never Loved A Man (The Way I Loved You)* as if Aretha was in the room, then she went down the singer-songwriter route, serving them a version of Carole King's *(You Make Me Feel Like) A Natural Woman* that made grown men weep. No one in the bar who was there to witness this magic would be foolhardy enough to step onto that stage and follow her. The night was entirely hers.

Jo sang and sang, people danced, laughed, and sang along. Some bought her drinks, keeping that fire in her belly well stoked. It should have been terrifying, but she was loving every second, riding high on the cheers of the crowd. As she finished a rousing rendition of Adele's *Rolling In The Deep* the call for last orders came. Jo was well aware that all performers should know when to stop, leaving their audience wanting more.

'Thanks everyone, you've been so lovely. That's it, I'm knackered, good night.'

Now the boos came, but they were good natured. These people couldn't get enough of her.

'No, seriously,' Jo said, gesturing at the bar staff. 'These people have homes to go to, even if you reprobates don't.'

No one cared. The cheers for more kept coming, and it reminded Jo of trips to the park when her daughter Ellie was a toddler. Telling her, 'We're going home now,' would only ever result in demands for more time. Saying she could have one more go on the swing, *then* we're heading home always worked, so Jo relented to the crowd's demands.

'Okay, okay, one more, and that's it. Understood?' Jo said, waiting expectantly for a response.

'Yes, Mum!' someone called back, getting a laugh.

'Good enough,' Jo said, tapping the touchscreen for the final song.

As the guitar arpeggio of the new song began to play there was a discernible intake of breath throughout the room. The kind of sceptical whistle beloved of plumbers confronted with what will surely be an expensive, tricky, if not downright impossible, job.

Stairway To Heaven was a regular undoer of karaoke singers. Those foolhardy enough to attempt this classic always forgot that, despite the soft start, it ends with Robert Plant screaming with fervent passion to Valhalla about shadows taller than souls, ladies who shine white light and other such eldritch nonsense, like it was gospel truth. There are few mortals walking the Earth who can pull that off with any conviction.

Jo handled the opening beautifully, sang about bustles in hedgerows with a straight face, played some sterling air guitar in the solo, and tackled the climactic verses like a pro, her voice finding that fine line between passion and heavy metal screeching. There wasn't a single person present who didn't believe her urgent request that they be a rock and not to roll, whatever that meant.

Despite the protests from the bar staff about fire regulations, many of the patrons were holding the decorative table candles aloft as she finished, and the room exploded in thunderous applause.

And then it was over.

Jo was mobbed. People rushed the stage demanding selfies and autographs on beer mats. A hand grabbed her wrist and she squealed, but she was relieved to see it was Michela who split the crowd by bellowing, 'That's enough. Make a hole. Move it!' as she shoved them aside and bustled Jo behind the bar, through the kitchen and out the back door.

They stumbled into a back alley, the brisk night air littered with the incessant ding-a-ling of the loitering rickshaw taxi bikes. Jo found herself shaking with pent-up adrenaline, and wondering what the hell had just happened. On stage, she'd been in complete control, but now the world began to swim again, her mind became fuzzy, and it took her a moment to realise that Michela was talking to her.

'Whassat?' Jo replied, with a little more of a slur than she would have liked. 'I should prolly go home. It's my birthday and Nick'll be going mental.'

Michela, whose astonishment levels were already peaking in the red, now looked like she was going to spontaneously combust.

'It's your *what?*'

FORTY-TWO

'You. Get on, now.' Michela manoeuvred Jo towards a rickshaw bike decorated with blinking fairy lights. Jo could see someone helping a grinning Pete into a black cab, and the rest of her colleagues were waving as they headed home.

'Is't time a go home?' she asked, again mildly amused that her words were stumbling over one another. She was about to apologise and point out she couldn't possibly be that pissed, when she tumbled forward into the seat of the rickshaw cab with all the grace of a crash test dummy. Singing had kept the drunkenness at bay, and now it was back with a vengeance.

'You all right, love?' the rickshaw driver asked. Jo hated being called 'love' by complete strangers, especially by handsome young men in short denim shorts, with well-toned legs and gym-nurtured biceps. Those she definitely hated the most. So why was she looking at him for so long? Michela's face popped in, blocking the view.

'London Bridge station, and step on it,' she ordered the driver, letting her eyes linger on the virile young man.

'Not to do myself out of a fare, ladies, but it's, like, two minutes that way.' He nodded up the street.

'Just go round Borough Market a few times will you?' she told him. 'We need to talk.'

'Whatever you say, love.' He flashed Michela a dazzling smile, and she smirked back at him.

As they began juddering down the cobbled streets, Michela managed to pull her eyes off the driver and turned to her friend with a look of astonishment on her face. 'When were you going to tell me it was your birthday? And what the bloody hell happened back there? I didn't know you could sing. And I certainly didn't know you could sing like *that*.'

'Too many questions.' Jo winced.

'Singing,' Michela said. 'Start with the singing. Fear of singing, my arse.'

'Yeah, s'been a while.' Jo shrugged. 'And the gin kinda helped.' A loud and rare combination of a hiccup-belch had the driver turning, his face concerned for the back of his white shirt.

'We should get you on The Voice or something. That was incredible.'

'Oh Lordy, no, no, no.' Jo shook her head far too many times, making it spin. 'No way. No reality TV meat factory, thank you. Can't stand it. Fifteen mins of fame, followed by a lifetime opening supermarkets. And the judging. I can't be doing with the judging.'

'But you should be famous,' Michela declared. 'Your voice... I've never heard anything like it.'

Jo dismissed her with a wave. 'I'm just lucky. My music teacher told me I had perfect pitch.'

'It's a gift. You should use it.'

'Well, I did sing a bit when I was younger. Professionally, y'know? I wrote songs, too.'

'Whoa, back up. You sang professionally? When? Where? I want all the details.'

'Oh, there's nothing to tell,' Jo said.

'You should be on a way bigger stage than a flipping karaoke bar.'

'Glastonbury.' Jo's eyes glistened as she spoke. 'That was the dream. Greatest music festival in the world. The Pyramid Stage.

Thousands of fans singing along. Music that moves people. That's all I wanted. Watched it on TV whenever it was on. It was always my secret dream to sing at Glastonbury.'

'Stuck in a muddy field in the pissing rain with a bunch of druggies?'

Jo started ticking off names on her fingers. 'Adele, Beyoncé, Bowie, U2, Neil Young, the Stones, Springsteen, Who, McCartney, Johnny Cash, The Bee Gees, Tony Bennett, the Dalai Lama, the Wombles and even Dolly bloody Parton have played Glastonbury. It's not all Radiohead going blinkity-bonk, y'know. It's three days on a different planet where anyone can be whoever they want to be.'

'Did you ever go?' Michela asked.

'No, I wish. Hundred and fifty thousand tickets and they always sell out in seconds. Could never afford it then and don't have the time now,' Jo said. 'Bloody hate camping and getting wet, too - so why bother? Don't tell anyone, please.' Jo took Michela's hand. 'No one at work knows. Promise me.'

'I promise.'

'Is that a real promise, or a Michela promise?'

'You hurt me, girl,' Michela said in mock offence. 'I swear. I won't tell anyone, but why not?'

'It's a stupid dream,' Jo said. 'And whenever I think of it, I feel like a complete bloody failure, so can we stop talking about it now? And can we please stop this bike thing?' Jo felt something stir in her intestines. 'There's a rather large chance that I might end up giving it a puke makeover.'

'Drink this.' Michela produced a bottle of Evian from her bag and thrust it into Jo's hand. She took a sip and was disappointed at first to discover that it really was just water, but it helped push down whatever was trying to rise up from inside her.

'Were you in a band?' Michela persisted. 'Did you ever record anything?'

'No.' Jo's voice dropped to a mumble as she allowed herself to be hypnotised by the rickshaw's fairy lights. They became softer, out of focus, and her mind drifted as the rickshaw gently rocked her. 'I made a choice,' she said, then whispered, 'And I chose her.'

'Who?' Michela asked. 'Who?'

Jo snorted and giggled, 'You sound like an owl.' Her head turned from the lights to Michela, who looked like an eager detective about to get a confession from a suspect. Even in Jo's fuzzy state, she realised she was saying too much. 'Doesn't matter,' she said. 'Forget I said anything. And let's be honest, it would've all gone tits-up anyway, so why bother?'

'Why bother? Your voice is amazing, Jo. You should—'

'Shhhh.' Jo pressed her finger up against Michela's lips, smudging her friend's lipstick. 'Whoopsie,' she said, trying to make good, but just smudging it all the more. 'You were right, it's a laugh, but now it's over, they've all gone home, they'll forget it by the morning. It means nothing. So, let's enjoy what happened, put it behind us, and never speak of this again. Taxi biker man,' she called to the denim-shorted driver. 'Pull over, please. Sorry, Michela, I need to walk this off.'

'Sure thing,' the rickshaw driver said, pulling up in front of a taxi rank, much to the annoyance of the onlooking licensed cab drivers. 'Fifteen quid, please.'

'One sec.' Michela raised a silencing hand to the driver. 'Jo, why didn't you tell us it was your birthday?'

Jo blew air through her lips, stopping short of blowing a raspberry. 'It's just another day. Can't be bothered.'

'Is it a biggie birthday? Forty? Is that why you're depressed?'

'Forty-two,' Jo said. 'Meaning of life and all that. And I'm not depressed. Birthdays are for kids, y'know? When I was a kid I loved birthdays. At fifteen I could get into the movies, at eighteen I was free, y'know? To do whatever I wanted. The whole world at my feet. Unlimited potential.'

'What did you do?'

Jo opened her mouth to answer. 'I... I don't know. Look, forget I said anything. I have to go home now to my family. They might even still be awake.' Jo swivelled round in her seat to negotiate the perilous journey from the rickshaw to the pavement, but Michela took her hand again.

'Sweetheart, I want to you to promise me two things: first, please consider using your gift. The world is a miserable place sometimes and your voice made all those people back there so happy. You must have seen that? Felt it?'

Jo rolled her eyes, 'Yeah, I'll... I'll think about it. And what was the second thing?'

Michela glanced at the rickshaw driver, 'I'm out of cash, so will you join me in a three-way with this fella so we can split the fare?'

HOME AGAIN

Jo negotiated the sticky gate and slippy path to her front door with relative ease, only once wavering off course and into the hydrangea bushes. When she actually made it to the door, slotting the key in the lock turned out to be a lot more challenging. Jo created a whole series of drunken etchings and divots on the front door around the lock before sliding the key in.

Only to find it was the wrong key and wouldn't turn.

'Buggery balls,' she muttered, jiggling the key to take it out. It was stuck firm. 'Okay, Jo. Come on, girl. You can do this.' Jo grasped the key in both hands, pressed a knee against the door, and pulled hard. The world spun around her as she fell and found herself lying flat on her back, looking up at the eaves and wondering when they had last been painted.

The door, miraculously, was open. And Nick stood there, silhouetted in a yellow glow, framed by the doorway.

Jo propped herself up on her elbows and smiled. 'Hello, sweetie,' she giggled. 'This is *exactly* what it looks like.'

'I've been texting you all night,' Nick hissed in a low whisper, folding his arms.

'Oh, that's adorable, thank you.' Jo tried to right herself and failed. 'I don't suppose you could help me up, could you?'

Nick hesitated. He actually bloody hesitated. The man who vowed to take her for better or worse took a moment to think about helping his wife off the ground. Jo made a mental note to file that away for future arguments, then began to wonder how much of tonight she would, in fact, remember at all.

Nick stepped out onto the path, glancing left and right to ensure No one was looking, before yanking on Jo's arms. She yelped as he hauled her to her feet, and she fell into his embrace. Jo gave him a smile, but still his eyes were elsewhere, scanning the street to ensure no one had seen them.

'Worried about the Net Curtain Nazis, Nicky dear?' Jo gave a sloppy grin, turned to face the rest of the terraced homes in their street and gave them all a sweeping one-finger salute. 'Screw 'em all,' she cried, before being hustled inside by Nick.

'Where the hell have you been?' he said, his voice returning to a standard angry volume now. 'I've been worried sick.'

Jo oh-so-casually sauntered along an uneven parabola from the hall into the living room, flopping onto the sofa to find a repeat of *Bake Off*, one of Nick's favourite shows, playing on the TV.

'I'm sorry,' she said, trying to look at her husband properly as the walls began to revolve like a carousel. 'The evening sort of got a bit amazing, and I had lots and lots of gin, and if it's any consolation I'm going to be paying for it big-time tomorrow.'

Jo's gaze fell on *Bake Off*'s Mary Berry, who was inspecting a fondant fancy on the TV. 'Oh no, can't do sugary treats tonight, Mary. Nick turn this off please, there's a love.'

'Why didn't you answer your phone?' Nick scooped up the remote and switched off the TV, looking like an oppressive father from the fifties in his cardigan and slippers. Nick was about eighteen months younger than Jo, but he had always been a bit of a young fogey, which had been charming when they were in their twenties. While Jo's other boyfriends wore torn jeans and plaid shirts in an attempt to look like Kurt Cobain, Nick preferred tweed jackets with leather patches on the elbows in a completely un-ironic way. He knew more about pensions than anyone rightly should before the age of thirty, and there was an honest-to-God period of about three months when he actually started smoking a pipe. Not a hookah, or a water pipe, but a proper wooden pipe and all the mucky goo that involved. This was back when Ellie was a toddler. Jo put an end to it when Ellie had started walking and was able to grab the abundance of brown, sticky pipe cleaners left on the dining room table, and tried to stick them up her nose.

Jo had known Nick since they were at college together, and he was very funny at first, and so smart and knowledgeable about the world and politics and ideas, that she completely fell for him. He used to ask questions as if he already knew the answers, and Jo would feel obliged to fill his thoughtful silences with her own half-baked philosophy, desperate to impress him. But now he spent much of his time looking baffled, as if he had walked into the wrong room, or even the wrong life. His laugh, which used to be an unaffected car crash of giggles and hoots that trailed away then returned when the humorous thought came back to him, had slowly devolved into a single, mirthless *HA!*, which he would hack like he had been shocked with a taser.

It would be their eighteenth anniversary in a few weeks. If Jo could keep things together tonight, that was. For all his faults, she still loved Nick and needed him around. He and Ellie were the glue keeping her life together. Why else would she endure such a godawful commute and tedious job, if not for them?

'I made you a special birthday dinner.' Nick gestured to the dinner table, currently bereft of any plates, cutlery or food. Jo must have looked confused, because he added, 'It's in the microwave. Your favourite. Spaghetti bolognese.'

'No, Nick, it's not my favourite,' she said, and decided to confess something she'd been meaning to tell him since he first cooked for her over twenty years ago. 'I only tell you that cos it's the one decent thing you can cook. And where are the flowers and candles, darling? If it's a birthday dinner, make an effort, just a little one.

'Think of what I get you for your birthday. Special dinner, cake, candles, proper Champagne, posh napkins and, if it's a significant birthday, a blowjob. Sorry, but your student-digs-spag-bol just won't cut it, babes.' Jo felt a pang of guilt as she saw a crestfallen look cross his face. Was it a pang? Or something bad stirring in her belly?

'I got you a cake,' Nick said, rushing to the kitchen.

Jo tried sitting up, felt her brain try to leak out of her ears, then flopped back down again as Nick returned with the confection on a plate.

'That's the cake?'

'Yes. What's wrong?'

'Darling, it's a Marks and Spencer's chocolate caterpillar cake.' She looked at the smiling face with its chocolate button eyes. 'It's a cake for children.'

'But we were at that party once and you said you liked them?'

'That was years ago. Ellie was a child. It was a children's party. And expressing delight at a fun cake does not necessarily mean I want one for my forty-second birthday, sweetheart.'

Jo released a wordless noise of anguish made up of decades of pent-up frustration. 'Nick, I know your heart is in the right place, but it's been an eventful day and I need some time to think. Also, I don't think I can get up from the sofa without feeling like I'm going to vom, so please go to bed and we'll talk about this in the morning.'

Jo's eyes were closed, so she didn't see him leave, but she could tell from the way his feet scuffed on the stair carpet that he was upset, and as she heard the bedroom door slam, Jo was certain she heard him cry out, 'HA!' But not one of his ridiculous laughs, instead it sounded like something inside him had snapped.

Jo knew how he felt.

Something special had happened tonight.

She could sing.

She'd always known she could sing, and wasn't averse to a tune in the shower. But she'd given up on it professionally, and just assumed her voice had gone along with her ambition.

But it was still there.

Jo had control of her voice and the audience, and it felt good. A blissful sense of belonging, and she wanted to get up there again.

She was surprised to find a tear trickling down her cheek and wiped it away, cursing her silliness, blaming it on the gin. As she did, a few notes popped into her head. Then a melody. She hadn't thought of it in yonks but it felt so familiar. What was it? Where had she heard it before? It came to her. It was one of hers. Jo had written it just after Ellie was born eighteen long years ago. It was the last song she'd penned, and it was the one she was most proud of. It didn't have a proper title, it was always just *Ellie's Song*.

As the notes drifted around in her head, she began to remember the lyrics, recalling how easy they had been to write at the time. Everything; chords, verse, chorus, words, that heart-stopping bridge, all came without any struggle, as if they had been waiting to be found in the depths of her brain like diamonds in a mine. Jo was overcome with an urge to sing it once more. Or the song was trying to break out of her.

She took a breath.

'Huck...'

Okay, that didn't go well. She noisily cleared her throat and tried again.

'Huck...'

And again.

'Huck...'

With each attempt, she found the words got stuck in her throat. A sudden wave of emotion would wash over her, and she simply could not get the words out. This was ridiculous. Jo had belted out some of Led Zep's most arcane gibberish earlier tonight, but her sincere song, the one she'd written about the birth of her daughter, made her all soppy and emotional. She just could not get beyond the first word of the lyrics.

The word 'I'.

One short syllable, but whenever she tried to sing it she could only manage a breathy noise that came out as a strangled 'huck'. The word was trapped in her oesophagus.

'Huck... huck... huck... bollocks.' Swear words posed no such problem. 'Twatty, balls, arse,' she spluttered, then, confident that the blockage had been cleared, tried again.

'Huck.'

Jo knew when to give up. She closed her eyes, and tried to get the song out of her head, but the melody kept looping, a repeating earworm. She sang herself *Happy Birthday*, trying to rekindle that brief moment of happiness she'd felt when she was singing in the bar. But that feeling wouldn't come. Soon she fell into a deep slumber, glad to see the back of yet another birthday, curiously satisfied that it had actually been quite extraordinary, and blissfully unaware that tomorrow would be even stranger.

ELLIE AWAKES

The front door slammed, waking Jo. Nick usually tiptoed out the door to work. Not today. Jo felt a black hole of swirling nausea in her belly. It twisted and tightened, eating her from the inside. Her back was a rigid plank and her bum had gone uncomfortably numb.

Through the pain, fragments of random drunken memories came and went like the transparent floaters in her eyes. Jo felt a tantalising remnant of bliss from her onstage adventure stir inside her, but it was soon overwhelmed by the sensation of being repeatedly tapped on the forehead by a ball peen hammer.

She decided to try opening her eyes.

It was like lifting a rusty garage door. Fortunately, the dim morning light only made her *wish* she was blind, and it kept the throbbing behind her eyes to a steady pulse, but she found herself totally confused as she looked up to see a Barbie doll hanging from a noose attached to a dusty light shade.

Jo craned her head round to see Ellie's arm hanging awkwardly over the side of the cabin bed above her.

Jo vaguely recalled waking on the sofa downstairs, staggering to the kitchen, drinking water, throwing up in the sink, cleaning up the mess, throwing up again, cleaning it once more, clambering up the stairs like Mallory braving Everest, and all the time trying to sing that stupid song, but never getting beyond that first word.

And now she was in her daughter's bedroom, having popped in to say goodnight.

Ellie's room was baffling to Jo: posters for muscular German metal bands with far too many umlauts in their names, bookshelves teeming with strange manga comics where the characters were always trying to stab one another, and a wallpaper on her laptop with a scary-looking tall, thin man called Slenderman. It was a far cry from the George Michael posters Jo had had as a teen.

Ellie was eighteen. When Jo was eighteen she had felt like she could conquer the world, and anything was possible, but at eighteen Ellie was still a child. That wasn't just Jo's protective parental instincts at play. Ellie still cherished the childish things - comics, animated movies, books and action figures - that eighteen-year-old Jo would have spurned. Her friends were the same. A whole generation too scared for the real world of work and taxes, the 'entitled' generation, clinging to their childhoods in the vain hope of putting off the inevitable. Jo didn't blame them. An education would put you in debt for most of your working life, and they could forget ever earning enough to buy their own home. No wonder Ellie's generation would hole up in their bedrooms, dress in slankets, and devour comic books.

Jo glanced at a photo of her and Ellie taken at Climping Beach over a decade ago. It was her favourite photo of the two of them. Ellie was wearing a pink tutu swimsuit, and proudly displaying a starfish she'd found in a rock pool. Jo couldn't remember the last time Ellie had worn something pink, or smiled with such undisguised glee. Jo felt an overwhelming urge to take the photo and snuggle with it like a teddy bear.

She felt a very different urge gurgling in her belly. She would need to find something long and distracting to read on the loo very soon.

As Ellie started to rise from slumber, with grunts of increasing awareness that someone might be in her room, Jo was surprised to find her old Surf Green Fender Squire Jaguar guitar looking sorry for itself under a pile of Ellie's discarded t-shirts, jeans and knickers in the corner of the room. Jo had loved it once, but now it just reminded her of past failures. It had been languishing in its case in the loft for years, and she vaguely recalled Ellie asking about it one morning over breakfast. Jo had blithely said Ellie could use it whenever she wanted, but she'd never thought that she would actually take her up on it. It was plugged into a box that was connected to her laptop. *Had Ellie been practising? Was she recording? Was she writing songs?*

Jo knew there are some things a mother should never do, like look in a daughter's diary, or scroll through her search history, but she had to know. She stroked her finger across the laptop's touchpad for a sneaky peek.

The noise that erupted from the device had Jo staggering back, wincing, and clutching her ears. She must have triggered play on a music app. It was some kind of megadeath metal and it sounded like the singer had swallowed the microphone and the rest of the band were attempting to bring it up using the Heimlich manoeuvre while still playing their instruments.

'Mu-um!' Ellie launched herself with uncharacteristic verve from under the sheets and across to the laptop in the blink of an eye. With deft fingers she shut off the noise. 'What are you doing?'

'I saw the Jag and I wondered if you were... y'know... recording something?'

'You said I could use it.' Ellie multi-tasked by rubbing her eyes and immediately going on the defensive.

'You're playing then? That's nice.'

Ellie ducked back under the covers and moaned some sort of reply.

'That was your music?' Jo asked.

'Yeah,' came a voice from under the sheets. 'Mum, I'm knackered, so can we have this conversation when I'm feeling more human, please?'

Jo opened the curtains, which she instantly regretted as bright daylight stabbed into her pupils.

'Is he ill?' Jo said, trying to blink away the pain.

'Who?'

'The singer.'

'Ha ha, very funny. *She.*'

'Sorry, she, of course.' Jo glanced at the guitar, recalling the late shifts she worked in a chicken battery farm to save up for it. It was the summer she'd discovered songwriting and turned vegetarian. Neither passion lasted as long as it should have. 'You in a band or on your own?'

'Band.' Ellie sat up cross-legged on the bed, looking askew at her mother.

'What are you looking at me like that for?' Jo asked.

'Just waiting for the lecture.'

'I'm not going to—'

'You are. You can't help yourself. That's why I kept this a secret.'

'How long have you been doing this?'

'A year, maybe.'

'A *year?*' Jo tried not to screech, so it came out as a gargled cry. 'How have you kept this secret for a year?'

'You know when you thought I was doing Duke of Edinburgh's Award? Rehearsals.'

Jo gasped, lost for words at her daughter's duplicity, but also slightly impressed with her nerve.

'Wasn't difficult, Mum. You're always late home or knackered, and Dad's always out with Andy, so it was easy to slip out with the guitar to Lizzie's.'

Lizzie. Ellie's friend with the tattoos, piercings and a resting bitch face that made Jo think of serial killer mugshots. Jo's own face instinctively contorted into an expression of disapproval.

'There. See?' Ellie jabbed an accusing finger. 'Your face. That's why I kept it secret.'

'Sorry, pickle, but Lizzie's weird. She's got more metal in her body than Darth Vader.'

'Yeah, well, you're wrong, actually. She's a genius, a visionary. We're writing songs.'

'That's great. Really, I'm happy for you. Just... Don't get your hopes up.'

'What do you mean?'

'Pickle, let me tell you now... It's going to be hard. You'll work your bum off, and for what? You'll play a few crummy gigs to an audience smaller than the band, make not quite enough money to cover your travel expenses, you'll be fighting off lecherous musicians, leeching promoters, paying to play, you'll spend a fortune recording a few songs that no one will ever listen to...'

'Jesus, Mum, who died and made you morale officer?'

'I know I sound cynical, but I've been there. I just want to save you the trouble of years of delusion and disappointment. If you want to succeed you have to be prepared to screw people over and... and make terrible, terrible sacrifices.' Jo gently stroked Ellie's face.

'Mum, you're being really weird.' Ellie leaned forward and sniffed. 'And — *eww* — you smell like a tramp.'

'That's...' Jo tried to surreptitiously sniff her own armpits. 'That's putting it a *bit* strongly, pickle.'

'Oh my god, you're hungover, too.' An astonished grin crept across Ellie's face. It wasn't often she got one up on her Mum. 'And where were you last night, young lady? Dad was well pissed off. He cooked and everything.'

'What was it like?' Jo asked.

'Like pasta Haribo, but don't change the subject. How come you can go out on the lash, but not me?'

'This was a one-off, it was my birthday. And if it's any consolation, my head is currently hosting a drum circle for hyperactive toddlers.'

'Ha, good.' Ellie ducked back under the covers. 'I'm going back to sleep and there's nothing you can do about it.'

'What about college?'

'What about work?'

Jo hadn't had time to consider that. She glanced at a clock on the wall. It was nearly half-eight. She'd already missed her regular train, and it would take at least three showers to wash last night away. More than anything, Jo desired a day in her pyjamas doing precisely sod-all.

But not with Ellie in the house tormenting her.

'I'll be off to work, soon, and you'll be at college, too,' Jo lied with conviction. 'C'mon, up you get.'

'No.' Ellie peered out from under the sheets and her eyes flitted to the Jaguar guitar. 'Think I'll stay in and practice.'

Jo's brain throbbed at the thought of sharing the day with a heavy metal teenager. 'College first, practice later,' she said. 'With headphones.'

'You're clearly trying to get rid of me, Mum. Do you hate me? You do, don't you? Bet you wish I'd never been born.'

'What? No. All I want is for you to be happy. If you want to play in a band, fine, great, fill your boots, just don't expect to get rich and famous, because it won't happen.'

'You don't know that. You *can't* know that.'

'I do, because I've been there. I nearly had a record deal with EMI, did you know that?' That shut Ellie up for a second, and Jo enjoyed the baffled look on her daughter's face. 'Course not, I never told you, so that was an unfair question, but I was lined up for the big time. Big contract, recording at Abbey Road, big tour, festivals, the whole shebang.'

'Bullshit.'

'No, for real. And don't swear.'

'That's not swearing. What happened?'

'Doesn't matter, boring legal stuff,' Jo said, trying not to look like she was lying. 'The fact remains, I've seen failure up close and it wasn't any fun at all, so have your fun now, but have something you can fall back on too. Believe me, the fall is long and hard. What about your coding? You're really good at that. And it's the future. Stock options like Mark Zuckerberg. You'll make a fortune.'

'Sitting hunched in front of a screen all day like you?'

'I made my choices for a reason, and one of those reasons was to ensure that you never wanted for anything. You've got a loving mother and father. I never had that.'

'Oh god, here we go again. The Orphan Annie sob story.'

'No, not a sob story, just fact. I never really knew my Mum, and that makes me a nervous parent.'

'What about that Frederica woman you keep going on about?'

'*Fede*rica,' Jo corrected her, warmed by the thought of her last foster mother. Federica would know what to do. Jo made a mental note to call her. 'She was brilliant, but I can never tell if I'm doing this right or not. I've never had an eighteen-year-old. I don't have much to compare it to, and if you're anything to go by then I've messed-up big time.'

'Get over yourself, Mum. You've done fine. You should see some of the screw-ups at college.'

'Really?'

'Yeah. It's nice to have a boring mum.'

'Oh, so that's how you see me? A boring mum?'

'Boring. Safe. I mean you never let me do anything.'

'You never *want* to do anything.'

'What about that skiing trip with school?'

'You? *Skiing?* You're the clumsiest girl I ever knew, Ellie. I might as well send Jar Jar Binks. I saved you from being airlifted off a Swiss mountain in a body bag with multiple compound fractures. You should be grateful.'

'And what about when I wanted to go to Glastonbury?'

Ellie hit a nerve mentioning the G-word.

'You were fourteen. What responsible mother would let her daughter run rampant in the world's largest music festival when she couldn't even get out of bed five minutes earlier to catch the school bus, let alone three trains to Somerset?'

'You screwed up the tickets on purpose.'

'I did not. I clicked refresh and they were gone—'

'And I wasn't going alone. I was going to go with Clifford.'

'Clifford is a pervert, Ellie. He was excluded from school for sticking his willy in his lunch yoghurt.'

'That was at playgroup. He was four.'

'Once a deviant, always a deviant,' Jo said. 'Why don't you go this year? I'll pay.'

'It's not on this year, Mum.' Ellie rolled her eyes. 'Anyway, what if I wanted to tour Eastern Europe with this band?'

'If you *what*?'

'Yeah, it's all booked. This kind of music is huge in the Ukraine.'

'So's background radiation, Ellie, but that doesn't make it a good thing. You booked a tour?'

'Lizzie did... Well, *will*. Soon. She's booking the flights and everything.'

'Just make sure she gives herself an extra two hours to get through the metal detector at customs.'

'You don't think we'll do it?' Ellie hopped off her too-small bunk bed, the one she'd had since she was twelve which was plastered with half-ripped stickers of boy bands she now hated. She grabbed some clothes from a pile on the floor.

'You can't get on a bus to town without asking me to top up your card,' Jo said. 'So a European tour with a metal band feels like a bit of a stretch for you, pickle.'

'God, *stop* calling me pickle.' Ellie snarled. 'You know why it's a stretch?' she continued, trying unsuccessfully to put her skinny jeans on back to front. Cursing, she wriggled out of the jeans, turned them round as she ranted. 'You never let me do anything, Mum. Just because you failed and never got on the Pyramid Stage at Glaston-bury, you've kept me locked in here like Rapunzel. I want to see the world, I want to run naked into the sea, do class B drugs, get piercings and tattoos, have sex with strangers, and, yes, if I want to, tour eastern Europe with a band and my messed-up friend Lizzie.'

'I'll do you a packed lunch.'

'Oh, ha ha. God, you're so funny, Mum. Forgive me while I split my sides.' Ellie managed to do up the final button on her jeans and shook her hair with both hands. 'Y'know, just because you were a complete failure, doesn't mean I will be, too. I'm going.'

'To college? Or the Ukraine?'

'Neither. I'm leaving and I'm never coming back. Fuck you!'

The door slammed, and Jo was alone once more.

A moment later, the door swung open again.

Ellie snatched up her bus pass and exited with a flounce, and an even bigger slam of the door, making the partition wall shake. Something toppled off a high shelf and jabbed Jo on the head.

'Ow!' she rubbed her stinging scalp and turned to find the offending object.

A photo frame lay face down on the carpet. Jo picked it up and turned it over to find the photo of her and Ellie at Climping Beach. A crack in the glass ran between the two of them.

THE GLOWING LIGHT

*F*uck you? Eighteen years of sleepless nights and worry, and Jo was rewarded with a big fat *fuck you*. A tear trickled down her cheek, that triggered a sob and before she knew it she had gone through a whole box of Kleenex, overwhelmed, emotional and hungover, lying in her daughter's bed and weeping.

Crying in a teenage girl's bedroom. *Haven't done that for a while*, Jo thought, as she wiped the tears away. She'd no idea what to do next. Usually her day was dictated by a non-stop routine, but she was utterly lost now.

Jo glanced down at the guitar. Like a neglected child it was looking up to her, asking to be held. Played. Gently.

Heaving herself off the bed, she picked it up by the neck, ducking her head under the strap, feeling its once-familiar weight pull on her shoulders. The fingers on her left hand instinctively found chord shapes and she began to strum. Something was off. The bottom E was tuned to a D, a common tuning for heavy metal, so she twisted the tuning key till it sounded right.

'Close enough.' She cleared her throat and continued playing. Nothing in particular, just a twelve bar blues, and a couple of mashed-up Beatles songs she half-remembered.

She was rusty, but it felt like putting on a comfy pair of old shoes. She could do this, and after last night's singing she began to wonder why she'd ever stopped.

Time. There was never enough of it. Not for her, anyway.

No, that wasn't it. That wasn't the only reason.

Jo began to play the opening arpeggio of *Ellie's Song*. She opened her mouth to sing.

'Huck...' she managed.

That mental congestion was still there.

She stopped strumming. The indentations from the strings on her tender fingertips looked like parallel tram lines. Her shoulder already ached from the weight of the guitar. She tuned the E back to a D and took it off, leaning it carefully against the bed exactly as she'd found it, not wanting Ellie to know that she'd been playing it. Assuming, of course, that she was coming back.

Don't be stupid. She always came back. Just like the time when, aged eleven, Ellie had filled a backpack and stomped out in a huff. Two hours later Jo had just started to get worried when the phone rang. The police? No, it was Pam next door calling to say she'd found Ellie hiding behind their greenhouse, finishing off the last crumbs from a pilfered packet of chocolate Hobnobs. Only last summer, Ellie had run off to Margate with no money to join an artists' collective and ended up hitching all the way home the next day. Ellie always came back.

Jo let her throbbing head fall on the bunk bed's sheets. A face-plant into a fading floral duvet. She closed her eyes and took a breath, taking in the smell of Ellie's hand cream mingled with the scent of deodorant. Ellie was a woman, Jo could no longer deny it. But Ellie wasn't ready for the world. It would eat her alive. Jo had plenty more work to do to prepare her girl for the realities of life, but didn't have enough time to do it.

Time. Jo needed more time, and she would give herself some *me time* today.

She emailed in sick, wrapped herself in the fluffy dressing gown that Nick got her for Christmas last year, embraced a hot water bottle to her tummy, grabbed her emergency box of Maltesers from the cupboard and shuffled into the living room for a day of self-indulgence.

There were about seven series on Netflix that she had to catch up on. She'd tried to keep up, she really had, but she would get home exhausted from being crammed on the train like cattle, cook dinner, wash up, and find Nick glued to *Strictly*. By the time she got to watch what she wanted, she could only stay awake for about fifteen minutes before falling into a slumber, waking at midnight and sloping off to bed.

Today would be different. *Breaking Bad* season one, episode two. As she curled up on the sofa, unwashed, hair a mess, faint whiff of body odour in the air, Jo felt a pang of sadness. While Ellie was doing goodness-knows-what, this was Jo at her most rebellious. This is what passed for a good time these days.

As she navigated the Netflix menu, Ellie's bloody song started playing in her head again. She dropped the TV remote, stomped back up to Ellie's room, grabbed the Jaguar and soon found herself back on the sofa, ignoring Walter White's descent into hell playing out on the TV, and strumming *Ellie's Song* again and again, trying, and failing, to sing it.

The chords were a pretty straightforward ballad progression, the melody wasn't difficult, and it was a memorable tune. So why couldn't she tackle her own silly little song? Jo tried whistling it, which worked. That was fine somehow, strumming the chords and whistling the melody, but as soon as she tried to sing any words...

'Huck,' Jo choked. Blood boiling, she cursed, unravelled herself from the guitar and its strap, and was ready to forget about it and give Bryan Cranston her undivided attention when she became aware of a strange glow coming from within her dressing gown.

Wondering if she'd switched her mobile phone's torch on accidentally, she opened it up - to find a rainbow light emanating from her belly.

The kind of glow you got from a disco ball, but just... *there*, radiating from her midriff like she was a middle-aged Teletubby.

At first, there were no words, no pain, just guttural expressions of fear and bemusement from Jo as she kicked and thrashed, trying to bat the light away, but her hands passed straight through it as it continued to expand.

She pushed down her panic and confusion as she jumped to her feet, turning and twisting in every direction to throw it off, but it remained tethered to her, extending like a finger towards the kitchen. Jo puffed her cheeks, took rapid breaths, and wondered just what the hell Michela had put in her drinks last night. This couldn't be real, it had to be a psychedelic experience. Jo had taken a few puffs of some sweet-smelling roll-ups at college and they had made her giggle a lot and tell everyone she loved them, but she'd never experienced anything like this.

Then came a new sensation, like someone tugging at her belly from the inside and she had flashbacks to carrying Ellie, the unborn girl wriggling and kicking inside her. But this was different, pulling her along. The finger of light wanted to go into the kitchen.

Jo was compelled to follow. She moved on the balls of her feet across the living room carpet, across the hallway's wooden tiles, unsure what to expect. Was this her mind's way of telling her that she was dying? Was this the last thing people saw before they kicked the bucket?

What she hadn't expected to see was a young woman looking equally befuddled and lost, standing in her kitchen, inspecting the fridge magnet photo of Jo, Nick and Ellie screaming on the log flume at Chessington World of Adventures like a curious art lover in a gallery.

For a moment, Jo could only watch as the tendril of light gently connected with the other woman's body, coiling around her, illuminating her like a Christmas tree angel. The girl, surprised by the light, spun round to see Jo staring open-mouthed at her. The girl was much younger than Jo and looked vaguely familiar. Her hair was frizzy — something Jo had considered in her youth — and she wore a crop top, faded jeans with holes in the knees, and a pair of bright pink Doc Marten boots.

The light connecting them reminded Jo of a picture she'd once seen online, of a black hole swallowing a star.

'Who...?' Jo's voice was dry and choked, so she worked her tongue around her mouth and tried again. 'Who are you?'

The girl narrowed her eyes and looked Jo up and down as if seeing her reflection in a mirror and not liking what she saw.

'I'm you,' she said. 'I'm dead, and I need your help.'

THE GIRL IN THE KITCHEN

Jo could try and deny it all she liked, but the more the girl spoke, the more she knew she was her younger self. Though not one she recognised. Jo had never worn clothes like that, and she'd chickened out when it came to frizzing her hair.

'That song,' the girl said, a puzzled look on her face. 'The whistling. Was that you?'

'What... What's this? Who...' Jo babbled. She stopped, took a breath, and started again. 'I've heard of out-of-body experiences, but that happens to people when they're on their deathbed, or...' A thought chilled her. 'Oh god, I'm dead, aren't I? I'm Bruce Willis in the *Sixth Sense*. I'm dead and I don't know it. Oh, Christ, I don't remember much about getting home last night. I was mugged, wasn't I? Oh shit, shit, what do I do?'

'Will you calm down and relax?' her younger self snapped. Her accent had a peculiar mid-Atlantic twang to it. 'Listen to me, I'm you... and I'm not you, okay?'

'Oh yes, that clears everything up, thank you. *What the fuck is that supposed to mean?*'

'Okay, let me start over, and I'll make this as simple as possible,' the young woman said. 'I am not here to hurt you, I'm not even sure why I came here to your house, but I won't be here long. I just want to go home.'

'Fine,' Jo said. 'Go. Click your heels three times.'

'I wish,' the younger her said. 'I was driving a bus, when I lost control and it went over a cliff.'

'You're a... bus driver? What cliff? What on Earth are you talking about?'

'I know this all sounds crazy, and it's weirding me out, too, but please listen. For most people, driving a bus over a cliff would be game over, but I learned something that saved my life and, for some reason, it brought me here. To you. Another version of me. I heard my song in the darkness, I heard you whistling, and it drew me to you, and here I am. How do you know that song, by the way?'

'You said you were going to make this simple?' Jo said.

'Okay, if I'm understanding this right, I think I came here from a parallel universe,' the young woman said slowly. 'Do you know what that means?'

Jo shrugged, 'I've watched *Back To The Future*.'

'No, that's time travel. This is different. Kinda. You and I are the same person, but you live in this world and I live in mine. We exist side-by-side, infinite numbers of us, each one created by a decision you or me made at some time in the past.'

'Okay, if you're me, when did I become Stephen Hawking?'

'My guru told me this.'

'Oh, this is insane.' Jo began pacing back and forth, the glowing light following her like a faithful puppy. 'I must be dead. That can be the only explanation. I've died and this is some kind of terminal brain fart as I finally kark it.'

'Will you calm down and listen?' the younger her snapped. 'I need you relaxed and I need your help. The bus came off a tight curve near Big Sur, I was flying through the air, I was gonna crash on the rocks, and—'

'Why were you driving a bus? Maybe I've had a stroke?'

'It was Lawrie's idea, a publicity thing—'

'I've never driven a bus. You can't be me. My god, you're so young, what's the insurance like?'

'Will you shut up, woman? I was about to die, but my guru, he was helping me with stage fright - you get stage fright, too, right? - and I was doing these breathing exercises, where you go into, like, a trance, and I was able to get into a bardo state. Do you know what that is?'

'You... dress up like Bridget Bardot?'

'It's from Tibetan Buddhism. It's the state between life and death, but Ronnie says it's also a way of travelling between universes.'

'Ronnie?'

'My guru.'

'Your guru,' Jo said, frowning, 'is called Ronnie?'

'I just need to get back into the bardo state...'

'Ronnie, the guru?'

'... and I'll return to my universe before any of this crap ever started and I'll fix everything.' The young woman adopted a yoga tree pose. Jo instinctively backed away.

'At the risk of sounding racist, but aren't gurus normally called something Indian? Ronnie doesn't sound particularly—'

'Shh. Concentrating.'

'Sorry.'

Nothing happened.

They both stood there for an excruciating minute before the younger one rested her hands on her hips.

'Problem?' Jo asked.

'No, no, I got it.'

'Look, Joanna—'

'Yohanna.'

'Yo-what?'

'I call myself Yohanna. It's my name. My stage name. One word branding, like Meatloaf, or Cher.'

'Or Stalin.' Jo emitted a short, hysterical laugh. This was beyond insane. She closed her eyes, pinched her nose and sat back on one of the kitchen stools. 'You wrote a song. You're a... You're a singer? Like me? Like I was?'

'Singer-songwriter, but my manager Lawrie just wants to push me as a singer. He says credibility can come later.'

'You're famous?'

'Yeah. Lawrie says I'm on the verge of breaking through to the big time. We're in L.A., and I screwed things up a bit and need to go back and make it right, so *please* help me.'

'L.A.?' Jo's skin tingled. She'd always wanted to go to L.A., but Nick's aversion to anything American had always put a block on it. 'You're recording in L.A.?'

'No, the single's recorded, but I did a few nights at the Troubadour, and now I'm doing the PR schlep, y'know, pushing the Yohanna brand big time on the long road to Glastonbury and superstardom and all that crazy shit.'

'That... that...' Jo struggled for the words, still hungover and in a state of befuddled shock. 'That was always *my* dream,' she said. 'To be a singer-songwriter, to record music, to play Glastonbury. How do you know all this? How can you be me? Why are you living my dream?'

Yohanna shrugged, 'Guess I just wanted it more.'

'Okay, Yohanna.' The name sounded weird when Jo said it. 'Just go, please, and hurry up. Nick's home soon. It's bad enough that he thinks I'm a disaster without a younger, sexier, more successful version of me to distract him.'

'Nick's your husband? You're married?'

'For the moment, yes.'

Yohanna scrunched her nose, 'Yeah, maybe it's best that you leave me to do this in peace? It's kinda weird.'

'*That* we can agree on.'

'I gotta say, you're being pretty cool about all this.'

'Oh no, I can assure you that beneath this calm exterior I'm going batshit crazy and worried that my brain is about to leak out of my ears. But that's my problem, not yours.'

'It'll be over before you know it.'

'Lovely. I'll be in the living room wondering where I went wrong with my life if you need anything.'

'Thanks, I'll be gone in just a sec, I promise.'

'Delightful. And lovely to meet you.'

'Nice to meet you, too,' Yohanna said, becoming a yoga tree once more.

Jo took a breath, stepped off the stool, and the light that surrounded her began to swirl like an eddy in a pool. It felt so real, but it had to be some kind of hallucination. It couldn't be a dream. No dream was this vivid, and Jo's dreams jumped around from place to place and skipped through time. What was happening to her now moved at the pace of reality. She could feel the floor beneath her feet, hear the burble of the TV in the other room, the hum of the refrigerator. There was no way her brain would remember to add all that detail. This was really happening.

As Jo tried to make for the door, the light intensified and encircled Yohanna, tethering the two of them. Jo was frozen to the spot. 'What are you doing?' Jo cried. 'Stop it.'

'This isn't me.'

Jo began to feel weak. She stumbled breathlessly to the tiles as the light became unbearably bright.

'I'm sorry.' Yohanna began to glow, rising off the tiles and into the air. 'I'm not doing this, I promise.'

'I can't...' Jo could barely keep her eyes open. 'Help me...' Jo saw flashes of another life. Flying across the Atlantic, a limo at the airport, palm trees along Santa Monica Boulevard, endless blue skies, the strobing flash and click-snaps of press photographers all jostling to get the best possible shot, adoring fans reaching out to her. She was standing on stage and singing, and that feeling of happiness was rising within her once again. Yohanna's life. The life that Jo might once have had. It was real, tangible, she could smell the humidity in the air, mingled with the fresh breeze from the Pacific brushing against her skin. All she had to do was step through.

Jo thought of her own life. An overpriced house in the suburbs, an indifferent husband, a hormonal daughter. The desire to turn back the clock and start again was overwhelming her and the light intensified. Jo had always had the talent to do something with her music, but had never used it, and now the universe was punishing her.

A memory came to her. Ellie giggling as a baby, her tiny face scrunching into a smile, her eyes shining. Ellie fell into a shadow, the memory began to cloud and Jo knew it would be gone forever any second now.

'NO!' Jo cried and, staggering to her feet, she reached out and dragged the light back towards herself. It was a tangible thing now. She tugged on the light, snapping it like a bed sheet and folding it over, and Yohanna disappeared in a blinding flash.

CEILINGS

'Jo? Jo, what happened?'

Nick's voice came to Jo in the darkness. How on Earth was she going to explain this to Nick? She could feel his face move closer to hers. He was sniffing. The cheeky sod was checking her breath to see if she'd been drinking.

'Hey,' she said in a gentle croak as she snapped her eyes open. This had the desired effect of startling Nick and making him jerk upright in surprise. Behind him, Jo could see the kitchen ceiling and despaired that they still hadn't sorted the flaky paint around the light fittings.

'Are you okay? What the hell happened?' He took her hand and helped her to sit upright. No yanking on her arm this time. Jo's head spun a little as she sat up, but at least she remained conscious.

'Nothing, I... I was doing some yoga and I had a funny turn,' she told him, hoping this would be enough to sate his curiosity, but from his unconvinced pout it clearly wasn't. 'Really, I'm fine. What time is it?'

'Seven. How long have you been here?'

'*Seven?* Shit.' Jo had been spark out for over nine hours, and she was about to say as much when she decided that Nick really did *not* need to know that. 'Where's Ellie? Is she home?' She brushed her hands across her face in an effort to massage some life into it. Nick helped her to her feet and she wobbled upright with all grace of a newborn giraffe.

'You're sure you're okay?' he asked.

'Yeah, yeah. Ellie, where's Ellie? ELLIE?' she called at the top of her voice. No reply. 'Phone. Where's my phone?'

Jo made her way on legs of jelly through to the living room where her phone rested on a sofa cushion. She grabbed it and checked for messages. There were a couple from Michela, taunting Jo for skiving off, but nothing from Ellie. She thumbed the phone, calling her daughter. It went straight to voicemail. *Shit.*

'Ellie, call me please. I'm worried. I don't care if you hate me, I just want to know that you're okay. Okay? Love you.' She hung up and turned to find Nick looking more confused than his usual state of perma-befuddlement. 'Long story.'

'I'm all ears.'

'It's nothing, really. Just the usual mother-daughter ding-dong.' Jo moved past Nick and headed upstairs. 'Did she tell you she wants to tour the Ukraine in a rock band with mad Lizzie?'

'Ellie's in a band?' Nick said, two steps behind her.

'Apparently so.'

'Okay. I can see why that sparked a row.'

'What do you mean?'

Nick stumbled to a halt on the landing, like a man who had just discovered to his utter horror that he had strolled into the middle of minefield. 'Nothing. Forget it.'

'You think I'm jealous of my own daughter?'

'I didn't say that.'

'You were about to.'

'That's not the same as *actually* saying it.'

'No, it might *actually* be worse.' Jo marched into Ellie's room and turned on her daughter's laptop. 'I'm not jealous of Ellie's ambitions to be a musician, I just warned her that it's a dog-eat-dog world and she should be prepared for disappointment.'

'I bet she took that well.'

'If storming out and vowing never to speak to me again is taking it well, then yes, she did.' The laptop pinged into life.

'What are you doing?'

'I'm going to call Lizzie and see if she's seen her. Oh, Christ. What's her password?'

'Tell Mum I hate her.'

'You're not helping, Nick.'

'No, it's a text from Ellie.' He showed her his phone, displaying the message. 'See, she's fine. She's just in a huff.'

Jo's relief was instant. 'When did she send it?'

'Just now.'

'Good, good.' Jo slumped against Ellie's cabin bed, exhaling loudly.

'You're not right, are you, babe?' Nick offered Jo a hand. 'You want something to eat?'

'God, yes, I'm starving.'

THE EVENING CONTINUED to play out like any other. They ate reheated leftovers, watched repeats of *Bake Off* while idly thumbing their devices in silence. Jo's memories of what happened with her younger self began to fade to the point where she was ready to dismiss the whole episode as a really weird and vivid dream.

Ellie sent no further texts. Jo left around a dozen messages on her phone, but to no reply.

During that evening's third repeat episode of *Bake Off*, just as Jo was nodding off, her phone pinged.

STAYING AT LIZZIE'S TONIGHT.

.   .   .

Jo SHOWED IT TO NICK, jabbed more buttons on her phone, and muttered, 'Oh, balls.'

'What?' Nick said, eyes still fixated on a Victoria sponge being inspected by Mary Berry and Paul Hollywood.

'Ellie's deactivated the *find a friend* thing on her phone. I have literally no idea where she is.'

'She's at Lizzie's. She just said so.'

Jo rolled her eyes at her husband's naïveté. 'Our daughter could be halfway to the Ukraine with a van full of drugged-up roadies.' Jo got to her feet. 'I'm going looking for her.'

'No, stop, Jo, c'mon...' Nick was on his feet and stood between her and the door. He gently took her hand in his, and gave her the doe-eyed look he reserved for when he fancied sex. 'It's not often we get a night in together.'

'You're kidding me, right?'

'What? Hey, it doesn't have to be sex. I know you've had a weird couple of days, I just think we should have some quality time. In bed.'

'It's Mary Berry, isn't it?' Jo glanced over at the TV where the octogenarian goddess of baking was critiquing a jam roly poly with Paul Hollywood. When Jo turned back to Nick, he was blushing.

SEX WITH NICK HAD BEEN 'PERFECTED' about twelve years into their marriage. At least, that's how Nick saw it. He had read Nancy Friday's dubious sex letter books cover-to-cover, and devised a couple of routines where he proudly declared to Jo that, by the end, everyone would be happy and satisfied. The first began with a few orgasms for her, a happy ending for him, and was all sorted in under fifteen minutes.

'Only you could see sex as a time management efficiency challenge,' Jo once told him, but Nick was so happy with it that he wanted to write to Cosmopolitan and share his gift with the world. Jo made it very clear that such an action would result in a stern letter from a divorce lawyer. Nick's second routine was the full Olympic marathon of tried and tested positions, all choreographed like a medal-winning gymnastics routine. That was usually reserved for birthdays and weekends away, and became increasingly exhausting with each passing year.

Jo was in no mood for that tonight. 'Use a condom, I only changed the bed sheets yesterday,' Jo said as she flopped into bed. 'And let's pass on the foreplay, all right? It's late. And I'm keeping my socks on. My feet are cold.'

'And they say romance is dead,' Nick said, tugging at his trousers.

'Or I could go straight to sleep right now, and leave you with your unrequited Mary Berry fantasies? Up to you.'

Soon, Nick was on top of Jo, grunting like a wounded werewolf. This was the second time today that Jo found herself staring up at a ceiling in her home.

'Is this okay?' Nick asked, slightly short of breath.

'Uh-huh,' Jo murmured. 'Can you lean over a bit...? Your elbow's sticking in me...' Jo asked, and Nick shifted his position. 'That's better.'

Flakes of paint here, as well. Jo suppressed a sigh as she tried to work out just how many hours a complete ceiling repaint would take, and how much of her hoped-for Christmas bonus it would cost.

'Are you okay if I do this? Faster...? Or slower...?'

'Hmm.'

Nick resumed his grunting and pelvic thrusts.

Lie back and think of... Facebook.

Jo turned and reached for her phone. Maybe Michela's tales of kissing in the back of a Rickshaw would spark her libido into action. As she suspected, Michela had spared no details. Jo had become quite versed at one-handed finger controls on her old iPhone. This new phone from work was slightly larger. She held it above Nick's back and kept the screen dim so he wouldn't notice. The sad thing was that she'd been reading messages during sex for months now and Nick, who insisted on keeping his eyes closed for the duration of all their intercourse, hadn't realised. Jo had broken her high score on Candy Crush three times.

Why does Facebook keep changing their layout? She fumbled with the phone screen and a small red light came on. She squinted, extending her arm. *What the hell's that?* Jo wondered if the battery was about to die. The screen suddenly flicked back to the main menu, the red light still glowing. Deep down she knew she needed reading glasses, but was not ready to acknowledge that one quite yet. Annoyed with the app's refusal to let her reply to Michela, Jo instead decided to check on Ellie's status. Nothing. She hadn't posted for two days. Jo had an idea. She would check on Lizzie. Ellie might be smart enough to hide her movements online, but Lizzie had nothing to hide.

Nick was in full swing now, 'Oh yeah. I can feel it building. Are you close, too?'

'Almost,' Jo muttered as she thumbed Lizzie's name into the search.

'Oh god, oh god.' As Nick became more excited, his weight began to crush Jo. She couldn't help but breathe harder, before long she was puffing like she was in labour.

Lizzie's Facebook timeline scrolled into life. She'd just checked into *The Muddy Middle*, a nightclub in town with a one-and-a-half star review average, and she'd posted a photo of herself and Ellie downing tequila shots.

'Oh, you...' Jo hissed.

'Yeah,' Nick managed to utter, before he climaxed in a shuddering mess of noises, including what sounded like a familiar name.

'What did you say?'

'Nothing.' Nick's voice was already drowsy.

'Sounded like... Paul?'

'Hmm?'

'Did you say the name Paul?'

Nick was already breathing heavily, mouth open, eyes closed. Jo shifted his weight off her, and checked the phone again, but the battery had died. She dropped the phone on top of the pile of unread Richard and Judy bookclub novels on her bedside drawers. Jo had a daughter who hated her, lied to her, and was frequenting nightclubs that had regularly failed food hygiene and fire safety examinations.

Whatever weirdness had happened in the kitchen today was a sign that things had to change. Tomorrow, Jo was going to take back control of her life, she was going to make things right with Ellie, and nothing would ever be the same old routine ever again.

JO GOES VIRAL

The next day Jo went to work with her mind firmly stuck in a life-changing mode. Her commute, so familiar that she could do it blindfolded, passed by in a blur as she thought of ways to reconcile with Ellie. Of course, first she had to get in touch with her, but all channels were silent. Jo tried checking Facebook for more updates, but the 4G was so strangled by her fellow passengers all doing the same, that all she got was two blobs of signal and the dreaded whirling update spiral of infinity. All her calls and texts to Ellie went unanswered, and Nick - who had seemed unusually agitated that morning - dismissed Jo's worries outright.

'Leave her be,' he told Jo as he bustled her out of the house. 'She just needs to get it out of her system.'

As Jo pushed through the revolving doors of the Mayer Marketing offices, she consoled herself that at least Michela would be a sympathetic ear. Jo hopped from the lift, strode through reception, and made her way to her desk in the big open plan office. She would make a cup of tea and start to make some sense of what was going on in her life. It also occurred to Jo that word might have got around about her big karaoke moment the other night. Perhaps her blank-faced colleagues might start to see her in a different light? Having had a taste of the limelight, would sitting at a desk all day begin to feel like even more of a chore than it already was?

SHE REALISED something was wrong as she switched on her PC. The office was unusually subdued - there was no tap-tapping of keyboards, casual chatting, or phones ringing - and when she finally popped her daydream bubble and took a moment to say hello to the people around her, Jo realised with a creeping sense of unease that everyone was looking at her.

Everyone.

Every single pair of eyes in the office.

Jo felt a pang of guilt, like a child caught playing truant. Then she remembered she was forty-two and not to be so stupid. What was wrong with these people? Had they never had a hangover day off?

She glanced over to Michela, who could only gawp at her with a look of pity that made Jo's stomach sink. In the next row, Pete snapped his head away from her, avoiding eye contact like a schoolboy caught looking at a nudie mag. No, this wasn't anything to do with her day off, this was something bad. Very bad. Jo felt a chill run down her spine. The air conditioning in here had been in dire need of repair for some two years, but it had never been as cold as this.

'What's going on?' she asked, her voice sounding flat in the silence around her.

'Jo, could we have a moment, please?' the calm voice of Mayer Marketing's CEO Nigel Mayer came to her from his glassed-off soundproofed office at the far end of the floor. He was the only one in the company who had the privacy of an actual office, and people only ever went in there when they were due a bollocking. Michela and Jo had a good view from their desks, and many was the time they had witnessed the silent movie drama of someone getting a dressing-down from Nigel.

Jo was further perturbed by a nagging realisation that Nigel was accompanied by Sandra, the company's human resources manager, and that Jo was about to star in her own short glass room drama, *Jo Gets Sacked For Skiving*.

Jo looked again to Michela for help, but her friend was, for the first time in her life, speechless.

'Quick as you can please, Jo,' Nigel said, raising his voice.

Jo, her mouth dry and her heart thumping, could only nod and run the gauntlet of the open place office of judgement with all the dignity she could muster.

'I'm sure I don't have to tell you what this is about,' Nigel began, confusing Jo even further.

Jo looked for clues from Sandra, who sat next to her boss with pursed lips, clasped hands, and a barely concealed disdain for Jo.

'If it's about yesterday, I'm really sorry, I was sick,' Jo said. 'I probably got food poisoning but if I'm honest I might have over-done it at the bar on my birthday. I'll take a day of unpaid leave, I'll—'

'No, no, no.' Nigel looked to Sandra for some kind of guidance, but she just shrugged. 'Okay, uh, you really don't know?'

Jo shook her head.

'Facebook?' he prompted. 'The video?'

Jo still had no clue, but she couldn't ignore the growing sensation of nausea in her belly. 'Nigel, I've no idea, and I'd rather you got to the point as you're weirding me out,' she said.

'At about eleven thirty last night this video was posted on the company's Facebook page...' Nigel spun his laptop to face Jo and, thanks to the miracle of autoplay, a video was already rolling. It showed someone who looked a lot like Jo peering over the hairy shoulder of a man as they had sex.

'Holy fuck!' Jo jolted to her feet, her hand going straight to her mouth, as the dread realisation set in.

Somehow, she'd filmed herself and Nick having sex last night.

And posted it on Facebook.

On the company's Facebook page.

'*Oh yeah.*' Nick's tinny voice came from the laptop's speaker. '*I can feel it building. Are you close, too?*'

'*Almost,*' sex-tape Jo replied, sounding more bored than she remembered.

'Turn it off. Turn it off!' Jo screeched.

Sandra's hand hovered over the laptop's tracker pad, 'Uhm, ooh, what one do I press?'

'Just— oh, fuck it.' Jo slapped the laptop lid shut, but the sound was still playing.

'*Oh god, oh god!*' cried sex-tape Nick from within the folded computer.

'WHY IS IT STILL MAKING NOISES?' Jo wrenched the laptop open and started mashing buttons in a desperate effort to silence the bloody thing.

Nigel came to her rescue, tapped a key and paused the video. 'Jo, please, calm down, take a breath.'

'I'm sorry, I'm so sorry, oh my god.' Jo fell trembling into her seat. 'I've no idea why that... There was a red light on. Christ, I thought that was strange. Oh shit, oh shit, oh shit. Nigel you have to believe me, I had no idea. I was checking on my daughter. She's run away, and I had to know where she was. I know that sounds weird, y'know, during sex and all that, but... well, yes, it's weird, but my life's suddenly very complicated, and I'm very, very sorry.'

'Jo, it's okay, we all make mistakes,' said Nigel, which seemed an unusually reasonable thing to say.

Another thought occurred to Jo, 'Why is it still on there?' she asked. 'Why haven't you deleted it? Delete it now, please.'

'Well, that's the thing...' Nigel said, biting his lip.

'What? What's the thing?'

'It's gone viral,' he said, turning the laptop back so he could see it, squinting at some text on the screen. 'According to this, we've had over three million shares, and five-point-two million likes. We've already had several enquiries from some major potential clients - ones we've been chasing for some time, actually - and they seem to think this is some genius viral marketing campaign. They want to talk to us about doing something similar. So, the thing is Jo, we'd like to keep it live for a bit longer if that's okay with you?'

'No. No, it's not okay with me. Take it down now.'

'Hmm, trouble is, the internet doesn't work like that, Jo.' Nigel angled the laptop around revealing a browser with a dozen live tabs. He moved the cursor across them and with each tap he revealed the video playing on every single one of them - Huffington Post, the Mail Online, LadBible and a whole bunch of sleazier sites, all accompanied by a click bait headline:

MILF MARKETING GOES viral
   Whatever she's selling, I'm buying!
   Who's Paul?
   Housewives in your area really <u>are</u> looking for fun!

'WHEN I SAID it had gone viral,' Nigel said, 'I meant viral. It's everywhere.'

'Graham Norton and James Corden have asked to use a clip. We're in a bidding war.' Sandra perked up.

'How... how do we stop this, Nigel?' Jo pleaded. 'Surely we have lawyers who can get these taken down?'

'I'm afraid we've gone beyond that, Jo.' Nigel shut the laptop again. 'I suggest we harness this for the company's benefit.'

'We do *what*?'

'This is an incredible digital marketing opportunity, Jo. We've never managed to make a video go viral. We've been trying for a year and never got close. Look.' He spun the laptop again, revealing a spiky, vertical chart. 'With this video we can make inroads to new markets, and attract top clientele for years to come.'

'You want to use my...' Jo almost said the words 'sex tape', but it made her bilious. 'This... video to promote the company?'

'Promote the company? *Save* the company, Jo. You've seen our revenue graphs. Steeper than a black run. All these New Media companies have been whittling away at our client base. This could finally turn things around and make such a difference to all our lives.'

'You can't,' Jo said, sitting upright. 'I mean... what if I refuse?'

Nigel sat back in his chair, clearly some kind of pre-rehearsed signal for Sandra, who took a printed letter from a file and slid it across the desk to Jo.

'Joanna.' Sandra tilted her head like a mother gently chastising a child. 'I'm afraid you must realise that what you did, however accidental you claim it was—'

'It was.'

'Nevertheless, it was a misappropriation of company resources and would be considered gross misconduct and cause for instant dismissal.' Sandra tapped a finger on the letter, and with a glance Jo could see that she was quoting from it.

'Gross...? What? You can't do this. This is blackmail. I want a lawyer.'

'Hey, whoa, Jo, that's a lot of scary words. Look, no one wants this.' Nigel raised his palms, something he'd been doing a lot since he went on a 'Difficult Conversations' course last year. 'All I'm asking you to do is sign a waiver to allow us to use the video to further the ambitions of the company.'

'We're under no obligation to do this,' Sandra said, her face pinched.

'No, no, we're not,' Nigel agreed, playing the good guy. 'But I prefer to have everyone on board and happy. We just want to make the best of a tricky situation. This could be very beneficial for everyone. The additional revenue from new and affluent clients could mean bonuses for all your friends and colleagues out there - and you, of course - and it will make this company great again.'

'I can't... I can't begin to process this Nigel. I need time to think.'

'Sure, sure, take a day, get some legal advice. I think Sandra has some leaflets. Think about what's best, not only for you, but this company and your colleagues.'

Jo glanced through the glass to the rest of the office where everyone was pretending to not look at them and failing miserably.

'Also, while you're mulling this over, can I ask you to consider this thought?' Nigel leaned forward, fingers tented. 'What does WWW stand for?'

'Wrestling... something? No, wildlife. Uh...'

'No, Jo, when we talk about the internet?'

'Oh, uh, World Wide Web.'

'*World!* Yes, the World Wide Web, well done. That video, for better or worse, is out there in the *world* - the whole wide world - and there's nothing we can do about that, short of asking every person on the planet to wipe their smartphones, laptops and tablets. There could be tribespeople in rainforests watching you right now, Jo. I know that's not an easy thing to live with, but that's the reality of the twenty-first century.

'The other reality is that this will be mercifully brief. In a few days people will be fixated on something else, and your little mishap will be forgotten - yesterday's news. Which is why we need to pounce on this now. I'm sure your colleagues would be most distressed to learn that we missed out on such a lucrative opportunity because of your indecision.'

'Let me get this clear, Nigel, because I really don't want to misconstrue this,' Jo said, trying not to let the tremble in her voice become tears or anger. 'You're saying that if I don't cooperate, you'll fire me, and you'll tell everyone out there that the company will go bust because of me?'

Nigel splayed hurt fingers across his chest. 'Sandra, did you hear me say that?'

'No, Nigel, I did not,' Sandra replied, lips drawn tight.

'All I'm asking, Jo, is that you think about it. Get on board the Mayer Marketing train to success, or clear your desk and go.' Nigel's smile remained in place, but his eyes were all business. 'You have till end of business today.'

IT'S A CRUMMY LIFE

When she was a teenager, Jo had harboured secret ambitions to be famous. She had a guitar, a few songs, a bit of talent, a good voice, and an ambition for a smidge of fame. Not too much. Just enough. She'd no desire to endure Beatlemania levels of adoration, but just having someone stop her in the street to tell her that her song had moved them would be all she longed for. A Goldilocks level of renown.

As she walked in a dreamlike daze back to the station, Nigel's words about her newfound worldwide infamy rung in her ears. He was wrong. This wasn't fleeting. How could this ever go away? Oh, yes, other people would forget it, but *she* never would. And neither would her family. Oh shit, what would she tell Nick? Was there any way that she could possibly keep this from him? For all she knew, he had seen it already. He worked in the IT department at a bank for God's sake, of course he'd seen it already. And Ellie. Oh dear god, Jo would be lucky if her daughter ever spoke to her again.

She tried to call her three times on the train home. 'Ellie, please call back, I need to speak to you urgently. This isn't about Lizzie or the band, it's... it's complicated. I've made a terrible mistake and I need to explain. Just call me back. Please.'

Jo ran through last night again and again, wondering where she went wrong, wondering what she could have done differently. But every time she came to the inescapable conclusion - she should never have been born in the first place. She shook the thought away as an immature, self-indulgent whinge, but she'd seen *It's A Wonderful Life* enough times to see the appeal of disappearing off the face of the Earth in order to make life easier for the ones she loved. But she was no George Bailey, and no angel would come and show her the error of her ways.

'Hey, it's you, isn't it?' A stranger, a man in a denim jacket and faded, paint-spattered jeans, stopped as Jo passed him in the street. 'Oh shit, it's you, it really is. I can feel it building, baby. Can you? Eh? Eh?' He cackled like a hyena, and Jo's heart raced, her cheeks burning with shame as she walked faster, turning the corner into her road.

That's it. That's how people would remember her. If she died right now, she would forever be that MILF who was shagged on Facebook. And who was that bastard? Why would he take so much delight in the humiliation of someone he didn't know?

Jo knew why. She'd been one of them, laughing at the online videos of countless poor souls who had fallen flat on their faces, and now it was her turn. That guy in the double denim was her audience now. Her fan club.

She tried calling Ellie again as she swung the gate open and rummaged through her coat pocket for her keys, but stopped when she heard the *thud-thud-thud* of nineties house music coming from inside the house. Jo hung up, turned the key and dashed inside. 'Ellie? Ellie? Are you home? Pickle? Ellie?'

Jo followed the music, dashing from the hall into the living room.

Where she found her husband Nick on his knees, enthusiastically fellating Andy, his bearded work friend. Both men were stark bollock naked, eyes closed in sexual bliss as the music pounded from the Sonos speaker.

The noise Jo made was not actual words, but the kind of talking in tongues that you might hear in some of the more hysterical churches on a Sunday. 'WhatthefuckisohchristNickJesus!' was just some of the garbled screech of horror the men heard coming from the doorway.

Andy, startled, jumped back from Nick, his erect penis slapping against his belly. He grabbed a cushion from the sofa, covering his privates.

'No. Not on my new cushions,' Jo snapped. 'No man juice on my cushions. Off, off, get it away.'

'Sorry,' Andy apologised, dropping the cushion and covering his humility with his cupped hands.

'Better. Now, fuck off,' Jo told him and jabbed a thumb at the door.

'I... I need to get dressed,' Andy said, edging towards his suit and boxers. He was a handsome fellow, she couldn't deny that. Always friendly and going on golf weekends with Nick, and...

They weren't golf weekends, idiot.

... and with his neatly-trimmed salt and pepper beard and flinty eyes, Andy reminded her of someone...

Paul Hollywood, you fool. Nick wasn't turned on by Mary Berry, but by her stud muffin sidekick.

It had been there in front of her all this time.

'Fine, whatever,' Jo told Andy. 'Do it in the hallway, I've seen enough of your hairy balls today, thank you, Andy. But I swear to God, if you're not gone in five minutes I'm getting the carving knife from the kitchen and you won't *have* anything to cover up. Understood?'

'Yes,' he said, snatching up his clothes and scurrying from the room, shutting the door behind him.

Nick remained on his knees on the floor, his head bowed low.

Jo slumped on the sofa. She waited for her heart to slow from a rapid thrumming to a steady metronomic beat before she spoke in a gentle, calm voice, 'Do you have any idea what kind of day I've had today?'

Nick looked up at her from where he knelt. 'I didn't think you'd be home so early.'

'Neither did I. I'm a meme,' she told him. 'An international joke. We both are, actually.'

Jo took a moment to enjoy the look of bafflement on Nick's face. He had no clue what she was talking about and clearly hadn't been online all morning, preferring the company of Andy and his member. All Jo's previous concerns for Nick's reputation and humiliation took a back seat for a moment. She would let him find out about their little video for himself. Why should she be the only one having a crappy day?

'How long has this been going on?' she asked Nick.

'Physically?' Nick's voice was dry and quiet. 'About... six... seven months, I guess.'

Jo thought back to every time he was late from the office, every work away day, every golfing weekend, every night when he claimed to be drinking with friends... And every time she'd fallen for it. No, that wasn't right. She wasn't a fool. She must have somehow known, but buried it deep down in a file marked 'Denial'.

'But I've known how I felt for longer,' Nick said. 'Much longer. I just never... acted on it.'

'Put something on.' The idea of seeing him naked seemed wrong and strange. Jo found herself staring at the family photos on the wall instead of Nick as he dressed.

The door opened a crack and Andy peeked in, 'I'm, uhm, I'm off. Shall I...?'

'Yes, fuck off, Andy, there's a good chap,' Jo said.

'Yeah, you'd better go,' Nick told him.

'Will you call me?' Andy asked Nick.

'Are you for real?' Jo turned her gaze of righteous fury on him. 'Fuck the fuck off.'

Andy ducked away, the front door opening and shutting an instant later as he fled the scene.

Nick finally had his trousers and a shirt on and sat on the armchair across from her. For a long time they said nothing.

'I'm sorry,' Nick said, tears welling in his eyes.

'Y'know what? Don't be.' Jo took a deep breath and shook her head. 'Actually, this explains an awful lot. Our whole marriage, in fact.' She idly brushed her hand on the sofa arm, and straightened a few cushions as her eyes fell on their wedding photo on the wall. The happy couple, though the smiles struck her as insincere in a way that had never been clear to her before, but now seemed so obvious. Like finally deciphering one of those Magic Eye puzzles.

'Did you ever really love me?' she asked him.

'Of course,' Nick said. 'It's just... I never knew who I really was. My whole life has been like there's two of me, and because everyone expects me to be one thing, I've had to keep this other me a secret.'

'Sounds like a well-rehearsed answer,' Jo said. 'Been working on that for a while?'

'A bit.' Nick smiled sheepishly. 'Never could fool you.'

'Apparently, you bloody well can.'

'You're being very calm about all this.'

'Yeah, I really am, aren't I?' Jo said, 'I could start screaming and smashing stuff up, but what would that achieve? It's not going to change a damn thing and I'd be the one who had to tidy up afterwards. And I can't blame you. It's me. I'm safe. I'm boring. Believe it or not, this might not be the worst thing to happen to me today.'

'Why are you home? You haven't been sacked, have you?'

'Not yet.' Jo could see that he wanted to know more, but she wasn't ready to give it to him. 'My whole life I've been sleepwalking,' she continued. 'Every day is a living dream. I couldn't tell you what was different about last Tuesday from the Tuesday before. Forty-two years of nothing in particular, and even when I come home to find my husband sucking off his boss, I—'

'He's not my boss.'

'I don't care. See, I don't care, and that's the problem. When did I stop caring? And now it's too late to even...' Jo drifted off, thinking of yesterday and the strange incident in the kitchen and that glimpse of another life of fame, fortune and luxury. It made her feel both sad and nostalgic for something she'd never actually had.

'Too late to what?'

'Hm? Oh, nothing.' Jo waved the thought away. 'Are you happy, Nick? Does he make you happy?'

A wan little smile crept on Nick's face. 'Yeah. Yeah, he does. We click, y'know? I feel totally comfortable with him. We make each other laugh, we like the same stuff, he's a great cook, we just enjoy each other's company, we—'

'All right, all right, you can shut up now, you've made your point. I feel inadequate enough already, thanks.'

'I'm sorry, but I can't pretend to be someone else any more.'

Jo looked at the man who was her husband. It was true. He even *looked* different to her now. The way he spoke, the way he sat, his posture and gestures. Like an actor being interviewed about a role he had once played in a movie.

'I understand,' she said. 'I really do.'

'What do we do now?'

'You're going to get out, and then I might do a bit of shouting and screaming. Maybe find some chipped crockery to fling around.'

'Are you going to be all right?'

'No, probably not.'

'I won't leave you alone if you're going to do something stupid.'

'No. You'd really better leave, Nick, because I can feel the calm starting to fade, the anger beginning to rise, and any minute now I could turn into Lady Macbeth. So, please, go.'

Nick wouldn't listen, however, and kept insisting on staying until Jo started screaming. She hated herself when she got like this, though she supposed that she should be grateful that there was some kind of passion inside her still. It always ended the same way, with her crying and getting the shakes. She should have known better, but something in her snapped. The argument reached its climax with her grabbing Nick's clothes from the wardrobe and throwing them out of the bedroom window, where they billowed into the street below.

'No, wait, not my Paul Smith!' Nick cried, dashing from the room, stomping down the stairs and out of the door.

Jo closed the curtains and fell back onto the bed, wondering what else could possibly go wrong. Her life had been a comfort blanket. Existence for the sake of existence, going through the motions until the grim reaper turned up on the doorstep of her semi-detached with a scythe, an empty hourglass and an apologetic shrug. Was this it?

Was this all she had to look forward to? An empty nest full of stuff she didn't need?

Jo rolled over on the bed, picked up her phone and called Federica. It went straight to messages.

'Hey, Federica, it's Joanna. Sorry I've not been in touch, and sorry to call only when I need something but... I've had a really—'

The phone buzzed. Another incoming call.

Ellie.

Jo hung up on Federica and answered Ellie, 'Hey, Ellie? Say something, pickle.'

She could hear her daughter's breathing brushing against the receiver.

'Please say something. Even if it's to tell me that you hate me. I just want to hear your voice.'

Jo filled the silence with her own fears: *she knows and she hates me.*

'Ellie, let me explain. It was a mistake—'

Ellie hung up, and Jo finally crumbled. A warm flood of tears rushed down her cheeks and she curled into a foetal ball, fists clenched, nails digging into her palms, her body shuddering with sobs.

Jo, exhausted with rage and sorrow, exploded in a primal scream that came from the very essence of her soul and, in a twist of metaphysics that would have fried Stephen Hawking's brain, crossed dimensions.

The silence was broken by a humming voice drifting up the stairs.

Jo sniffed and wiped the tears away. She recognised the melody.

Ellie's Song.

Shadows began to shift across the walls. The rainbow light was back, rising from Jo's belly and homing in on the source of the song.

Jo pushed herself off the bed, tripped her way down the stairs, chasing the snaking light as it swerved into the kitchen to where she found her younger self glowing like an angel on a Christmas tree. She was sitting on a stool, humming to herself as the light from Jo's belly wrapped around the pair of them, joining them together.

'Hey.' Yohanna looked up and rushed towards Jo. 'Thank God, you're here. I need your help.'

ACROSS THE UNIVERSE

J o found herself considerably less freaked out than with her first Yohanna encounter. Hallucinating a younger version of yourself *once* can be written off as the psychedelic after-effects of a hedonistic night out, but seeing this doppelgänger in her kitchen a second time was reassuring for Jo. Yohanna couldn't possibly know about Jo's terrible Facebook debacle, and it would be a relief to spend a little time with someone blissfully ignorant of what a complete idiot she'd been.

'Didn't expect to see you again,' Jo said, wading through the rainbow light that drifted around them. 'I thought you wanted to get home?'

'I do, but something got screwed up,' Yohanna said, hands in her hair as she paced. 'You saw me, right? I started floating up, everything went really bright, and I was back in the bus, but just before I lost control, which is exactly what I wanted.'

'Great, so why're you back?'

'I was there, but I wasn't there. It's hard to explain, but I couldn't get back into my body. I was floating like a ghost, it was all like a dream, and I found myself in the dark. I thought I was dead. I... I could hear someone crying. I heard your scream and I ended up in your bloody kitchen again. What the hell is going on?'

'Don't ask me,' Jo said. 'You're the one with the guru.'

'Guru.' Yohanna snapped her fingers. 'Yes. Ronnie says all things happen for a reason. There must be a reason why I keep coming back to you.'

'Well, you and me are technically the same person,' Jo ventured.

'Yeah, but there are billions of yous and mes across countless parallel universes,' Yohanna said, gesturing at the light that gently ebbed around them. 'Why us, specifically? Why are we linked like this?'

'The song you were humming... You wrote it?' Jo asked.

'Yeah,' Yohanna said. 'You know it?'

'I wrote the same song when I was about your age.'

'That's it, that's the connection.'

'Okay, okay, great. But how does that help us?'

'The universe has chosen you to help me,' Yohanna said, with a certainty that Jo found unnerving.

'I'm not sure you can speak for the universe, Yohanna,' Jo said. 'That's hubris on an intergalactic level, and can only end in tears.'

'What other explanation is there? I tried to get home, and I get bounced back to you again. You're my saviour.'

'I'm happy to help, Yohanna, but I wouldn't know where to start.'

'Take my hand.'

Jo started to reach out, but then hastily withdrew her hand. 'What's going to happen? Are things the same in your world? It doesn't, I dunno, rain anvils, or anything weird like that?'

'No, we're just like trains running on parallel lines,' Yohanna said, clapping her hands together. 'Ronnie told me once that matter can only occupy a moment in time once. I can't go back to that moment, but you can. You enter my body, and save my life.'

Jo considered the offer as if she understood the mechanics of moving between universes. 'Aren't you scared?'

'Yeah, sure, but Ronnie's been trying to figure out how this works for years and I finally did it. I proved him right. We can do this.'

She looks so young, Jo thought as she looked back up at herself. There was a fragility to Yohanna, but also a strength. An unconquerable naïveté mixed with confidence that the world was hers for the taking. No one was going to mess with this kid.

'How old are you?'

'Twenty-four, I guess.'

Jo's heart burned. The year she got pregnant with Ellie, 'You guess?'

'I don't do birthdays.'

'Why not?'

'Who's counting? Live in the now.'

'Got a boyfriend?' Jo asked, trying to make the enquiry sound as innocent and casual as possible.

Yohanna pulled a face like a child confronted with sprouts for the first time. 'Ugh. No time for that shit,' she said. 'I need to get back. Lawrie's waiting for me.'

'Lawrie's your manager, right?'

'He reckons I can be huge, so long as I don't fuck things up. I need this week so much. I've got TV lined up, the single's ready, we've got a record company on the hook. This is just the start. That's kinda why I really don't need to be dead, or in limbo, or whatever this is right now.'

'When you were last here, and we... connected, I saw things. Flying first class, adoring fans, stuff like that. Is that your life?'

'Not all the time, but it has its moments.'

'And you're happy?'

'Hell, yeah.' Yohanna beamed a grin of pure joy, and Jo wondered if she'd ever been that happy about anything. Yohanna exuded invincibility. Fame and fortune for her were inevitable. 'It's awesome.'

'You're not worried about intrusion from the press? Crazy fans? The pressure?'

'Bring it on, lady. It's all the fun of the fair, and all I ever wanted.'

That made Jo's forehead crinkle. Was it everything she wanted when she was that age? This version of her had grabbed life by the balls and wasn't about to let go. 'So, why were you running away in a bus?'

Yohanna's facade dropped for a moment. 'I had a freak out,' she admitted with a shrug. 'A little panic attack, that's all. Things were moving a little fast and I just needed space to think, that's all.'

'No one's trying to murder you, or anything like that?'

'Oh god, no, just a ton of stress. It happens. Please help me.'

'And what happens if I can't get back?'

'Tell Ronnie. He'll know what to do.' Yohanna bit her lip, then asked, 'You're gonna help me?'

There had been a few moments in Jo's life when she knew it would never be the same again. Walking through her foster mother Federica's front door for the first time. Saying, 'I do,' to Nick. Agreeing to start a family. This felt bigger, weirder and more unreal than any of them. Besides, Jo was convinced that she would soon wake up on the sofa with a hangover. Either way, she really had nothing else to lose.

'Yes, fuck it, why not? I was going to change my life today, anyway. Let's live a little.'

'Okay, close your eyes, and take my hand.'

'You're positive you know what you're doing?'

'Yeah, yeah. Me and Ronnie have run through this dozens of times. Trust me.'

'Who is this Ronnie anyway, is he qualif—?' Jo was silenced as Yohanna squeezed her hands, triggering a tingling sensation that flushed through her in a heartbeat, then surged back from the tips of her toes, up her legs and body, finally making her hair stand on end.

'You feel that?' Yohanna grinned as the light around them began to intensify. 'Pretty orgasmic, huh?'

For a moment, Jo could only utter consonants. 'That was... What was that? What do I do now?'

'Just relax. Do you get a feeling that there's, like, water rising around your body?'

'I do.'

'Good, I had that before, just let it happen and—'

· · ·

THE UNIVERSE MOVED AROUND JO.

THANKS TO POPULAR CULTURE, most people are convinced that the best way to travel through time and space is to construct some kind of warp speed spaceship, ask your navigator to punch in a few coordinates, hit a big button and *whoosh* through hyperspace. These people are wrong. It's actually best to sit down in a comfy chair, create a wormhole to your destination, and let the universe do all the hard work.

That said, it's not entirely without trauma.

Jo found herself at the centre of the universe, with every galaxy, star, planet, moon, sentient being and mote of space dust whirling around her. It was over in the blink of an eye, and that's an awful lot to cram into a single human brain in such a short space of time, but Jo had seen enough repeats of *Doctor Who* to get her head around something like an infinite number of parallel universes jostling for her attention.

Somehow, Jo could see Yohanna on the far side of the universe. She was both infinitesimally distant and in Jo's face at the same time. Wormholes, Jo reflected, can really mess with a person's sense of perspective.

'What's happening?' Jo's voice reverberated like god in a Hollywood golden age Biblical movie, and with all the Old Testament righteousness and anger that entailed.

'I don't know.' Yohanna became a tiny speck in the darkness, her voice tiny and distant. 'It wasn't like this before.'

'What have you done?'

Yohanna began to streak towards Jo. She was a comet with a dazzling rainbow of light behind her, like the split beam of light through a prism. Jo felt the sensation of movement. There was no rushing air, but the heavenly bodies around her began to shift perspective before falling out of sight. More came and went, rushing past with increasing frequency until they became nothing more than light streams, pulsating around her like the trippy bit at the end of

2001. Jo saw her younger self heading straight for her. She and Yohanna were going to collide. There was nothing either of them could do other than scream as they were drawn to one another.

WITH A SOUND like someone slurping the dregs of a drink through a straw, everything went black.

REALITY CAME CRASHING BACK with the clatter of a double-decker bus engine, the screech of tyres on Tarmac, and the wind howling around Jo, mussing her hair like a maniacal barber as the bus she was driving spun out of control.

THE EDGE OF DARKNESS

Yohanna was not where she was meant to be.

She'd been ready to breathe in the warm and welcoming waft of Pacific Ocean air, but instead she found herself in darkness once more.

Her older self had let her down twice - or the universe just wasn't playing ball. Either way she seemed to be stuck in this abyss. She couldn't even be sure how long she'd been here, but any time at all in this place was too long.

'Hello?'

Her voice was deadened, and she was reminded of the insulated vocal booths in recording studios. This was more oppressive. The darkness was smothering her. There was no light, taste, touch or scent. Just a big, fat nothing. Yohanna suppressed the rising panic within her and tried to figure out how to break free.

The sound of sobbing came to her ears. One moment it seemed to be right behind her, the next it echoed like someone crying in a church.

Definitely time to leave.

There was no point trying her older self again. There was only one woman who always came through for Yohanna. She closed her eyes and tried to visualise the only place she ever called home and hollered her name into the darkness.

'FEDERICA. HELP ME!'

A DARK DESERT HIGHWAY

Jo was driving a double-decker bus at high speed, at night, snaking around the teetering cliffs of a rugged coastline. Gravity and centrifugal forces pulled her in every direction, and she gripped the oversized steering wheel like her life depended on it, which it surely did. Jo could feel the wheels juddering as they rubbed against the shoulder. She took her foot off the gas, careful not to brake suddenly, and started to slow down.

A truck came hurtling around the bend, blinding her with more lights than a Pink Floyd gig, its deafening horn a panicked morse code warning. Jo yanked the steering wheel and lurched away from the truck.

Jo had never driven anything more complicated than her Ford Focus, and this out-of-control behemoth had momentum on its side. But she knew enough to steer into the skid and she pumped the brake with a rabbit foot rhythm. Nevertheless it continued to whirl out of control, the tyres grinding on loose stones on a stretch of moonlit gravel, stirring up a dust cloud as the rear of the bus swung around. Debris flew around the driver's cab, including a chunky old Nokia phone that whacked Jo on the temple. The warm night air whipped her frizzy hair over her eyes, and she got a faint whiff of sea breeze from the Pacific Ocean. Any moment now the bus would fly into empty space and gravity would do its stuff, sending her plunging onto the rocky shore below, where she would surely perish in a fiery ball of death.

Jo gritted her teeth and yanked hard on a lever she was relieved to discover was the handbrake, slowing the bus as it scraped against a boulder, finally coming to a stop. The impact shook her like salt in a shaker and as the dust cloud settled, a wave of adrenaline flooded her as the shock set in.

The truck continued speeding away from her on the highway, its horn blaring angrily as it faded into the distance, leaving Jo trembling in a stalled bus, its orange hazard lights winking.

Jo blinked the dirt from her eyes, and dared to peer downwards out of the driver's window. The bus was parallel with the sheer edge, inches from plummeting over. Below, the ink-black ocean mingled with the teeth of the jagged cliff face. *The Pacific?* She was in California. Her whole body tingled, her heart pounded in her ears. *Yohanna was right.* She looked around the bus for any passengers, but she was alone.

And that's when she caught a glimpse of herself in the large side mirror.

Her frizzy hair.

'What the f...?' Jo's voice wasn't her own. Well, it was, but one from eighteen years ago. Lighter in tone, higher in pitch. Jo leaned closer to the mirror for a better look. No crow's feet around her eyes, no bags, no flecks of grey in her hair. A few more zits than usual, but all buried under foundation, and she had bright crimson eye shadow caked on like a Cyndi Lauper tribute act. The make-up was a day old, slept-in and streaked where she had been crying. She gently touched her face. The skin on her hands was smooth - apart from calloused fingertips she instantly recognised as guitar string blisters - and the post-pregnancy belly she'd spent the better part of two decades trying to shake off was nowhere to be seen. She had abs. When did she get abs?

Jo was in Yohanna's body. *How was this even possible?*'

'Yohanna!' Jo stumbled out of the bus, calling her younger self's name again and again, trying not to be too weirded out by the sound of her girlish voice. 'Yohanna? Where are you?'

More cars whooshed by on the Pacific Highway. A few honked their horns, no doubt wondering why a large London bus was parked so dangerously close to the edge. The sea continued to crash on the rocks far below, a warm breeze ruffled her hair, the gravel crunched under her bright pink Doc Marten boots. If this was a dream, then it was a bloody vivid one.

Jo walked in confused circles as she tried to figure out what to do next. If this was real, if she was in Yohanna's body, where was Yohanna? Had they swapped bodies? Or was Yohanna dead? Or still in limbo? And if she really was here, would she ever get home?

That last thought chilled her. She couldn't be stuck here - not only on the other side of the world, but in a parallel universe.

It didn't take her long to realise that wandering round in a state of increasing bewilderment and panic wasn't going to solve anything. She needed to take action.

Ronnie. Yohanna had told her that her guru, saddled with the unlikely name of Ronnie, would help. Jo needed to find this Ronnie guru person, fix this mess and get back home.

Jo dashed back to the bus, clambered back into the driver's cab and retrieved the Nokia phone that had whacked her on the head. She thumbed the device's buttons, trying to recall how these old Nokias worked, wondering why Yohanna didn't have a smartphone. There were a few texts, and all from the same number. No name. No Ronnie. They all said variations of the same thing:

CALL ME.
Where the bloody hell are you?
Call me now. Urgent.
If there's so much as a dink on the bus, you're toast...

. . .

JO GLANCED BACK at the big dent in the side of the bus where it had scraped against the boulder, and winced.

Taking a deep breath she decided to call her mysterious texter. The phone rang. That unfamiliar long drone of American phone lines.

'Finally.' A voice crackled at the other end of the dodgy signal. 'Where the bloody hell have you been? What's the point getting you a bloody mobile phone if you never bloody answer the bloody thing?' He was British. A Londoner. Bit of a cockney geezer, even. Fond of the word bloody. 'And where the bloody hell is the bus? Get your arse back to the hotel, pronto. If the press call, say nothing. And if there's even the smallest scratch on that bus—' The call dropped.

Jo turned to watch another truck roar by in the opposite direction, its headlights sliding across a road sign, revealing she was ninety-nine miles from Los Angeles.

'Oh shit,' she muttered, ready for the long drive to L.A.

There was no key. No ignition. How was she supposed to start this thing? There was a big red button that looked like a petrol cap. She twisted it and the orange indicators blinked.

'No, that's not it.' Jo pressed and twisted every button, honking the horn and scraping the wipers across the glass as she did. Nothing. Memories came to her of watching the film *Summer Holiday* with Federica when she was younger. 'If Cliff Richard can drive one of these things, then so can I,' Jo said, trying to recall the film. Cliff would always reach up to start the bus. She looked up and found a lever to her left. She gave it a tentative pull. The bus shook into life with a coughing metallic rattle, vibrating every bone in her body. 'Yes.'

Jo had passed her driving test on the first go, but her examiner had somehow failed to cover the basics of turning a double-decker bus around on a narrow cliff edge. And here, instead of hitting the curb, she had a much bigger problem. Back up too far and the bus wheels would drop off the edge of the cliff. With more experimental lever-pulling she put the bus in reverse. She had inches to manoeuvre.

Eight mini back-and-forths later, Jo had the bus straddled across both lanes on a tight bend. In the distance she could see the glow of swooping headlights across the rocks as a vehicle negotiated the coast road's curves at very high speed. Whatever it was, it was heading this way and she and the bus were sitting ducks.

'Move,' Jo muttered as she stepped on the accelerator.

The bus stalled - and headlights came careening round the corner.

THE HAPPY PHANTOM

Yohanna felt woozy. A dazzling glare left streaks of green and blue through her closed eyelids. They darted in sync with her panicked eye movements. She began to fear that she was going to be permanently blind, but the glow began to fade and the streaks disappeared soon after. Only then did Yohanna dare to open her eyes again, feeling them pulse in time with her heart as they adjusted to the daylight around her. She half-expected to find herself back in that damn kitchen with her older self complaining, but instead Yohanna was standing alone in a field of wheat that came up to her belly. The sky was bright blue, dotted with puffy white clouds.

She wondered if she was dead and if this might be heaven, but a lark sang - spiralling above her - and as Yohanna followed its flight she found criss-crossing vapour trails in the sky. The distant whisper of traffic carried from an unseen motorway, and a dog's barking drew her eye to the edge of the field where she saw a woman walking her golden Labrador. The woman waved at a car that drove by as she posted a letter in a red Royal Mail letter box.

This wasn't the afterlife. It was somewhere in Britain, and there was something familiar about the place. She hoped this was where she wanted to be.

Yohanna tried to wave at the woman to catch her attention, but she was already turning off down a footpath.

'Hey. Excuse me.' Yohanna took a step to follow her, but found herself floating on air, drifting through the rows of wheat like they weren't there. They looked solid, but when she moved her hand to touch them, her fingers passed right through.

Whoa, whoa, whoa. Yohanna looked down at herself properly for the first time since arriving. She was a pale ghost of herself. Not transparent, but bleached of colour like a photo left in the sun. And she was floating about an inch off the ground.

Oh god, oh god, oh god, what's happened? This isn't right.

When Yohanna had met her older self in the kitchen she'd felt perfectly normal, she could feel the floor beneath her feet and the gentle brush of air across her lips and tongue as she breathed.

She took a deep breath.

Nothing. No air entered her lungs, there was no sensation of movement in her mouth and nostrils. It was as though her whole body was numb. She ran her hands through her hair, pinched and pulled at the skin on her face, and tugged on her ears. They were all solid enough, but she couldn't touch or interact with anything around her. She was a ghost. She was dead, and she was a ghost.

Shit.

How had this happened?

Yohanna had visualised Federica's home in the darkness, a place where she had been happy, a place where she knew she could get help. She'd figured there might be a high price to pay, but she hadn't imagined this. She didn't want to end up in some pointless bit of boring farmland in the middle of nowhere, just like the place where she last...

Oh.

No, she was in the right place after all.

Yohanna turned a hundred and eighty degrees before finding something she recognised. A place she hadn't seen for about five years. A small row of red brick houses backed onto the field. They had once been farm buildings, long since converted into homes. The house on the end had a number of extensions protruding from it: a glass conservatory with Victorian ironwork, a garage converted into a playroom, a loft converted into bedrooms with a row of Velux windows. The garden had a low hedge, so Yohanna could clearly see the small, familiar space peppered with colourful plastic toys, ball pools, slides and swings, and a washing line weighed down by kids' pyjamas, socks and school uniforms.

'Madame Federica, yes.' Yohanna smiled to herself. Federica was the only person who would understand what the hell was going on and get her home. Yohanna stretched her arms wide, hoping this would send her gliding across the wheat towards the house, but she didn't move.

Oh, are you kidding me?

She tried flapping. Nothing. Yohanna lowered her arms, and began walking. She couldn't feel the ground beneath her feet, but it somehow gave her the momentum to move.

Great, so I'm a ghost, but I can't float, and I still have to walk? Brilliant. What's the point of that?

Yohanna silenced her grumbling as she floated closer to the house. Figures moved around inside the kitchen, and overlapping voices clamoured for attention. A girl in a school uniform hurried into the garden with a dog's water bowl.

'Poppet,' the girl called, and a dog came running, tail wagging as the girl put the bowl on the ground. Since when did Federica have a dog?

'Hey, kid,' Yohanna called, waving her hand. The girl didn't look up, but Poppet the dog started barking at Yohanna.

'What's up, Poppet?' the girl asked, completely oblivious to Yohanna's presence, but Poppet kept up his enthusiastic woofing. 'Silly dog,' the girl said, before stepping back inside.

Okay, I'm invisible, except to dogs, Yohanna reasoned as she moved through the hedge towards the back door of the house. Poppet continued to bark at her.

'Oh, shush,' she said as she stepped inside.

Yohanna walked into organised chaos, and felt a pang of nostalgia for days like these. A boy and the girl she'd just seen with the dog, rushed around stuffing textbooks into bags, complaining about - and swapping - the contents of their lunch boxes, wondering aloud where their shoes/shirts/blazers/ties might be, and creating the kind of frenetic energy that Yohanna had only since seen backstage, minutes before a gig was due to start, and no one could find the bass player.

And there, a figure of calm in the centre of it all, was Madame Federica.

A wiry woman with a nose that could only have been sculpted in Rome, Federica stood with her hands on hips, occasionally gesturing to steer a child towards whatever it was they were looking for. She wore a pink dressing gown, a matching towel was wrapped around her head like a whipped ice cream, and there was an unlit cigarette tucked behind her ear. Her Italian accent was as thick as ever.

'They're in the wash, Ben, so wear those today... Do they smell? Then you can wear them again. Robin, darling, your shoes are drying in the airing cupboard. Ben, if you keep picking at it, it will never go away. Robin... Don't do that. Ben, turn that off, no phones while eating,' she said to the teenage boy sat at the breakfast table who was staring at a tiny rectangular TV as he ate her cereal.

About the size of a cigarette packet, the device was playing some kind of prank show where people were falling flat on their faces in a quick succession of clips. The words *Epic Fail* bounced across the screen and the teen giggled. Yohanna, perplexed by the device, moved in for a closer look, but Federica walked right through her to address the teen more sternly.

'If I have to ask you again, phone privileges will be denied for the rest of the week, and I know how disastrous that would be to your social standing. Neither of us want that, do we?'

Ben looked up from the phone, considered it, and laid it face down in the breakfast table and blew Federica a wry kiss. Yohanna liked the boy's aura of rebellion mixed with affection, and recalled many mini-confrontations just like this with Federica when she was that age.

'Thank you.' Federica caught the kiss and blew one back, before beckoning over the other teenage girl. 'Robin, darling, did you finish your homework?'

The girl who had given the dog the water bowl found herself the unwilling focus of Federica's attention. She scratched her nose and avoided eye contact as she said, 'Ye-es.'

'I'm a psychic, Robin, you know that means you can't lie to me, don't you?'

Yohanna belly-laughed. Federica didn't need any psychic powers to spot a fib, she just used a lifetime of experience fostering and caring for more children than most local authorities.

Aunty Fede, or Madame Federica as she was known to those who crossed her palm with silver, was Yohanna's last foster mother. The one who had prepared her for the big, bad world. Yohanna - or plain old Joanna, as she'd been then - felt a wave of guilt wash over her. When had she last called Aunty Fede? Yohanna noticed that Federica looked old. Older than she had any right to be. It had only been a few years.

Robin confessed to not doing her homework, and promised to do it right now, rushing to the kitchen table, whipping out a notebook and scribbling intently.

That was Federica's real talent. She never once had to shout at her foster kids. To do so would have been a failure. Federica treated each one of them with respect, giving them the full attention they needed, whipping them into shape and taking no nonsense, getting them to help around the house, but making it fun and co-operative. This may have looked like bedlam, but Federica had everything under control and, at 8:15 precisely, both kids were dressed and marching out of the door to the bus stop, fully prepared for their school day. She shut the door with a gentle click.

The silence they left behind was almost tangible. Chaos to serenity in under six seconds. Already Yohanna missed them, though Federica was clearly relieved to see them go as she exhaled loudly, took the cigarette from her ear, placed it between her lips, took out a lighter, and paused. Her head angled to one side, like a fox catching a scent. Federica turned in her pink slippers, looking around the hallway.

'Federica?' Yohanna rushed to her foster mother's side, waving her hands to get her attention. 'Can you hear me? Aunty Fede? I'm right here.'

Federica only narrowed her eyes. Leaving the cigarette stuck to her lower lip, she put the lighter back in her dressing gown pocket and strode through to the living room, hurriedly tugging the heavy curtains closed, leaving a small crack of mote-infested light as the only illumination.

'I need your help, Aunty Fede. Please. Can you hear me?' Yohanna pleaded, following Federica as she took a candle from above the fireplace, placed it on a coffee table in the light beaming through the crack in the curtains. Federica lit the candle, took a seat in the same battered recliner armchair that she remembered from her time here. Federica pulled on a lever, releasing a pop-up footrest, lay back, closed her eyes, and took a deep breath. Was she going to sleep?

'Aunty Fede.'

'Bloody hell, spirit, give me a chance.' Federica snapped, eyes still closed.

Yohanna couldn't help but smile at hearing the wonderful way Federica said 'Bah-luddy,' giving the word that extra Italian syllable. 'You're a strong one, but I want to know who you are before I just let you in. Be patient.'

Yohanna tingled with excitement. She began to wonder if Federica even remembered her. Aunty Fede had been a foster mother to so many children, would she recall one who had only been with her for a couple of years? For a teenage Joanna Adams it had been the happiest two years of her life. After being bumped from one foster home to another, she'd found a place that finally felt like a home.

The candle's flame began to dance, twisting and jerking like a needle in a compass. Federica raised her arms from the recliner, and the crack of light through the curtains began to move, a searchlight in the darkness. It passed over a wall festooned with framed photos of all the children that Federica had ever loved, over a bookshelf crammed with dog-eared copies of children's books, over a pile of toys teetering in the corner, before finally settling on Yohanna.

'Stop.' Federica commanded, and her eyes blinked open. Federica gasped as she recognised her old foster child, 'Joanna Adams. What bah-luddy trouble are you in now?'

L.A. WOMAN

'Come on, you big, red bastard.' Jo tugged on the bus's starter lever, but the vehicle remained a motionless hunk of metal blocking the road. A beam of light shone around the curve and a motorbike swerved at high speed between the bus and the wall of rock looming above the road. It skidded to a halt on the same outcrop that she'd been reversing off and then, through the grit and dust circulating in the night air, it began flashing red and blue lights.

Jo had been here barely five minutes and she was going to be shot by Erik Estrada from CHiPs.

She slid the bus window down, and did what any British tourist did when confronted by American law. She went super-English.

'I say. Hello.' She waved, sounding like Mary Poppins as she opened the door and began to clamber down.

'Stay in the vehicle, please ma'am,' the cop said, striding towards her.

'Righty-ho.' Jo did as she was told.

'You need to move the vehicle from the road, ma'am.' The cop looked up and down the road for any more incoming cars. 'Quickly.'

'Yes, I had just stalled, when I—'

'Start her up and let's get you off the road, right away,' he said, pointing to his bike. 'Pull up over there, please, ma'am.'

Jo did as she was told, eventually realising that she had to push a brass switch before pulling on the starter lever to bring the bus to life. She was more nervous about driving a few yards with the cop looking on than when she was trying not to reverse over the edge of a cliff. Once she parked, he approached her cabin again. He was tall, black and the owner of a moustache that would have made Tom Selleck's Magnum shave his off in shame at its inadequacy.

'Licence, registration and insurance, please.' He extended a hand.

'Oh, yes, of course,' Jo said, inwardly cursing as she suspected she had no such thing. She rummaged through the backpack in the footwell, nudging aside a hotel key for the Beverly Wilshire, sunglasses, a purse, several tampons, blue lipstick and mascara, and about three dollars in change. She was overwhelmed with relief when she opened the purse to find a lot of complicated insurance documents and a UK driving licence with the name Joanna Adams on it. Jo noted with muted disapproval that it was an old-school paper licence that Yohanna hadn't updated yet.

She handed it over and the cop examined the licence, unfolding it like a map, and looked up at Jo. He hadn't seen the damage to the side of the bus in the darkness.

'Are you the owner of this vehicle, ma'am?'

'No, it's a... a friend's,' she ventured. 'He let me take it for a spin and I got a bit lost, I'm afraid.'

'Where you headed?'

'Los Angeles.' Her mind scrabbled as she tried to remember the name of the hotel on the key in her bag. 'The... uh... Beverly Wilshire, actually. I could do with some directions if that's not too much—?'

'What's the purpose of your journey this evening?'

'I've always wanted to see Big Sur.' She smiled, relieved to recall Yohanna's mention of her runaway destination.

'Big Sur's some two hundred miles that way.' The cop pointed north.

'Oh.'

'And you're from the UK?'

'Yes. Have you ever been?'

The cop didn't answer, still studying the licence, turning it over.

'Is everything all right?' Jo asked.

The cop took a breath through the nose mounted on that magnificent moustache.

'Ma'am, I just found an English woman stalled in a London bus on one of the most dangerous stretches of highway along the Pacific coast in the dead of the night. Does that sound all right to you?'

'Like I said, I'm a bit lost, I'm afraid. I'm jolly sorry if I've caused any sort of kerfuffle, but there's no harm done and I simply need to get back to—'

'Ma'am, I could write you up for about fifteen traffic violations, y'know that?' the cop mused and Jo's heart threatened to stop. He handed her a ticket. Then his serious face cracked into a smile looking up at the side of the bus. 'But, dammit, my kids are fans. We saw you play at the Troubadour, and they'd be super-excited to hear I met you. Can you sign this for them, Yohanna?' He handed her a pen. 'On the back.'

'Erm, sure.' Jo wasn't quite sure what to do. 'What are their names?' Yes, that sounded good.

'Jennifer and Michelle.'

'Righto, To Jenn-i-fer and Mich-elle.' Jo drew a heart and signed her name. Joanna. Shit. It was the signature she used when signing for online deliveries, and it was a scribbly mess, so not immediately recognisable as a Joanna. As she was about to pass it to the cop, she quickly pulled it back and morphed the J into a Y and added an X at the end.

'Forgot the kisses.' Jo handed over the autograph feeling like a fraud, yet strangely exhilarated at the same time.

'Thanks.' The cop grinned. 'I'm not gonna give you a ticket, ma'am, but I will give you a warning that these roads can be extremely dangerous for a vehicle of this size. Your hotel's the Beverly Wilshire?'

'Yes, and I'm a bit vague on the directions.'

'Okay, tell you what I'm gonna do,' the cop said. 'The thought of you lost in this thing on these roads make me nervous, and it's the end of my shift, so I want you to follow me, okay?'

'What? Like a police escort?'

'No, a police escort for real.' The cop started putting his gloves back on. 'Stay on my tail, and honk if you got any problems.'

AND THAT WAS how Jo found herself entering Los Angeles in a red double-decker Routemaster bus with a mini police cavalcade in front, as the heat of the morning sun intensified.

They had driven through a dusty landscape with silent and still oil derricks dotted across the horizon, all casting long, sentinel shadows as the sun was coming up. Jo kept sleep at bay by singing along with the various non-stop rock stations she found by twirling the dial on a transistor radio that had been left in the driver's cab. Tom Petty, The Eagles and the Beach Boys each saved her from swerving off the road at some point.

They left Highway 101 just in time to hit thick morning commuter traffic on the outskirts of Los Angeles, but with a few flashing lights and the *whoop-whoop* of his siren, the cop cleared the way. Jo sensed hundreds of eyes on her. There was a mustard smear of pollution lingering over the city and she began to wonder about the wisdom of having the window open - the smell of car fumes was overwhelming.

The blazing sun was already beginning to leave an impression on her forearms, so she was grateful for the pair of Ray-Ban Clubmasters she found in the handbag. Now she could see where she was going without squinting like Nick trying to do the *Times* crossword.

Nick. Oh, Nick. Stupid bloody Nick. Would she ever see him or Ellie again? Her insides churned, and tears began to well, but Jo took a few deep breaths and pushed her sadness back down again. She knew she couldn't let herself get consumed with the grief of missing her daughter and errant husband. She had a mission to get home, and if she didn't focus on the task at hand she might never see them again. Glancing in the mirror to change lanes, she kept catching sight of her younger self, and every time it made her heart trip over.

On top of all that, something wasn't quite right. Everyone was driving really old BMWs, Mercs and Fords. Old cars, many of which were in surprisingly good condition and, if she didn't know better, looked brand new. This triggered another thought, one that sent a chill down her spine. It shouldn't be possible, but neither should she be in the body of her younger self, thousands of miles away from home. Jo twisted the dial on the radio, switching off the classic rock and searching for voices.

'... peak of eighty degrees in downtown L.A. today...'

'... Dodgers play the San Diego Padres at...'

'... President Clinton spoke to the Washington Post about his Defense of Marriage act, saying...'

Clinton?

His?

Unless Hillary had gone through a very quick sex change and won an election without Jo knowing, or the American people were suddenly ready to forgive an impeached president, Jo realised with a flush of dread that she was somehow in the nineteen-nineties. Of course she was. If she was her younger self she had to be, didn't she? The old cars, the lack of any new music on the radio, Yohanna's babbling about travelling through space *and* time. It made as much sense as anything else that had happened to her in the last twenty-four hours.

She was on a wide boulevard, one as big as the motorways back home, but that didn't stop the other drivers from staring at her and wondering why the hell a bus was getting the presidential treatment of a police escort. Some people standing on the road edge waved. Jo was half tempted to stop and pick them up, but a glance at the sinking petrol gauge told her to keep going. Eventually they found themselves on Rodeo Drive, and something in Jo's mind clicked as she saw a familiar building on the corner of Rodeo and Wilshire.

'*Pretty Woman*,' she blurted to herself. 'The Wilshire is the hotel where she stays in *Pretty Woman*. Oh my god.'

She followed the cop off Rodeo Drive back onto Wilshire, passing the legendary hotel with its domed awnings - yellow and white stripes today - elaborate carvings, sandstone columns, and tidy topiary. They couldn't make a left turn, so took a diversion around the block, but Jo eventually pulled up outside the hotel's entrance, finding all her energy draining from her. That had been one hell of a drive.

'Morning, ma'am.' A valet parking boy came running to the bus, sliding open the door for her and Jo had to stop herself from flopping onto the sidewalk. 'How are you today?'

'Rather exhausted, truth be told,' Jo said, waving at the traffic cop as he pulled away. 'Thank you!' she called after him and he waved back before disappearing into the morning traffic. She spent a few moments explaining to the valet boy how to start the bus before leaving him to fend for himself.

Jo felt a wave of tiredness come over her. Cosmic jet lag. She really needed to sleep. She faced the grand entrance of the Beverly Wilshire, where a smiling doorman was holding the door open for her. Jo smiled back, then hesitated. How was this now normal? She had to stop for a moment, to take stock and feel the ground beneath her feet, the air brush against her face. This was real, not a dream. She'd arrived from nowhere in an out of control bus, made friends with a traffic cop, been escorted into a city that was completely alien to her, and now found herself about to step into a luxury hotel from a movie that she loved. This had to be an hallucination, but it was all too real.

The doorman continued to wait patiently for her to come in.

'Sorry,' Jo said. 'Just getting my bearings.' *And making sure I'm not completely mental*, she thought as she crouched down to the sidewalk, feeling the grit of it under her fingers, watching ants as they scurried between the cracks in the paving slabs. She could smell bacon and glanced over to see a couple enjoying breakfast on one of the tables outside the hotel. Yup, this was as real as it got.

The doorman was looking concerned.

'Anything I can help you with, Miss? Have you lost something?' he asked, closing the door and crouching down to help her.

Jo straightened up, brushing the dust from her hands on her jeans.

'No, it's fine. This is real,' she said, flinging her arms wide. 'It's all real, isn't it?'

The doorman's smile returned. 'Certainly is, Miss.'

'It's just a little overwhelming at first, isn't it? Hollywood, L.A. and all that?'

'It can be, Miss. The City of Angels, land of dreams.' The doorman opened the door again and, reflected in the glass, Jo saw her face.

Twice.

One face was hers.

The other was plastered all over the side of the bus.

The entire thing had been covered with an image of Yohanna singing her heart out and thrashing an electric guitar, and it announced without any shame whatsoever, 'Brace yourself, America - Yohanna is here!'

Her face was on the side of a big fucking red bus.

'What did I say?' An angry voice hollered from the hotel lobby through the open door. 'Not a bloody scratch. And you bring it back with a dent as big as a boulder. Where the fuck have you been?'

Jo didn't need to turn round to figure out that she was about to meet Yohanna's manager, Lawrie. And she didn't need to be psychic to sense that he might be a little upset about something.

MADAME FEDERICA'S PANTOMIME

'Y ou're not lying,' Federica said, lips pursed after hearing Yohanna's story. 'But something's not right. I'm still not convinced.' Federica stepped up to Yohanna, inspecting her like a card-sharp looking for tells. Federica was proud of her Sicilian heritage, and she would tell her foster children that she'd been taught the many pantomimes of liars by her grandmother. Every gesture, every involuntary blush, blink, and fluctuation of the iris was part of the pantomime, and no liar could escape the scrutiny of someone who knew what to look for. And Federica was looking very closely indeed.

'You could be a jinn, a ghostly doppelgänger, a trickster. I'm very careful about who I let cross the divide from the other side. Please don't make me regret that decision.'

'I swear, it's me,' Yohanna pleaded. 'I'm the same girl, I've just been away for a while.'

'The girl I knew never dressed like this, never drove buses off cliffs, never believed in what she called my 'superstitious twaddle', and what the bah-luddy hell have you done to your hair?'

'Forget my hair,' Yohanna snapped. 'Why the fuck am I a ghost?'

'Language, young lady. None of that in my house.' Federica threw the curtains open, filling the room with light and a galaxy of dust. 'You should go back to where you came from.'

'That's what I'm trying to do. I don't know how.'

'Leave my house, spirit.' Federica pointed at the door.

'Christmas, nineteen-ninety,' Yohanna said. 'You caught me snogging Deon Fenwick in the driveway and you scared him off with a curse. Who else would know that?'

'Deon Fenwick would.' Federica blew out the candle.

'It's me, Aunty Fede, only...' Yohanna looked around her, at the flat screen TV, and what she figured was some kind of phone resting on the mantle. 'I might not be *your* Joanna Adams. This doesn't feel like my world, or time. And that's the problem, I need to get home.'

'You, but not you?' Federica said as the snuffed candle smoke swirled around her. 'Another Joanna?'

'Yes, finally, you're getting it.'

'And your home is this other universe? A parallel dimension, you said?'

'My guru said I could travel through parallel universes using the bardo state.'

'A guru?' Federica's face contorted into a sneer. 'Beware false prophets, darling. Especially ones who call themselves gurus.'

'I met another me. We were flying across the universe, and then I ended up standing in the middle of the field out there.'

'And where is she? This other you?'

'No idea, but it's exactly as Ronnie described it,' Yohanna said. 'He was right about everything.'

'Ronnie?'

'Aaronovitch. My guru. I call him Ronnie.'

'Aaronovitch? What's his first name?'

'Dunno. He's Doctor Aaronovitch.'

'A Doctor of what?'

'I never asked.'

'I hate him already,' Federica said.

'Okay, he's a bit of a dick- a clever dick, but he's the only one who understands this stuff. I need to find him here, in this universe, and he can send me home.'

Federica took a pair of reading glasses from a pocket in her dressing gown, a phone from the other, and started thumbing the phone's screen.

'What are you doing?' Yohanna asked.

'Googling him.'

'Sounds painful.'

Federica peered at Yohanna over the rims of her glasses, 'You're really not from around here, are you?'

'Yesterday I was in California, it was the nineties, and I was on the verge of the big time. Now I'm back home, you're telling me it's twenty years later, and I look like a bad photocopy of myself.'

'We all have bad days, darling. It's how we cope with them that counts. Ah, here we are. That him?' Federica angled the phone's screen for Yohanna. It was a book cover for something called *The Infinite Power Of You*. A garish jumble, the cover featured a portrait photo of a balding, bearded man with piercing blue eyes looking directly at the camera. Behind him was a backdrop with a prism floating in clouds, and a rainbow of colours beaming from it. He was grinning with all the sincerity of a fox in a chicken coop.

'No, that's not Ronnie. Wait, it *is* him, just older.' Yohanna's eyes flitted to Federica.

'We all get old, darling,' Federica said, continuing to thumb the phone's screen.

'Where is he now?' Yohanna asked.

'Looks like he owns a bookshop in Hastings,' Federica said. 'The Prism Power Bookstore and Esoteric Emporium. Catchy.'

'We have to go.'

'We? Me?' Federica said. 'I have a house to clean, I've got washing to do, the toilet's blocked and the car's being serviced. Do I look like someone who has time for a day trip to Hastings?'

'But I need you,' Yohanna said, waving her hands through Federica's face, making the older woman flinch. 'Look, I can't touch anything, can't write anything down, I've got a memory like a sieve, and you have that clever little thing.'

'iPhone.'

'Do you? Who?'

'No, that's what it's... Never mind.'

'I need you and that phone thing, and I can fix this.'

'I was always very impressed with your self-confidence, darling, but coming back from the dead might be a push, even for you.'

'I'm not dead, just in this weird limbo. Please, Aunty Fede. I came here for a reason. I thought of you, I visualised this house, and the universe, fate, God, the spirit world, whatever you want to call it... it dropped me on your doorstep, because you're the only person who can help me.'

'I'm still not convinced you're my Jo. She had no time for spirits. She always had her feet on the ground. A practical girl.'

'That's why she's living in a suburban coffin, waiting to cash in her pension and die.'

'What?'

'The Jo I met was me if I gave up on life. I dunno, maybe that's why I made contact with her? Maybe the universe decided she needed a few thrills?'

'Is she in danger?' Federica's face darkened.

'Maybe, I dunno.' Yohanna shrugged, then saw Federica bite her lip. 'I mean, yeah, she could be. Big danger. Stuck in limbo, lost, afraid, dying. Who knows? We're not gonna find out standing in your living room, are we?'

'Wait.' Federica moved to a landline phone by the TV. 'You called me last night.'

'What?'

'You, or one of you, left a message.' Federica pressed a button on the answerphone. The digitally compressed sound of Jo's voice filled the room.

Hey, Federica, it's Joanna. Sorry I've not been in touch, and sorry to call only when I need something but... I've had a really—'

The message ended with a beep.

'Okay, good, she's fine, cool,' Yohanna said. 'Let's find Ronnie.'

'Maybe she can help us?'

'I've freaked her out enough,' Yohanna said. 'Trust me, she doesn't me need spooking her again. We need Ronnie.'

Federica glanced at the clock on the wall.

'Nearly nine,' she said, and Yohanna felt a thrill of excitement as her old foster mother began to give the idea some serious thought.

'Just get me to the bookshop in, where was it? Hastings?' Yohanna said, treading very carefully. 'Once I find Aaronovitch, I'm out of your hair, and you'll be home before school's out.'

Federica looked up from the phone and once again scrutinised her former ward. 'You're just as stubborn as your other self.'

'You'll help me?'

'Back before school's out?'

'I promise.'

'Don't make promises you cannot keep.' Federica unwrapped the pink towel from her hair, whilst still thumbing the phone. 'Fine. Let me get my face on and we can go... Oh dear.'

'Oh dear, what?'

'Your guru... He's the only one who can get you home?'

'Yeah, without him I'm screwed.'

Federica held up the phone's screen, swiping through headlines that chronicled a scandal, with accusations of fraud, womanising, bankruptcy, drug abuse and heavy drinking.

'Your guru is an alcoholic, bong-toking, shag monster, darling,' Federica said. 'Your guru is a crook.'

HEY BULLDOG

'Where the bloody hell have you been?'

Jo entered the lobby of the Beverly Wilshire like an extra from the *Walking Dead*, to find a roly-poly little man barking at her. Jo didn't think of herself as tall, but she was a good foot taller than this guy, and some bit of lizard brain was telling her that he was maybe a little dangerous. She had no doubt that he was Yohanna's manager Lawrie.

'Do you have any idea of the heritage of that bus, Yo-Yo?' He was still going on about the bloody bus. 'Elton John arrived in that bus in 1970. It announced him to America, the biggest British artist since The Beatles. I try and do the same for you and this is how you repay me?'

He left a space to take a breath and Jo realised she was expected to speak. She thought back to what Yohanna had said in her kitchen.

'Sorry, I... I had a little panic attack, that's all.'

'Then get a paper bag and take a few breaths.' Lawrie took her elbow and pulled her closer. 'Don't go running off with a priceless piece of rock history and putting a fucking great dent in it.'

'It's a bus, it's hardly Jimi Hendrix's codpiece.'

'A bus that cost me two grand to rent, young lady, and that was mates' rates. That's coming out of your first royalty cheque,' he said. Lawrie took a deep breath, his scowl softened. He stood and looked at her like a museum exhibit.

'Gordon Bennett, you look like you've been dragged through a hedge backwards. Look at your barnet.' He had to reach up to tame her windswept hair. 'Alright, let's focus. You must be cream-crackered. Let's get you to your room, get you well-rested. Big day today. Big day. Got your room key?'

'Oh, shit.' Jo's hands went to her jeans pockets, but she already knew it wasn't there. 'I left it in the bus.'

'No problem. Oi. Garçon.' Yohanna's manager hollered across the lobby and snapped his fingers at the reception desk. 'Room key for Yohanna, mate. In the big red. Quick as you can, son. Chop-chop, wicky-wicky.'

The man behind the reception desk bore this onslaught of bossiness with a lifetime of service industry experience and deference.

'Of course, Mr. Grant.'

'Listen, girl.' Lawrie rested an arm on Jo's shoulder. 'I know all this hullabaloo can be a bit scary first time round, but it'll all be worth it in the end.' He gently prodded the end of her nose with his index finger, which she didn't much appreciate, especially as he really needed a manicure. 'You are gonna be a megastar, young lady. Huge. The biggest, the best.'

'The key, Mr. Grant.' The hotel bellboy arrived, breathless.

'Nice one, sonny Jim,' Lawrie said, peeling a ten dollar bill from a roll in his pocket. 'Stick that in the piggy bank, eh?'

'Thank you, sir.'

As the bellboy retreated, Jo watched Lawrie stuff the notes back in the depths of his trousers. Lawrie's suit was off the rack, Miami Vice pastel blue, and unforgiving around the midriff. There were beads of sweat on his forehead, and his receding hair was waxed back in the Phil Collins style. His trousers were a little too short in the leg and a little too tight around the waist. His shirt and tie were loose, and he wore scuffed Hush Puppies that Jo suspected were older than her. The forty-two-year-old her.

Jo followed him through the lobby to the elevator. The way he walked, his shoulders rocking like a boxer's, suggested he could be quite handy in a ruck. Yet there was also something Churchillian and British bulldog about Lawrie. Not a man to mess with, and not a man to be fooled easily.

On top of all this there was something very familiar about him. Jo was sure she'd met him before, but she couldn't put her finger on when or where.

'Home sweet home.' Lawrie unlocked the door to a penthouse suite.

She was about to gasp, but she realised that Yohanna would have already seen this, and so Jo did her best to stay in character. But, bloody hell, it was fantastic. The aroma hit her first. The sweet perfume of Calla lilies welcomed her to the main room, bursting from every table in vivid shades of white, orange and pink.

Floor-to-ceiling windows lined one wall, giving her a panoramic view of Los Angeles. There were enough sofas, couches and soft furnishings to fill IKEA, and more decorative vases than the British Museum. Tastefully framed and inoffensive watercolours of even more flowers filled gaps in the wall, and discreet lamps and lights were tucked away in every corner. The penthouse was perfect for keen botanists who hated to move more than three feet to dim the lights.

Jo casually explored further, trying not to look like this was all new to her, finding a fully-fitted kitchen, a dining room, and a terrace. It was almost bigger than her house.

'Press pack's on the table here.' Lawrie briefly picked up a paper-stuffed folder for her to see before letting it slap back on one of the suite's many coffee tables. 'Give it a quick shufty before this afternoon. Car's coming at three, I'll come and get you at about quarter to. Be ready. Repeat that back.'

'Hm?' A bubble burst around Jo and she snapped out of her penthouse trance.

'Yo-Yo.' Lawrie growled in frustration, nails digging into his palms. 'Yohanna, listen to me, all right. You listening?' Lawrie took her arms and looked her in the eye. 'I know you had a wobbler yesterday, and I understand the last few days haven't quite been what we wanted, so this afternoon is important. More important than ever. You've got fans, girl, a growing committed fan base. Something we can build on, we know that. But we need the single to hit that magic tipping point to take you mainstream. The music press loves ya, but we need the great unwashed to fall in love with you, too. This is where we announce you to the world. We get this right, and we'll have the record companies fighting over you like dogs over meat.'

'Ew.' Jo grimaced at the metaphor.

'You know what I mean. This is the crunch, so I need you with it, focused, on the ball. *Capiche?*'

'Lawrie?' Jo was struggling to piece together the breadcrumbs of clues that he was leaving her. She'd thrown a wobbly of some sort, the trip so far had been a disappointment, and she'd run off in a bus for some reason. There was someone important missing in all this. Someone she needed to find.

'Can I ask you a question?'

'Course you can, girl.'

'It's a weird one.'

'Wouldn't be the first. 'Specially not from you.'

Jo wondered how to phrase this, so took her time.

'My guru—'

'You keep the fuck away from him.' Lawrie shocked Jo with the intensity of his anger. 'It's him putting all that bollocks in your head that made you all doolally yesterday. Let me make myself clear - you are barred from talking to him, okay? I know you think he's the Dalai bloody Lama and all that, but he's bad news. This charabanc is costing me a fortune, and I will not have some stuck-up tosspot with his crystals and ley lines bollocks put it in jeopardy. Understand? And he's been warned, too. I've told him that if he so much as calls you, I'm gonna take his chakras and shove 'em up his arse. Savvy?'

Jo nodded, dumbstruck.

'Good.' Lawrie puffed his cheeks and relaxed a little. 'Right, scrub yourself clean, get some kip and I'll see you later for a major life-changing event. Okay?'

'Uh... yeah.' Jo watched him head to the door, patting his jacket pockets, finding his phone and dialling with his chubby fingers.

'Oh, yeah.' He paused and jabbed the phone in the direction of the bedroom. 'I got your baby back from him. She's in there. Ta la!' And with that, Lawrie was gone.

STRANGERS ON A TRAIN

Yohanna rocked with the crowded suburban train as it ambled towards Hastings. Quite how she was moving *with* the train, even though her feet were floating two inches above the stained floor of the carriage, was a mystery to her. But, like gravity, time, and the enduring appeal of dinner jazz, it was a mystery that worked without her having to worry about it, so she accepted it as another freakish by-product of her current predicament.

What was more troubling was that Federica was now blanking her. The old lady had been aloof since they left the house. Yohanna, worried that she'd upset her somehow, tried to break the ice with some casual conversation.

'I guess we'll have to take the bus or a taxi to the bookshop?' Yohanna said. 'Or maybe we could walk? Weather's good, so...'

Federica continued to stare impassively out of the window, but a series of self-absorbed boyfriends had given Yohanna all the experience she needed to know when she was being ignored.

'Or do they have, like, beaming technology in the future now? Like *Star Trek*? No? Course not, or we'd be using it now wouldn't we? Silly.'

Federica glanced at her phone, much like every other passenger on the train.

'Christ, what's on those things that's so interesting?' Yohanna peered over the shoulder of a young woman and recoiled. 'Bloody hell, she's watching zombies rip people to shreds. Have you seen this? Aunty Fede? You've got gory zombie movies on telly during the day?'

Yohanna moved to the next passenger, who was watching a show where a dragon was burning people alive. 'When I was a kid it was repeats of *Sesame Street* and *Home and Away*. Daytime TV's gone hardcore.'

Federica said nothing, but her eyes briefly met Yohanna's. *She can hear me.*

They came to a stop and as the commuters shuffled around to let people on and off, Federica turned her back on Yohanna.

'Fine, okay, ignore me.' Yohanna pouted as they set off again, peering over Federica's shoulder, finding her thumbing her phone. 'Yeah, that's it, keep fiddling with your phone. See if I care. Clearly, *Zombie Jerry Springer* is on, and you watching people being burnt to a crisp by dragons for entertainment is more important than me. I just want to know if the whole trip is going to be like this, and then I can—'

Federica held the phone at eye level, at an angle where Yohanna could see it. She'd written her a message:

I CAN'T TALK to you, or even acknowledge you, without looking like a crazy lady who talks to thin air on the train. So, please be patient. Say, okay, when you've finished reading this, so I can put the phone down.

'OH,' Yohanna whispered. 'Okay. I mean, okay, I've read it.'

The hypnotic rumble of the train moving filled the carriage, a backdrop to the chattering *tsk-tsk-tsk-tsk* of headphones. No one spoke.

'Sorry,' Yohanna said breaking her own silence. 'It's just I get bored easily, and I like to talk, so I'll just keep talking if that's okay with you?'

Federica exhaled heavily, and held her phone to her ear, 'Yes? Oh, Yohanna, how lovely to hear from you.'

Yohanna was momentarily puzzled, but then Federica's eyes locked onto hers, 'Oh, I see. You're pretending to be on the phone while actually you're talking to me.'

'Yes, that's it,' Federica smiled, though her eyes betrayed impatience.

'That's quite cool, actually.'

'I'm glad you think so. Now, what do you want?'

Yohanna opened her mouth. Then closed it again.

'Oh, so *now* you're lost for words?' Federica twisted her lips.

'No, no...' Yohanna looked at the other commuters around her. 'So, they're watching telly?'

'Yes, mostly they've downloaded shows they recorded or are watching on catch up. Is that really the burning topic you needed to discuss?'

'No one has Walkmen now? Do I have a future? Do people still listen to music?'

'Of course, yes. Well, on iPhones, mostly.'

'Why does everything start with an 'i'?'

'Blame Steve Jobs.'

'Who?'

'Doesn't matter.'

Yohanna squinted at some of the phone users around her and saw the cover art for *Goodbye Yellow Brick Road* on one commuter's iPhone, 'Did CDs get really small, or what?'

'It's all MP3s, or streaming. You can have all the music in the world on one of these.' Federica saw a man look up from his newspaper and frown at her. She looked directly back at him with a glare that made him decide that minding his own business would be the best course of action to ensure a peaceful journey to work.

'Empy-whats?' Yohanna asked.

'M-P-threes. Look, can we change the subject? Tell me more about Jo? Was she okay when you saw her?'

'Yeah, I think maybe we swapped places?' Yohanna said. 'Did you ever see that film, *Freaky Friday*?'

'No.'

'Jodie Foster when she was really young.'

'I didn't see it.'

'Oh, well, it's like that, but with more inter-dimensional travel.'

'I just said, I didn't see it. *Oy.*' Federica briefly took the phone away from her ear in exasperation. More passengers looked up at her. 'Mind your own business,' she said, laying the Italian accent on thick, then returning to her call. 'Okay, okay. You were in California, and my Jo was here and you think you swapped?'

'Yup.'

'How does a nice girl like you end up with a...' Federica chewed on the next word, '...*guru*?'

'It's California. Everyone has a guru out there.'

'And the bus? Tell me about that.'

'What about it?'

'You were running away?'

Yohanna became evasive, looking out of the window.

'You still there...?' Federica raised an eyebrow. 'The line's breaking up.'

'Yeah.' Yohanna's voice was quiet. 'I'm here. I wasn't... I wasn't running away. I just needed a little air.'

'There she is.'

'Who?'

'The Joanna I used to know. Quiet, thoughtful. Why were you running away?'

'Can we not talk about this?'

'I'll hang up, shall I?' Federica moved the phone a little away from her ear.

'Yeah, you do that.'

. . .

HASTINGS WAS BASKING in bright sunshine, the promenade playing host to dawdling holiday makers. A group gathered around street magicians and human statues, and a busker playing *A Whole Lotta Love* on the pan pipes.

'People keep walking through me,' Yohanna complained. The first words she'd spoken since the train.

'Do you feel anything when they do it? Does it hurt?'

'Apart from a creeping sense of detachment from reality? No.'

'Then stop complaining.'

'Hey, how come you're okay talking to me here, but not on the train?'

'It's Hastings,' Federica said. 'People will assume you're either crazy and should be left alone, or talking on bluetooth.'

'I'm just going to assume that a bluetooth is a kind of tiny phone that you stick in your molars like a filling and it tells you the weather whenever you chew gum.'

'Yes, that's it exactly.'

Yohanna was about to ask if that was really true, when she caught Federica's withering look and decided better of it.

'What do you want me to say to this guru man?' Federica asked.

'You? Why are you speaking to him?'

'You're a spirit,' Federica said, just as a group of oblivious teenagers walked through Yohanna. 'He won't be able to see or speak to you.'

'Ronnie is one of the smartest and most spiritually aware guys I've ever met.' Yohanna raised her chin as she spoke. 'He's completely tapped into the universe and its workings. He'll figure out a way to speak to me, and he'll get me back. Like I said, you'll be on the train home in no time.'

'Oh, so I'm not needed now, am I?' Yohanna's dismissive tone made Federica stop in her tracks. 'I'll go now, shall I?'

'No, no.' Yohanna scurried back to her old foster mother. 'Let's make sure he's there first, huh? He might have popped out for a sandwich or something, or it could be his day off.'

'You mean this god-like man needs to eat, just like us mere

mortals?' Federica opened her mouth in mock astonishment. 'You're in for a big disappointment, young lady.'

'Hey, he got me this far, didn't he?' Yohanna protested.

'Stuck in the wrong universe as a disembodied spirit? Nice work, Einstein.'

'He saved my life.' Yohanna cried, immediately regretting it.

'How?' Federica stepped up to Yohanna, aware now that she was getting funny looks from passersby. 'And why would your life need saving, Joanna?'

'That's not my name any more,' Yohanna said, wandering aimlessly. 'Is it this way?'

'This way.' Federica pointed in the opposite direction towards the centre of town.

'He's a good man,' Yohanna finally said as they turned into a narrow road, crammed with gift shops selling buckets and spades. 'And this is the future. You're older, so he'll be older too. Older and wiser. He's probably expecting us and will know exactly what to do. He'll probably send me home using a bluetooth or something, and you can get back to your life and we'll all be happy.'

'I doubt it,' Federica said, stopping and checking her phone.

'My god, you are so negative, you know that?' Yohanna turned on her, hands on hips. 'A little positivity goes a very long way. So much of our lives is dictated by the way we think. If we think we're going to fail, we will. But if we prepare ourselves for success, we're far more likely to succeed. That's why I'm going to be a star and why that other loser me will always fail.'

'I certainly failed when it came to teaching you manners.'

'I'm sorry, but it drives me mad. Why are you so sure that he can't help us?'

'Because this is his bookshop.' Federica tipped her phone to the facade of the building they had stopped by.

It was a nice enough shopfront. Big windows, plenty of room inside. It would have made a wonderful bookshop.

But above the door it had a name that was unfamiliar to Yohanna.

'Who's Nando?'

YOHANNA'S BABY

B *aby?*
Yohanna had a baby.
In the next room.
Ellie!

Jo rushed to the master bedroom, flung the double doors open and, once she'd got over the huge size of the bed, realised with a wash of disappointment that there was no cot, playpen or baby in the room.

There was, however, a guitar on the bed.

A battered Martin acoustic guitar. Three-quarter sized, with a sun-bleached spruce wood top, faded maple wood neck and steel strings. There were dinks and chips all around its poor body, and a scar running the length of its top, a botched crack repair, where...

Holy shit.

Jo knew this guitar.

But this was impossible. How could it be here?

When Jo was sixteen, she would make pilgrimages to Hill's Music in town every Saturday morning. Mr. Hill was a kindly man who couldn't have a single conversation without eventually steering it round to The Beatles and their genius and influence on everything from popular music, film and comedy to politics and merchandising. He would gladly let Jo practice with any of his guitars, then try to sell her something from his extensive range of Beatles mugs and T-shirts. Jo would politely decline as she was saving to buy a very specific guitar. A battered Martin acoustic that belonged to Mr. Hill himself. He kept it in the back room and would only show it to his most trusted customers. The story was legendary. He had found it tossed in a skip outside a house on his walk to the shop one winter morning. A gem, discarded by someone who had no inkling of its value. He had been restoring it over a number of years between paid jobs, and he confessed to Jo that it was a job that he hoped would never end.

Each week Jo would make an offer for the guitar, and each week Mr. Hill would politely decline.

That spring, Mr. Hill's wife passed away. Both were elderly, and her illness had been a long and painful one, but something in him died, too. In a change of heart, he offered Jo first refusal on the guitar. They agreed a fair price - which was still beyond her means, but she knew how much of Mr. Hill's love had gone into its restoration and would save every penny until she had enough.

After thirteen months of pre-dawn paper round deliveries in rain, sleet and snow, the guitar was finally hers. That was the guitar she taught herself Beatles and Bowie songs with, the guitar that replaced the broom handle she'd previously practiced with in front of the mirror, and the guitar that almost convinced her she could be a star one day. She called it Ziggy, and sang for Federica and her friends at weekends. They started with polite applause and words of encouragement, but by the end of her eighteenth summer, they were urging her to write songs and apply to music college.

Ziggy was like an extension of Jo, and when she had it strapped over her shoulder and resting on her belly, she felt supremely comfortable and confident. Nothing was impossible with Ziggy in her arms.

Until a boyfriend sat on it only nine months later while trying to entice her into bed. The loud hollow crack broke the guitar and her heart. Jo wept like she'd lost her best friend. It was the end of two relationships, as her boyfriend tried to use the trauma as an excuse for make-up sex - turning her tears to anger.

'The only thing you're getting on tonight is your bloody bike.'

'It's just a bloody guitar.' Jo could still hear his words even now.

He was wrong. It was her first true love.

Or was it? Jo picked it up, turning it over, sniffing the sound hole and getting a whiff of bronze and furniture polish. It was uncanny. She ran her thumb over the strings - *thrang* - and winced. It needed tuning. She sat at the end of the bed, thumbing the strings and turning the tuning keys with ease until it was near perfect. After strumming a few chords, there could be no mistake. This was the guitar. Ziggy lived. Both she and Yohanna had toiled for this beauty - but where Jo had all but given up after its encounter with her boyfriend's backside, Yohanna had carried on.

Yohanna told Jo that *Ellie's Song* had called to her across the universe, so maybe this was it? Maybe a magic guitar was what she needed to go home? All she had to do was play the song, hand the guitar back to Yohanna, swap places and she'd be back in her little terraced house before tea time.

Jo played the opening arpeggio, took a breath.

'Huck...'

Oh, for God's sake.

'Huck...'

She still couldn't sing it. Whatever mental block she had was still in place, and no amount of interstellar time travel could change that.

She would hum it.

It was a beautiful guitar, with a fast neck and full, bright tone. It responded to her every strum and bend, making Jo sound better than any other musical instrument she'd known. Jo also found the tips of Yohanna's fingers were hardened due to regular playing, and her nails were trimmed back so she could really dig into the strings and go for it.

Jo continued to play, and hum, and play, and hum.

Nothing. No glowing light, no angelic apparition of her younger self. Just a lost and lonely woman in a hotel room that smelled like a florist.

Jo was tired to her bones, and the bed was soft. She lay back, cradling the guitar, promising herself just a half hour nap and then she would shower, find her guru, and figure this thing out once and for all.

Six hours later she awoke to Lawrie yelling in her face.

TRULY OUTRAGEOUS

'Wake up. Yo-Yo. Upsy daisy.'

Jo had hoped for more familiar voices, perhaps a vision of Ellie, but it had been a dreamless slumber.

'C'mon, girl, move your arse, or you'll be late.' Lawrie's voice popped Jo's bubble, and she struggled to reboot her brain. It was difficult enough waking in a strange room, or a new country, but she was also in the wrong universe with pan-dimensional jet-lag.

'Wakey-wakey, eggs and bakey.'

Lawrie was shaking her now, which she really didn't appreciate, and only added to her confusion.

'All right, all right, I'm up. Christ, it's like being back at school.' Jo sat up and blinked her eyes to focus on this strange pear of a man marching around this extraordinary bedroom dressed in a blue pastel suit with the sleeves rolled up.

'Car's here in ten minutes, girl, and you're not even showered,' he growled. 'Up. Now.'

'Yeah, yeah.' Jo took a breath and the bizarre reality of her situation took hold once more. She was stranded. She was Yohanna, this man was her manager, she'd had a press conference, and she had to find a guru. She stretched her arms and caught a whiff of her body odour. Most deodorant could handle forty-eight hours' protection, but not eighteen years.

'Shower, yes,' she agreed. 'I'll meet you in the lobby in ten minutes.'

Lawrie didn't leave, but opened the wardrobe, grabbed some clothes from the rack and tossed them on the bed, next to the guitar.

'What are you doing?' The words tumbled from her mouth in a semi-conscious jumble.

'Try the crop top with the shredded jeans,' Lawrie said, clacking through the hangers, looking for other options. 'Or should we go with hot pants?' He was half talking to himself now. 'Yeah, the hot pants,' he decided, hurling a tiny pair on the bed next to the crop top and shredded jeans. 'Ooh, hold the phone, I like these.' He turned to Jo, holding up a pair of stars and stripes leggings for her to admire. 'Bit of local colour. The Yanks love bollocks like this. Try 'em on and we'll see what works.'

'What... what are you doing?' Jo repeated, still too befuddled for complex conversation.

'You're right.' Lawrie glanced at his watch. 'Not enough time. Leggings, crop top, red stilettos, and wear those big strawberry earrings. I reckon they could be your trademark. Y'know? Strawbs and cream, tennis, English rose and all that.'

'Fine, whatever.' Jo waved him towards the door with no intention of wearing any of that tat. 'I'll see you downstairs.' He still didn't move. 'Lawrie, I'm going to shower. I need you out of my room, please.'

'Not with your track record, girl,' he said.

'What?'

'You're a flight risk. I don't wanna be humping my way back up here in ten minutes to find you've legged it, or that you're having a kip.'

'I'm not a bloody toddler.'

'Events of the past few days suggest otherwise.' Lawrie's lower lip jutted out like a bulldog's. 'Sorry, love, but you made your bed, now sleep in it... Though, not literally, I need you up and at 'em.'

Jo realised he wasn't going to budge.

'Compromise,' she said in an even voice, though her anger was simmering. 'You wait in the hallway. If I'm not out in eight minutes, you can come and get me.'

Lawrie folded his arms.

'Lawrie, the clock is ticking. The longer we piss about, the later we'll be. You're a manager, a negotiator, yes? Then you'll know that a successful negotiation is where both sides come to a happy compromise.'

The wrinkles on Lawrie's face folded in on themselves. 'When did you swallow a bloody dictionary?'

'Lawrie. Trust me. I'll be out that door in eight minutes, ready for action.'

Lawrie glanced at his watch. 'Seven,' he said, turning on his heels, scooping up a folder stuffed with papers from a dressing table, and making for the door. 'One second longer and I'm coming in.'

EXACTLY SEVEN MINUTES LATER, Jo, true to her word, emerged from her suite showered and refreshed, wearing a plain white T-shirt, un-shredded jeans, Nike sneakers, no earrings, her chunky Nokia 2110 wedged in her jeans pocket, and her Ray-Bans resting in her hair.

'Come on, Lawrie, car's a-waiting,' Jo said, beaming and moving quickly past him and striding down the hall towards the elevator.

She didn't need to look back to sense his fury, 'What're you wearing?' he called after her. 'Where's the stars, stripes and strawbs?'

Jo hopped into the elevator just as the doors were closing, leaving him stranded in the hallway like a jilted groom.

JO SMILED at the doorman as she stepped out into the L.A. sunshine. She caught a glimpse of herself reflected in the door's glass once more. It was an out-of-body sensation that she would never get used to. Seeing yourself in old photos was one thing, but actually inhabiting your younger body was strange beyond anything she could have imagined. She had more energy for a start, but she was paddling in an unfamiliar hormonal wave pool, experiencing brief, overwhelming washes of anger and sadness that threatened to engulf her. The trauma of her teenage years had always been a vivid memory, but she'd forgotten just how unsettling and terrifying her early twenties had been.

So much uncertainty and suddenly being responsible for your actions can send a person into a spiral of despair. But would she have ever let herself be bossed around? Or have her clothes picked out for her by an older man? And the rose tattoo she had found on her right buttock while showering confused her more than anything else so far. Jo hated tattoos, and had lectured Ellie time and again about how she'd regret getting one when she was older. Jo had read once that the body replaced all its cells every seven years or so, and that technically you weren't the same person as you were then, which explained a lot. But she was disappointed with this version of Yohanna so far.

Burying the dismay with her younger self, Jo donned her sunglasses, ready to play the part and ride out whatever the universe had in store for her today with a determined smile. She wouldn't find her guru stuck in a hotel room, that was certain. She needed to get out in this world, learn all she could, and get home as soon as possible.

There were three black Mercedes limousines parked outside, all with tinted windows. The driver of the first one greeted her by name and smiled as he opened the door for her. The morning was already heating up and the car was stuffy. The black leather seats creaked as she shuffled across, but it was comfortable and springy in a way that only limousines ever are. Inside, there was a telephone on a wire, a TV with a VHS player, and a refrigerator that was depressingly empty. Jo hadn't been in a car this posh since her wedding day.

The door was yanked open again, and a breathless Lawrie was glaring at her with a face like a slapped arse.

'You're going out looking like that?' he said in a tone not dissimilar to one used by Jo when scolding Ellie prior to one of her nights out clubbing.

'Lawrie, I won't be dressing like a tart, and I won't be taking fashion tips from a man who looks like a cut price Miami Vice tribute act,' she said as sweetly as possible. 'Get in, we'll be late.'

There was more teeth grinding from Lawrie, but he obviously knew she was right about being late. He slapped the roof of the Mercedes. 'Tower Records, Sunset,' he barked at the driver and flumped inside next to Jo.

As the car pulled away, he shuffled through his paper-stuffed folder with angry vigour. 'I have a plan,' he fumed, shoving some of the papers into Jo's hands. 'A very detailed and thorough plan, *that I thought we had discussed*, to propel you to stardom, young lady.'

Jo started leafing through the papers he had given her. There was a detailed schedule of events for the next few days. It looked busy on the page, but the gaps between events were hours long. It looked like Lawrie was struggling to get her booked.

'Part of that plan,' Lawrie found what he was looking for and flourished a sheet of paper like Chamberlain returning from Munich, 'is to present you to the world as the most outrageous pop sensation since Cyndi Lauper. Now how the bloody hell am I supposed to do that when you go round dressed like a middle-aged mum shopping for big knickers at Marks and Spencer?'

'Outrageous? Why do I need to be outrageous? That's just a few adjectives away from 'zany' and 'madcap', and then I'm afraid I shall have to kill you.' Jo crinkled her nose, still reading the press release. 'Bloody hell, Lawrie, you're laying it on a bit thick, aren't you?'

'What do you mean?'

'*The songwriting talent of Lennon and McCartney, wrapped in a bod built for sin, topped off with the voice of an angel.*' Jo curled her lip in disgust. 'How is anyone supposed to live up to that? No wonder she...' Jo managed to stop herself before she said something weird or incriminating. But it was true. This was freaking her out as a mature woman. What would something like this do to the mind of an impressionable, butt-tattooed, twenty-four-year-old? Would it send her driving away in a double-decker bus, never wanting to come back?

'This was your bloody idea.' Lawrie said.

'*A bod built for sin* was my idea?' Jo saw the look of suspicion on Lawrie's face and realised she was sailing a little too close to the wind. 'On reflection, let's steer away from the body image stuff, shall we? It's not a great message for young girls, is it?'

'What's happened to you?' Lawrie said. 'You've changed.'

'I'm still a little jet-lagged, that's all.'

'No, no, girl, this is different,' he said. 'You're a lot more lippy for a start. Lippy, smartarsey, and now you've got all political. Give me your phone.'

'What? Why?'

'Hand it over.' Lawrie snapped his fingers.

'No.'

'See. This *defiance*. This is exactly what I mean. This is him, isn't it?'

'Who?'

'That twat of a guru.' Lawrie scowled. 'He's been filling your head with all this hippy-dippy shit, and it's turned you into a lairy little cow. I never had any of this backchat before you met him. Phone,' he demanded. 'Come on.'

Jo leaned over, tugging on the Nokia jammed into her jeans pocket. It was small for a nineties cell phone, but still a sizeable chunk of plastic when compared to a smartphone. She yanked it free like a dentist removing a stubborn molar and turned it over in her hand. Lawrie made a grab for it, but she shifted around so he couldn't reach. With her thumb she detached the battery from the main body of the phone and gave it to him.

'Half and half,' she said, knowing that she would pinch it back from him later. 'Compromise.'

Lawrie opened the car window a crack and tossed the battery out the window.

'Lawrie! What the fuck?' Jo spun round, craning to see out the limo's tiny rear window. The battery clattered on Santa Monica Boulevard and was flattened by a Coca Cola truck. Jo's heart froze. The phone was her only way of finding Ronnie, and now it was just a powerless lump of plastic.

'That's that sorted.' Lawrie cleared his throat, turning his attention back to his papers. 'Here's the running order. We play the new single — the big one — and then announce you. I've got a couple of plants in the audience who'll lead off with some easy questions - the ones we rehearsed, remember?'

'Er... okay.' Jo's mind drifted back from thoughts of where to buy a Nokia battery in L.A. to the conversation at hand. She wondered how she could break it to Lawrie that she had no memory of a rehearsal that Yohanna attended. She could wing it. How hard could it be? She'd seen enough press conferences on TV to know that it was all positive platitudes and smiling for the cameras.

'Then it'll open to the floor.' Lawrie continued. 'But by then we'll have set the tone. Easy peasy, bright and breezy. You all set?'

'Ready as I'll ever be,' Jo sighed, as the car pulled up outside the huge Tower Records on Sunset Strip. There was already a small flock of teenage girls waiting in line.

'There's a crowd.' Jo was puzzled. 'Wow.'

'Central casting.' Lawrie smiled at his own ingenuity. 'Play along.'

'Fake fans? You got me fake fans from a casting agency?' The driver had the door open, and Lawrie waved Jo into silence.

'Course I did,' he said in a sotto voce. 'You get a photo op with adoring fans, we get a puff piece in Billboard, and they get fifty bucks and a free T-shirt. Everyone's happy. Now will you trust your manager?'

The teens waiting outside the store looked bored and confused and none of them recognised her.

'Hey kids!' Lawrie called to them. 'Yohanna. She's here,' he cried, throwing his hands at her like a circus barker.

On cue, the kids began to whoop and cheer with big grins on their faces and a few rushed her with Yohanna postcards to sign.

'Oh, er, hello,' Jo said, quite taken aback by the attention. 'Has anyone got a pen?' Lawrie handed her one over the kids' heads, and she scribbled her name on the first one.

Joanna.

Shit. Again.

She would have to work harder on remembering that she was Yohanna, the bubbly young woman with strawberry earrings beaming up at her from the postcards.

'All right, all right, break it up.' Lawrie waded through the modest crowd of ersatz admirers as a photographer snapped away, took her by the arm and steered her towards the record store. 'She'll be signing more after the press conference, thank you, thank you.'

It was like a movie director had called cut on a scene. The fake fans dropped out of character and looked at each other as if to say, *When do we get paid?*

Jo knew in that moment that poor Yohanna's career was doomed.

THE PRISM BOOKSTORE

'Piri piri chicken?' Yohanna stood stranded with Federica outside Nando's, once the location of Aaronovitch's esoteric bookshop, now full of exhausted holidaymakers getting their carbs fix after a day at the beach. 'An entire chain of restaurants dedicated to piri piri chicken? That's bloody genius.'

'Where the hell is your guru man?' Federica walked over to a door just to the right of the Nando's, where she found a damaged entry-phone hanging askew on the brickwork. She leaned closer and inspected the faded names next to the buzzers.

'Here, Prism Power. That was the name of the bookshop, wasn't it?'

Yohanna nodded as she joined Federica. 'Buzz us in.'

'It's in the basement, must be his office.' Federica pushed the buzzer.

No answer.

Three more times, still no answer.

'Buzz them all,' Yohanna said. 'Say we're delivering flowers.'

Federica mashed the buttons and cocked her ear, waiting for a reply.

'*Eeyo?*' a voice replied, so distorted by the knackered entry-phone it could have been a Dalek with laryngitis. '*Eeyo? Ennyfobby dere? Eeyo?*'

'Flowers.' Yohanna insisted.

'Hello,' Federica said. 'I'm a psychic accompanied by the disembodied spirit of one of my former foster children. Can we come in, please?'

'Oh, nice one, great,' Yohanna sneered. 'Like they'll ever—'

BZZT!

The door latch clicked, and Federica leaned on the door, swinging it open. 'I couldn't hear them, they couldn't hear me. Why not tell the truth? Come on.'

Federica stepped into the tiny hall, rucking the loose carpet, kicking up dust. There was a flight of rickety old stairs that led up to the other offices. There was also a flight hiding in the shadows, leading down into the basement.

'Oh, great,' Yohanna muttered. 'A creepy staircase leading into a basement.'

'I've seen it all now. Why are you frightened? You're a ghost.'

'I am not a ghost. I'm in limbo. There's a crucial difference.'

'Quickly.' Federica beckoned her to follow. 'Before someone from upstairs gets suspicious.'

Federica moved stealthily, barely creaking the stairs as she headed down into the basement. A musky, damp odour assaulted her nostrils and she took a hanky from a pocket and covered her nose and mouth with it.

'Smelly?'

'You don't smell that?'

'Can't touch, smell, or taste,' Yohanna said. 'Kill me now.'

Federica tried the door at the bottom of the stairs. It was sticky, but unlocked. She gave it a shove. '*Che palle*,' Federica said, taking a step back.

'What? Oh, god, it's a body isn't it? He's dead. Please don't tell me he's dead.'

'No, don't be silly. It's flooded,' Federica said, shoving the door harder. As it opened, light reflected on ripples. An inch of water covered the whole basement. Federica tentatively flicked a light switch. A pale yellow bulb apologetically glowed into life.

The low ceiling was dotted with flaky paint and damp stains the colour of builder's tea. Federica's eye was drawn to a tall bookcase, empty except for a row of Aaronovitch's books.

A few had toppled to the floor, a mouldering pile of papiermâché. There was a cheap computer desk, the kind you got from a DIY store with handy shelves and slots for CD cases you never used, and it leaned at an angle that suggested a slow death by collapse was inevitable. A cork board hung above it, festooned with clippings from newspapers, and Federica recognised some of the damning headlines from her Google search of Aaronovitch's downfall. She took a few steps into the water and it lapped over the uppers of her boots. Her foot knocked something. A desk spike, impaling a soggy collection of final demand bills, rolled on its axis.

'I have to ask, darling,' she said, the hanky still over her nose and mouth. 'What it was you saw in this man?'

'This doesn't make sense.' Yohanna drifted over to the cork board. 'He's such a great guy, so wise and confident, y'know?'

Federica took one of the clippings off the wall. The headline read *Disgraced Guru Guilty Of Fraud*, and there was a photo of a haggard, bearded man leaving court with his lawyer. 'Is that him?'

Yohanna moved closer for a better look. 'Older, but yeah.' Her voice began to crack. 'How are we going to find him, Aunty Fede? There must be a clue here somewhere? Keep looking, please. I can't just be stuck here. I can't.'

'It's okay, calm down,' Federica said, her voice softening as she continued to look through the clippings. But all she could find were allegations of the gullible rich being fleeced by Aaronovitch, whose ability to hoodwink them for large sums of money in return for his guru services ran out once the fraud squad got on his case.

There came a series of creaks from the floorboards above them, accompanied by tiny dust showers from the peeling ceiling.

'Someone's coming,' Yohanna whispered. 'We need to hide.'

'You're invisible,' Federica reassured her, as the footsteps groaned their way down the stairs. 'And I can play the eccentric foreigner card. We'll be fine.'

A shadow filled the stairwell, large and ominous, and Federica thought about grabbing the bill spike as a weapon.

'I reckon you must be the psychic,' said a voice with a light Edinburgh rhotic roll. In the doorway stood a woman much smaller than her shadow, older than Federica, with heavy eyelids that suggested there wasn't a single thing you could surprise or shock her with. 'Course, you'd know I was coming, wouldn't ye?' she cackled. 'Your disembodied spirit about?'

'Right next to me.' Federica smiled, 'Thanks for letting us in.'

'Pal of yours?' The woman gestured straight at Yohanna who looked down at herself and wondered if she was suddenly visible.

'Aaronovitch?' Federica said, glancing through Yohanna, back at the cork board of press clippings. 'I need to find him. Do you know where he is? It's quite urgent.'

'Take a ticket and join the queue,' the woman said, taking a puff on her electronic cigarette device, filling the doorway with white coils of vapour. 'Owes me six months' rent, the old bugger.'

'He's been gone that long?'

'Maybe longer.' The woman leaned against the door jamb. 'He was reclusive. Even when the bookshop went tits up, he didnae care. Spent all his time down here.'

'That doesn't sound like Ronnie,' Yohanna whispered in Federica's ear. 'He wasn't a recluse and he wouldn't run away.'

'He just disappeared?' Federica asked.

The old woman nodded. 'Lassies in the office upstairs said they heard a wee bit of argy-bargy one afternoon. Your fella shouting and hollering and smashing the place up.' She looked around at the mess. 'Which might account for the state of the place.'

'He flooded it, too?'

'Oh no, that's just a burst pipe. Meaning to get that seen to.' The old lady dipped a booted toe in the water, testing its depth. 'So, what's he to you? You a detective?' she said, a glimmer of excitement crossing her wrinkled face. 'Has he gone and murdered someone? Did he murder your ghost?'

'What would make you say that?'

'Angry fella, full of the rage. Glad to see the back of him, frankly.'

'That is not my Aaronovitch,' Yohanna protested. 'We've made a mistake.'

Federica held the clipping with the bearded Aaronovitch under the light for the old woman to see. 'We're talking about this man, yes?' she asked the old lady.

'Aye, that's him.'

'I don't believe her,' Yohanna said.

'Will you be quiet,' Federica snapped at Yohanna.

'You talking to me or the ghost?' the old woman asked.

'Ghost,' Federica said. 'Did he ever mention any friends or family? Any names we can look up?'

'Let me see. Someone called Sam regularly got a bollocking on the phone,' the old woman said. 'Could be their other name was Forfucksake, as that's how our mutual friend often addressed them. That sound familiar?'

Federica shook her head. 'No, sorry. What did they argue about?'

'Money, mostly, from what I could gather,' the woman said. 'He was paid for a book he never finished, or something.'

Federica glanced at the mouldy books on the shelf. 'Do you mind if we keep looking for a while?'

'Fill your boots. You won't find nothing,' the old lady said as she took a puff from her e-cigarette, sighed and started to head back upstairs. 'Now, if you'll excuse me, I've got to call a plumber.'

Federica waited until the shadow had drifted away. 'Know anyone called Sam?'

'I had a boyfriend called Sam.' Yohanna twisted her lips as she thought. 'Saxophone player. Complete tosser. Sat on my guitar once.'

'I meant a Sam associated with Aaronovitch.' Federica waved the press clipping to make her point.

'No,' Yohanna said. 'Shit, this is it, isn't it? I'm screwed. A dead end in a flooded basement. Shit, shit, shit.'

'*Uno momento*.' Federica sploshed across the room to the book-case, picked up one of the less damp books and flicked through its pages.

'What are you doing?' Yohanna peered over her shoulder.

'If he argued with Sam about books, he could be... Ah. Here,' Federica said, her finger tracing the words on a page. 'The acknowl-edgments. *As always, love and good vibes to my editor Sam Ewers, the only man who can make sense of my ramblings. Shine on you crazy diamond.* That's our Sam.'

'Brilliant. How do we find him?'

'First, we go somewhere dry,' Federica said.

'Dry? The desert, maybe? Does he mention that in the book?'

'No. My socks are soaked.'

TEN MINUTES LATER, Federica had an espresso, got connected to the Nando's Wi-Fi, found the number of Aaronovitch's publisher online and called them. She leaned back in her chair, punctuating her side of the conversation with a series of regular assertions.

'Yes... uh-huh... I see... okay...'

On the chair next to her, a pair of red and black plaid socks were drying out. Yohanna didn't need a seat, but took one out of habit, only using the edge of it as she awaited the outcome of the call.

'Oh, really?' Federica tucked the phone between her head and shoulder and scribbled something in her notebook. 'That's helpful.'

Yohanna leaned forward for a better view, but Federica's spidery handwriting had only got worse in the last eighteen years. 'What? What's helpful?'

'Okay.' Federica held up a silencing hand, which must have looked peculiar to other customers in the coffee shop. 'Thank you, goodbye.'

'What did they say?'

Federica gave her an exasperated look, and put the phone back to her ear again. 'Hello? Yohanna?'

'What? Tell me.'

'Sam Ewers died about six months ago,' Federica said.

'When Ronnie disappeared.'

'He left no living relatives, but he did have one final, peculiar request,' Federica said, leaning closer to Yohanna. 'He asked that his ashes be spread on Glastonbury Tor.'

'Glastonbury,' Yohanna said, getting excited. 'You think that's where Ronnie is?'

'If I were a fraudulent guru on the run with delusions of grandeur, it's where I'd go.'

'Cool, let's go.' Yohanna got up and found herself standing halfway through the coffee table.

'Wait, wait, sit down,' Federica said.

Yohanna did so. 'What? What else?'

Federica took a breath. 'Darling, look, I know this is important, but I can't go with you.'

'What? You have to.'

'I'm sorry,' Federica said. 'The children will be home in a couple of hours. They're depending on me. There's dinner to be made, uniforms to get ready... Sorry, darling, but from here you're on your own.'

THE TOWER RECORDS REVELATION

'Okay, okay, what do I do again?' Jo trailed behind Lawrie and a Tower Records member of staff who introduced himself as Duke, but reminded her of Shaggy from Scooby Doo. They took arbitrary lefts and rights in the stock room's maze of shelves that teetered with CDs, cassettes and VHS tapes.

'Just stick to the script,' Lawrie muttered.

Ah, the script, Jo thought. The one with the rehearsed answers, the one she knew nothing about. 'And what if I want to, y'know, improv a bit?'

'Improv?' Lawrie chewed on the word like a Haribo sour.

'Yeah, freewheel it.' She shrugged. 'Be honest, maybe? Wouldn't that be refreshing?'

Lawrie turned on her with a pointy finger. 'No. No, it would not be refreshing. It would be a bloody disaster. This has been planned to the nth degree, and you will be sticking to the script. *Capiche*?'

'Just trying to keep it real,' she said.

'They don't want it real. No one wants it real. There's the real you and the publicity you. The real you wouldn't last five minutes out there. But be Yohanna for a little while and fame and fortune will soon come calling.'

'There's more to life than that surely, Lawrie?'

That stopped Lawrie in his tracks, 'Do not flake on me now, girl.'

'Uh, dudes.' Shaggy Duke was waiting for them by a fire door. 'Just through here. You cool?'

'Are we?' Lawrie glared at Jo, and she knew he would only be happy with one answer.

'As a cucumber.'

SHAGGY DUKE USHERED Jo behind a Tower Records press conference display, where they hid in silence as Lawrie strode out to address the gathered press in the store's events area. Duke and Jo were an awkward duo, staring at their feet or the wall, unable to make any small talk as Lawrie picked up a microphone with a whistle of feedback.

'Good morning, everyone.'

Jo noticed something had changed in his voice. Lawrie had adopted a nasal, breakfast radio DJ tone. Not the real Lawrie. The publicity Lawrie.

'And what a very special morning this is. I'm here to introduce you all to an incredible new talent, one that is going to change the land-scape of the pop firmament, a singer-songwriter of such virtuosity that, in the future, her name will be mentioned in the same breath as Lennon, McCartney, Brian Wilson and Bob Dylan.'

'Are you fucking kidding me?' Jo whispered, burying her face in her palm.

'I'm her manager, and so of course I'd say that, but you should judge for yourselves. So, before we meet the pretty little lady...'

Jo's embarrassment flashed to anger.

'... let's hear what all the fuss is about and listen to her debut single *Only You*. Roll tape.' Lawrie ordered.

There was an excruciatingly long period of nothing happening.

Someone in the press seats coughed.

Others fidgeted, making their seats creak.

Jo imagined some poor Tower Records flunky scrabbling to find a demo tape or CD.

Then, finally, mercifully, the music began.

It was up-tempo, poppy, peppy, overproduced, drenched in compression, slick - and designed to be a chart-topping hit.

It was also, without any question of doubt, *Ellie's Song*.

The lyrics had changed, with more references to sexual desire than the love a mother has for her child, all mixed in with a clunky message of world peace rather than inner calm, but it was the same song - the song that Jo had written when she was pregnant with Ellie, and the song Yohanna had been strumming in her kitchen. A version corrupted by the pop machine. Jo felt a tiny bit violated and angry at the thought of someone tinkering with her song, but then she got a terrible sinking sensation in the pit of her stomach.

Jo now remembered where she'd met Lawrie before.

She'd been playing in a covers band at a wedding and this guy had somewhat drunkenly offered to make Jo a megastar. He showered Jo with flattery, eulogised about her gift, and promised a life of fame and fortune. All she had to do was sign on the dotted line. He wore a pastel suit with the sleeves rolled up, had a Phil Collins brushback hairdo and cursed like a docker. Lawrie. No question.

Jo turned him down.

She'd been tempted, of course. She had more ambition back then, and knew she had the talent, but she'd been seeing Nick for six months. They were serious.

And she was pregnant.

Jo had chosen Ellie and a life of suburban comfort.

Yohanna had chosen to trust Lawrie and follow a dream.

And yet, somehow, they had both written the same song.

'You okay?' Shaggy Duke looked concerned, and Jo realised she was leaning on the wall for support as if the room were tilting over.

'Uh, yeah, yeah,' Jo puffed, righting herself and shaking her head clear. 'Just a bit... overwhelmed.'

The song was reaching its climax and Lawrie hollered, 'Ladies

and gentlemen, here she is, the superstar sensation of tomorrow...
Yohanna!'

I guess that's my cue, Jo puffed her cheeks and took a step.

'Uh, wrong way.' Shaggy Duke pointed her back to the store.

'Yes, yes, of course, thank you.'

'You're welcome.' He grinned. 'Good luck.'

'Ta.' Jo rounded the display, finding herself bombarded by a
strobing display of flashbulbs - and her mind decided to take a vacation. Any plans she'd had for this moment, any clever little witticisms,
any thought of improv' or winging it all just took a long hike down
Sunset Boulevard, and she realised exactly why Lawrie had insisted
that she stick to a script. Because this is what happened when a
regular human being was presented with an intense moment of fame.
Their brain turned to mush, they became a deer in the headlights,
and it wouldn't be long before they became gibbering roadkill.

Jo had given birth, travelled through time and space, and seen
Nick clipping his toenails in the bathroom, but she'd never, ever been
as terrified as she was now.

Waving to the cameras, Jo wished she'd worn something a little
more exciting. Not the teen hooker look that Lawrie was going for,
but something that wouldn't make her look like she'd just popped to
the shops to get some milk. As she took her seat behind a table decorated with a microphone and a glass of water, Jo was dismayed to see
that only a third of the seats laid out were occupied. All this hassle
and stress, and for what? Maybe a dozen journalists scattered about
the room. Lawrie stood at the side of the table, hands clasped across
his belly like a pregnant mother.

'Hi,' Jo said into the mic, thrown by the booming sound of her
voice coming from the PA flanking the table.

A journalist raised a hand, and Lawrie pointed at him with the
finger of benediction. 'Yes, Terry.'

Terry, clearly one of Lawrie's plants, looked bored as he asked, 'So,
what's the song about?'

Oh god. They were actually asking her questions. Asking her
questions that they expected her to answer like she knew what she

was talking about. She tried to imagine in her mind what Lawrie's script might look like, but all she could envision were the words *What's the song about?* repeated over and over like Jack Torrance's *All Work And No Play* in *The Shining*. It was at this moment that she realised she'd been gaping like a landed fish for about ten seconds, and her brain gave up and shifted into neutral.

Jo was certain that someone had just asked her a question, but she could not for the life of her remember what it was, who she was, what she was doing here, what country she was in, the name of the planet, how any of her limbs worked, how to speak, or use the big lolling thing in her mouth that she thought was called a tongue, but that's a ridiculous name for a thing in a mouth, and who's Jo?

'First love and innocence,' Lawrie growled from the corner of his mouth.

'Uhm.' Jo's mouth was sand, her lips uncooperative flaps of skin. 'It's, uh... about...'

'First love and innocence,' Lawrie repeated like a bad ventriloquist.

'First love and innocence,' Jo croaked. It was pathetic. Meek. She could see the disappointment in the journalists' faces. This girl was no pop megastar, she was just another lucky singer with an ambitious manager whose big plan for fame was yet another song about first love and innocence. Lawrie's plan was doomed to fail and Yohanna's career was about to die and be buried in this very room. For all Yohanna's faults, Jo thought the poor girl deserved better than that. Jo could feel the world falling beneath her feet, and she could sense Lawrie's anger radiating from the end of the table.

At the back of the room, a couple of journalists got up to leave.

Jo turned towards Lawrie, hoping for a bit more help, and her foot brushed against something under the table. She glanced down to find a small trash can. She knew exactly what to do with it.

'Will you excuse me a second?' she asked those assembled, before sliding the can from under the table, holding her hair back, and vomiting vigorously into it. The splashing sound was accompanied by camera shutters clicking like castanets. She heaved loudly a couple more times, but nothing more was forthcoming. It had, however, done the job. Her mind was clear once more. She grabbed the bottled water, rinsed her mouth out, spat it into the bin and felt herself again.

'So sorry about that,' she said to no one in particular. 'Touch of the collywobbles.' She picked up the trash can. 'Duke? Are you there, sweetie?'

Shaggy peered around from the behind the Tower Records back-drop. 'Uh-huh?'

'Sorry, dear, but do you mind...?' Jo offered it to him. 'And could you get me a napkin, please?'

'Sure thing,' he said, backing away out of sight.

The journalists who were halfway out the door, paused and kept watching. Most of the photographers were standing, not wanting to miss the next projectile event.

'Right, someone had a question about the song's meaning?' Jo squinted out into the astonished audience. Terry hesitantly raised a hand. 'Yes, sorry, no it's not about first love and innocence, that's just the bollocks my manager wanted me to say. It's actually about a baby,' she said, before realising that Yohanna never had that baby. 'A baby I... never had.'

The cameras were clicking in a frenzy now, and the journalists were frantically scribbling in their notebooks. It was now Lawrie's turn to be the deer in the headlights.

Duke arrived with a big pile of napkins.

'Lovely, thank you, poppet,' Jo said, dabbing her lips with one.

'Tell us about the baby,' a voice called.

'You had an abortion,' a woman asked.

Jo was in the middle of a minefield. She truthfully had no idea what choices Yohanna had made.

'I didn't say that. And I won't say any more till someone pays more money and puts me on the cover of their magazine.' There were a few nervous laughs. Jo reflected that jokes about abortion probably weren't the best way to win Americans over. 'My songs come from the heart and they all tackle difficult emotional ideas. I prefer that they speak for themselves.'

'But in an interview with *Smash Hits*...' A British home counties accent came from the throng. 'You said they were all, and I quote, *catchy pop songs designed to get you bopping.*'

'Nah, that sounds like something he would say.' Jo jabbed a thumb at Lawrie and got a bigger laugh. 'Anyway, who said you can't boogie and be a bit emotional? Ask ABBA for God's sake.'

'What other emotional ideas do you write about?' another journalist asked.

'Oh, er...' Jo began to miss Lawrie's script here as she realised she was being asked to invent a back catalogue of songs on the spot. 'My guru says not to discuss it.'

'You have a guru?'

'Yeah,' Jo said, thinking back to what Yohanna said in her kitchen. 'He's been helping me with my stage fright. I wish he were here now.' This got a laugh from the crowd. Jo leaned closer to the mic. 'Ronnie, my phone's broke so come and find me at the Beverly Wilshire.' She dared to glance at Lawrie, who was like a firework about to go off. 'I repeat, the Beverly Wilshire.'

Some of the crowd laughed, as if sensing there was some kind of in-joke. One man asked, 'Are you seeing a guru because of the baby?'

'No more baby questions,' Jo said, almost enjoying this. 'Next.' She pointed at a woman with a raised hand.

'What makes you different to today's other megastars? Like, Diemond?'

'Who?' Jo asked, and got another laugh. 'No, seriously, I've no idea who that is. Who is he?' The laughs became embarrassed titters as people began to realise that she was serious.

The woman who asked the question looked around for help. 'Diemond? She's... on the cover of every magazine, hits like *Vacation, A Fair Maiden, Catholic High School Girls*...? First female artist to sell over a hundred million records worldwide...'

The overlapping snap of camera shutters went into overdrive as Jo began to realise the huge error she just made. This Diemond person was this universe's equivalent of Madonna, and Jo had just made herself look like a complete spanner. 'Oh... *Die-mond!*' she nodded a little too vigorously. 'Of course, sorry, I thought you said... something else...'

'She really doesn't know,' one of the journalists whispered with a baffled grin.

'Diemond will totally shit,' said another with undisguised glee.

The photographers surged forward, and the journalists' voices merged into a cacophony of questions.

Lawrie was Jo's unlikely hero. 'Okay, that's it for today, thanks very much. Hope you got everything you need. Any questions, all contact details are in your press packs, thank you, thank you.'

Lawrie scooped Jo up by her arm, and steered her behind the Tower Records display, growling in her ear, 'What the fuck was that about? What part of stick to the script did you not fucking understand?' He barged the door open into the stockroom.

Jo wriggled free of his grip, 'My mind went blank,' she lied, still none the wiser about who this Diemond really was. Then she looked up and around her to find CDs and VHS tapes racked to the rafters with the name Diemond on their spines. There was also a cardboard standee featuring the megastar glaring straight at Jo like a judge about to give a death sentence. She looked like a cross between Lady Gaga and Tim Curry in the *Rocky Horror Picture Show*. Whoever Diemond was, she was clearly a massive megastar and she looked fucking terrifying.

'Still.' Jo put a brave face on it. 'Could've been worse, eh?'

The garbled holler of the clamouring journalists returned for a second as Shaggy Duke slipped through the stockroom door.

'Lady,' he puffed, leaning against the closed door. 'That was the best. Barfing, babies, gurus, therapy and dissing Diemond. Man, that had everything.'

'See,' Jo said, brightly. 'Duke liked it.'

'You, young lady, are under house arrest,' Lawrie said through a snarl. 'You don't do anything, don't say anything, don't talk to anyone, don't even leave the hotel without my say so. You're on lockdown.'

FADE TO GREY

Yohanna returned home with Federica.

She could only look on, silent and unseen, as Federica performed her parental duties for Ben and Robin, eventually sending them off to their rooms after *Game of Thrones*.

Satisfied they were asleep, Federica returned to her favourite armchair, snug in her dressing gown, swirling a brandy in a glass.

'I see you watching me, spirit,' she said to Yohanna. 'I know you're impatient, but these children have come from homes where their lives were full of disruption. Abusive parents. Anger, violence. If I cannot provide stability for them, then I've failed. They need me as much as you, if not more.'

'I know,' Yohanna said. 'You were a good mother, Aunty Fede. The best.'

'Thank you, but it's not a competition.' Federica took a sip of the brandy. 'Why a bus?'

'Hmm?'

'You were running away in a bus. Should I read any significance into that?'

'It had nothing to do with Mum, if that's what you're thinking.' Yohanna sighed as if she'd been expecting this question. 'It was just another of Lawrie's big ideas. He knows the guy who still had the bus that Elton John used when he arrived in L.A., and he wanted me to arrive with a bang.'

'Did you tell him?'

'About Mum? No,' Yohanna said. 'No one knows.'

'It's nothing to be ashamed of.'

'I know.'

'It was an accident.'

'Yeah.'

'And nothing else.'

'How do you know?' Yohanna snapped, then flushed with shame. Federica didn't deserve her anger now.

'I know because I read all the reports before you came to me.' Federica remained calm. 'Your mother's death was an accident. A painful, unfair and horrible accident. No one is to blame. Especially not you.'

'Can we not talk about this,' Yohanna said, doing her best not to raise her voice again. 'I need to get to Glastonbury, and I can't do it on my own.'

'And I cannot abandon those children upstairs to travel halfway across the country,' Federica said.

'They're not children, they're teenagers.'

'Robin's eleven.'

'And more mature than I'll ever be.'

'They are my responsibility.'

'They'll be fine.' Yohanna threw her hands to the ceiling and began moving in impatient circles. 'I was fine.'

'Hmm,' Federica said, putting her brandy down and looking closely at Yohanna.

'What?' Yohanna shifted, uncomfortable at the sudden scrutiny.

'It might just be my imagination, or it could be that it's night time, different light and all that, but...' Federica hesitated, squinting. 'You don't look as... *solid* to me as you were before.'

'What?' Yohanna hopped to her feet, turning in a circle as she looked at herself.

'In fact, and don't take this the wrong way, but I can see right through you.' Federica bit her lip.

'No!' Yohanna cried, but it was true. She could see the carpet through her own feet. She was like a frosted glass version of herself. 'What's happening to me?'

'Darling, darling.' Federica got to her feet, her hands reaching out for Yohanna's, but unable to take them to comfort her. 'We're not going to fix this by panicking.'

'Don't panic? I look like a glass fruit bowl.'

'Do you feel tired? Weak?'

'I don't know. I don't feel anything really. Numb.'

'Wait.' Federica scuttled over to one of her overloaded book-shelves, and snatched up a couple of water-damaged copies of Aaronovitch's books that she'd taken from the Prism Power Bookshop basement. She began thumbing through the index of *The Infinite You*.

'What? What's up?'

'Something I read.' Federica flicked through the book. 'So much of this is complete egotistical nonsense, but he said... Yes. Here.' Federica began to read, and Yohanna hurried to read over her shoulder.

'*A traveller's strength and ability to move between universes depends on their relative position to their sun. For example, if the planet's rotational axis is inclined towards the sun, those in the bardo state can find themselves weak and detached from our world, fading from sight and trapped in limbo forever. It is not safe to travel at these times. The ancients knew this and ceased all bardo activity during these periods. Instead, they celebrated what we now know as the solstices.*' Federica slapped the book shut. 'The summer solstice is two nights from now. If we don't get you home before then...'

'I'm stuck like this?'

'Worse than that. You will fade to nothing.'

'I NEED you two to be sensible while I'm away,' Federica told the yawning children as they propped themselves up on the kitchen table. 'I could be gone all weekend, and that means taking care of the meals, the washing, and making sure you do your homework, and that school uniforms are ready by Sunday night. Got that?'

'I completely understand.' The younger of the two was sitting upright in neat, striped pyjamas, hands clasped before her and as bright a button as one could be at this hour. Robin had read so much *Famous Five* she now spoke like a World War Two evacuee. 'Would it be too much to ask where you are going, Aunty Fede?'

'One of my children is in trouble,' Federica said. 'She needs my help.'

'She's a grown up, right?' Ben, who hid hunched under a blackened hood of hair, punctuated each word with a jerk of his gangly arms. 'Can't she sort herself out?'

'What sort of trouble is she in, Aunty Fede?' asked Robin. 'Is it ghastly?'

'Big trouble,' Federica said. 'I wouldn't be leaving you otherwise.'

'Is it drugs?' Ben was suddenly interested. 'Or she's run off and become a terrorist? Or she's murdered someone and written your name on the victim's body and you have to help cover it up.'

'Have you tried reading something other than gory horror comics, Ben?'

'Yeah,' Ben shrugged. 'And they're all rubbish.'

'Will you be safe, Aunty Fede?' Robin asked. 'It would be simply awful if anything were to happen to you.'

'I'll be fine. I just need to drive to Glastonbury to meet someone. No danger at all, so please don't worry. You've got my number if you need me, and Mrs. Fenwick is next door for anything urgent, but don't tell her how long I'm away. She's looking for an excuse to call social services after Ben broke her greenhouse window. You got all that?'

Robin nodded. 'Cooking, washing, homework, don't tell Mrs. Fenwick.'

'And...? Come on, this is my most basic rule, even if I'm just going to the supermarket.'

'Don't burn the house down,' Ben muttered.

'Yes. Especially, don't burn the house down.' Federica hurried around the kitchen gathering her bag, phone and keys. 'I promise I'll be back as soon as possible,' she said, kissing them both on their foreheads.

'Who is she?' asked Robin. 'Why does she need your help in Glastonbury at this unGodly hour?'

Federica glanced over to where the pale spirit of Yohanna watched from the shadows.

'When she came to me, she was lost. Her mother had died, she never knew her father, and I worked harder getting her back on track than any other child before or since. And now she's lost again, and time is running out. I want to get her home.'

Ben and Robin let that sink in and both turned to look at each other.

'She's totally murdered someone.' Ben grinned.

'She has not,' Federica insisted. 'Ben - you're demoted for being silly. Robin - you're in charge till I get back.'

'What?' Ben whined. 'Not fair.'

'Jolly good.' Robin immediately perked up and saluted. 'You can rely on me, Aunty Fede.'

'I know I can.' Federica smiled and added, 'And all my children can rely on me. No matter how much trouble they're in.'

RAPUNZEL WITH THE FRIZZY HAIR

J o knew that, as prisons go, the penthouse suite of the Beverly Wilshire wasn't exactly Robben Island, but she resented Lawrie's idea that she couldn't be trusted to venture out on her own. However, she couldn't deny that the press conference had been a bit of a disaster. If someone in her world had gone on record as not knowing who, say, Madonna was, she would have written them off as either a wilfully eccentric attention-seeker, or a complete loon. Either way, she wouldn't be rushing out to buy their records.

Lawrie had checked in with Jo just as room service arrived with her breakfast. He'd laid down the law once more - she was not to leave the room, she was not to answer the phone. His job today was to pick up the pieces from her debacle and promised to be back for lunch. Until then, she was to do nothing.

And so Jo was left alone with crappy cable TV, and she did what anyone else would do in this situation. She watched MTV in the vain hope that something she liked might come on. Jo was in for quite a wait. She only knew about half the bands and singers. In this parallel universe they had Prince, but Michael Jackson was nowhere to be seen. Jo was about to turn it off when a newly-familiar face burst onto the television.

Diemond dominated the screen in an artistically shot black and white music video. Gender-ambiguous dancers snaked around her body as she sang. And she really could sing. Her incredible vocal range punched through the heavy production of the song. Diemond wore a short peroxide wig, and moved like an Olympic gymnast as she danced, hurling herself into impossible shapes, barely breaking a sweat. It was powerful, and so different to the rest of the crap on MTV. No wonder she was a megastar. Like Madonna or Bowie she was a pioneer, breaking down barriers, pushing the envelope, and all the stuff that other artists only ever talked about. A graphic flashed up in the corner of the screen announcing that this was the first video in the Diemond Power Hour on MTV.

Jo heaved herself off the couch and picked up the suite's phone, dialling zero.

'Reception, how may I help you?' asked a voice saturated in California customer service.

'Hi, it's Jo... uh, Yohanna in the penthouse suite. I wonder if you could grab me some trashy magazines please?'

'Trashy...?' The receptionist said it in a way that made Jo wonder if he was smirking.

'Yeah, gossip magazines, celebrity stuff, anything you can get your hands on asap, please.'

'Certainly, Miss,' the receptionist said. 'I'll have someone bring you a selection.'

Within half an hour a porter arrived with a range of glossy magazines on a silver platter. Jo went through the excruciating British agony of not knowing whether or not to tip him, and then apologising for not having any cash anyway. The porter told her it was no problem and left her alone with the mags.

It was like bingeing a soap opera on Netflix. Affairs, betrayals, accusations of plagiarism, numerous image changes, the Diemond story had it all.

In every copy of *Hello* or *Variety* there was always at least one story about Diemond. An incident in a restaurant where she took a layer of clothing off after each course and was in her underwear by the time coffee arrived, a concert where she stopped everything and refused to continue singing until a bickering couple in the front row kissed and made up, and the time she paid for a hat to be flown first class from L.A. to Cairo for a video shoot. Diemond - real name Diana Mondale - was a club singer from Miami who struck it lucky when a producer took her into the big time with a single called *Vacation*. This was followed by her first number one hit, *A Fair Maiden*, a song about virginity that shocked the world in the mid-eighties. More hits, a few movies and a shocking book called *Vulva* followed, and now Diemond had the world at her feet.

Central to the Diemond story was a torrid affair with a dishy actor called Rand McManus. Born in London, his American mother moved them to California as a teen to get him into acting. He started out in a series of terrible horror movies - *Head In The Refrigerator*, *Head In The Freezer* and *Head In The Washer-Dryer* - and his career seemed to be over before it had even begun. Eventually, he got a break starring in a low-budget action movie called *Taskmaster*, in which his character, a rugged explorer called Butch Task, gunned down vast swathes of villains and caused billions of dollars of property damage to save the day and the girl. It made hundreds of millions of dollars at the box office, propelling him to stardom. He starred in three sequels, making him the highest-paid Hollywood actor for the last three years in a row, but now he was looking to be taken seriously. His upcoming film was *The Watcher*, about a terminally-ill lawyer determined to save a small town's water supply from wicked developers. It was pure Oscar-bait and after the end of his affair with Diemond he was hoping to—

'Holy shit, that's me.' Jo jolted upright on the couch.

There was a photo of Jo in the *National Enquirer*.

More accurately, there was a photo of Yohanna in the *National Enquirer*.

It was a long-lens paparazzi shot of Yohanna and Rand in the double-decker bus. They were laughing, and clearly looked like a couple enjoying a blossoming romance. The copy under the photos clearly thought so too, and wondered what Rand's ex, Diemond, would think of him dating this mysterious girl so soon after their split.

Jo was having a fling with the biggest star in Hollywood.

And had got him on the rebound from Diemond.

The magazines and Diemond didn't know who she was yet. Though after yesterday's press conference it wouldn't take them long to add two and two.

She really should have stuck to Lawrie's script.

There was a knock at the door.

'Come in.' Jo called, scouring the magazines for more information. Jo didn't think Diemond would be the type to take it well, but you never know, she could be completely grown up and magnanimous about it. This sort of thing happened in Hollywood all the time, surely? Still engrossed in the magazines, it took Jo a few moments to register that whoever had just come into the room was now just standing there, completely still. Probably room service for her lunch order. Jo looked up.

'Hi, would it be possible to get some sandwiches and some tea, please? Proper tea, with... oh.'

Standing before her was a man in a bright pink suit, with greased-back hair and a pencil-thin waxed moustache. He carried a briefcase in clasped hands before him and his face was baby-bottom smooth.

'I've an important message,' he said in a voice that reminded Jo of the cartoon character Droopy. 'May I?' he asked, gesturing to one of the suite's many coffee tables.

Jo, too dumbfounded to speak, nodded.

He opened the suitcase, revealing a chunky, plastic device with a fold-up LCD screen. She could make out the words Sony Video Walkman, and found herself charmed by the twee technology.

'Aww, look at that,' she said.

Without another word, the man in the pink suit pressed play and the tiny screen was filled with an angry face.

'If you thought your little prank would go unnoticed, young lady, you are greatly mistaken.' It took Jo a moment to realise that this was

Diemond, minus her make-up and strategic lighting. There was a hint of a Southern manners drawl in Diemond's accent that made Jo think of Scarlett O'Hara. Onscreen, someone in the background urged her to calm down. It sounded like Droopy. 'Fuck you, Ricardo. This bitch needs to be told.'

There were crashing noises and yelps of pain, and Diemond's face returned to the phone again. 'My man wasn't enough for you, hmm? I warned you, didn't I? I told you to stay away, and when I saw you scurry away in that bus, I thought that would be the end of it. But no, you had to try and humiliate me at your pathetic little press conference. Well this, my little English rose, is a declaration of war.

'I will fucking destroy you. Future pop stars will tell their children horror stories of the girl from merry old England who tried to mess with the biggest star in the world and was sent home weeping, ruing the day that she ever fucked with Diemond. Not only will you never work in this town again, you'll be reduced to busking on the streets of London like an organ grinder's monkey.

'You've one chance left. Leave town. Today. And never return. No explanations. Just go. Or I swear to you, little girl, all they will find of you is a smear on the sidewalk. Revenge is a dish best served with diamonds!' Diemond declared, bringing her speech to a climactic, if somewhat confusing, conclusion.

Her face remained on screen. 'How the fuck do I turn this thing off?' she barked, before Droopy leaned into the shot to help and the screen went dark.

The man in the pink suit folded down the LCD screen, put the video Walkman back in the briefcase and left the room.

Jo chased after him. 'Wait. Please, I didn't mean to insult her, I just went blank. Tell her I'm sorry, please.' But he ignored her, stepping into the elevator without a word, the doors closing.

Jo had been in L.A. less than twenty-four hours and she already had a mortal enemy.

She dashed back to the suite and picked up the phone.

'Reception, how may I help you?' It was the same chirpy receptionist as before.

'Hi, I need to call my manager, but I don't have his number, could you—?'

'I'm sorry, Miss,' the receptionist interrupted and switched to a neutral voice, all the chirpiness gone. Getting trashy magazines was one thing, but this was the kind of difficult conversation that he had trained for on a concierge course. 'Mr Grant left strict instructions that no calls be made from the penthouse suite.'

'What?' Jo's blood boiled. 'None at all? Not even to him?'

'His instructions were somewhat blunt, Miss. No calls.'

'What if the suite was on fire?'

There was a brief pause.

'Is it on fire?'

'I'm being hypothetical.'

'That's a no?'

'Yes, it's a no. The room is not on fire.'

'I'm very glad to hear that.'

'Yet.'

'In the event of an emergency, you can call me,' the receptionist said. 'Just dial zero.'

'Can you get him to call me, please? I guess he left a number so you could call him?'

'He did not, Miss.' The chirpy receptionist was a long and distant memory. Jo was now dealing with an automaton in disappointment mode.

'Then how am I supposed to...?' Jo stopped herself. She was on the verge of screeching. 'Never mind, never mind. If he checks in, can you get him to call me straight away, please?'

'Of course.' The receptionist was on surer ground now. Happy to help. 'Is there anything else I can assist—?'

Jo hung up with a little too much anger and stood rooted in the middle of the suite, thinking hard with her hands gripping her frizzy hair. How was she supposed to make a call without a phone? Actually, that wasn't true - she had half a phone. And, more importantly, she had the phone half. All that was missing was the battery.

She rushed to her bedroom, turning out her cases and opening drawers.

'Yes.' She found what she was looking for in her knickers drawer. The Nokia's charger.

She grabbed the half-a-Nokia from beside her bed and found a power socket in its base. She plugged it in, connecting it to the wall socket, and thumbed the On button.

'C'mon, c'mon,' she growled under her breath. Would this work directly from the mains without a battery?

The pale green LCD screen pulsed into life. She had three bars of signal.

'Fab.' Jo began nudging her way around the clunky menu. There was no search facility and Yohanna had only saved a few names in the address book: Aaronovitch, Ben, Bryan, Nigel, Erica, Grant, Joe, John, Rand. All unknown to her apart from Rand. And no Ronnie. That was weird. What was the point of having a guru if she didn't have his number? Maybe he didn't own a phone? Whatever. That had to wait. Jo kept thumbing through the names. She came to Lawrie, called him, but it just rang off. No message service. She tried again. Nothing.

'Bollocks,' she whispered to herself, nudging her way back through the menus to find the texts. She nudged the number one button three times for the letter C, once again for the letter A, the number five three times for the letter L. *I'd forgotten this was such a bloody faff.* She cursed as she typed, eventually managing:

CALL ME. DIE MOND W*NT S TO K ILL MF

Bloop.

The noise came from somewhere in the suite. It triggered memories of her own first mobile and the electronic announcement of a text arriving.

'No, please, no.' Jo spun to see Lawrie's phone resting on the arm of a couch. He'd left it charging.

'Fuck my life,' Jo declared, matter of factly, hands on hips.

Jo continued nudging through the address book till she saw the name she really needed. Rand.

Heart thumping, she pressed the green call button. It barely rang once before he picked up.

'Hey,' he said with a familiarity that suggested he knew exactly who was calling. 'You okay? You just took off the other night.'

'Uh.' Jo knew what she wanted to say to Lawrie, But now she was talking to someone she'd probably been intimate with recently, and that's when her brain went into overdrive. 'Wehavetocalitoffi'msorry-butDiemondwantstokillme.'

'Okay,' he said eventually. 'You saw the National Enquirer?'

'And so did she. She knows,' Jo said, regaining her composure a little. Realising she was entering into a relationship she knew nothing about, she decided to fall back on a strategy she'd used on boyfriends past. 'You're a lovely guy and everything, but let's, y'know, stop before someone gets really hurt. We can stay friends.'

'She threatened you, right?'

'A man in a pink suit came round and delivered a message,' Jo said.

'Pink suit?' Rand said. 'Little pencil moustache?'

'That's the guy.'

'That's Ricardo. Her eunuch.'

'That seems about right.'

'What was her message?'

'She was definitely in the anti-Yohanna-and-Rand camp. Promises were made regarding my wellbeing, and, look, this seems silly now. I'm sure she didn't mean it, and—'

'Oh no, she means it,' Rand said. 'And she'll do it, too. Remember that rapper who died in the drive-by last summer?'

Jo didn't, but played along. 'That was her?'

'I can't prove it, but for a whole week after that, I never saw her happier.'

'Shit.'

'You said it,' Rand said. 'Yohanna, you're a wonderful girl, and a huge talent, but I don't want you to get hurt. It was fun while it lasted, but let's walk away Renée and live to love another day.'

'I think you might be right,' Jo said. 'A shame, as it's been nice talking to a grown up, even for a brief moment. This town is crazy.'

'Tell me about it,' Rand said, and Jo imagined him smiling. 'But, just to be on the safe side, you might want to get on the first plane home and let's not speak again till she's dead.'

'That's a joke, right?'

'Kinda. Oh, and is Lawrie done with my bus?'

'Ah.' Jo managed to stop herself from blurting, *The bus is yours?* 'Yeah, sure. There's a bit of a dink, I'm afraid.'

'Dink?' For the first time, Rand seemed annoyed, 'What kind of dink?'

'Just... a little one,' Jo said, not wanting to add that she'd nearly driven it straight into the Pacific.

'Seriously, how big?' His voice was trembling now. 'You don't just dink an AEC Routemaster, the same way you don't dink the Mona Lisa or the Taj Mahal.'

Jo's next mistake was to laugh.

'You think that's funny?' Rand's voice tightened as he got more apprehensive. 'That's an RMC Coach. Y'know how many they made of those?'

'I... uh—'

'Forty-two,' Rand snapped. 'I had to outbid some sonofabitch from Japan to get that bus, Yohanna. It's the best one in my collection.'

'You... have a collection?'

'It's a thing. My uncle drove a bus, he let me ride up front, it's the one happy memory from my childhood, okay? I wouldn't expect anyone to understand.'

'Actually, I do.' Jo's voice softened. 'I really do. I have a thing about buses, too. I'll... I'll tell you about it one day.' The suite's phone started ringing. 'Oh, that's my other phone,' Jo said. 'I'd better get this. Bye, Rand.'

'Okay, I'm sorry I went a little nuts,' Rand said, still a little terse. 'I'll send a guy to collect it later today.'

'Thanks, Rand, I'm really, really sorry. I need to take this call. Bye.' Jo really didn't want to hang up quite yet, but she was already dashing across the room, shutting off Rand and answering to Lawrie.

'You, my girl, have the best manager in the world,' he announced with zero modesty.

'Lawrie, Diemond sent a—'

'Your little debacle at Tower Records is actually the best thing that could have happened. The press are going mental, and - brace yourself - they want you on *The Tonight Show*.'

'When?'

'Tonight,' Lawrie said. 'That's why it's called the—'

'Lawrie, I'm not sure I can. Diemond wants to kill me,' Jo said.

'I know how she feels,' Lawrie said.

'No, she really does. She sent a man with a little video player thingy and everything.'

'Don't you worry about her. I can handle that mental case. We have history,' Lawrie teased. 'This is no time for nerves, girl. All that matters is that six million people hear you sing. I can't begin to tell you how important this is for your career. You gotta start out the gates with a bang, love. This is your moment. Your Golden Ticket. This is it.'

Jo thought about Yohanna's dreams and ambitions. Jo had done enough damage to the girl's future as it was, and it would be ridiculous to be cowed into submission by a bully like Diemond. To come all this way and waste an opportunity like this seemed frivolous.

'Tonight, and then we're done?'

'Done?' Lawrie's angry voice returned.

'Not done,' Jo lied to appease him. 'It's just we need to fix the Diemond situation. She kills people.'

'She does not, don't be ridiculous,' Lawrie scoffed. 'Maim, yes. Kill? No.'

'Oh, I feel so much better.'

'You'll be safe with me, girl,' Lawrie said. 'I'm one of the few people she's scared of. I know all her secrets.'

'Really? Like what?'

'Never you mind,' Lawrie said, shutting down the thread of conversation. 'Start picking out an outfit. Tonight you're introducing yourself to America.'

Goldfish flipped in Jo's tummy. National television, an audience of millions. One show and she could reach out to Ronnie live on TV, get him to get in touch and she could be home tomorrow *and* save Yohanna's career.

'Who's presenting *The Tonight Show*? Is it Jay Leno? He's nice.'

'Yeah, but he's off this week. They have a stand-in presenter. Your mate and London bus enthusiast, Rand McManus.'

The banshee-like wail that assaulted his ears bequeathed Lawrie a lifetime of tinnitus.

THE RAINBOW CONNECTION

Federica's ancient Fiat Punto didn't have much in the way of horsepower or legroom, but it had the tenacity and endurance of a Chieftain Tank, and it clattered down the A303 towards the West Country. They left home a little after four in the morning and arrived on the outskirts of Glastonbury just as the roads were beginning to fill with coaches full of curious tourists, Hells Angels on Harleys, and seekers of solstice enlightenment.

'Where do we even start?' Yohanna asked as they wandered the streets of the town, a jumble of colourful shopfronts festooned with hanging baskets of spring flowers, buskers preparing for a day of Beatles and Oasis covers, and tourists consulting maps. The distant Tor and the towering remains of St. Michael's church suddenly dominated the horizon when they turned a corner, and the sensation that they were somewhere ancient was inescapable.

'I think in detective books they call it shoe leather,' Federica said. 'Meaning we go from door to door and we ask everyone we meet.'

'Brilliant, and here I was thinking we would just wander around aimlessly hoping to bump into him.'

'If you have a better plan, I'd like to hear it,' Federica said, eyebrow raised.

'Fine. Just remember I'm turning into the ghost of Anne Boleyn.' Yohanna gestured at her fading body. Federica could see right through her now. 'And once I'm gone... Actually, I don't know what happens then, but I doubt that it's good. People fading to nothing is never good, is it?'

'I know, darling, I know,' Federica said. 'We move fast, we turn every stone, we start there.' She pointed to a gift shop selling dream-catchers, candles shaped like human skulls, and other paranormal ephemera.

They spent the whole morning going from bookshops to pubs to vegan cafés with no joy. No one had seen the bearded man in the newspaper clipping that Federica showed them. It started to rain around noon and Yohanna took some little comfort in not getting drenched as the raindrops simply passed through her.

Federica dashed back to the car to fetch her umbrella.

As she waited, Yohanna drifted to where four streets met by the old stone Market Cross. A vivid rainbow split the heavens above. On one side the sky was slate grey, on the other lapis blue, shimmering with countless dots of falling rain. Then, as fast as it appeared, the shower was gently blown away on a wisp of wind. The rainbow faded and the blue skies returned.

'Oh, bah-luddy typical,' Federica said as she marched up the high street to join Yohanna, brolly in hand. 'As soon I get an umbrella, the rain buggers off.'

Yohanna turned, expecting to see her old foster mother, but blocking her view was a beam of rainbow light glowing along the high street.

'Are you seeing this?' Yohanna said, her voice hushed.

'Seeing what?' Federica stepped through the light, completely oblivious to its presence.

'You don't see that?' Yohanna frowned. It was the same light that emanated from her body when she met her older self, only much more intense. 'That bright, blinding rainbow light shooting down the street like a big gay pride laser beam, you don't see that?'

Federica shook her head. 'No, I...'

Yohanna reached out to touch it, 'Look, it's right there. How can you not?'

SHE WAS two years old again.

Standing at a zebra crossing, holding her mother's hand and slurping on an orange ice lolly as it melted in the summer heat and its juice dripped onto her fingers, 'Mummy, she said, splaying her fingers wide. 'All sticky.'

'Oh, Yo-Yo, what are you like?' Her mother crouched down, shaking a handkerchief open, smiling as she wiped the goo away. Her head was silhouetted by the sun like a halo, giving only a hint of her features - a loving smile, round cheeks, brown eyes, frizzy hair. Yohanna desperately wanted to see more, but however much she moved, the sun was always directly behind her mother.

'Mummy,' she said. 'Are you real?'

'Of course I am, silly Yo-Yo,' her mother said cheerily, using her pet name for Joanna again. Yo-Yo was what Mum always called her when she was being silly.

Always? It seemed like it now. The memory settled into place. A trespassing thought, claiming every right to be here and refusing to budge. It felt right, so she let it be.

'Sorry, Mummy.'

'That's okay, we all get messy.' Mum leaned forward and kissed her on the forehead, wafting a scent over Yohanna that sent her into a nostalgic spiral. Mummy's special smell. A milky hint of Pond's skin cream and the tang of Superdrug's own-brand hairspray. This had to be real. You couldn't smell in dreams. She wanted this moment to last forever.

'I love you, Mummy.'

'I love you too,' Mum said, brushing her hands on the pleats of her skirt and standing upright.

'Mummy, Mummy, I forgot my dolly.'

'Oh no, darling. Where is it?'

'I lost my dolly, I lost my dolly.' Toddler Joanna was getting agitated, her mouth pouted and buds of teardrops glistened in her eyes.

'It's okay, poppet, it's probably back in the shop.' Mum glanced at the newsagent's just across the road. 'I'll get it.'

This was how it happened.

'No, please Mummy, stay.'

And nothing that Yohanna could say would stop it from happening again.

'Wait there and be good,' Mum said, calmly stepping out onto the road into the path of a speeding red double-decker bus. A horn blared, brakes screeched.

YOHANNA CAME to by the Market Cross in Glastonbury. Her eyes watered, and she covered her mouth with her hand, but it couldn't stop the sobbing. The beam of light was still shining, but she was on the other side of it, sat on her bottom, wondering what had just happened. Federica once again passed through the light as though it wasn't there.

'You disappeared.' Federica looked worried. 'Where did you go?'

Yohanna could barely speak without a shudder. 'Mum. I... I saw my Mum. She said goodbye to me and...' She melted into tears again.

'It was just a... a bad dream, a hallucination or something.' Federica looked around, getting funny looks from passersby as she talked to thin air. 'What happened? You said there was a light, and then you were gone.'

'How long for?'

'A few seconds, that's all.' Federica turned around. 'Is the light still there?'

'Yes.' Yohanna looked up and down the street. The rainbow light seemed as permanent, intense and immovable as the sun and it crackled with energy. 'What is it?'

'I don't know, I... I can't see it,' Federica said. 'I wish I could help, I really do—'

'We follow it,' Yohanna said. 'We follow it, and we find him. I'm sure of it.'

TONIGHT, TONIGHT, TONIGHT

'I can't do this, Lawrie.'

'Give me three good reasons why not.'

'One, Diemond has made it very clear that if I ever speak to Rand again she'll kill me... Ow!'

Jo was going through the push and pull of hair and make-up at the NBC Burbank studios. She suspected their resident hairdresser was trying to scalp her.

'Sorry, hun,' the hairdresser said, continuing to assault Jo's frizzes like a stable boy brushing a horse. 'It's kinda knotty.'

'Don't you worry about Diemond,' Lawrie said. 'Her bark is worse than her bite.'

'That's easy for you to say,' Jo snapped. 'You're not the one on her death list.'

'You reckon you're the only one who's been threatened by her?' Lawrie had his feet up, leafing through *Rolling Stone* in the next chair. There was a row of six, all facing mirrors framed with lightbulbs. 'If I had a pound for every time she threatened to castrate me,' he said, 'I'd have two pound fifty.'

'How do you know her?' Jo asked, recalling his comment that he and the megastar had history.

'Know her?' Lawrie peered over the top of the magazine. 'I was her manager once upon a time.'

'No way.'

'Terrific singer,' he sniffed. 'Great dancer, amazing songwriter, a proper once-in-a-lifetime talent—'

'I feel so much better about myself, great pep talk. Thanks, Lawrie.'

'She's a complete narcissist,' he said. 'That's not uncommon in this business, but she took it to a whole new level. Completely incapable of showing any kind of empathy for other human beings.'

'She should've been a manager.'

'Ha-ha. Thanks very much, I love you too. No, she dumped me as soon as she got a whiff of interest.' Lawrie's gaze turned from Jo to some imagined future. 'Could've been amazing. Could've been the big time.'

He stayed like that for a while, just staring into space, his face becoming more and more still until Jo began to wonder if he'd fallen asleep.

'You okay, Lawrie?'

'Hmm?' He jolted out of his daydream. 'Yeah, fuck her. Like I said, I can handle anything she throws at us.' Lawrie's phone rang. 'Yeah,' he answered while digging in his free ear with his little finger. 'She's what? How can she—? For what? Ah, fuck. Get me another. What do you mean, you can't? No. No, no, no, no, no, no, no, no. No. Yeah? Fuck you, Tommy.' Lawrie hung up, tossed the phone across the room where it clattered into pieces, jumped to his feet, kicked his chair over and punched the wall. 'Ow! Fuckit.'

Jo and the hairdresser could only look on in astonishment.

'Problem?'

'How can she steal an entire band?' Jo stood with bits of highlighter foil in her hair and protective tissue tucked into her collar. She was in the TV studio's music rehearsal room. A small bunker, with foam soundproofing on the walls, a house drum kit, backline amps, mic stands, but no instruments apart from her little Martin acoustic.

And no band.

Jo had rushed here straight from make-up, not wanting to believe what they had just learned. Lawrie had gone to find someone to shout at.

'She hired them for a charity gig.' Lawrie crashed through the door, a lit cigarette dancing on his lip. 'Some kind of double-booking. Their manager said he was oh-so-fucking sorry. Don't you worry, I'll teach him the meaning of sorry.'

'Can they do this? Weren't they under contract?'

'Not exactly.' Lawrie didn't do squirming, but he was uncomfortable at being outfoxed. 'They were doing me a favour. A few session musicians I know giving me a freebie in return for a bit of exposure.'

'And they'll get more of that at a charity gig with the biggest star in the world than they will with me.'

'Exactly.'

'And if I try and get them back, I'm denying a charity their headline act and suddenly I'm the bad guy,' Jo said. 'She's a clever little minx, you've got to give her that. What did the floor manager say? We can postpone it, right?'

'Not unless you want to completely ruin your reputation.'

'What do you mean?'

'Oh, they'll let us off the hook.' Lawrie took a drag on his cigarette. 'But it's too late to replace you with anyone, which leaves them in the lurch, and it'll be all over the trades tomorrow that you're a flake who bails at the first sign of trouble, and no one will touch you with a barge pole.'

'That's not fair.'

'Yeah, y'know, cos the music industry is normally so egalitarian. *Course it's not fucking fair!*'

'What am I going to do, Lawrie?'

'You'll have to go solo,' Lawrie said. 'You and your guitar. We'll call it Yohanna Unplugged or something.'

'I can't.'

'Course you can.'

'No, that's what I've been trying to tell you,' Jo said. 'Reason two why I can't do this. I can't sing that song.'

'What are you on about? I've heard you sing it a million bloody times.'

'Yeah, well, not any more. I have this... mental block.'

'Don't worry about it, seen it all before. Doctor Adrenaline cures all known stage fright.'

'It's not stage fright, it's something more than that.' Jo jabbed at her throat. 'I literally cannot get the words any further than my oesophagus. Look, lemme show you. Give me that.' Jo scooped up her Martin guitar, and played the opening of the song. She took a breath, hoping she would be wrong, and... 'Huck... huck.'

'What's that? What's wrong with you?'

'I told you, it's a mental block.'

'It's mental, all right. Get over it. Try it again.'

And she did. 'Huck... huck.'

'Are you winding me up?'

'I'm telling you, Lawrie,' Jo insisted. 'This is real. I cannot sing this song.'

Lawrie's voice was quiet and calm, which was always worse than his shouting tantrums.

'I don't know what's wrong with you, and frankly I don't care, but six million people will watch this show and they'll tell six million more about it at the water coolers tomorrow. Record companies will call us and make offers and you will make the big time. That's what you want, isn't it? That's what we agreed when you signed up for this. If it's not, then we'll go our separate ways.'

'Really?' Jo wondered if this was some kind of olive branch.

'Sure. And I'll sue you for breach of contract and recoup the losses I've made on this little jolly. You want me to do that?'

'Not really.'

'Then sing. Tonight.'

A heavy silence filled the air.

'How about a backing track? I'll mime to a backing track.'

'I'm trying to bill you as a credible recording artist,' Lawrie said. 'And they don't do backing tracks on *The Tonight Show*.'

'I could sing another song?'

'I want you singing the single, the song we worked on for six months. 'It's the reason we're here, unless you can suddenly pluck something better out of your arse?'

'I hate to break this to you, Lawrie, but songs aren't just plucked - especially from bottoms.'

'I know that,' he raged. 'So, sing the bloody song.'

'I need the backing track, Lawrie,' Jo pleaded. 'I'm sorry. Tell them I've lost my voice or something.'

'Lost your voice?' Lawrie was struggling, 'Are you out of your tiny little mind? How am I meant to promote a singer without a voice? What the fuck is wrong with you?'

'It's a mental—'

'—block, yeah, right.' Lawrie checked his watch, 'Half an hour till you're on,' he said. 'All right, I'll get you your fucking backing track, but you have to fix this, Yohanna. I don't have any use for a singer who can't sing.'

Jo rushed back to hair and make-up, got rid of the foil in her frizzes and went looking for the one person who might just have the clout to get her out of this, also the one person she wasn't supposed to speak to.

The heady whiff of incense came from the other side of his dressing room door. The floor manager had said something earlier about Rand liking to meditate before a show, but Jo didn't have much in the way of time, and she rapped on the door.

'Come,' Rand said.

Jo opened the door a crack and popped her head around the door. 'Hey, look, I know we're not supposed to—'

'What are you doing here?' Rand was sitting in the lotus position in the middle of the amber glow of his dressing room. Candles and incense sticks were positioned in every corner. He wasn't wearing a shirt, only a prism pendant on a chain around his neck. Jo noted that he was ripped, his body smooth and tanned nut brown. She was surprised by the intensity of the lustful urges that clamoured for her attention.

'You're not supposed to speak to me,' he yelped, unfolding himself and rushing to the door. Jo darted back into the hallway as he slammed it shut.

'I'm sorry,' he said from the other side of the door. 'But I promised her. I told her that you were already booked to come on the show and that we would only speak on screen where she could see us. I thought I made that clear?'

'Oh, come on, Rand, just two minutes. She'll never know.'

'Are you kidding? She's like the CIA. She has eyes everywhere.'

'That's ridiculous, don't exagg...' Jo glanced up as a production assistant with a clipboard passed by, taking a little too much interest in their conversation. 'Okay, I'll be quick. I can't do the show tonight.'

'What do you mean you can't do the show? We're on in twenty minutes.'

'I can't sing the song. I cannot physically do it. I have a mental—'

'Fine, use a backing track.'

'Really? I thought that wasn't allowed?'

'Probably. I don't care. I'll talk to the producer. *Just leave me alone.*'

'FIVE MINUTES.' Jo's handler for the show was a super-enthusiastic Asian-American woman called Kate who looked barely old enough to order a beer, let alone work a headset. 'You're gonna be awesome,' she added in her Valley girl drawl, doing little to calm Jo's nerves as she stood in the wings. 'Rand's amazing. Mega-friendly. So chilled, y'know? You'll be fine.'

'Have you seen my manager?' Jo asked, checking the tuning on the guitar slung over her shoulder. 'He's supposed to be sorting the backing track.'

'What backing track?'

'I'm singing to a backing track.' Just saying the words made Jo blush with shame. 'It's because... of a... thing.' She gestured at her throat in the hope that would explain everything. Kate continued to smile.

'I haven't seen your manager.'

'Why are you smiling? That's a bad thing. I need to see him.' Jo started to move, but Kate zipped in her path with astonishing speed.

'I'm sorry, you're on in four minutes.' She continued to smile. 'We go to commercials in two.'

'I have to know!' Jo pleaded.

'One moment.' Kate raised a cheerful finger and spoke into her headset. 'Bobby, can I get a location on the music artist's manager... Yeah... something about a backing track... No, me neither... Cool, roger that. Over.' Kate finished the conversation, and returned to her smiling.

'And?'

'Bobby's on it.'

'What does that mean?'

'Bobby's super-cool. You'll be fine,' Kate said. 'Relax, enjoy the show. You're on in three.'

Jo considered running, but where would she go? And who was to say that Bobby wasn't about to turn the corner with Lawrie hand-in-hand. Jo took a deep breath, remembering her old voice lessons and pilates, jumbling them up and nearly hyperventilating. She tuned her guitar some more, but the little LCD on her tuner insisted that the instrument was as in tune as it possibly could be. She gave up on that and tried to enjoy Rand's interview with fellow movie actor Harrison Ford. This wasn't the Harrison Ford that Jo knew. He was animated and eager, almost happy-go-lucky.

'You've made some interesting choices,' Rand said to him. 'There was that space movie, what was that?'

'Uh... *Star Wars*.'

'Yeah, what drew you to that?'

'Y'know, it was an interesting script, taking mythology into space, knights and laser swords. It coulda worked.' The audience sniggered at the silliness of the very idea.

'And rumour has it you were nearly Indiana Jones? That would've been cool.'

Ford shrugged, 'Tom Selleck was always Spielberg's first choice. I... I can't comment on that.'

'But you'd like to work with him one day?'

'Spielberg? Sure, who wouldn't?'

Jo couldn't believe what she was hearing. '*Star Wars* was a flop?'

'I never saw it,' Kate shrugged. 'Sounds kinda corny.'

Rand continued his conversation with Ford. 'Would it be fair to say getting the role of Tim Whatley in *Seinfeld* is something of a comeback for you?'

Ford gave a wry smile, and Jo got a glimmer of the star she knew.

'How can I come back if I've never been away?'

The audience murmured, sensing tension.

Ford waved a dismissive hand. 'Yeah, not everything works out. It happens. But I love the work. I love working with the directors, the writers, and the actors to create a story. I see myself as a kind of assistant storyteller, and I'll keep doing it while they still let me.'

'No chance you'll go back to carpentry?' Rand joked.

Ford smirked. 'I doubt it. It's very satisfying, but I love my work now. If a movie's a success and makes money, great, everybody's happy. For me, the work is everything. Find happiness in your work, and you'll always be happy.'

Jo was less concerned about happiness, and more worried about making a complete idiot of herself in front of six million people in about—

'Two minutes,' Kate, the speaking clock, announced.

'Give it up for Harrison Ford, everybody!' Rand cried and the audience applauded along with some half-hearted whoops. Most of them didn't really know who Ford was, and were worried that they'd got a filler episode while Jay Leno was away. The next guest had better be good.

Rand announced a commercial break. 'And we'll be back with music from the UK's latest sensation, Yohanna!'

The studio's electronic sign flashed 'Applause' and the audience obliged in anticipation. Jo nearly blacked out from the rush of adrenaline. Her heart was playing a paradiddle under her sternum, and she realised why so many musicians did hard drugs.

'Well done, Mr. Ford,' Kate chirped. 'That was super-cool.'

'Thanks, kid. Anybody got a cigarette?' Harrison Ford said as he strolled off the set, hardly a care in the world. Jo thought about telling him that he was a huge megastar in her universe, but she had a peculiar feeling that this would only pop his bubble. He had the talent, but little luck, yet he was happy. At this moment, Jo would settle for just a little luck. Fate owed her some. Backdated.

'Thirty seconds,' Kate said in an excited whisper. 'This way, please.'

'No, wait, I can't go on till I hear from... *Lawrie!* Where the hell have you been?'

Her manager came stumbling around the cameras on the studio floor, breathless. Beads of sweat sat on his forehead, and Jo caught a warm waft of stale body odour that hit her like an overripe cheese. He rested for a moment, bent over, hands on his knees.

'Lawrie, is the tape ready?' Jo said, but he only expanded and contracted like a bellows.

'Ma'am, this way, please.' Kate took the crook of Jo's arm, her smile now a *please-co-operate-or-I-get-fired* grimace.

'Fifteen seconds,' someone called from beyond the cameras.

'Lawrie, are we good?'

Lawrie gave a thumbs-up, and Jo was shuffled into the limelight, the guitar around her neck.

'When you hear three, two, one, the lights come up and you're on, okay?'

Jo nodded, like a condemned woman going to the chair.

'Ten seconds!'

The world slowed around Jo. For a moment she wondered if she might be in the middle of an out-of-body experience and about to be transported home. As a child she'd watched shows like *Top of the Pops* and dreamed of singing on TV, and here she was ready to swap everything to be back in the karaoke bar with a few gins warming her insides.

A roadie dashed over to her, adjusted the height of her mic stand and plugged a cable into her guitar.

Kate placed a bottle of water by her monitor.

'Do you have any gin?' Jo asked.

'Don't worry. You're gonna be awesome.' Kate scurried back to the wings to enjoy the sight of another young musician about to have their big breakthrough. There she was, this Yohanna, alone in the spotlight, just her voice, a microphone and a guitar.

'Aww, she's gonna be fine.' Kate beamed at a job well done, and turned to where Lawrie was slowly returning to an upright position.

'Bobby came through?'

Lawrie still had trouble breathing, but he managed to speak between gasps. 'Bobby... fucked up. There's no... There's no backing track.' Lawrie nearly died again when he saw Yohanna standing in the spotlight.

'Five seconds.'

'You have to stop her.' Lawrie lunged forward, but Kate threw herself between him and the stage.

'Three. Two. One.'

OH WELL

Yohanna led Federica out of the town centre of Glastonbury, following the beam of rainbow light up the hill to the Tor. From here, they looked down on a ramshackle camp in the corner of a sympathetic farmer's field. Yohanna could see a few people milling about, hanging up laundry and chatting. There were three dilapidated caravans, and a number of pop-up tents scattered in a horseshoe shape. A few sheep gathered in a pen, hens pecked at the ground, and two cats, one black, one ginger, stalked each other in the shadows underneath the caravan. A woman in dungarees was chopping vegetables on a camping table outside a tent.

'He's there,' Yohanna said. 'I'm sure of it. The light cuts straight through the camp.'

'Who do you think they are? Gypsies, maybe?'

'If I know Ronnie, he's probably set himself up as their god or something,' Yohanna said, heading down the hill.

KAT SHELLEY HAD LEARNED to find simplicity and happiness in the simplest of tasks. Cutting carrots, for example, now gave her all the pleasure she needed these days. Once upon a time she'd indulged in ecstasy and cocaine in search of euphoria, but these days all it took was the satisfaction of slicing the carrots into perfect little wedges to give her a hit of contentment.

'I can smell lentil soup,' an Italian voice said. Kat looked up to see a wiry little woman strolling into the commune and sniffing the air. 'Lentils... and marijuana. Hippy cologne.'

The woman seemed to be having a conversation with herself.

'Can you see him? Is he here?' the woman asked the air around her, nodding when she got a reply. 'Okay, okay, I'll ask.'

As the woman moved through the commune, the cats hissed and darted under the caravans. The other commune members backed away, and Kat found herself in the woman's sights.

'Hello,' the woman said with a smile as she approached Kat. 'My name is Federica. I'm looking for someone called Ronnie Eades. Do you know him?'

Kat shook her head, and Federica reached into her pocket, producing a newspaper clipping with a photo of a balding, bearded man. 'He looks like this.'

'Don't know him,' Kat said with as much certainty as she could muster.

'What's your name?'

'Kat.'

'Kat.' Federica spoke calmly as she folded the newspaper clipping as carefully as a flag at a military funeral. 'I know that you're lying, and I'm sure that you think you're helping him, but I can assure you I am no threat. A friend of his desperately needs his help. This is a life or death situation, and I would be grateful if you could—'

'We don't know him.' Julie, another commune member who had been hanging out the washing, spoke up. 'Please leave.' Julie used to scare Kat. She was pale, freckle-faced, with one eye squinting while the other stared in amazement. Julie used to work in the City and closed multi-million dollar deals. She also used to live in a big house before divorcing her husband and selling everything to come here to find happiness in laundry, but she could still be Scary Julie From The City when she wanted to.

But this Federica woman wasn't listening to Julie. She seemed distracted by something in the air beside her, and she was talking to herself again.

'Where are you going? No, don't...' She stopped when she caught the puzzled looks of the people around her.

'You all right, love?'

'Yes, fine, thank you. Now, once again, can you tell me where to find Ronnie Eades?'

'We don't know no Ronnie Eades,' Kat said.

'But you know the man in the photo?'

'Listen, missus—'

'Federica.'

'Listen, Federica, we've all come here for a reason.' Kat placed her knife on the table next to the carrots. One of her wedges was bigger than the others and that made her cross. 'The world out there has nothing for us. We don't want money, we don't want big houses or land, and we don't want people thinking they can just wander in here and start calling us liars. We have come here for peace and quiet and contentment. So please, leave us alone.'

'I'm sorry to intrude, I truly am.' Federica clasped her hands together, then placed them over her heart. 'But I wouldn't be here if it wasn't important. There are times when we need to put aside our own needs, there are times when we must risk our own peace and solitude to help those we love, there are times when we must put everything on the line to save a life. This is one of those times, and I implore you to look inside your hearts and ask yourself...' Federica's head tipped as if someone was whispering in her ear. 'Okay, thank you, bye,' she said to Kat and the others before turning and leaving the commune.

Kat looked over to Julie, whose big eye was bigger than usual, 'What the bloody hell was that about?'

FEDERICA HURRIED to keep up with Yohanna, who was leading her back the way they came.

'I hope you're happy,' Federica said. 'They all think I'm crazy.'

'I'm sorry, but I needed you to keep them busy while I snooped around.'

'What did you find? Is he here?'

'No, but the big caravan had his maps and copies of his books, so he lives here - he's just not here now.'

'So where are you taking me?'

'He had a calendar on his wall.' Yohanna grinned. 'His weekly routine all written out in biro. Today is bath night, and he uses a very exclusive establishment.'

THEY FOLLOWED the narrow path down from the Tor to where it mingled with the edge of the town, eventually finding themselves on a steep hill called Well House Lane.

'This way,' Yohanna said, heading up the incline of the narrow road.

'You've been here before?'

'I came to the festival a few years back,' Yohanna said. 'Never had a ticket, couldn't get in, so I dossed around town for a couple of days. And this place is legendary.'

They almost walked past it. An unremarkable nook just off the road, with red tiles on the ground and damp stones framing a darkened doorway. Beside the door was a carved wooden totem pole with swirls of blue and white, and above the door, on the lintel, were the words The White Spring. Through the doorway was an iron gate.

'Quick, inside.' Yohanna passed through the gate. 'They'll be closing soon.'

Federica slipped inside, looking for some sort of ticket office. 'How much is it?' she called after Yohanna.

'Nothing,' Yohanna said. 'It's an old Victorian well house and local volunteers keep it running for free. It's bloody brilliant. Follow me.'

'Wait, slow down,' Federica called after Yohanna, as she took a moment to let her eyes adjust to the gloom inside. She descended the steps carefully behind Yohanna, gripping the handrail, listening to the sound of splashing and singing coming from the depths. It was a man's voice, and he was singing an old Fleetwood Mac blues song. Something about not caring about what shape he was in, not being pretty, unable to sing, and having thin legs. She couldn't make it all out as he broke off every few seconds to splash in the water. Candles lit the way, and the stones on the walls shimmered, almost in time with the man's blues vocals.

'C'mon,' Yohanna said. 'This has to be him.'

'I know you're excited, but I won't be any good to you if I slip and break my neck.'

'Okay, okay, I'll slow down, but... but hurry up!'

'I'm coming, hold your bah-luddy horses.'

Yohanna and Federica found themselves in an oubliette. A stone-walled sanctuary where the candles gave the pool a comforting amber glow. It should have been the perfect venue for solitude, meditation and reflection, were it not for the stark bollock naked man vigorously scrubbing his testicles in the water as he sang.

'*Oh, my god!*' Federica crossed herself as they were treated to a view of his shining buttocks and more as he bent down to rinse his flannel in the water. He seemed to sense their presence, turned to them and smiled.

'Good day to you, madam.' He bowed to Federica. 'I heard you chatting and assumed you were with a friend, but I see you are alone. Talking to one's self is often seen as a sign of madness, but I find it rather comforting. Perhaps you are touched with the power of the psychic? This place is something of a magnet for those sensitive to the more esoteric vibrations of the universe, and you strike me as a remarkable woman.'

He flashed a flirtatious grin, and Federica realised that this man was coming on to her.

'In fact, I should say that there are few women I know who can match your beauty or allure, and that accent. *Oh.*' He pursed his lips in appreciation. 'Rome, of course, yes? With a dash of Sicilian, perhaps? Might I interest you in an espresso? There's a marvellous Italian café just around the corner, away from the tourists and all the other riff-raff.'

Federica carefully took the news clipping from her trouser pocket, unfolded it and glanced at the face in the photo. There was some stubble around his chin, but his head was as smooth as a billiard ball. You could take the beard and the hair away, but you would still be left with those cunning eyes and that chancer smile. There could be no doubt.

'Aaronovitch Eades?' she asked, certain of the answer.

His good humour vanished and he did his best to pretend he hadn't heard her, suddenly gathering his clothes piled at the edge of the pool. 'Perhaps another time?' His voice hardened, his charm evaporated. 'This has been lovely. Good day to you.'

'Ronnie.' Yohanna said. 'God, you got real old. Can you hear me? It's me, Yohanna.'

Aaronovitch showed no sign of hearing her or seeing her move as he strode away, doing his best to cover his nakedness with his damp smalls.

'Her name is Joanna Adams.' Federica marched after him.

'Forgive me, I thought you were someone else.' Aaronovitch began to walk faster. 'I was clearly mistaken. Goodbye.'

'You might know her as Yohanna,' Federica persisted.

'Is that a real name?'

'Yes!' Yohanna snapped.

'Yes!' Federica echoed.

'I'm afraid I've never heard of her.'

'Well, she knows you,' Federica said. 'It was your theories that got her in this situation in the first place.'

'My theories?' Aaronovitch stiffened, glancing back at Federica as he walked. 'You're too short to be a bailiff. Are you the police? A private detective?'

'No, but I can call one if you don't start being helpful.'

Yohanna glided to Federica's side. 'Tell him about California. That's where we met. Venice Beach.'

'She says you met on Venice Beach,' Federica said, and Aaronovitch's eye twitched involuntarily with recognition.

'That's where he taught me how to assume a bardo state,' Yohanna said. 'He was helping me with my stage fright.'

'That's where you taught her about the bardo state, to help with her stage fright,' Federica repeated.

'Please leave me be.' Aaronovitch grimaced, and marched up the steps, trying to wriggle back into his clothes as he did, but the Italian woman kept calling after him.

'She says you showed her how to travel between parallel universes.' Federica closed in on him. 'She says you showed her how to enter the spiritual plane, and she actually did it... It was a song that made the connection. Not voices, but a song.'

'Tell him it's all about pairs,' Yohanna said.

'It's all about pairs,' Federica echoed.

Aaronovitch stopped, turning back to Federica. 'Pairs? A song?' he asked, suddenly interested. He watched as the woman seemed to take dictation from the air.

'She made a connection with another version of herself,' Federica said. 'They wrote the same song. Your theories were right, Aaronovitch. And she can help you prove it.'

'She?' He gestured at the empty air next to Federica. 'Who is she?'

'A young woman who needs your help to get her home.'

'You're too late,' he said, his voice trembling. His charm left him and he became a defeated old man. 'If there's one thing I've realised out here, it's that the longer you stay in isolation, the more the world goes on without you. I'm surplus to requirements, and I don't have to be that person anymore.'

'No,' Federica said. 'You can be better.'

SIX MILLION PAIRS OF EYES

The lights bloomed into life. Jo winced as the brightness stabbed into her pupils. The audience, prompted by the studio's 'Applause' signs, put their hands together in anticipation of enjoying something new and dynamic from a rising star. Some had even heard of this singer's weird press conference yesterday and knew they were in for a treat.

Jo waited for the playback to start.

And waited.

And waited.

A glance over to the wings confirmed her worst fears as Lawrie, face as red as a beetroot, made a throat-slitting gesture.

And Jo realised with a cold twist in her gut there would be no playback.

She was going to have to sing.

As she wished for the world to open up and swallow her whole, Jo recalled a secondary school production of Macbeth where she'd bagged the role of Lady Macbeth (much to the annoyance of her drama rival Vics Pinborough, who went on to appear in a TV commercial for Tampax before getting a semi-regular role on *The Archers*).

It was in front of the whole school. Jo had rehearsed for weeks, stayed up nights to learn the lines, all in the hope of turning in an award-winning performance and, more importantly, being able to rub Vics' nose in it. She'd been doing fine until the 'Out damn spot' scene, when she suddenly blanked. Completely word blind. Could not remember what came next for the life of her.

All in front of every kid she knew.

And Vics Pinborough.

Jo's audience back then was about twelve hundred kids at her local comprehensive school. There were fewer people in the TV studio now, but she also had at least six million pairs of eyes watching her in close-up, who would all tell their friends what an utter disaster she was tomorrow over the water cooler.

Jo could hear frantic whispers of '*Roll playback,*' but no sound was forthcoming. She could see panicked faces in the crew. Kate was pacing back and forth, muttering into her headset, her smile now a grimace.

In the school play Jo was eventually rescued by the drafted-in prompter, little Tony Edwards from class 3BNR, who boasted he knew all the words and didn't need a script, so she'd been surprised to see him frantically flicking through one when she blanked.

There would be no prompter to save her now. Jo leaned into the mic.

'Okay folks,' she said, trying to keep it chirpy. 'Bit of a technical problem, apparently, so, uh...'

'Sing!' someone in the audience cried, then began chanting it over and over, 'Sing! Sing! Sing! Sing!' They were soon joined by whoops and cheers of encouragement from the audience. Unlike Lady Macbeth, where the audience took great delight in seeing her fail, these people were on her side.

Also, unlike her Lady Macbeth, Jo was strangely calm now. The thing that could have gone disastrously wrong *had* gone disastrously wrong and no one had died, no one was pelting her with rotten fruit. They just wanted to hear her sing. But what could she sing? She'd nothing else to offer them. Well, nothing she'd written herself. Then she remembered it was the nineties.

'Okay, screw it,' she said. 'Let's try something different. This is a new one I just, uh, pulled out of my bottom.' A strange choking noise came from the wings, and she glanced over to see her manager making a throat-cutting gesture. New material on a live TV show was not part of his plan.

Only this wasn't a new song. Not to Jo, anyway.

She could just about remember the chords and lyrics to Adele's *Rolling In The Deep*. Jo reckoned Adele might be nearly ten years old now and hadn't written it yet, so why the hell not use it to fill a hole in the schedule?

Jo started pounding the body of the guitar, a steady rhythm. The audience clapped along. Brilliant. Confident they had the beat, she stopped her guitar thumping and sang *a cappella*. There was no mental block here, and the words came easily. It could have been just another karaoke night with friends from work, or a sing-along with her iPod as she readied Sunday lunch in her kitchen. Her voice soared and the audience went nuts, clapping harder and jumping to their feet. Jo began strumming the guitar, and that blissful feeling of happiness engulfed her like a wave, making her skin tingle, making her heart fly. All the tension in her voice vanished.

While her technical hitch had lasted an eternity, the song was over in a flash. She brought it to a thunderous conclusion and everyone in the studio, crew and Rand included, were on their feet, roaring in appreciation of the girl who had just clawed a triumph from disaster.

Jo wasn't sure what to do other than take a bow. As she did, she caught sight of more frantic movement and crew members chatting into headphone mics. Rand strode across the studio floor and addressed one of the cameras directly.

'A-mazing! Huh?' The crowd cheered in agreement. 'We'll be talking to Yohanna right after this break. Don't go changing.'

'And we're out,' someone cried, and a make-up lady hurtled towards Jo and began dabbing her face with a sponge.

'Holy shit, that was incredible,' Rand beamed, and Jo wondered if he was about to embrace her, but he hesitated, still afraid of Diemond's spies seeing him get too intimate.

'Thank you,' Jo puffed, still buzzing from the high.

'You're gonna put me in an early grave, girl.' Lawrie scowled as he hurried over like a football coach at half time. 'Cracking song, though. Where'd you get that from?'

'My arse,' she said. 'Where you told me to get it from. You're dead to me, Lawrie. What was that bloody thumbs-up about?'

'You asked if I was good.'

'I asked if *we* were good. Meaning, was the bloody backing track ready? Which it clearly wasn't. I wasn't concerned with your general bloody welfare.'

'One minute!' someone yelled.

'This way, please.' Kate gently took Jo's elbow and steered her towards the guest's leather chair next to Rand's presenter desk.

'You'll have plenty of time to hate me later,' Lawrie said, chasing them to the chair. 'Just tell them you're looking for a record deal and you want to play Glastonbury.'

'I *do* want to play Glastonbury, actually,' Jo said, as if half-remembering an idea.

'You've told *me* enough bloody times,' Lawrie said. 'Now tell them.'

Glastonbury. Jo's childhood dream. Yohanna's, too.

'Thirty seconds!'

Lawrie was hustled away by Kate, and Jo found herself sitting opposite Rand as a stage manager fitted her with a tie mic.

'Uh, what happens now?' Jo asked. Kate had given her a full and thorough briefing before the show, but she'd been somewhat distracted by the backing tape situation, and couldn't remember a single thing she'd told her.

'We just shoot the breeze,' Rand said. 'It's okay to be nervous. I was too, the first time. You know how I dealt with it?'

'Meditation? Hard drugs? Bit of both?'

Rand grinned, newly infatuated. 'I just looked into Johnny Carson's eyes, told myself I was chewing the fat with a buddy in a bar, and it was all over before I knew it. You'll be fine.'

'Three. Two...'

The audience drowned out the 'one' with their enthusiastic hollering.

'And we're back!' Rand announced, his voice becoming drowned out by the rush of blood in Jo's ears as she allowed herself to revel in the moment, noticing little details - the little red light on top of camera one, the exhausted floor manager chewing gum, the heat of the studio lights on her cheeks, the smiling faces in the audience, Ellie sitting in the front row.

Ellie.

Jo shielded her eyes, squinted, and leaned forward for a better look. No, it wasn't Ellie. It wasn't even a girl, just a boy, half Ellie's age, leaning against his mother as they watched. Great, now Jo was seeing things. She became angry with herself. When was the last time she'd given Ellie any thought? If Jo was so desperate to get back to her, what the hell was she doing on *The Tonight Show* pretending to be a rock star?

Jo became aware of Rand asking her a question, and it took her a second to pop out of her bubble.

'Hmm? Sorry, love. Miles away,' she said, and the audience laughed.

'I gotta say that was one of the most amazing things I've ever seen,' Rand said. 'Can we be honest with the audience here? You were going to sing to a backing track, is that right?'

Jo blushed and wondered what kind of follow-up fit Lawrie might be having in the wings. But she found herself enjoying the sensation of honesty, even the jocular noises of disapproval from the audience. It was liberating. One of her early foster families was Catholic and they made her take confession every Sunday. Jo, weirdly, liked it. The act of unburdening all your sins to some stranger was simply a precursor to therapy as far as she was concerned.

'Yeah, the truth is I can't sing my new single live,' she said. In her peripheral vision, Jo was sure she caught a glimpse of Lawrie burying his head in his hands. There were some nervous laughs from the audience. 'I have a kind of... mental block. Whenever I try and sing it, it just gets stuck in my throat. It's really weird.'

'Why is that? You said something at the press conference about a baby?'

Jo felt her belly churn. She'd forgotten about that. A throwaway comment just to annoy Lawrie had now come back with a vengeance. The idea of pretending to be a pop star was one thing. Pretending to be another person, even another version of herself, now felt all kinds of wrong.

'Okay, look, let me be honest. This is going to sound weird, but I'm a kind of time traveller,' she announced, drawing giggles from the audience. 'I'm not the Yohanna you think I am, okay? I'm really a forty-two-year-old mother from England who somehow ended up in the body of a pop star sexpot.' More laughs. Jo realised they thought this was some kind of comedy bit, a publicity stunt to get attention, and that suited her fine.

'That song just now? *Rolling In The Deep*. It gets written by someone called Adele in about eighteen years or so from now.' Jo looked for a camera with a red light. 'Which camera am I on? This one?' Rand nodded, and Jo spoke directly to the camera. 'Adele Adkins, sweetheart, you're just a kid now, but if you're somehow watching this, take the song. It's yours anyway.'

'Kinda like the Chuck Berry bit in *Back To The Future*?' Rand's arms were folded, though he was smiling.

'You have *Back To The Future* here?'

'Of course.'

'Who's the star?'

'Eric Stoltz.'

'See, in my world it's Michael J Fox.'

'The kid from *Family Ties*?' More laughter.

'Yeah, and Harrison Ford? Huge in my world. Massive. *Star Wars* was a colossal hit, loads of sequels, and *he* played Indiana Jones, not bloody Tom Selleck.' The audience was hooting with laughter now.

'That's one hell of an imagination. Ever thought of writing a movie?'

'I'm not making this up, honestly,' Jo said. 'Okay, take Diemond. You probably heard about the press conference yesterday, where people are saying that I pretended not to know who Diemond was? Yeah? I wasn't pretending. I genuinely had no idea. We don't have a Diemond where I come from, which is why I hadn't the first bloody clue who she was.'

'There's no Diemond in your world?'

'No, our pop megastar is Madonna. Do you have Madonna?'

Rand shook his head.

'No?' Jo turned to the audience. 'Okay, so maybe there's a Madonna Louise Ciccone out there who's a singer and hasn't had her big break, or maybe she never tried? Maybe... maybe she settled down, got married, had kids and is in a boring job? Bloody hell, I just described me.' A big laugh.

'So, who sent you on this time travel mission? What's your purpose here?' Rand asked. 'Have you come here to assassinate a future Hitler?'

'Ah, no, but that would be Donald Trump.' The audience roared with laughter. 'I'm serious. Don't let him anywhere near the White House. Oh, do you have Harry Potter yet?'

'No, who's he?'

'Okay, okay.' Jo turned back to the cameras. 'If there's a single mum in Edinburgh called Jo Rowling and she's thinking of writing a book about a boy wizard and she hasn't done it yet? Do it. Do it now, girl!' The audience was just confused now, and Jo began to feel that she was pushing her luck. 'I'm sorry.' She turned back to Rand. 'I just want to go home. In my world that song - the one I can't sing - is about my daughter, Ellie, who I love and miss terribly.'

'You have a daughter?' Rand frowned. 'You look barely old enough to—'

'Yohanna doesn't have a daughter. Does this body look like it's had a baby? But I do. Joanna Adams, the forty-two-year-old woman that's stuck inside Yohanna's body has had a baby. I don't belong here. This world doesn't know Ellie. It will never know her smile, her honking laugh, her terrible macaroni and cheese, her ability to fly off the handle in mere milliseconds, and the way she cries whenever she watches *The Lion King*.'

Jo was annoyed to find herself crying, and she hurriedly brushed the tears away from her cheeks. Rand looked concerned and almost reached out to take her hand, but the fear of Diemond's reprisals remained. The audience loved it, and started cheering Jo in support. Jo could see on the monitors that the cameras cut to women in the audience crying too.

'I'm sorry,' Jo sniffed. 'Is it too late to say that my manager told me to say I need a record deal, and tell you all that I want to play Glastonbury?'

'No, that's fine.' Rand was smiling again. 'How do we get you home, Yohanna? Is there a space ship? A time machine?'

'No, apparently I have a guru who can do it, but I don't have his number,' she shrugged. 'Ronnie, if you're out there, please get in touch. No weirdos, though.'

'Oh, that's fine,' Rand said with a wry grin. 'There are zero weirdos in California. I'm sure he'll get right in touch. Ladies and gentlemen, that's all for tonight's show. I want to thank my guests - comedian Bill Hicks, actor Harrison Ford, and the extraordinary Yohanna. Give it up!'

THE NEXT FEW minutes were a blur for Jo as she was shepherded away from the stage, through to her dressing room. Her mind began to come down from the high of the show, and she tried to recall half of the insane stuff she'd said.

Lawrie was sitting waiting for her, feet on the table, phone at his ear.

'Yeah, yeah, I'll see. No promises. Yeah.' He saw Jo and gestured for her to sit on the leather couch in her dressing room. She flopped on it, exhausted. 'Okay, fine. Speak tomorrow.' Lawrie hung up, turned the phone off, and for a moment they sat alone in silence. Jo had half-expected a bollocking from Lawrie, but she couldn't read him now. His face was a blank.

'Lawrie, I'm sorry, but it's true. I—'

'Ah-cha-cha,' he said, shushing her into silence like she was naughty pup. He bit his lip, thought for a moment, and took a cigar from inside his jacket. Jo was about to object, but remembered it was the nineties.

'I've been in this business nearly thirty years,' he said, snicking his Zippo into life and bringing the flame to the cigar's tip. 'I've seen it all. The drugs, the sex, the self-destruction, Keith Moon's arse... But I've never seen anyone want to so wilfully destroy their own career like you, girl. Refusing to sing, deliberately screwing up a press conference, bad-mouthing your peers and competitors, and now making a complete fool of yourself in front of an entire nation.'

'Lawrie, it's—'

'Ah-cha-cha,' he said again, raising a finger. 'If I had the first clue how mental you were going to be when we first met, I would never have taken you on. It's like you're a different person.'

'I am a different person.'

'Yeah, so you said, time travel, blah-blah-blah.' Lawrie's cigar crackled and blossomed orange as he sucked on it. 'Fact is, I should drop you like a turd sandwich. Walk away and count my blessings, but here's the thing...' Lawrie heaved himself out of the chair in a cloud of his own cigar smoke and moved uncomfortably close to Jo, his eyes fixed on hers.

She glanced at his fists. They weren't clenched, so she hoped this wouldn't get violent, but looked around the room for weapons just in case it did. There was a hairdryer. Maybe she could melt his face with it? But something strange happened. Lawrie's face went from baggy to taut, and she realised he was smiling. Not his usual conniving grin, but a proper beaming shiner.

'Whatever you're doing, it's bloody working,' he hooted, grabbing her by the arms and kissing her on each cheek, nearly setting her hair alight with his cigar. 'I've just had three of the major labels on the blower and they all want meetings. They want you, girl. They said you had the most amazing voice, you're a breath of fresh air, you're not just another manufactured pop star.'

'Ironic, really,' Jo said, brushing cigar ash from her hair. 'As that's exactly what you were going for.'

'Don't ruin it,' Lawrie snapped, his old self again. 'Okay, so this kooky thing is working for you, just give me some warning when you do something mental, will you? It's not good for my dicky ticker.'

'I'll try.' Jo tried to be happy, but she wasn't sure all this extra attention was going to be good for her. All she wanted now was to head back to the hotel and sleep for a week. 'So what do we do next?'

Lawrie's conniving grin returned.

'We party like it's 1999.'

THE INNER LIGHT

'Is this nonsense really necessary?'

Yohanna looked on, silent and unseen, as Aaronovitch pulled the curtains closed in his caravan back at the commune. A futon was propped up against one wall, piles of half-read books dotted the threadbare carpet, and a dusty laptop lay askew on a deckchair. There were several small hillocks of laundry, and a kitchenette area with a line of ants marching along the edge of the cabinets.

'In order for this to work, you must be open to the spirit world.' Federica lit a candle on a coffee-stained green baize card table. As the flame grew she perched herself on the edge of a red and white striped collapsable garden chair. 'Are you?'

'Oh, I am, I am.' Aaronovitch pulled a paint spattered stool over to the card table, sitting opposite Federica. He watched as she produced an unlit roll-up cigarette and let it sit on her lips. 'Is that part of the ritual?'

'It helps.' Federica closed her eyes, then, a moment later, opened one to check if Aaronovitch was doing the same. He wasn't. 'Close your eyes,' she snapped. He did so. 'Yohanna, darling.' Federica pointed at the far wall, which was a blank space as far as Aaronovitch was concerned. 'Wait there,' Federica told Yohanna. 'Please don't move.'

Yohanna was still hurting from her encounter with the rainbow light in the street earlier. Her mind trying to separate what was real from the dream-like bardo state in the light. Mum had died when she was just a toddler. Yohanna told people she was too young to remember her. What if she could know her mother again? Even if it was the most painful, heartbreaking experience she'd ever known, who wouldn't want a moment to say a few words?

'Concentrate,' Federica snapped at Aaronovitch who was yawning.

'Forgive me,' he closed his eyes. 'I was simply waiting for something to actually happen.'

Yohanna wondered how any of this going to get her back home. This wasn't even *her* Aaronovitch. He was the same guy - just as the older Joanna was a version of her - but this Aaronovitch was a kooky old man. He had no hair and no neck and looked like a thumb in a shabby suit. Her Aaronovitch had vision and energy to spare and a well-groomed beard. He would figure out the riddles of the universe and get her back in L.A. before tea time.

Yohanna had been away from her old life - her *real* life - for too long. A part of her brain, the bit that regularly made her feel like a fraud, was beginning to question if she really was a rising star. It was telling her that she was just a silly little girl following a stupid dream.

Yohanna shook the thought away and clung on to memories - her suite in the Beverly Wilshire, Rand and his smile, even Lawrie's temper was worth recalling.

The candle's flame danced as before. Yohanna recognised its unnatural jerk as it encountered whatever strange force that Federica was summoning. The light through the curtains swept across the room, faster than before, possibly because Federica knew exactly where to find Yohanna. It settled on her youthful face and she glowed amber, surrounded by countless dust motes.

'You can open your eyes now.' Federica's voice was barely a whisper.

Aaronovitch's eyelids opened, heavy and slow. 'I prefer my naps to take a little longer, but any opportunity for a rest is always... BUGGER ME, IT'S A GHOST!'

His eyes bulged when he saw Yohanna floating in his caravan, and he stumbled back over his stool, tumbling into a pile of old *Fortean Times* magazines. 'How...? How did you do that?' he asked Federica when he eventually got his breath back.

'A few of us can see, others just need to be shown.' She took the unlit cigarette from her lip and put it back in her pocket.

'Oh, spirit,' Aaronovitch called to Yohanna like he was auditioning for an amateur dramatic production of *A Christmas Carol*. 'Can you hear me?'

'Oh, for God's sake, Ronnie, yes,' Yohanna said. 'Can we just get on with this?'

'Uh, oh yes, of course,' he said, a little thrown. 'Federica said you and I have met, but I must confess I do not recall us ever meeting.'

'Maybe not in this universe,' Yohanna said. 'But in mine you're my guru.'

His face lit up. 'Really?'

'Ugh,' Federica sneered. 'Don't inflate his ego any more than it already is. He'll burst.'

'You mentioned Venice Beach before.' Ronnie ignored Federica and focused on Yohanna. 'I had a practice there, some time ago I must say, but I'm sorry to say that I don't remember you.'

'I'm a singer,' Yohanna said. 'I'd read your books when I was recording my demo tracks, and I wrote to you a few times and you said if I was ever out in California we should meet, and I was and we did and...'

Yohanna let it hang there for a moment, hoping he would remember her.

'And?'

He didn't.

'You were amazing,' she said. 'I was totally stressed out by my manager, and the pressure, I wasn't sleeping, I was a complete mess, I had the worst stage fright. You improved my yoga, Alexander technique, meditation, and we started talking about life and death, my... *huck.*'

Yohanna stopped, took a moment to compose herself, cleared her throat, and continued. 'My mother. In less than a week you had completely changed my life. And you told me that you were looking for a way to cross between worlds. You were studying this lost chapter from the *Tibetan Book of the Dead* and you said I was the best subject you'd encountered yet.'

'In what way?'

'I can go into a bardo state just like that.' Yohanna snapped her fingers. 'I don't know how, but I can.'

'Remarkable.' Aaronovitch pulled himself out of the pile of magazines. 'I've never met anybody who could do it without hours of meditation.'

'I just closed my eyes, breathed like you told me, and I'm there, transcendentally floating between worlds,' she said, gesturing at her opaque form. 'At least, I could. Something went wrong, Ronnie, and I need you to fix it. I need you to get me home before I'm gone for good.'

Aaronovitch clambered to his feet, his forehead wrinkling as he tried to piece together all this new information.

'There's something else,' Yohanna said. 'Just now, out there, I had a really weird experience with this beam of rainbow light.'

'Rainbow light?' Aaronovitch said, intrigued. 'Show me.'

THEY RETURNED to the Market Cross. For Yohanna, the beam of light was as solid and real as ever, but Federica and Aaronovitch still couldn't see it. Federica and Yohanna looked on as Aaronovitch wandered back and forth through it with his prism.

'Yes,' he said. 'Yes, I see it. Come here.' He beckoned over Federica and Yohanna, dangling the prism from his hand and squinting at the refracted light inside. 'Do you see it?'

Federica had to step on tip-toes. One pane of the prism showed the Market Cross as she saw it, but the other had a blinding light splitting the street in two.

'Bah-luddy hell,' she gasped.

'I know what this is,' Aaronovitch said, suddenly animated, and Yohanna saw a little of the man she knew. 'A ley line runs right through here. It's been right in front of us all this time and we couldn't see it.'

'Maybe you just needed to be shown?' Federica smiled.

'Oh, shush,' he said, before returning to squinting at the prism. 'My theory is ley lines are streams of tachyon light, gateways between parallel universes. One can only enter when one is in a bardo state, and even then you risk being swept away like a swimmer in rapids. You could find yourself in another time, place, or even another body. It's incredibly dangerous.'

'You might've thought to mention that before encouraging me to play with them,' Yohanna said.

'I suspect that version of me had little idea of what he was dabbling in,' Aaronovitch said. 'I'm older now and, I like to think, a little wiser. I'm delighted that my theories have been proven to be true, but this sort of thing is dangerous and must be avoided at all costs.'

'But you're gonna get me home, right?'

'I can't see how.' He frowned in deep thought. 'As you've seen, just hopping in can be traumatic and perilous. I suppose I could direct the energy of the light using a prism, but one would need a vessel in which to focus its power.'

'A what?'

'He means a body,' Federica said.

'Yes.' Aaronovitch began pacing again. 'You and your older self were attracted to one another via this song. My theory is that similar pairs are bound to one another when moving between universes. I could never prove it, of course, but if your transfer between universes had been controlled, you should have swapped places, but like the aforementioned swimmer in rapids you were thrown around in the stream and found yourself in a less than corporeal state.'

'I'll ask again,' Yohanna said. 'A what?'

'A ghost,' Federica said.

'No, not a ghost,' Aaronovitch growled. 'A manifestation of your spirit.'

'Yeah, a ghost,' Federica repeated.

'No, she's not dead, but she's close to it.' Aaronovitch ran his hands over his smooth head. 'Oh, goodness, there's one more thing.'

'The solstice?'

'You know about that?' Aaronovitch grimaced. 'That could be very bad indeed. It weakens you, and, if you cannot return home before the sun disappears over the horizon, you might not get home at all. We need to find this other you, bring her here, or to any ley line, and we can switch you back to your rightful place in the universe.'

'Perfect, let's do it!' Yohanna jumped and clapped her hands together excitedly.

'Excellent.' Aaronovitch smiled. 'Where is she?'

Yohanna's excitement left her like the air from a balloon. She didn't have the first bloody clue.

RAND'S INNER SANCTUM

'Get in there, girl, make yourself known. Every hello is an opportunity and all that.'

Lawrie was coaching Jo on the show's after party networking opportunities as they followed Kate through the labyrinth of backstage corridors of the TV studio. 'Stay on message for once. Record deal. Record deal. Record deal. Record deal. Repeat that back to me.'

'Something about... a record deal,' Jo quipped. 'Not sure. Can we run through that again?'

'Ha ha, very funny,' Lawrie said, gripping her biceps as they walked. He dropped his voice to a harsh whisper. 'You've just made an impression out there, not the one I wanted, but you made one all the same. People are gonna want to know more and it's up to you to deliver.'

Jo stopped in her tracks, slapping Lawrie's hand away from her arm, 'Will you stop grabbing me and leading me around like a bloody dog?'

'All right, love, calm down,' Lawrie said. Jo saw an expression of surprise she hadn't seen on him before.

'Love?' Jo took a breath. 'Right, let's establish a few new rules, shall we? You do not touch me, dress me, tell me what to say or what to do, okay? You are my manager. You will manage my career. I will listen to your advice, but I won't promise to take it. You will follow my instructions. I'm the talent and you're the management and you can be fired. Understood?'

Jo hated to admit it, but she really enjoyed watching Lawrie's face fold into its angry bulldog mode. The capillaries on his nose were turning purple and she could see he was about to explode. But she could also see Kate opening the door to the green room where the party was, so Jo marched off before he could begin to rage.

'I'm knackered and time-lagged, Lawrie. I'm not in the mood for networking. I'm actually going to have some fun, I might get pissed, I might even get laid, it's been that sort of week. It's time to paaaartay!' she yelled as she shoved the green room doors open and marched in.

Jo stopped in her tracks. 'Oh, for fuck's sake.'

The smell of microwaved chicken wings wafted over Jo as she saw seven people standing around a poor excuse for a buffet. They nibbled on the wings and one of them tried to open an enormous bag of potato chips with his mouth. The bar was just a foldout table with a few cans of diet coke. Most of them had crew lanyards. Harrison Ford was nowhere to be seen, presumably in a limo headed to a hotel or the airport. She scanned the room quickly for Rand who was notable by his absence.

She turned to find Lawrie looking a lot more smug than he had any right to be. Hands in his pockets, he shuffled up to her and whispered in her ear, 'I think that fella on the end by the cheese and crackers is from Columbia Records. Works in the mail room. I could introduce you if you like? I am, of course, but your humble servant. Please don't fire me.'

Jo fought the urge to thump him.

'I need a pint,' Lawrie said, mopping his brow with a handkerchief. 'There's an English pub in Sherman Oaks. Fancy a drink?'

'I'm going back to the hotel.'

.   .   .

JO WANDERED off alone in a huff, and it didn't take her long to get lost. The corridors were lined with framed portraits of previous guests, but signs to the exit were non-existent. She found herself passing Rand's dressing room once more and decided to give him a try and knocked on the door.

'Jesus Christ!' his voice yelled from inside. 'What does a guy got to do to get five minutes' meditation around here?' Rand whipped the door open in anger. He was shirtless once more, and Jo's eyes were drawn to the little prism pendant dangling around his neck. His fury faded when he saw it was her.

'Oh, shit, Yohanna, sorry.' He glanced up and down the corridor for Diemond's spies, then beckoned Jo. 'C'mon inside, quickly.'

'Sorry.' Jo did as she was told, and he locked the door shut behind her. The sweet smell of incense floated around the room. 'I'm not stopping,' she said, trying not to linger on his bronzed skin, toned pecs and tiny shorts. She concentrated hard on keeping her eyes on his face. 'I'm just lost. How do I get out of here?' Jo felt her cheeks blush.

'Huh? No, stay, stay. Drink?'

'No-I-really-shouldn't-okay-just-one,' Jo blurted.

Rand poured her a glass of champagne, and refilled his own from an already opened bottle that was obviously part of his 'meditation' ritual. Real champagne, not the cheap prosecco that she and Nick were keeping for a special occasion that was now never going to come.

'So what was that, huh?' he said. 'Amazing, or what?'

'What?' Jo asked, necking the entire glass and enjoying the tingle of the bubbles in her nostrils combined with the fug of his incense sticks and candles.

'*Wot?*' Rand grinned topping her up. 'Love your accent. That voice, girl. I knew you could sing, but that was incredible. And that shit about time travel...? You should do comedy. No, you should do a movie. I can get you meetings. You're a natural. I just don't know where it all came from. You're not the same girl I dated last week.'

'The thing is, Rand...' Jo took another sip to help loosen her tongue, 'I'm not the girl you dated. We switched places. I really am a forty-two-year-old woman.'

He chuckled again, 'Cool. You're really funny.'

'No, please believe me. I arrived here two days ago in Yohanna's body. She's probably at my place now wondering how she suddenly put on so much weight and trying to explain who she is to my daughter and husband.'

'Cool. Astral planing?' Rand asked, genuinely interested. 'So you're married in this other life? You got a kid?'

'Yes,' Jo said, and caught sight of her younger self in the dressing room mirror. 'My name is Joanna Adams, I'm forty-two, I'm married to Nick and I have a daughter called Ellie and, god, I miss her so much.' Jo's cheeks burned, her eyes swelled and she chewed on her bottom lip to stop the tears. 'I just want to go home.'

'Hey, hey,' Rand said gently. 'It's okay.'

'You must think I'm mad.'

'A little, yeah.' He moved closer, took her hand and led her to a leather couch. As they sat down, she could detect a hint of moisturiser on his face, mixed with a cologne so subtle that she knew it had to cost a fortune, or was probably made exclusively for him mixed with ambergris and his own sweaty musk. 'But I understand. I really do.'

'You do?'

'Yeah, we all feel like we don't belong,' he said. 'Imposter syndrome. My therapist says it's very common with creative people. It's perfectly normal. It'll pass.'

Jo considered persisting with the truth, but thought about how she would react if someone she'd just met started telling her they were from a parallel universe. 'Yeah, I... I guess so.'

'I'll give you his number.' Rand rested his hand on her arm and she shuddered at his touch. She was thrilled, but also annoyed at herself. She couldn't let him get to her. She had a mission, she had to get home.

'I should probably go,' Jo said without moving.

'Yeah, you probably should.' Rand leaned in closer and she let him kiss her. His lips were soft, welcoming and, unlike Nick's, weren't slathered in lip balm.

She pulled away as Nick's dopey face appeared in her mind and she flushed with guilt.

'What's wrong?' Rand looked confused. 'Are you fucking with me, Yohanna? Because I don't want to play any games.' His eyes glistened and he took a cleansing breath. 'I've had my heart broken so many times already and I don't wanna—'

Jo couldn't resist any longer and launched herself at him, to shut him up if nothing else. They fell back on the couch. Why should she feel guilty? Nick had Andy. Jo had nothing except this adorable, hunky, willing, successful actor, and so she snogged him with vigour. The passion lasted about thirteen seconds before something jabbed into her chest.

'Ow! What the...?' It was the prism around Rand's neck. 'Would you mind taking that off? It's a health and safety passion killer.'

'It belonged to my Dad.' Rand moved it around to the side of his neck. 'It's kinda important to me and I never take it off.'

'It's so pointy. How are you not full of holes?'

'It gives me energy,' he said, and added with a mischievous grin, 'It sustains me.'

'Oh, yeah?'

'Yeah.'

'Let's see how long for,' Jo giggled, pulling at Rand's shorts, finding them difficult to get unwrapped around his erection.

There was a knock at the door.

'Mr. McManus?' It was Kate. 'Your car's here.'

'Dammit,' Rand muttered as Jo continued to pepper his chest with kisses. He called to Kate, 'Uh, y'know what, I'm good. I'll grab a cab.'

'Okay,' Kate said. 'Oh, and Diemond is in the green room. She said she wanted to say hi before you left.'

Jo had never known an erection to die so quickly.

Rand began to tremble, he shoved Jo off him and scrabbled around the dressing room looking for his clothes. 'Tell her I'm not here,' he yelled at Kate. 'Tell her I'm—'

'Screwing the special guests?' Diemond's voice came from inside the room. Like a ghost she'd somehow appeared in the doorway without making a sound. Kate could be seen gawping in the hallway behind her. Jo remained on the couch, grateful to be fully dressed if somewhat flustered, but poor Rand was frozen with one foot in his jeans and a semi-on bulging in his shorts for all to see.

DIEMOND'S GIFT

Rand's sizeable dressing room was still too small to contain Diemond's presence. The megastar wore an incredible dress made of strategically-placed palm leaves that left little to the imagination. She was almost wearing less than Rand, but on her it looked like a fully-fledged outfit with eye-popping slits along her thighs and a plunging décolletage, all balanced on gravity-defying heels. The fascinator that adorned her head was a living piece of millinery, with undulating coils of beads beckoning all who gazed upon it like Medusa's snakes. She didn't appear to have any make-up on at all, but Jo knew that it took an awful lot of slap, and maybe even a dextrous surgeon, to look that good. Jo had read that Diemond might be in her forties, but she looked fantastic for someone even in their early thirties.

Rand covered the bulge in his shorts. 'What the hell is this? You can't just barge in here, Die. We broke up and... and that's the end of it. We're—'

'Be quiet, silly boy, I'm not here for you.' Diemond waved him into silence, then turned her attention to Jo. 'My darling, I've come to apologise for my overreaction. You caught me at a bad time and I wish to offer the olive branch of peace.' Diemond's Southern Belle accent was even thicker in real life and Jo had to fight the urge to join in with an *I do declare!*

Jo had never met anyone really famous before today. She'd got a book signed by Michael Palin in her local Waterstones - but that was just a quick hello, -and had almost been run over by Prince Philip whilst jogging in Windsor Great Park. Most recently she'd seen Boris Johnson cycling over Waterloo Bridge and somehow resisted the urge to shove him in the Thames.

But she'd never been in the close presence of someone who had such a surefire reassurance that the universe revolved around them as Diemond did.

'Think nothing of it,' Jo said. 'It livened up my afternoon no end.'

'I'm delighted to hear it.' Diemond moved around Jo like a duellist looking for weaknesses. 'Young Rand here is an intoxicating specimen, don't you agree?'

'He's a very charming young man.' Jo realised she was beginning to sound like a middle-aged housewife, so added, 'A hot bod, and pecs you can bounce coins off.' And immediately regretted it.

'I caught your performance,' Diemond said. 'Very impressive, young lady. A beautiful voice and you have a singular imagination. A universe without me. Can you imagine such a thing?'

'Huh, yeah, I should apologise, too,' Jo said. 'I'm working out some... issues.'

'I'm sure you are.' Diemond licked her perfectly arranged pearly teeth as she smiled. 'I brought a few friends along from my charity concert tonight.' She gestured down the hallway back to the green room. 'Producers, songwriters, musicians, come and say hi. I'll introduce you around.'

Every instinct Jo had was telling her to leave now, go back to the hotel and get a good night's sleep. Diemond was up to something, that much was clear, but the megastar also thought she was dealing with a naive twenty-four-year-old, and not a cynical mum in her forties who had seen enough weird shit in the last two days to last her a lifetime. Also, Jo's desire to cop off with Rand had faded. She was feeling a little silly and, figuring she might as well salvage something from this evening, followed Diemond out of the room.

The green room was transformed.

A party was in full swing. The music was pumping techno. A DJ with a mohawk twiddled dials and punched the air as the room - now heaving with the young and the beautiful - yomped in time to the beat under the swirling light reflected off a mirror ball.

Diemond glanced at Jo's astonished *Where did all these people come from?* expression. 'Just a few close, personal friends,' Diemond told her. 'I call them the Die-Hards. They're always ready to party.'

The Die-Hards whooped as they sensed the aura of their leader in the room, and they beckoned the megastar to join them. Ricardo, Diemond's friend with the pencil moustache and droopy voice, rushed forward with three flutes of champagne. He wore a black suit with lemon piping tonight.

'Make sure everybody gets a glass. Quick, quick,' Diemond commanded and Ricardo scurried away. Rand took a glass and was swept away by admirers. Jo remained under Diemond's feather boa wing.

The next few minutes were a whirlwind. Wherever Diemond went in the room, people stopped what they were doing to talk to her. Jo saw people completely blank who they were chatting to in order to make themselves available to the star. Most were blatantly obsequious, angling for something from her, but without quite knowing what they wanted yet. Others were just too excited to be close to their hero. A few tried to be cool and diffident, but Jo could sense their desire to impress.

At first, Jo thought Diemond knew everybody by their first name, but she began to note an increasing number of 'Darlings' and 'Sweeties' for those a bit further down the food chain. Record executives and producers, those with the money and the power, got Diemond's full focus and she graciously introduced Jo to them all.

'This is Yohanna, wasn't she marvellous? Did you see her tonight? Just extraordinary. She's a star, I'm telling you. Snap her up now. No, this is *her* party. Nothing to do with me. This is Yohanna's party. Celebrate.'

Diemond repeated this again and again, 'This is Yohanna's party. A new star has arrived.' Its repetition began to set off little alarm bells in the back of Jo's head, but she dismissed them. She told herself she was being too cynical and she should just bloody enjoy herself for once. Whenever she was dragged along to a party by Nick she'd had to listen to other people drone on about their boring kids or house prices, but here everyone wanted to listen to her. They asked the same questions again and again, and she soon got the knack of giving the same answers as though she was being asked for the first time. She made them laugh, she had them on tenterhooks with her stories, and they all wanted more. Complete strangers were praising her, beautiful men and women were giving her the eye, and Diemond was now her official best friend ever.

Diemond raised her arms to the ceiling. 'Darlings!' The DJ killed the tunes and the room fell into rapt silence. 'Honeys, it's so wonderful to see you all this evening, but for once tonight isn't all about me.' There were some titters from the crowd and Jo caught sight of Rand chatting to a pair of very glamorous young ladies and felt a pang of jealousy. 'No, really, it isn't. It's about a new talent and I know you all saw her extraordinary performance on the show tonight. Come here, Yohanna!'

Diemond led the applause and beckoned Jo towards her. Something felt wrong all of a sudden, like she was being set up, like this was all a big practical joke and in a moment they would all be laughing at her. Jo was reminded of visiting a store Santa when she was a child and that terrible anticipation of not wanting to go near the scary thing, but knowing that there might be a gift at the end of it.

She remembered Rand's words about creative people feeling like imposters and shook her doubts away. This was her moment, and she wasn't about to let her own paranoia sabotage it. Diemond was being amazing, welcoming Jo into the fold. Jo, or Yohanna, had arrived and she was about to become a star.

'Ricardo, how are we doing, sweetie? C'mon, chop-chop.' Ricardo and a handful of Diemond's acolytes hurried through the crowd handing out more champagne.

Up close, Diemond was truly beautiful with hypnotic sapphire eyes. Jo felt the star's hands on her shoulders and felt a special warmth rise through her.

'A toast,' Diemond announced. 'To a new star in the firmament. May she burn... brightly. Yohanna!'

'Yohanna!' everyone cheered back. Jo took a sip of the champagne along with everyone else.

Diemond did not.

Jo didn't take much notice at the time, but looking back she realised this should have been her big clue of what was to come. Instead, Jo revelled in the moment, downed her own glass and gave Diemond a hug.

The party resumed. Diemond snapped her fingers at Ricardo, who bustled to her side. 'Yohanna, darling, I can't stay, I'm rehearsing for Glastonbury this weekend, but I hope you have the time of your life. Let's do lunch.' She gave Jo three air kisses, turned and made for the exit at speed. Jo knew this was her cue to back away, but she followed Diemond out to the artiste's entrance around the back of the building.

'Look, I just wanted to say thank you,' Jo said, almost running to keep up. 'I know we got off on the wrong foot and everything, but tonight has been just amazing. I think it's really kind of you to have done all this. Lawrie said you—'

'Ah, yes, our mutual friend,' Diemond purred. 'How is the poisoned dwarf? Tell him I haven't forgotten that he nearly destroyed my career before it even started.'

'Really?'

'Ask him where he gets his money from.' Diemond beckoned Jo closer and whispered. 'His mother. She's loaded. He has to go begging, cap in hand, to her mansion in the country and she makes him beg like a dog. Everyone knows this. He's a laughing stock. Go on, ask him, I dare you. Then fire his ass.'

Photographers were gathered on the other side of a chain-link fence, their flashes strobing as Diemond strode out to her waiting limo. Ricardo rushed ahead to open the door. Diemond slipped inside, and Jo found herself looking at a reflection of her younger self in the tinted glass. The window slid down, and Diemond peered at Jo over her sunglasses.

'Now run along little girl. Get back to your party.' Diemond grinned a 'gator smile. 'They'll need someone to clean up the mess.'

'Mess? What mess?' But the limo pulled away and as the photographers' clicking ceased, Jo felt something churning in her belly. She was nauseous, dizzy. Something wasn't right. She staggered back into the studio, its maze of corridors began to tilt and sway. Ahead of her, the mohicaned DJ burst through the green room doors, projectile vomit ejaculating from his mouth in a perfect arc, splashing on the wall. More followed him, clutching their bellies and shoving one another aside as they ran for the bathroom.

Jo fought her own belly as it began to spasm, but she knew it would be in vain. One way or another, something would be ejected from her very soon.

Rand staggered from the green room, falling to his knees in front of Jo, clutching his stomach. His once-tanned face was now the colour of a vanilla candle as Jo barfed all over him.

FINDING JOANNA

Federica fired up the most essential tool that every twenty-first century journalist and missing persons investigator used when looking for someone. 'I'll look her up on Facebook,' she said, tapping the screen of her phone.

'You'll do what now?' Yohanna asked, drifting to look over Federica's shoulder.

'We have this thing now called social media, where people spend most of their life posting silly things like funny videos of cats, music, film clips. But eventually it all descends into people sending pictures of their genitals and accusing each other of being worse than Hitler.'

'They do this for fun?' Yohanna looked puzzled.

Federica shrugged, 'I stopped using it myself a long time ago. Some of my grown up children would come looking for me, and many of them were lovely, but there were always a couple who... Well, let's say I have first-hand experience of the genital-Hitler thing.'

'A pox on them all.' Aaronovitch growled as he checked on his own laptop. 'I was guilty in their eyes long before I even went to trial. A gushing sewer of filth and depravity.'

'I'm guessing you're not on this social media thingy then?' Yohanna asked.

'One must keep with the times, of course,' he said. 'I have well-disguised voyeur accounts.'

'Okay, that sounds a little creepy,' Yohanna said.

'It's nothing sordid, thank you very much,' Aaronovitch sniffed. 'It's simply a necessary measure to keep the scavengers and opportunistic journalists at bay. If any of them got a whiff of where I was, they would descend upon me like a pack of wolves.'

'Or flies to dog mess,' Federica said.

'I will have you know, my good lady, that to a certain kind of journalist I am like Howard Hughes or the Yeti,' he said.

Federica bristled, 'I am not your good lady.'

'What did you do wrong?' Yohanna asked Ronnie.

'I promised people hope,' Aaronovitch said. 'I offered them solutions to their woes.'

'For a fee,' Federica said, not looking up from her phone.

'One must earn one's crust,' he said.

'These self-proclaimed gurus always promise the world,' Federica said. 'But all they ever give you is re-heated Ancient Greek Philosophy with new names they can trademark and sell. And when it doesn't work, they accuse you of not understanding and make you feel even more stupid and worthless than you were before. They put the blame squarely back on you, and still cash the cheque. Very clever.'

'I was funding my research into the very thing that will help this young woman return home.'

'By ripping off the gullible.'

'I will not take these insults from a reader of tea leaves.'

'That I may be, but no one's ever tried to sue me.'

'I paid my debt,' Aaronovitch began to rage, but his voice softened to a tremble. 'Lost my flat, the car, my books. I lost everything, but that will never be enough in their eyes.' Aaronovitch's face became puffy and red, but all the fight had gone from him. Resting his chin on a fist, he slouched on the deckchair and joined in the hunt on his laptop, his eyes glazing over.

'There are too many Joanna Adamses,' Federica said, scrolling through Facebook. 'And I don't recognise any of them. Yohanna?'

Yohanna scanned the profile pictures. None of them looked like the woman she'd met in her kitchen that fateful morning.

'Keep going,' Yohanna said. 'Did she ever write to you?'

'Christmas cards,' Federica nodded. 'For a few years, but they stopped coming. They always do.'

'That's so sad.'

'No, no, that's good. If my children go on to their own lives, with their own families, I've done my job.'

'Still, you'd think they might make an effort.'

'Do you write to your Federica?'

Yohanna was about to declare that sure she did, every year, but then she realised she couldn't remember the last time she'd written anything to anyone other than Lawrie. 'I've been busy,' she said.

'Exactly,' Federica said. 'And that's how it should be.'

'Good gracious,' Aaronovitch sputtered, turning his laptop round to face them. 'Is... is this her?'

The screen was filled with the hairy back of a man having sex with a bored-looking woman who was staring directly at the camera as if checking something online.

'*Oh, yeah,*' said the man in the video. '*I can feel it building. Are you close, too?*'

'*Almost,*' the woman replied.

'Oh my god, that's her.' Yohanna covered her mouth in shock. 'What's she doing? How did you find her?'

'Some of us simply have the investigative skills to... hey!'

Federica snatched the laptop from him. 'Or maybe you were attracted to the trending topic 'Bored Housewife Sex Video Goes Viral'?' She pursed her lips and narrowed her eyes. 'You dirty old man.' Federica hit pause and scrubbed along the video to find the best shot of Jo's face. 'That's her?'

'For sure.' Yohanna nodded, bemused.

Federica started tapping the laptop keys.

'What are you doing?'

'I want to see if I can find the account it originated from,' she said.

While Federica diligently worked, Yohanna drifted away to watch

Aaronovitch make some tea. 'I don't get thirsty anymore,' she said. 'Or hungry.'

Aaronovitch nodded sympathetically. 'You have no physical form to drive those urges.'

'I do,' she said. 'Someone else is using it.'

'I'm sure she's taking good care of it.'

'I still get scared,' Yohanna said. 'That's a good thing, right? Means I'm still me, not just some ghost.'

'I suppose.' Aaronovitch gave it some thought. 'It suggests there's some other part of us that does not inhabit the corporeal. A spirit, if you will.'

'But mine's fading.'

'Indeed,' Aaronovitch said. 'Which says to me that one needs the other to survive. You cannot remain as a ghost indefinitely, just as the older Joanna will not be able to survive parted from her body.'

'She seems to be doing just fine to me,' Yohanna said. 'I never had her pinned as a porn star.'

'Aha!' Federica turned the laptop to Yohanna. 'This her?'

It was a Facebook profile page with the face of the woman Yohanna met just the other day. 'Yes,' she said. 'That's her. Where is she?'

Federica turned the laptop back to inspect the screen. 'She's set privacy to full, but let's look at her friends.' She tapped the keys and stroked the mouse. 'Michela... who are you to her, hmm?' Federica scrolled through Michela's posts. 'Cat video, cat video, share if you hate cancer, Coldplay video, ugh, attention-baiting complaints about minor illnesses, more cat videos... Ah, yes. Oh no.'

'What?'

'Please pray for my good friend Joanna who has...' Federica faltered. 'Oh.'

'What?' Yohanna flew to Federica's side. She was joined by Aaronovitch who read aloud what they could not.

'Please pray for my friend Joanna who has been in a coma for two days. Doctors are completely baffled, but say that if there's no improvement in the next seventy-two hours she could be in a permanent vegetative state.'

'What the fuck?' Yohanna cried. 'What does that mean? What do we do?'

'When was that posted?' Aaronovitch asked.

'Two days ago,' Federica said. 'She's in Guy's Hospital in London.'

'What do we do? If she's not awake by the end of the solstice, what does that mean for me?' Yohanna paused. 'What if she dies? What do we do?' Yohanna's hands were in her hair, she floated in little panicked circles.

'What do we do?' Federica slapped the laptop shut. 'We find her and we save her.'

IS THIS THE REAL LIFE?

Mum?

Jo was in that beautiful womb-like refuge between sleep and waking.

The doctors say you can't hear me, Mum, but I'm going to talk anyway.

Jo was becoming increasingly aware of the world around her. The bed, the pillows, her breathing.

Dad and I love you. We wish... we just want a sign...

There was something else. Something important she needed to cling on to.

We just want you back.

Light was pressing on her eyes.

I miss you, Mum.

Light, and a pounding headache.

JO WANDERED her suite in the Beverly, pouring black coffee from a cafetière. She had no memory of actually waking up or ordering breakfast, only that she needed copious amounts of coffee to combat her hangover, a very plain breakfast of high-fibre cereal, and a vague recollection of a dream about Ellie.

'You're having a laugh?' Lawrie's voice drifted in from the suite lounge loud enough for any nearby audience to hear him. 'I ain't just got off the boat y'know, Keith. I want serious offers, not this Mickey Mouse bollocks.'

Nursing her coffee, Jo shuffled into the lounge and perched on a couch.

'Yeah, you do that, sunshine, you think about it. Think about it long and hard. In the meantime, I'll be looking at the other offers on the table, so don't dilly-dally, eh?' Lawrie gave her a wink as he spoke. 'Yeah, love to Suzy and the kids, yeah, bye.' He hung up. 'Ponce.'

'Morning,' Jo said, her voice a regretful death rattle.

'Closer to noon, actually.' Lawrie grinned, helping himself to a coffee. 'And how are we after last night's little adventure?'

'It wasn't me,' Jo said. 'I know it sounds pathetic, but it was Diemond. She spiked the drinks.'

'Colonic cleanse. She's done it before. Elton's not been the same since. Told you not to mess with her, didn't I?' Lawrie cackled. Was it Jo's imagination, or was Lawrie actually happy today? 'How was the rest of the evening? Make any contacts?'

Jo began to recall some of the detail from the party, but there were only fragments and they all ended with Jo covering Rand in his very own technicoloured dreamcoat. He had been very understanding, but she couldn't help feel that it might have put a crimp in their burgeoning relationship.

'Yeah, I met lots of people,' she told Lawrie. 'And they all said they loved me, and they all asked nice questions, and I loved it at the time, don't get me wrong... But I feel totally stupid, like I've fallen for some sort of con, y'know?'

'Well, it worked. We're getting offers, girl. You can have today off.' Lawrie dialled his phone, and adopted his bossy voice when he got an answer, 'Yeah, Lawrie Grant... Yeah, I'll hold.'

'That's nice,' Jo said. 'All it cost me was my credibility, self-esteem and the biggest dry-cleaning bill in history.'

'Don't worry about that. The studio are blaming the caterers.'

'That's not fair. It was that cow, Diemond. She should pay for it.'

'You can prove that, can you?'

'I have a mortal enemy, Lawrie. I've never had one of those before. The worst I've ever had is that miserable old moo on the fish counter at the supermarket who keeps giving me the dodgy cod that isn't really cod.'

Jo sipped her coffee, and noticed Lawrie looking at her in a peculiar way, then realised that international music megastars probably didn't buy cheap cod from the supermarket. 'Diemond is an evil genius,' she said, getting back on track. 'No other word for it. They should put her in a Bond movie.'

'You're not alone, if that's any consolation. You won't find many people in this town who haven't been screwed over by her at least once.'

'She said you nearly ruined her career.'

Lawrie's default grouchiness returned in an instant. 'I paid for her studio time, her demo, costumes, session players, everything, and how did she reward me? Buggered off at the first sign of a deal, and left me holding the baby.'

'She had a baby?' Jo's brain still hadn't fully rebooted.

'The bill. None of that came for free, y'know. She owes me big time.' He raised a silencing finger as his caller replied. 'Pauly. So, you gonna shit or get off the pot? ... No, that sounds like the pot to me ... Why don't you think long and hard about how you're wasting my time, and then come back with a grown up offer? Good lad.' He hung up. 'Twat.'

Jo watched as he dialled another number, 'Lawrie, can I ask a personal question?'

'No.'

'Oh.' Jo took another sip of coffee and her brain began to return to some of its former sharpness. 'Can I ask you a business question?'

'Depends.'

'Who's paying for all this?' Jo gestured at the luxurious suite around her. 'None of this is cheap and we don't have a record deal. Are you paying for this out of your own pocket?'

'That sounds suspiciously like a personal question.' He scowled at his phone, 'Engaged,' and started dialling another number.

'I don't want you losing the family jewels because of me, Lawrie. We can stay in a motel or something.'

'A motel?' For a moment Lawrie looked like Nick when Jo had suggested switching to supermarket-brand toilet paper to save money. 'You met our Yankee friends last night, right?'

'Yes.'

'And what do you think impresses them most?'

'My English accent?'

'No.'

'My effortless charm?'

'No.'

'My ability to apologise profusely while simultaneously projectile vomiting over them?'

'I bloody wish. No, and it ain't talent. Throw a stick out that window and you'll hit a dozen Rand McManuses who can act and two dozen Yohannas who can sing. Yanks love nothing more than money, girl. They worship it. If you come to this town like a fucking panhandler they'll treat you like a leper. You come to town and shack up in the Beverly Wilshire and they sit up and pay attention.'

'And is that working?' Jo asked, her eyes turning to the phone in Lawrie's hand. 'You said we're getting offers. Are they good ones?'

'You leave the business side of things to me.' He grimaced again with the phone at his ear. Another engaged tone.

'What are they saying?'

'What do you mean?'

'Do they like me? Do they like the song?'

'They love you. Don't worry about it.'

'Don't worry about what?' Jo could see a wrinkle of doubt in Lawrie's facade. 'You can tell me. I'm a big girl.'

'They love your voice.'

'Good.'

'They love your song. Especially that new one last night.'

Jo winced and wondered how she should credit the young Adele,

'Oh-kay. What else? There's definitely something else. I can tell when you're agitated, Lawrie. The capillaries on your nose go red.'

'They think you're strange.'

'Is that all?'

'America doesn't do strange,' Lawrie said. 'Stevie Nicks only gets away with it because she's in Fleetwood Mac. Kate Bush is a cult over here, I need you to be more than that. They used the word *kooky*. I can sell kooky to college students, I can't sell kooky to the masses. I need more cutey and less kooky.'

'You're asking me to... not be me?'

'No, no, just dial down the weird time travel crap you were waffling on about last night, that's all.'

'But it's true.'

'I don't give a fuck,' Lawrie barked. 'Think of how close we are. How far you've come from that crappy little wedding band.'

'Hey, we were good.'

'*You* were good,' he said. 'The rest of them were a bunch of real ale drinking Fairport Convention wannabes. And you'd still be playing school fairs and open mic nights if it wasn't for me.'

'You said I'd be a megastar,' Jo muttered to herself, half-remembering.

'And you still can be,' Lawrie said. 'I just need you to be less of a weirdo for the men with the money. Can you do that?'

Jo saw the desperation in Lawrie's eyes. Whatever was motivating him - a debt to his mother, his giant ego, a genuine belief in her talents - he really needed this. And she couldn't tell him what she was really feeling. How the events of last night had only confirmed that she didn't belong here, that she missed Ellie more than ever. Jo had tasted fame and it made her sick. Literally. There was one woman right for the job and her name was Yohanna. Jo had to go home.

'Yes, Lawrie, I can do that,' Jo told him, and his chipper self returned.

His phone rang and he answered. 'Keith, speak to me, mate. What's the news? ... No, no, no. Not good enough.'

'I'm gonna have a shower,' Jo announced to no one.

'Dickhead.'

TEN MINUTES under a shower powerful enough to quell a city riot helped Jo begin to feel vaguely human again. Whatever emetic Diemond had put in the drinks, it didn't seem to leave any lasting after-effects, other than a nervousness on Jo's part whenever she thought about food. As she towelled her hair, she could hear the tinkle of her Nokia. It was still lacking a battery and plugged into the wall by the bed. If she understood the display, it looked like she had voice messages. Maybe a dozen of them. It took her a few minutes to negotiate the menus, but she soon began to hear voices over the phone's tinny little speaker.

Voices she hadn't heard in years - girls she knew from school, some of her old Mother Folker band mates, other foster kids, and a few men she didn't recognise at all, but were *very* familiar with her. They were all congratulating her on last night's appearance. How the hell had they got her number?

'Well, bah-luddy hell,' said a very familiar voice. 'Hello darling, it's Aunty Federica. I got the number from a nice lady at your management company. She said I wasn't to give it to anybody else, but I thought to hell with that and I sent it to everyone I know who knows you. I hope you don't mind, but I am so proud, darling. You've been on the *Big Breakfast*, in the papers, everybody here thinks you're amazing, which I've known for years, but now the world gets to know, too. Don't call me back. I know you're busy, but know that I love you, I'm proud and you're amazing. Love you, darling. Bye.'

Jo found herself wiping tears from her cheeks. Jo called her back, but there was no answer. It was the evening in the UK, so Federica should have been able to answer, but it just rang and rang.

There was one more message, and Jo eagerly cued it up, hoping it was Federica.

'Hello my dear, what a wonderful performance last night.' It was a man. English, well-educated. And not someone that Jo recognised. 'I was most impressed, I have to say. Though, there were several turns of phrase that surprised me. They showed an apparent maturity that I've not seen in you before. I know we've had our differences in the recent past, but there's something I have to ask you and I really need to do it in person.

'If you're free, come and meet me at the Griffith Observatory tomorrow at noon and we'll discuss it further. Good to speak to you again, Yohanna, if indeed that is really you. It's Aaronovitch, if you're wondering. Though you might only know me as Ronnie.'

GIRLFRIEND IN A COMA

'A re you family?' The receptionist at Guy's Hospital intensive care unit looked at the man and woman standing before her. The woman was short and Italian with an impressive schnozz and reminded the receptionist of a fortune teller she'd visited as a young woman. He was as bald as a cue ball and wore the faded, shabby corduroy ensemble of a geography lecturer.

'Yes,' the short woman said.

'Not exactly,' the man's words overlapped with the woman's and she shot him a spiteful glare.

'I am. He isn't,' the short woman said. 'It's complicated. Forgive us. We've been driving all night.'

The receptionist didn't doubt it. Guy's Hospital was one of the busiest hospitals in the centre of London and attracted all sorts. The people who came to visit this particular ward of the hospital were often distraught. The patients brought here were near death's door, and their families would express their despair in peculiar ways. Some would try and be jolly, but they would always leave in tears, others were angry or sad. Many were quietly baffled. Unable to process what was happening. This pair were fairly par for the course.

'I was her foster mother,' the woman said. 'Can I see her? Please?'

. . .

FUCK YOU.

Even in the dwindling twilight of her teenage years, Ellie still gave death a considerable amount of thought. Few of her friends were religious, but even fewer were out-and-out atheists. Most were like Lizzie and described themselves as spiritual. Mostly this meant they liked to smoke weed and try and make sense of the world with theories about souls and the afterlife that Ellie recognised as half-baked borrowings from flaky blogs, self-help books from the Mind, Body and Spirit section, and YA novels about angels.

Fuck you.

Ellie was certain of only one thing. She knew nothing.

A few years ago Ellie had decided that death was it. The end. The big off switch. But now, sat beside a hospital bed where her mother was being kept alive by machines and tubes, the idea of an afterlife felt warm and fuzzy in a way that Ellie hated. God and Heaven was too easy. A comfort blanket for those who couldn't face the fact that we were all here for a brief flash of pain and pleasure before disappearing into oblivion. But it was a comfort blanket she now really wanted to snuggle in, and never come out.

Ellie glanced to the bedside cabinet where she'd placed the photo of her and Mum at Climping Beach, the frame's cracked glass separating them both. She'd found it on her bedroom floor after the ambulance had left. Ellie had come home after arguing with Lizzie about their plans to tour the Ukraine and conquer the world. Much to Ellie's annoyance it was clear that Lizzie didn't have the first clue what she was doing. Then Mum had called. Ellie didn't want to talk to her, didn't want to admit that Mum had been right - but she knew she'd been forgiven and could come home.

That's when she'd found Mum. Lying on the kitchen floor. Silent. Barely breathing. The world unravelled that day.

Ellie had called an ambulance straight away. Immediately after, she phoned Dad who was angry and defensive when he met her at the local accident and emergency. For some reason he had brought his friend Andy with him. That's when he took a deep breath and tearfully confessed his affair with Andy to her. It was all too weird for one day. Ellie confessed back that she'd known something was wrong when she found a couple of naked photos of Andy on the family's iCloud library that had automatically uploaded from Dad's iPhone. Dad broke down at that point and begged forgiveness, but Ellie just held him tight. She couldn't bring herself to hate him because she'd done something much worse.

FUCK YOU.
> *Ellie's last words to her mother.*
> *No, not her last words. They couldn't be. She wouldn't let them be.*

IT WAS while they were transferring Mum to Guy's that Lizzie messaged Ellie about the sex video. Mum was a meme. A joke on everyone's Snapchat. Ellie thought that was the low point, where she'd actually looked skyward and cried, 'Anything else?' at whatever gods might be listening. Worse was to come. As she watched the hospital staff insert tubes into her mother, Ellie felt all the purpose drain from her. All her energy was gone, and she was utterly helpless.

That was the worst bit. Sitting and watching and waiting in the corner of a sterile hospital ward. They gave her Mum a quiet room away from the main ward, they experimented with changing the lighting levels, they played music she loved, they constantly prodded and poked her for any sign of a response, but there was none.

Ellie was not a sitter, a watcher, nor a waiter.

She told Dad she would be back soon, walked out of the intensive care unit, and jumped on a bus home. She returned a couple of hours later with her laptop and a broadband dongle, and began the process of removing the video from the internet.

Youtube, Facebook, Twitter and Vimeo all had ways of requesting takedowns and Ellie was relentless. One by one they were gone. She called Michela who put her through to Mum's boss Nigel, who stuttered as he tried to explain the marketing benefits of the video.

'Nigel, did you know my Mum is in a coma because of this?'

'Well, now, let's not get excited. I know you're upset. There's nothing to prove a link between—'

'That's how I'll explain it to the *Daily Mail*,' she said. 'The *Daily fucking Mail*. That's how desperate I am. I will pose for the photo of me and Dad looking sad by her bed for that hateful shit rag, and I will name you, Nigel Mayer, as the cause of her coma, and your company will be ruined. You'll lose your house, your wife, your car, and end up sleeping under a bridge somewhere - I will find you, and point at you, and laugh, and post a video on YouTube, and then *you* will be the fucking laughing stock of the internet.'

The video was gone from the company's website and YouTube page in minutes, cutting off hundreds of thousands of shares across social media. Ellie knew the job was far from done, and continued to search deep on Google. All she wanted was for her mother to wake up in a world where that bloody video was gone, or at least die in peace knowing the story had been put to rest.

All she wanted was for her mother to wake up.

'You wait here,' a voice snapped from outside the room.

'My good woman, I was not dragged halfway across the country to wait in a hospital corridor like a vagrant awaiting a tetanus jab.'

'You'll sit in the bah-luddy car park if you don't behave.'

Ellie stood a little too quickly, the blood rushing to her head after a whole morning slumped in an uncomfortable plastic bucket chair. She wavered to the door and opened it to find a short woman with a spectacular nose berating a bald man from a pensioners' corduroy fashion catalogue. The little woman saw Ellie and her angry expression was instantly replaced with one of sympathy.

'Oh my god, you must be Ellie.' Federica went to hug her but Ellie backed away. 'You look so much like your mother.'

'You... you know my Mum?' Ellie had never seen this pair before and tried to imagine a single thing that they had in common with her Mum that might possibly link them all.

'I'm Federica,' the woman said, taking Ellie's hand. 'I was her foster mother.'

'Oh, yeah, yeah,' Ellie said, enjoying the feel of Federica's hand in hers. 'Mum talked about you. She really liked you.'

'May I come in?'

'Erm, sure, it's nice to have some company,' Ellie said, and joked, 'Mum doesn't talk much.'

Federica turned to the man and pointed at a chair in the ward by a table of well-thumbed magazines.

'You. Sit.'

He sneered, panted like a dog, and did as he was told.

'How is she?' Federica asked in a hushed tone as she stepped inside the room, greeted by the gentle rhythmic beeping of the heart monitor. She held back a gasp as she looked down at the ageing corpse-like form of Jo. Her face was a deathly white. This wasn't the youthful Jo she remembered. Tears welled in her eyes and her hand covered her mouth.

'I'm sorry. She was one of my favourites. I know I shouldn't have favourites, but she was such a lovely girl. She'd every reason to be angry, but she always found a way to joke, y'know?'

'Yeah, that's Mum,' Ellie said, finding a smile coming to her lips for the first time in a long time.

'What do the doctors say?'

'They haven't got a clue.' Ellie sat back in one of the uncomfortable plastic bucket seats. 'There's no clot on the brain, no trauma, no damage, no possible reason for her to just shut down like this. But they say...' Ellie's voice trembled and she began to breathe erratically. 'Sorry.'

'No, it's okay.' Federica sat down beside her and took her hand.

'They say she's fading. That she's going to die.' Ellie wept. 'It doesn't make any sense. Why should she die? It's not fair.'

'Hey, hey, she's not going to die.' Federica brushed the tears from Ellie's cheeks. 'Listen to me, she's going to be okay.'

'How can you say that? How can you know? They say there's

hardly any brain activity. That machine is the only thing keeping her breathing.'

'What if...?' Federica hesitated. 'What if there was a place that we could take her? A place where she could be cured?'

Ellie's brow wrinkled at the word, 'Cured?'

'Okay, this is going to sound strange, but hear me out.' Federica squeezed Ellie's hand. 'We—'

'Sorry to interrupt, but...' the old man peeped his head around the door.

'What the bah-luddy hell?' Federica pivoted to scowl at the man.

'It's just our somewhat ethereal friend is—'

'I don't care. You sort her out. I'm in the middle of something.'

'But—'

'Aaronovitch, I swear I will take one of these tubes and shove it where the sun doesn't shine. Now, go away.'

'Right, well, don't say you weren't warned,' he muttered, backing out of the room.

'Who's he again?'

Federica dismissed the man with a wave. 'We'll get to him in a minute.'

'Where do you want to take my Mum?'

Federica bit her lip. 'Glastonbury.'

'Glastonbury?' Ellie's nose crinkled. 'To the festival? It's not on this year, is it?'

'No, to the town.'

Ellie was still confused. 'To what? Another hospital? A clinic? I don't understand.'

'No. Specifically - and I want you to keep an open mind about this - to the Tor.' Federica took a breath. 'Where there's a ley line.'

'Oh, Jesus.' Ellie shook her hand free of Federica's. 'For a second there I trusted you. I actually trusted you. How could I be so stupid?'

'Shh. Please, Ellie, listen.' Federica looked around hoping Ellie's raised voice wasn't going to bring a nurse running.

'Mum doesn't believe in any of that wishy-washy bullshit, okay?

And neither do I, so please... I know you mean well, but I don't need this right now.'

'If we do nothing.' Federica fixed her gaze on Ellie. 'She will die on the last light of the solstice. That's tonight.'

'The doctors will think of something. They'll find out what it is and they will help her.'

'Ellie, they're doing everything they can and she's still dying. Don't you want to take a chance?'

'A chance? Drive her all the way across the country to bloody Glastonbury? Look at her charts. She's breathing through a bloody tube from a ventilator. She can't be moved. They told me.'

'Ellie...'

'No, please leave.' Ellie raised her voice. She stood up, scraping the chair on the floor, and opened the door. 'Now. Or I call the nurse who will call the police.'

Federica grabbed Ellie's shoulders firmly.

'Listen to me carefully. You have to let me—'

'And it's all my fault.' In a crying rage, Ellie shoved Federica and ran out of the hospital room.

'Er... how did it go?' Aaronovitch joined Federica by Jo's bedside having watched Ellie run down the long corridor and into the toilets.

'I swear to God, Aaronovitch, I will—'

That was the moment that Joanna's body sat bolt upright in her bed with a choking gasp of air, her eyes wide open, fingers flexing, feet kicking. She pulled the ventilator tube from her mouth, retched, and cried, 'Holy shit, I'm in.'

She flung the sheets aside, hopped off the bed, and fell in a heap as her legs gave way like jelly.

'It worked,' she rasped, looking up from the floor, directly at Federica and Aaronovitch.

'We gotta get to Glastonbury. Right now.'

GRIFFITH OBSERVATORY

J o hung up on Aaronovitch and checked her watch. It was noon. She wriggled into jeans and a T-shirt and scooped up a handful of per-diem dollar bills on the bedside table, and paused at the bedroom door. Lawrie was still on the phone.

'How about a third,' he said, and Jo wondered if he had finally got a deal that he liked. 'Everyone remortgages their house in this business, Freddie... Yes, three times... You're my accountant, you work it out.... Yes, it's worth it. I'm on the verge of something really big here, mate.'

Jo felt a pang of guilt. He was remortgaging his house? For a third time? For her?

Jo took a breath and strode through the lounge towards the door.

Lawrie's hand covered the phone's mouthpiece. 'Where you off to?'

'You said I had the day off.'

'You're not gonna go running off in any buses, right?'

'No, no, I fancy a bit of sightseeing.' She shrugged as nonchalantly as possible. 'Thought I might pop up to the Griffith Observatory, see the Hollywood sign.'

'Be back by six. I reckon I'll have a deal for you then.'

'Nice. Thanks Lawrie, uhm...'

'What?'

'Are you remortgaging your house? For me?'

'Listen, you do what you have to do,' he said. 'And I'll do what I have to do, oh, and one more thing.'

'Yeah?'

'If you get mobbed by adoring fans, try and do it when there's a photographer around. Waste of time otherwise.'

'Oh, don't be ridiculous. Who would want to mob me?'

'CHEESE AND CRACKERS! THERE SHE IS!' a woman in a pink Minnie Mouse T-shirt, shorts and baseball cap ensemble was the first to spot Jo as she stepped out of the hotel into the sunshine. The woman had been lying in wait and charged at Jo with all the vigour of a rugby full-back, brandishing a pen and a copy of this week's *TV Guide*, which she asked Jo to sign.

'You have the voice of an angel,' the woman said. 'You touched me.'

'You can't prove anything,' Jo laughed nervously as she started to write a large J and awkwardly turned it into a Y.

'Huh?'

'Nothing, thanks for being lovely. Were you waiting long?'

'Since breakfast.'

'You've been here all morning?'

The woman rested a hand over her heart. 'You touched me,' she repeated.

'Oh-kay, we're back to that again.' Jo handed back the signed *TV Guide*. 'Have a nice day,' she added, feeling very American all of a sudden.

'I'll pray for you,' the Minnie Mouse enthusiast said as she backed into the crowd that had gathered around them. Jo was surrounded by a dozen people all demanding that Jo sign scraps of paper and body parts. Jo couldn't bring herself to think of them as fans based on a single performance of a song that wasn't even hers, but they had a fanatical energy to them. One man, sporting a scraggly ginger beard, Stonehenge teeth, and a tattered L.A. Olympics T-shirt leaned-in close. 'I'm a time traveller, too,' he told Jo.

'Oh, really?' Jo said as kindly as possible as she signed a teenage girl's bus ticket. 'That's nice.'

'You want I should kill Donald Trump?' He grinned with a little too much enthusiasm.

'No,' Jo yelped. 'Don't kill him. Well... maybe break his legs?'

The man's eyes darted as he considered this, 'Cool,' he declared and ran off.

'I was joking!' Jo called after him. 'It's called irony. Please don't hurt anyone.' But the would-be assassin was already gone.

More people thrust things at Jo to sign, newspapers, magazines - and they began to speak about her as if they were watching her on TV.

'I thought she'd be taller,' one woman said.

'Is that her real hair?' another asked. 'So frizzy.'

'I'm pretty sure she was miming,' one dude announced. 'That whole thing was a set-up from the start. Friend of mine works on the show told me.'

'I'm right here, y'know,' Jo said, seeing more passersby noticing the crowd and wanting to join in. If she didn't make a move now, she was going to be stuck here all day. But the truth was this was exhilarating, and a part of her didn't want it to stop.

'Okay, that's enough folks. I'm late already. *Taxi!*'

Jo broke through the crowd and waved down a cab. There was a chorus of *awws* from the huddle, though as Jo ducked into the taxi, she heard one voice, possibly the dude's, utter the word 'Bitch.' Jo felt the cold chill of fame's dark side flush through her.

THE CAB CLIMBED WINDING roads up Mount Hollywood, delivering Jo to the beautiful art deco observatory that stood sentinel over Los Angeles. Tourists milled around outside, posing for photos of the Hollywood sign on Mount Lee behind them. Jo looked around for someone who fit the bill of a guru and, not for the first time since arriving here, really missed her iPhone and the power of a quick Google search.

There were tourists aplenty, but no gurus. What did a guru even look like? Should she expect someone in robes, with an entourage of acolytes scattering rose petals wherever he walked? That's even if he was still here. Jo was forty-five minutes late.

Jo moved fast under the arches around the observatory's exterior, where tourists could take in the sprawl of Los Angeles. She took the winding steps up to the domes, but he wasn't there. She stepped inside, ignoring the Foucault pendulum that dominated the entrance hall, past the crackling Tesla coil and through to the gift shop, where she was recognised again by a woman who also claimed to be moved by her music, but was less manic than Minnie Mouse woman. Nevertheless, Jo invested in a baseball cap and a cheap pair of sunglasses from the gift shop as a quick disguise.

Failing to find anyone remotely guru-like, Jo returned to the pendulum, where school children gathered around it as a teacher explained how its motion demonstrated the movement of the Earth and its relation to the coming summer solstice. Just then the entrance hall was flooded with people leaving the latest show in the planetarium.

'Yohanna, my dear,' an English accent cut through the bustle to Jo. 'You missed the show.'

Jo turned to find a man in his early fifties with a trim beard and bushy head of brown curly ringlets fighting a losing battle against male pattern balding. He was dressed in a corduroy jacket in the L.A. heat. No robes or acolytes.

'Aaronovitch?' Jo asked, kicking herself. She should have said his name with more certainty.

'Indeed,' he grinned, enjoying her vagueness. 'You're alone as I requested?'

Jo felt a flicker of panic, but took some reassurance from the presence of the crowd around them. 'That's the sort of question a serial killer asks right before he bundles you into his van, but yes.'

Aaronovitch smiled, 'My apologies for the cloak and dagger nature of our meeting, but I assume you're still under the management of the malodorous Lawrie Grant? He and I haven't quite seen eye to eye since our first meeting.'

'He has that effect on people.'

'And what other effect might he have had on you?'

'What does that mean?'

'I must say I really did enjoy your little show last night, Yohanna.' He angled his head as if inspecting a specimen in a museum. 'But all that talk of time travel had me intrigued, and then you capped it all by declaring that you were in fact a forty-two-year-old mother, somehow transported through time and space from an alternate timeline where Harrison Ford, of all people, is a huge star.'

'It's true.' Jo lowered her voice, not wanting to attract any more unwanted attention. 'I'm not her, I'm not Yohanna, I need to get home now and she told me that you were the only person who could do it.'

'I just sat through a spectacular show that made it very clear that, while the universe is a wondrous place, time travel is an impossibility. What makes you think I can defy the law of physics as defined by a genius like Einstein?'

'Don't,' Jo warned him. 'Do not piss me about. I am not in the mood to play games or solve riddles. You brought me here. Just tell me how to get home.'

'*I* brought you here?'

'That's what she told me.'

'What who told you?'

'Yohanna.'

'But I see Yohanna before me.' Aaronovitch gestured at her. 'You look like her, you sound like her. If it looks like a duck, and quacks like a duck—'

'You have to believe me.'

'Yohanna, you're the one playing games.' Aaronovitch's tone changed now, like a teacher scolding a first year student. 'In the short time I've known you, you've demonstrated an incredible ability to tap into the bardo state, and yet you've failed to take my theories seriously or listen to my advice. How am I to believe this nonsense without thinking it to be another childish prank?' Tired of the conversation, he began to step away, but Jo gripped his arm.

'I saw the universe,' she told him. 'It was moving around me. For a moment I could see everything, then nothing, and then I saw her, the other me, flying by on a beam of rainbow light. Now why would I make up something as bloody stupid as that?'

Something changed in Aaronovitch, a flicker of recognition. Something she'd said intrigued him. He scratched at his beard, and asked in a trembling voice, 'R-rainbow light?'

KEEP VENICE FREAKY

Aronovitch's small apartment overlooked Venice Beach.
'It belongs to a client,' he told Jo as they weaved through the daily carnival of buskers, iron pumpers, skateboarders, basketball twirlers, breakdancers and crazies with signs declaring the end of the world. 'He's letting me have it rent-free for the summer, which is jolly nice of him.'

Jo couldn't help but wonder what kind of scam Aaronovitch was pulling with that particular client, then reminded herself to be charitable. When she told him that she saw her other self, flying by on a beam of rainbow light, his cool exterior dropped and he was clapping his hands like a child about to open his Christmas presents. He had hurried her to his car and jumped two red lights to get here in record time.

He'd bustled Jo around the back of a gift shop, squeezed past a man shrouded in a sweet fug of weed propped up by a 'Keep Venice Freaky!' placard, through a gate and up into his ramshackle apartment. This may once have been a smart place, but now there were musty-smelling books in teetering piles everywhere, and the bright Pacific sunlight was rationed into pale slices by dusty venetian blinds.

There was a yawn from another room and a young woman

dressed in a oversized Guns N' Roses T-shirt and a yellow bikini bottom shuffled into the kitchen area and started making coffee. 'Hey, Ronnie,' she said, her voice early-morning croaky.

'Good grief, Sarah, did you just get up?' Aaronovitch became flustered in the young woman's presence. Jo could see that he wanted to be sterner with her, but like most older men with a pretty girlfriend he didn't want to jeopardise a good thing. 'How's the meditation going?'

'Huh?'

'Sarah is a... a...' Aaronovitch struggled for the right word. 'A colleague of mine. She's researching the bardo state, too. It's exhausting work.'

'I bet,' Jo smiled at Sarah, who squinted at her.

'Hey, I know you from the TV,' Sarah smiled. '*Tonight Show*, right? Man, that was awesome. You can really sing. We were watching in bed last night, weren't we, Ronnie?'

Aaronovitch began to stutter, 'I-I-I-I, yes.' He directed Jo towards another room. 'This way, please.'

'Lovely to meet you,' Jo said, enjoying Aaronovitch's awkwardness.

'Oh, you're so sweet.' Sarah scrunched her nose. 'I love your accent. I have a thing for English accents.'

Jo glanced at Aaronovitch who was blushing like a beet. 'Tell me more,' she said.

'No time,' Aaronovitch blurted, shepherding Jo into his office.

'Make yourself at home,' he said, as he began to rummage through the books sprawled across his desk. There were more books and boxes in here, and no windows at all.

'I'd love to Ronnie, but I'm struggling to find a chair that isn't acting as a bookshelf.'

'Oh.' Aaronovitch swiped a pile of books from a stool, sending them tumbling to the ground and kicking up a cloud of dust. 'There you go.'

'Right.' Jo clapped her hands. 'Before we start, I want to establish one thing. You and Sarah have a thing, that's fine. All power to you. You and me... we never...?'

'Oh, good gracious no,' Aaronovitch said, and Jo flushed with relief. 'In fact, we had a very similar conversation to this one where she made it very clear that if my intentions were dishonourable she would kick my arse from here to Mexico.'

'Atta girl,' Jo smiled. 'Please continue.'

Aaronovitch pulled down a screen, unleashing a cloud of dust motes. On the screen was a map of California, covered in criss-crossed lengths of red string tacked to the map with pins.

'So, you're either a serial killer, or you're hunting a serial killer,' Jo half-joked as she examined the map.

'Hmm?' Aaronovitch followed her gaze to the map. 'Ah, no, yes, very funny.'

'So what it is?'

'You don't know?' For a moment, Aaronovitch was genuinely puzzled before slapping his forehead with the palm of his hand. 'Of course, you don't. You're not my Yohanna. She picked all this up very quickly, y'know. Quite the natural. One of my best students. What do you know about ley lines?'

Jo thought back to repeats of TV shows like *Arthur C. Clarke's Mysterious World* when she was a child. 'Oh, are they the invisible lines that run through places like Stonehenge? Druids and David Icke get very worked up about them.'

'Excellent, yes, ancient lines of energy, invisible to the naked eye, but very powerful. So much so, that our ancestors - who were far more attuned to these things than we are - built sacred sites on these lines. In particular, there are convergences where the lines cross, which is where their power is strongest.

'And there's one right here on Venice Beach. One line cuts through Santa Monica Boulevard, the Museum of Art and the Griffith Observatory, and the other line heads north to San Francisco. I worked with you, uhm, *Yohanna*, on channeling that energy to help with her stage fright.'

'And that's how she got into this bardo state thing?'

'Yes.' Aaronovitch pointed toward the beach outside. 'She stood directly on the point where the ley lines converge in a vriksasana yoga pose - standing on one leg like a tree - and I watched her stay in that position for at least thirty minutes. *Half an hour.* She didn't move. I became concerned and I approached her. She awoke as if from a dream. She told me that only a moment had passed for her. She described her experience as if stepping into a blinding beam of energy and crossing the universe...' Aaronovitch's eyes bulged as he paused. 'On a beam of rainbow light.'

'Oh.'

'Oh, indeed. Now you see why I was so excited. She'd somehow slipped into the bardo state and was on the threshold of something incredible,' Aaronovitch said with a delighted grin. 'And it somehow brought her to you, another version of her. Something very specific connects you, I think.'

'A song,' Jo said. 'We both wrote the same song. She says she heard me humming it and it drew her to me. There was this rainbow light splurging from my belly, and she showed up in my kitchen looking like a radioactive Teletubby. It snaked out of our bellies and wrapped around us.'

'Fascinating.' Aaronovitch's eyes lit up. 'Pairs. It's all about pairs of people. Your spectrum signatures must have resonated and they began to conjoin.'

'How does this get me home?'

'We exist in an infinite number of parallel universes, each of them slightly different to the next one. Some so similar as to be hardly any different. Maybe this morning I had a bagel instead of croissant? And so that choice creates a new universe. Every decision we make spins off into a new reality. And some are so far apart, like yourself and Yohanna, that you might not even recognise yourself. But you all share a resonance that connects you across every universe, and the ancient monks experimented with crossing from one reality to another using the concentrated energy at ley line convergences.'

'And these can get me back like a ley line superhighway?'

'I've long believed that the energy from the lines can be harnessed to travel between parallel universes, yes - but never been able to prove it. Then I meet you, *her*, a young lady whose experience in the bardo state bolsters my theories and everything began to fall into place. And now she's claiming to be a forty-two-year-old time traveller.'

'Okay, so do you need, like, a large Hadron Collider or something? Or a DeLorean at the very least?'

'No, that's the wonderful thing,' Aaronovitch said. 'All you need to do is master the bardo state to channel your energy and harness the ley line's power.'

'Cool, let's do it. Show me how.'

'Yes, there's just one problem,' Aaronovitch said. 'It can take years to master, and you don't have much time at all, I'm afraid.'

'Why not?'

'In two days it will be the summer solstice. After that the Earth will be in such a position in its relation to the sun that it will be impossible to get you home.'

'What? You might have fucking mentioned that before. What are we waiting for? Let's go!'

THE BODY SNATCHERS

Yohanna was still getting used to her new forty-two-year-old body.

Her eyesight wasn't as good as it used to be, there was a faint ring of tinnitus in her ears, and she now had a belly. Not a huge one, but big enough to make her wonder if she could ever touch her toes again, let alone do any serious yoga. Her whole centre of gravity had shifted from her sternum to her bum. Also, post-coma, she had all the floppy grace of a drunk scarecrow.

Yohanna had warned Aaronovitch that she was going to try and enter Jo's body, and he advised her to wait, but she knew her time was running out. There was no ley line here, no mysterious energy to tap into. But when she closed her eyes she could sense Jo's presence in the ward. The pale life light that they both shared. Yohanna found herself floating in a space above Jo, looking directly down at her body while Federica and Ellie argued. Yohanna thought back to school swimming lessons and diving off the top board at the pool. That fearful moment of anticipation before the dive, and the exhilarating thrill after jumping off, knowing that there was nothing you could do to stop yourself hitting the water. Ellie left and Yohanna took a similar dive from her ethereal plane into Jo's body. There was a flash of light, a cacophony of noise as the drum of a heartbeat pounded in her ears, a tingling sensation as billions of nerve endings sent signals of alarm to her host's brain, and the electric jolt of life colliding with her consciousness.

Yohanna found herself in Jo's body.

And it hurt like hell.

The intubation breathing tube had been stuck in her mouth, keeping her airwaves open. It left her with a sore throat. She pulled out the food tube that was stuck up her nose and fed down to her stomach.

'Close the door,' Yohanna said to Federica and Aaronovitch as they hauled her up from the floor. She had the voice of an old crone.

'Yohanna?' Federica said, still trying to make sense of what just happened.

'Clothes.' She gestured at the little cabinet by the bed.

'These are all I could find,' Aaronovitch said as he awkwardly held up a pair of training shoes and a large pair of beige Marks and Spencer's knickers.

'What the thunderfuck are they?' Yohanna asked in wide-eyed astonishment.

'There are no other clothes. Get them on.' Federica was nervously looking over her shoulder expecting Ellie to burst in any second.

Yohanna unceremoniously attempted to stand upright whilst she slipped on the knickers causing Aaronovitch to avert his eyes. Her knees were like jelly and her feet felt tied down as if laden with dead weights.

'I'm fading, Federica,' Yohanna said, wriggling a foot into a sneaker. 'We need to go, now.'

Federica turned and muttered to Aaronovitch. 'Get the car, bring it round the front and keep the engine running.'

'We need a plan first,' Aaronovitch said, 'We can't just stroll out with her in a hospital gown.'

'Just get the car.' Federica opened the door, peered out, and booted Aaronovitch to get him moving.

'No time. I'm outta here, bitches!' Yohanna cried, launching herself from the bed on legs of jelly, stumbling through the open door like a toddler, and careening out into the ward.

'Yohanna!' Federica cried, chasing after her.

Yohanna collapsed two strides into the corridor. Federica heaved Yohanna into a wheelchair that sat vacant outside the room.

'You okay?'

'Just...so...tired.' Yohanna's head was lolling. 'We have to go, please, Aunty Fede, we have to go now.'

'Sure, sure. Try to keep your head up and smile at anyone we pass, okay? Federica said, fumbling in her handbag. 'Here, hold these,' she said, passing Yohanna a packet of her cigarettes.

'We're going to get you some fresh air. Hold the doors,' she shouted to the porter who stood in the lift across the hallway, but the lift promptly shut. Federica hammered the button, cursing her luck as she watched the numbers sink three floors. Yohanna's head was now fully drooping and her body slumped forward in the chair. Federica ran around the front of the wheelchair and pushed Yohanna's shoulders back, trying to keep her upright.

'*Merda.*' Federica looked back down the corridor to see Ellie walking out of the washroom and heading toward the room.

Federica bashed the lift button again, her heart beating rapidly. She heard Ellie's scream reverberating out of Joanna's room and down the corridor.

'Mum!'

Federica wheeled Yohanna away as fast as possible, finding another lift. She jabbed this one's button and it came after the longest five seconds of the foster mother's life.

'There. Stop! They're taking my Mum, stop them.' Ellie rounded the corner. Federica hammered the ground floor button rapidly as if it would close the doors quicker. They shut just as Ellie slid to the lift. Federica's belly tightened with guilt as she heard the poor girl pounding desperately on the door. Ellie's screams faded as they descended to the ground.

The lift opened in the reception area with a jolt that awakened Yohanna, who launched herself from the wheelchair with a 'Let's go!', staggering through reception, pinballing off the main doors and stumbling into the drop-off lane.

Brakes screeched as Yohanna in Joanna's body gently bounced off the front of an incoming ambulance.

'Watch it.' Yohanna glared at the dumbstruck driver.

A pitiful horn beeped behind her. It was Aaronovitch in Federica's Fiat Punto, engine running in a spot reserved for ambulances. Yohanna flailed into the passenger seat window, face pressed into the glass, hands flapping as they tried to open the door. Aaronovitch tried from inside, but her weight was on it.

'Back off,' he hollered. 'I can't open it.'

'Yeah, I... Whoa!' Yohanna pushed herself away, falling on her backside.

Federica dashed out of the hospital and came to the rescue, helping Yohanna to her feet before yanking open the back door and bundling her into the rear.

'Move, I'm driving.' Federica shooed Aaronovitch out of the driver's seat over to the passenger side. She jumped in, rammed the gear stick into first, stomped on the accelerator, and peeled away.

ELLIE POUNDED on the door to the intensive care ward, buzzing the intercom and begging the nurses to let her back in. She told them what had happened, although when she did it made little sense, even to her, and she demanded that they call the police.

Ellie was lost. Her heart sank, but her mind raced. She made a call.

'Dad? Get the car. We're going to Glastonbury.'

MAKE LIKE A TREE

'Where do you expect me to stick this?' Jo asked, inspecting the sachet of colonic cleanse Aaronovitch handed to her.

'It's all in the instructions.' Aaronovitch hurried around the Venice Beach apartment gathering various bits of ley line ephemera. 'Sarah. Find my dowsing rod, pendulum, compass and maps.'

'Ronnie, why the hell do I need a clean colon to travel between universes? I managed perfectly well without it last time?'

'Where you're going you will need to travel light. Just mix it with water. It's very powerful and very fast-acting. Get thee to a lavatory and find something to hold onto. We'll meet you down at the beach in thirty minutes. *Sarah!* We have to leave now.'

Aaronovitch and Sarah bustled out of the apartment, leaving Jo alone with the sachet.

'Sod that for a laugh.' She tucked it into the back pocket of her jeans.

AFTER THE EXPECTED thirty minutes was up, Jo joined Sarah who looked on as Aaronovitch wandered up and down Venice Beach with his Y-shaped dowsing rod, taking little lefts and rights like a drunk heading home from a bender.

'You totally made me cry.' Sarah stood by, still burdened with Aaronovitch's pendulum, compass and maps, and still dressed in nothing but a T-shirt and bikini bottoms. 'Like, on the TV last night.'

'Sorry about that,' Jo said.

'No, I totally loved it. Ronnie says I need to get more in touch with my sensitive side.'

'You're a client of his?'

'Oh yeah. He's totally getting my shit together.'

'Jolly good.'

'*Jolly good.* Huh. Love your accent.'

'Totally.'

'Yeah... totally.'

Jo shielded her eyes and squinted as Aaronovitch shuffled into the gently lapping waves on the beach. 'How exactly is he getting your, uhm, shit together?'

'We use the energy of the convergence to strengthen my life force.'

'O... K... And how does that work exactly?'

'We come to the beach...'

'Yes.'

'He locates the convergence. The ley lines, y'know?'

'Uh-huh.'

'I move to the convergence, and I stand like this...' Sarah adopted a yoga tree pose.

'I see.'

'And I get into a meditative state. I have to totally empty my mind.'

'And that takes how long?'

'Oh, seconds.'

'Hmm.'

'And I stay like that for maybe a half hour.'

'And it works?'

'Oh, totally.'

'Splendid. And, if you don't mind me asking, what's Ronnie's fee for each session?'

'Eight hundred dollars.'

'Jesus wept!'

'Yeah. I get a discount, cuz I'm letting him use my Dad's apartment.'

'Sarah, will you excuse me for a moment?'

'Sure.'

Jo left Sarah and marched across the sand to where Aaronovitch was still turning in little micro-curves as he glared at his dowsing rod. He glimpsed her coming out of the corner of his eye and gave her an apologetic smile. 'Bloody thing can be elusive. Please bear with me.'

'Am I wasting my time with you?'

'Sorry?'

'Dowsing rods, ley lines... What sort of doctor are you, exactly?'

Aaronovitch looked over to Sarah. 'What did she tell you?'

'That you're charging that poor, gullible girl eight hundred dollars a pop to do piss poor yoga on the beach.'

'Oh, that,' Aaronovitch shrugged. 'She can afford it. Or rather, her father can. Silicon Valley millionaire, y'know.'

'And that makes it okay?'

'She's no fool. She's looking for happiness and I'm giving it to her.'

'I bet you are.'

'Young lady—'

'I'm forty-two.'

'So you say. It's not what it costs, it's what it's worth to the individual. You can't put a price on enlightenment, and it's always in the spirit of discovery. These people are patrons, and without them the world would be a far poorer place. Their donations thus far have enabled me to make incredible discoveries, and now - *finally* - I have something concrete that I can show to the world. I want enlightenment for all, not just those who can afford it. And you can help me achieve that.'

'And then you will write the book, make millions, and bugger off to Bermuda?'

Aaronovitch looked genuinely hurt, 'No. Is that what you think of me? After all we've been through.'

'*We* haven't been through anything. Hang on, what have we been through?'

'You, or at least your younger alter-ego, is a troubled young woman. She's spent her whole life thinking she's a talentless imposter, which is quite a common phenomenon among the very talented. Yes, she's very ambitious, but because of her drive and single-mindedness, she's unable to sustain relationships of any sort. She's desperately lonely.'

'She seemed pretty confident to me.'

'All bluster, I assure you. She came to me looking to add some meaning to her life. Make sense of the madness of the music industry. I was tasked with giving her the tools to allow her to take control of her life.'

'So why did she run off scared in a double-decker bus?'

'These things take time.'

'And money. How much are you charging her for all this?'

'If this results in validation of my research, absolutely nothing. Ah! Here, this is it, I've found the convergence.' Aaronovitch's dowsing rod was twitching, though Jo was sure he was doing it with his thumbs. 'Stand here.'

'And what? Stand on one leg, patting my head and rubbing my tummy?' Jo nodded towards where Sarah was now standing in a sun salutation.

'You want to get home, yes? See your family again?'

'Of course.'

'I can make that happen right now. Think of this convergence as a transmitter. We can harness its energy to move you into the bardo state, where you will connect with Yohanna and switch back into your own bodies and timelines.'

'Okay.' Jo was buzzing with excitement. This was it. She was going home. 'Let's do it... What do I do?'

'I require you to adopt a vriksasana yoga pose,' Aaronovitch said. 'That's where one stands on one leg like a tree.'

Jo took a deep breath and lifted one leg off the ground, finding it far easier to balance in a younger, more lithe body than her forty-two-year-old one.

'Excellent,' Aaronovitch said. 'Now close your eyes, slow your breathing and listen only to my voice. Gently repeat this mantra silently.'

'How...? Sorry to interrupt, but how do I repeat a mantra *silently*?'

'Say it in your head.'

'*Think* it?'

'If you like.'

'Why didn't you just say that?'

'This isn't helping, young lady.'

'Okay, okay, what do I say?'

'*Oh-ry-in-eye-yay.*'

'*Ory-in-aye-aye.*'

'Not quite right. *Oh-ry-in-eye-yay.*'

'*Oh-ry-in-why-yay.*'

'You sound like a Geordie. *Oh-ry-in-eye-yay.*'

'*Oh-ry-in-eye-yay.*'

'Yes!'

'*Oh-ry-in-eye-yay. Oh-ry-in-eye-yay. Oh-ry-in-eye-yay.*'

'Great. Now in your head.'

Jo did as she was told, Aaronovitch kept repeating it aloud to gee her along.

Oh-ry-in-eye-yay. Oh-ry-in-eye-yay. Oh-ry-in-eye-yay.

It wasn't working. Maybe she should have taken the dose of colonic cleanser after all?

Oh-ry-in-eye-yay. Oh-ry-in-eye-yay.

Or maybe it kept bothering her that she could hear inflections in Aaronovitch's voice that suggested he wasn't quite as posh as he made out.

Oh-ry-in-eye-yay.

For all his superior attitude, she could hear a working class boy who had worked his way into British academia, and had adopted a disguise in a way that someone like Lawrie never could.

Oh-ry-in-eye-yay.

Jo began to worry that Lawrie would be wondering where she was and sending search parties out for her. She had no phone and no way of getting in touch with him. But would that matter? If she could get home right now then Lawrie would be Yohanna's problem.

Oh-ry-in-eye-yay.

Jo wondered if Lawrie had managed to get a deal for Yohanna yet, and if Yohanna was even ready for one? If she was struggling to cope with success, was it wrong to throw her in the deep end like this? Jo reminded herself that she hadn't started this. She didn't even really know what *this* was. She was standing on a beach, pretending to be a tree in order to project herself across the universe.

Oh-ry-in-eye-yay.

This was ridiculous. It wasn't working and Aaronovitch was going to realise sooner or later.

Oh-ry-in-eye-yay.

'Oh, hey.' Sarah's unmistakable California voice came to her. Jo opened her eyes and found herself drifting in a dark void. She caught a glimpse of Sarah floating by in the dark, her incredibly white teeth shining like a lighthouse as she turned.

Jo felt a sudden pull of acceleration, and the sound of the waves became the rush of the universe swirling around her.

This was it. She was going home. She could make amends with Ellie, she could sort out her life, she could—

Everything stopped, and now it was so dark she couldn't even see her hand in front of her face. Her whole body suddenly felt numb. The blackness was oppressive, and she began to panic, suffocating.

There was a light. A tiny pinprick at first, like when she turned off her TV as a child and everything shrunk down into a couple of tiny blips in the centre of the screen.

Jo was sure she could hear someone sobbing.

The light now rushed towards her, filling the universe with noise.

Jo found herself sitting in the back seat of a tiny car. Or not quite sitting. She was floating. A disembodied spirit, and the world around her was fuzzy, vibrating like she had a massive migraine. Her heart was racing and she could feel her energy draining from her like water down a sink. She couldn't see the face of the driver of the car, but it was a woman, small and hunched forward in the seat like a racing driver. There was a strangely familiar old man in the passenger seat. He turned round. It was Aaronovitch, much older and balder. She tried to say something but no sound came from her mouth.

Jo glanced to her left.

And saw herself staring back at her.

There was a tiny moment of confusion. Followed by screaming.

CLOSE ENCOUNTER ON THE M4

'What? What?' Federica's eyes darted to the rear view mirror.

'Glastonbury.' Yohanna had stopped screaming and was now yelling at the empty air next to her. 'Go to Glastonbury.'

'What do you think we're doing?' Federica asked, puzzled.

'No, not you,' Yohanna said. 'Her. Stop the car.'

'Her? Who *her*?'

'Stop the car!'

'I can't,' Federica said. 'I'm on the motorway. I can't just pull over. Tell me what's wrong?'

'You can't see her? Ronnie, can you see her?' Yohanna said, then added, 'Oh shit, she's gone.'

AARONOVITCH'S GENIUS

J o found herself on the hot sand of Venice Beach, wondering what the hell she'd just experienced.

Aaronovitch stood over her with his dowsing rod.

'We have to go to Glastonbury,' she told him.

'It was me, but it was Yohanna.' Jo was pacing back and forth at Aaronovitch's apartment. 'I mean, it looked just like me, but I could tell it was her. She was in my body, but it was definitely her. She was in a car and she told me to go to Glastonbury. And you were there,' she told Aaronovitch. 'Only you were older.'

'How much older?'

'Bald older.'

'Bald?'

'As a coot,' Jo said. 'Sorry, it happens.'

'Oh.' Aaronovitch ran a hand across his thinning scalp.

'C'mon, Ronnie, stay with me,' Jo snapped.

'Let's try it again.' Aaronovitch was so excited he had snapped his dowsing rod. He was now twirling it through his fingers in a fidgety way that was annoying Jo. 'We can make contact and discover their plan.'

'No, it felt wrong,' Jo said. 'I was like - and this is going to sound ridiculous - but I was like a ghost. I was floating next to her, and she was the only one who could see or hear me. Everything was weird and fuzzy. It was like a bad TV signal, and I could feel all my energy just... have you ever had an anaesthetic for an operation? It was like that. I could barely keep my eyes open.' Sarah handed Jo a black coffee. 'Thanks. God, I really need this. There's no way I'm trying that again. Oh, and here's the really weird bit... I could feel our connection,' Jo said. 'That energy, that light. It's fading in her, too. Only she has it worse. She's weak and she was in a hospital gown.' Jo took a sip of her coffee. 'I don't think she has long left.'

'The solstice thing?' Sarah asked.

'Yes, bloody hell, it's affecting her, too,' Jo said.

'A moment, a moment.' Aaronovitch began pacing again, fingers pressed to his forehead.

'He's so cool when he does this,' Sarah said. 'He has this amazing, beautiful mind. Totally a genius.'

Jo smiled politely and downed the rest of her coffee.

'Curious.' Aaronovitch pursed his lips. 'If I was there, travelling with her, surely it was in some sort of advisory capacity. Perhaps, in the future, I have achieved a level of fame for my knowledge of the bardo state and she came to me seeking my wisdom.'

'Totally,' Sarah nodded.

'Yeah, thanks, Sherlock,' Jo said. 'If she knows you here, it would make sense that she would look for you over there.'

'Totally,' Sarah nodded again.

'Especially if she thinks you're some kind of guru who knows about this crap.'

'Totally,' Sarah agreed.

'Sarah, sweetie.' Jo rested a gentle hand on Sarah's forearm. 'That's getting a little tiresome.'

Sarah snorted a laugh, 'God, I love your accent. You're just like Mary Poppins, or something.'

Jo handed Sarah her empty coffee cup, 'Any chance of another?' she asked. Then, remembering who she was speaking to, added, '*Spit spot!*' in her best Julie Andrews.

'So cool,' Sarah beamed as she took the coffee cup to the kitchen area.

Jo turned her attention back to Aaronovitch who was still massaging his forehead. 'Why would we go to Glastonbury?' she asked. 'Why not, I dunno, Stonehenge?'

'The ley lines at Glastonbury are among the most powerful in the world,' Aaronovitch said. 'And your weak signal experience, as you put it, could be explained by the distance between us and your other self. If we were to travel to the right spot in Glastonbury, we could swap you over like you were walking through a door. And besides, who am I to argue with myself?'

'Glastonbury,' Jo mused, thinking of Lawrie's potential gig deals. 'I might have some good news for you, there.'

'I only ever travel first class.' Aaronovitch winced theatrically. 'My sciatica, you see.'

'You don't need to come,' Jo told him. 'Just write me some instructions and—'

'Oh, but I do,' Aaronovitch protested. 'It's not as simple as just walking through a door.'

'You *literally* just said—'

'It requires skill and equipment that takes decades to master.'

'What equipment?'

'There's one piece in particular...' Aaronovitch drifted off, before asking Jo with a raised eyebrow, 'How friendly are you with Rand McManus?'

'Hardly know him,' Jo said, trying not to blush.

'You looked fairly chummy on the television last night.'

'What's your point, Ronnie?'

'If I am to return you home, I need something of his,' he said. 'And I require you to get it for me.'

'If it's his bus, you can forget it,' she said. 'It's being repaired.'

'It's a mere trinket,' Aaronovitch said. 'A tiny little crystal prism, which can fit in the palm of one's hand.'

'He wears it around his neck,' Jo said. Aaronovitch and Sarah shared a brief and knowing look. 'Oh, stop, it was nothing like that... Well, it was a bit, but that's not the point. He showed it to me. He said it was his Dad's.'

Aaronovitch threw his hands to the sky and made a series of huffing noises as he stomped around the room like a middle-aged toddler.

'What's up with him now?'

'He gets kinda cranky on this subject.' Sarah scrunched her nose. 'Don't worry, you get used to it. Ronnie, honey, I can get you a prism.' She rummaged through a box full of dream catchers, scented candles and crystals. 'I'm sure I got one in here, somewheres.'

'No, it has to be the one Rand has.'

'His father's?' Jo teased.

'It's not his father's,' Aaronovitch declared, pointing to the ceiling. 'What do you know about Rand McManus?'

'Big movie star, bit insecure, but a nice guy. Fond of buses.'

'His family. What do you know about his family?'

'Nothing,' she shrugged. 'He's not a movie star in my universe.'

'Oh, really?' Aaronovitch grinned, taking more than a little delight in that.

'C'mon, Ronnie, skip to the end.'

'Rand McManus' father was Cygnus Macbeth, drummer for the band Khufu.'

'Okay, you're just making names up now,' Jo said.

'Oh, Khufu were totally awesome,' Sarah insisted. '*Spiritual Satellite* is, like, a message from the Gods. Totally opened my third eye.'

'They were the worst kind of hippy-dippy prog folk,' Aaronovitch said. 'And Cygnus, real name Keith McManus, knew Michael Eavis, who, in 1970, was trying to get acts for the Pilton Pop, Blues and Folk Festival.'

'The first ever Glastonbury,' Jo said, pressing her nose with one finger and pointing at Aaronovitch with the other. 'See, I know that much.'

'Exactly, and Khufu were supposed to be on the bill. Only Bill Harkin had them kicked off.'

'Too many Bills. Who?'

'Bill Harkin designed the pyramid stage.'

'Pyramid Stage?' Sarah frowned.

'The largest stage at the festival,' said Jo. 'All the big headliners play there to hundreds of thousands of fans.'

'The story goes that Eavis and Harkin were using crystals from Stonehenge to bless the site of the stage, which was placed on a precise spot...'

'Let me guess - it's on a convergence of ley lines?'

'Yes. Only Cygnus goes and pinches one of the crystals and buggers off back to London. It's never seen again.'

'And you think the prism in Rand's dressing room is the same crystal?'

'I *know* it is. I've been trying to buy it off him for years, but he won't part with it. A precious heirloom, he calls it. Rand gets a curious vibe from it. The word is it helped him recover during rehab.'

'And how badly do we really need it? I mean, what's wrong with one of Sarah's junk shop prisms?'

'This prism has ancient properties unlike any other. Without it, you'll end up drifting ghostlike as you were just now. This prism will not only boost your signal, but help steer yourself right into Yohanna's arms.'

'I swear to god, Ronnie, if I hadn't seen all this crap for myself, I'd think you were off your tits. This is insane.' Jo stood, ready for action. 'Okay, let me talk to him. Maybe he'll lend it to us?'

'I would recommend just stealing it,' Aaronovitch said.

'I am not stealing anything.'

'Borrow it, then. I'll give it back to him when we're done.'

'Sure you will.'

'His father stole it in the first place,' Aaronovitch snapped. 'Look, young lady, until some ancient druid turns up demanding their crystal back, it's all up for grabs as far as I'm concerned. Get me that crystal, Jo, and I can get you home. Before you and Yohanna fade away forever.'

BAND ON THE RUN

F ederica pulled into a service station on the M4 not long after Yohanna's encounter with Jo. The fuel light had been pinging since they left London's suburbs and she took the first opportunity she had to fill up the Punto.

'I know what I saw.' Yohanna popped her head out the rear window as Federica wriggled the petrol head into the car and started the pump. 'It was me, but it was her, because she had terrible make-up and looked like a nun and she's going to ruin my career.'

Federica and Yohanna had barely exchanged two words since their clumsy escape from Guy's Hospital, then Yohanna started screaming about seeing a ghost causing Federica to swerve across two lanes on the motorway, and intensifying her already foul mood.

'Are you angry with me?' Yohanna asked.

'Angry?' Federica said. 'Why should I be angry? I was going to convince Ellie to come with us, only you have to go and ruin everything. You can't wait can you? You have to have everything your own way. You were never this spoiled when you were with me.'

'There was no way she was coming with us,' Yohanna protested, her voice still raspy from the ravages of her hospital breathing tube. 'Would you? Whatever we say to anyone, no matter how convincing we think we are, we're always gonna sound and look like a bunch of weirdos.'

'We needed her on our side, and now she'll be coming after us.'

'You don't know that.'

'You're her mother.' Federica gestured to the front of the car. 'Look in the mirror. When she looks at you she sees the woman who sacrificed everything to bring her up. She's not going to sit on her bum while her crazy coma mother goes running off to Glastonbury. She's going to call the police and send them after us.'

'Oh,' Yohanna said. 'Okay, shit, that's a good point, but y'know, it was a stressful situation and we needed to take action. And anyway, what can the police do? She doesn't know what car we're in. And, important point, I *haven't* been kidnapped. I went willingly, and if they stop us I promise to behave like a normal person.'

'That will take years of training.'

'Federica, please don't be angry,' Yohanna said. 'I'm so tired I can barely keep my eyes open. I'm not entirely thinking straight.'

'Then leave the complicated decision making to us,' Federica said, yanking the petrol head from the Punto, and marching across the garage forecourt to pay. Aaronovitch was coming the other way, waving an Ordnance Survey map in his hands.

'Found one,' Aaronovitch called triumphantly. Federica blanked him.

'You look happy,' Yohanna said, glad just to have someone not yell at her.

'As I should be,' he said. 'Your little encounter back there proved we're onto something. The other side is trying to get through, and with this we'll make contact.'

'What is it?'

'Every inch of Glastonbury carefully mapped out for us,' he said, unfolding the map as he circled the car. 'I'll have to find the ley lines from memory, of course, but fortunately for you I can recite Pi to three hundred decimal places.'

'How does that help?'

'I don't recall.' Aaronovitch flopped into the passenger seat, becoming engulfed by the ever-unfolding map. 'However, I'm fairly certain I can pinpoint the convergence of ley lines we found in the centre of town.'

'No, we can't go there.'

'Why ever not?'

'Because I'm an idiot and ran away and they know where we're going, and they'll be there waiting for us.' Yohanna shuddered with exhaustion and fresh tears rolled down her cheeks. 'Oh god, Ronnie, I don't think I'm going to last. How long will this take?'

'We have another four or so hours' driving ahead of us,' he said. 'Do you think you can cope with that?'

Yohanna nodded, 'But where will we go if we can't go into town?'

'Oh, my goodness, Glastonbury is riddled with ley lines,' Aaronovitch reassured her. 'Glastonbury Tor, Worthy Farm—'

Yohanna perked up, 'Worthy Farm's where they have the festival.'

'Indeed, the site was chosen specifically for its location on a convergence.'

'There,' she said. 'We go there.'

'You're sure?'

'I told the other me to go to Glastonbury and when I think of Glastonbury I think of the festival. Let's go.'

'Might I suggest we wait until Federica returns,' Aaronovitch suggested. 'She's quite keen on being the driver.'

'Yeah, yeah, good call,' Yohanna said.

FEDERICA STOOD in line in the service station mini-mart waiting to pay for the unleaded, trying to calm down, wondering just how she'd ended up in this situation. Up ahead, a truck driver was querying something about his loyalty card points and the queue was going nowhere, so she dialled home and Robin answered.

'Gosh, Aunty Fede it's jolly good to hear from you,' the young lady said.

'Everything okay? No one burned the house down?'

'You'll be glad to hear that the house is spick and span and untainted by smoke or fire, and Mrs. Fenwick is blissfully ignorant of your absence.'

'Good work, thank you, Robin.'

'When's the mad old bat coming home?' Ben called.

'Ben has asked when you might be—?'

'Yes, heard him. Soon, darling, soon,' Federica said as the line shuffled forward, the trucker's dispute settled. As they moved, Federica glanced at the woman in front of her who was idly flicking through Facebook on her phone. And Federica saw something that made her blood chill. 'Bah-luddy hell.'

'Aunty Fede? Is everything all right?'

'Yes, yes,' Federica said quickly. 'I'll... I'll be back tomorrow. Day after at the most. I've something I have to do. Very important. Can you cope for a little longer?'

'Can do,' Robin said, and Federica hung up, immediately activating the Facebook app on her phone.

YOHANNA LEANED FORWARD in her seat, catching sight of herself in the rear view mirror. 'Jesus, look at me. I'm an old woman.'

'Don't be ridiculous,' Aaronovitch said. 'You're in the prime of your life.'

'I look old.' Yohanna raised her chin, tilting her head from side-to-side. 'I've got wrinkles. Chins, *plural*. Baggy eyes.'

'You're also recovering from a coma. Few can come away from such trauma with the glow of the supermodel. Give yourself time.'

'Don't have much of that.' Yohanna slumped back into her seat, hand resting on her belly. 'Actually, I'm not just old. I'm a mother. This body's given birth.' She peeked under her hospital gown. 'Stretch marks. Ugh. This is so weird. Never thought I'd have kids. But she did. I'm not being judgy or anything, but it's just... alien to me.'

Aaronovitch, unused to such conversations, and way out of his depth, wisely chose to remain silent with an encouraging smile.

'I guess it made her happy,' Yohanna said. 'Her daughter clearly loves her.'

'What brings you happiness, if you don't mind me asking?' Aaronovitch was satisfied he was on safer ground here.

'Oh, the gig, y'know?' Yohanna smiled. 'Getting up on stage and singing my heart out. Better than sex, drugs, booze. And I like getting it *right*. Perfecting it, getting better, learning my craft. You think you know it all, but you find there's just more crazy shit to get your head around. All this from a few notes on a scale. Infinite possibilities. It's magic.

'Course, there's all sorts of crap that gets in the way of me doing that, but I let Lawrie handle all that. He may be a bitter old sod, but he's also my shit storm umbrella. For all his faults, I love the guy. For God's sake don't tell him any of this, but I'd do it for free if they'd let me.'

The driver's door swung open and Federica jumped in. 'Put these on.' She tossed Yohanna a cheap pair of sunglasses and a straw Trilby hat from the service station's gift shop. 'We're in trouble.'

Yohanna peered out the car windows. 'The police?'

'Worse,' Federica said. 'Social media.' She held up her phone for Yohanna and Aaronovitch to see. It was a post from Ellie. It had received well over 2,000 likes and 20,000 shares. It was a picture of Jo grinning with a large glass of wine with the headline, 'HAVE YOU SEEN MY MUM?'

EMBRACE THE WOO-WOO

'Hey,' Jo beamed as Rand opened his dressing room door. He recoiled like a horror movie ingénue encountering a vampire, but covered it well. 'I know, I'm sorry.' Jo slipped into the dressing room, ignoring the seductive waft of Rand's incense, and closed the door. 'Things didn't end too well with us last time.'

'You barfed all over me.'

'I barfed on a great many people that night, but I wanted to say sorry to you in person.'

'You don't have to,' Rand said in a way that suggested she totally had to. 'Seriously, it's my last show tonight, I'm on in a half hour. Can we do this another... Hey, how did you even get in here?'

'Yesterday's pass and a big dollop of charm.' Jo winked. 'Freddie on security is lovely, isn't he? His parents and my completely made-up parents are from the same part of Ireland. Amazing coincidence, eh? Anyway, I bring gifts.' Jo offered Rand a plastic carrier bag.

'What is it?' Rand took it and peeked inside, 'Oh, cool. Where did you get this?' He took out a second-hand vinyl copy of Khufu's debut album *The Pharaohs of Albion*, the cover of which depicted a dramatic gathering of torch-bearing druids circling Stonehenge. 'Oh, man. Haven't seen this in a while.'

Rand grinned as he opened the gatefold. It featured a pale and rather chilly-looking naked woman lying on a pentangle in the centre of the ancient stone circle, suffering the further indignity of having the album's track listing printed over her in a papyrus typeface. 'Dad did some of his best work on this. Said it was all downhill from here. Where'd you get it?'

'Some little second-hand record store on Sunset. I was pootling through their prog section when I saw it,' Jo lied. She'd ordered her cab driver to take her to the best second-hand record store in town. 'I'm a fan,' Jo lied again. 'A big one, and I think it's a crime that it hasn't been reissued properly.'

'Yeah, a crying shame.'

'I know, and that's why I have an offer for you.' Jo took a breath before her really big lie. 'I'm playing Glastonbury this weekend—'

'Really? Wow, congratulations.'

'Thank you,' she said, without qualifying that she *hoped* she was playing Glastonbury, that she *needed* to play Glastonbury, or at the very least had to just *make it* to Glastonbury otherwise she would never get home. 'And I was thinking I could sing one of Khufu's songs at Glastonbury. Have a little tribute moment, y'know? Show the fans what real music used to sound like. Get them demanding a re-release of a lost classic, sort of thing.'

'That's such a cool idea, thank you.'

'No problem.'

Rand was looking at the back of the album which had a pyramid on it. 'Maybe the end of side two?'

'Uh, yeah?' Jo began to wish she'd memorised some of the song titles. Her mind scrambled, trying to recall what Sarah had said. 'Maybe... uhm...' Jo could see Rand fold his arms, enjoying her torment. '*Spiritual Satellite*?' she said, delighted with herself. '*Spiritual Satellite* is, like, a message from the gods. Totally opened my third eye.'

'Never had you down as a third eye kinda person.'

'Oh, yeah.' Then added for authenticity, 'Totally.'

'Though it does require a children's choir, a theramin, and a gong to really capture its majesty.'

'Well... they say any great song can be played on a guitar or a piano, so I could do it solo.'

'It's twenty-two minutes long.'

'A... uh... a seven inch remix, perhaps?'

There followed an awkward silence.

'You're not really a fan are you, Yohanna?'

'God no, I'm sorry, I just really need your crystal.'

'My what?'

'Your prism, the one you use for your meditation. I need to borrow it, just for a few days. I swear to God you'll get it back.'

Rand narrowed his eyes. 'Did Aaronovitch send you?'

'Nnnnno...'

'I knew it!' Rand snapped his fingers. 'Dammit, that son of a bitch has been trying to steal it from me for years. Sorry. No. He's not having it. Good to see you again, Yohanna, but I have a show to do, and...' Rand tried to shepherd her to the door, but she grabbed his lapel and slammed him against the wall. 'Jesus! What's—' Jo kissed him full on the mouth until they both had to come up for air.

'What did you do that for?' he asked - once he got his breath back.

'Seemed the best way to shut you up,' Jo said and kissed him again. He was very yummy.

'The answer's still no.'

'Please. My life depends on it.'

'I kinda doubt it. Anyhow, the crystal was my father's, it has great sentimental value and it's gotten me through some tough times.'

'And now it can get me through a tough time,' Jo pleaded. 'When I told you I was a forty-two-year-old woman I wasn't kidding, it wasn't imposter syndrome, it was real. Your little prism can get me home.'

'Aaronovitch told you that?'

There was a knock on the door, 'Thirty minutes, Rand!' Jo recognised the super-perky voice of Kate, the production assistant who had herded her around when she was on the show.

Rand hesitated before answering. 'Thank you.'

'I have to get home, and that stupid little crystal is the one thing that can help me,' Jo pleaded. 'I swear, I promise that you'll get it back.'

Another knock and Kate's voice seemed less perky now, 'Everything okay, Rand?'

'Yeah, I'll be right there,' Rand assured her, and placed a protective hand over the prism hanging from a silver chain around his neck. 'I'm sorry,' he told Jo. 'I can't let it out of my sight.'

'Then come with me to Glastonbury,' Jo said. 'This is your last show tonight, right? We fly out first thing. Please.'

'To England?'

'Yeah, why not? Aaronovitch reckons yours is the only prism that can steer the energy of the ley lines and get me home. Now if that means anything to you—'

'He's been talking about that shit for years, Yohanna.' Rand shook his head. 'Seriously, it doesn't work.'

'It does,' Jo said with a surprising amount of passion. 'I've done it, I just stood on a convergence of ley lines on Venice Beach, travelled through time and space on the back of a rainbow and saw myself in the back of a car in a parallel universe.' Jo let go of Rand's lapels. 'Jesus, I'm actually saying this stuff and believing it. Look at me. I know this sounds completely woo-woo, but it's real, please believe me.'

'A rainbow?' Rand was suddenly intrigued.

'What?'

Rand opened up the gatefold of Khufu's album *The Pharaohs of Albion* where all the tracks were listed over the naked lady's body. 'You never heard this before, right?'

'No, and I'm sorry,' Jo said. 'They actually don't exist in my universe.'

'No, no, no, look.' Rand pointed to the final track listed on the album, *The Druid's Journey*. 'My Dad wrote the lyrics for that song. They were the only lyrics he ever wrote, as a matter of fact, and he based them on an experience he said he had with the crystal. It goes, *I felt the universe move around me, the moon and stars intense and bright, I took a ride to another time, on a glowing beam of rainbow light.'*

'Holy shit. He did it, too?'

'Everyone said Dad was crazy, high on acid, but he always swore it was true.' Rand closed the gatefold, his eyes glistening. 'I... I never believed him.'

'Come with me, Rand.' Jo squeezed his hand. 'Prove your Dad was right. You can be the guardian of the prism. I'll make sure Aaronovitch gives it back to you, I swear. What do you say?'

'I can't, I'm sorry,' Rand insisted. 'It's a matter of principle. He's—'

'I'll take you on a hot date to the London Bus Museum.'

'I'm in.'

Jo DIDN'T GET BACK to the Beverly Wilshire till after dark and, as predicted, Lawrie was having conniptions. 'Where the bloody hell have you been, girl?'

'Sorting my life out.' Jo flopped onto one of the suite's many sofas.

'Get packing,' Lawrie said. 'We're on the first flight out of LAX tomorrow morning.'

'Brilliant!' Jo hopped to her feet and ran to her room. 'So, what stage are we on at Glastonbury?' she called as she yanked clothes from the wardrobe and tossed them on the bed. 'Acoustic? Avalon? Please not the kids' stage.'

'What planet are you on?' Lawrie frowned at her as he wandered into the room.

'Ooh, bigger? The Pyramid Stage would be awesome, I mean I don't ask much, but—'

'Yohanna, Glastonbury is *this* weekend. There's no way on God's Green Earth that I can get you into Glastonbury. It's been fully booked for months.'

'What? But you said—'

'Yeah, for next year.'

'No, no, no, I need to play Glastonbury. Like, now.'

'I've created a monster,' Lawrie muttered.

'You don't understand, I have to be there. It's the only way I can...' Jo stopped herself. She was pretty sure Lawrie didn't need a primer in pan-universal ley line travel right now. 'I'm hot. Hotter than hot, people love me, people write about me, and a spot at Glastonbury is exactly what I need to propel me into megastardom. We can't wait a year, Lawrie. You're the big shot manager. Make it happen.'

'I can't, I've already booked you for NanoMuFest.'

'Noo-noo-what-now?'

'NanoMuFest.'

'What the fuck is NanoMuFest?'

'It's a really cool alternative to Glastonbury.' Lawrie spread his hands like a magician about to do a trick. 'All the best up-and-coming unsigned acts in a field in Dorking, and the whole industry goes there to find new talent.'

'The same weekend as Glastonbury?'

'Yup.'

'How can the whole industry be in bloody Dorking when we know perfectly well that they're all at Glastonbury, Lawrie?'

'Not... *all* of them.'

'Just your mates? And every crappy manager who couldn't get their act booked for Glastonbury?'

'Don't start on me, girl. I've worked hard to get you a deal.'

'Clearly not hard enough,' Jo said. 'I was on *The Tonight Show*. I blew people away, you said.'

'You're a weirdo,' Lawrie snapped. 'Sorry, but there it is. They think you're strange. And not in the good Kate Bush, Stevie Nicks, Tori Amos way, but the *she-actually-believes-she's-a-time-traveller-so-she-must-be-mental* way. You're too much woo-woo for the industry.'

'How can I be too much woo-woo, Lawrie? What about Michael Jackson? He's very probably from another planet and people love him.'

'Who?'

Jo cursed, remembering that the King of Pop wasn't a thing here. 'Prince and his symbol. Is *that* mainstream?'

'He was mainstream, *then* he went woo-woo. You can't go full woo-woo from day one. There has to be something the masses can latch onto. The girl next door, the sexy girl, the bad girl. Not Wednesday fucking Addams with a guitar. The only reason people write about you is you're completely weird.'

'Isn't it up to you, as my alleged manager, to tell them I'm not?'

'I would, but you keep insisting it's all true,' Lawrie said. '*I'm really a forty-two-year-old woman*, you told me. What am I supposed to do with that? I try and steer round it, but they all heard you on live TV. Oh, and they all think you poisoned those people at the after party.'

'That was Diemond.'

'That's as may be, but getting anyone to take you seriously is an uphill struggle.'

'Me? Take a look at yourself, Lawrie. How does the scruffy cockney geezer look go down in the boardrooms of the multinational record companies? What do the public schoolboys who run the industry really think of you, eh?'

'I am respected, girl.'

'You're a laughing stock,' Jo spat. 'They all think you run to your mum, cap in hand after every one of your disasters, Lawrie.'

'My mum?'

'Yeah, you go to her mansion and she makes you beg like a dog.'

'My mum's dead,' Lawrie said, and it hit Jo like a slap in the face. 'What?'

'Died when I was a kid,' he said. 'Oh, yeah, I got a few quid in the will. It got me started, but I get my money from investors and some very understanding bank managers.'

Jo felt nauseous with guilt, 'I'm sorry, oh fuck...'

'Who told you all that bollocks? Diemond? Yeah, I fucking bet. Look what she does to people.'

Jo lowered her voice and took Lawrie's arm. 'Why not get back at the old witch? Why not take this opportunity to show her she's wrong? You and me, we're outsiders. I'm the woo-woo weirdo, you're the working class geezer. We don't have to play by their rules. We are getting on that plane tomorrow and we are going to gatecrash Glastonbury and we are going to be huge.'

'You're not even going to consider NanoMuFest?'

'Not even for a second. Can't even pronounce it.'

'Okay.' Lawrie inhaled loudly through his nostrils and puffed his cheeks. 'Sorry, Yohanna. I quit.'

ATOM HEART MOTHER

'Bah-luddy hell, look at the size of it.' Federica and Aaronovitch stood on a rise overlooking Worthy Farm. Fields bordered by ancient hedgerows rolled away under a blue sky dotted with puffy white clouds. Directly below them was a field populated with dairy cows happily chewing their cud. 'You're sure this is a farm? It looks like the whole countryside.'

'It's rather sizeable,' Aaronovitch said, turning the map in his hands as he tried to get his bearings.

Most years this land was host to hundreds of thousands of festivalgoers. But, this summer, the festival was taking its traditional fallow year. Today it was just another farm, albeit a bloody big one. 'Where do we start, Aaronovitch?'

'A moment, woman.' Aaronovitch turned the map again. 'Ah, here we are. Through these cows, and into the field beyond. That's the site of the Pyramid Stage and the convergence.'

'How do we get down there?' Federica gestured back to where the Punto was parked, and where Yohanna lay barely conscious in the back seat. 'That girl can hardly sit up straight. She definitely can't walk, and I'm not sure I can carry her.'

'And driving the car across private land will only attract the wrong kind of attention,' Aaronovitch mused.

'And wreck my car,' Federica said. 'Well, I guess it was time for a new one, anyway.'

She started walking back to the car, when Aaronovitch raised his hand, 'Madame Federica,' he called. 'I think I have a solution that will spare our backs and your vehicle.'

'MUMMY, I FORGOT MY DOLLY.' *Yohanna was two-year-old Joanna again, with pouty lips and tears in her eyes.*

'Oh no, darling. Where is it?'

'I lost my dolly, I lost my dolly.'

'It's okay, poppet, it's probably back in the shop.' Mum glanced at the newsagent's just across the road. 'I'll get it.'

This was how it happened.

'No, please Mummy, stay.'

But Yohanna would not let it happen again.

'Wait there and be good,' Mum said, calmly stepping out onto the road.

'No!' Yohanna was herself again. All grown up and frizzy hair, her voice trembling. 'Please don't. It doesn't have to happen. Leave the dolly, leave it, please.'

A speeding red double-decker bus whooshed by, missing her mother by inches.

'Gosh, that was close,' Mum said. Then faded to nothing.

'Mum!' Yohanna cried. 'Mum, no, please come back.'

YOHANNA'S MIND drifted in and out of deep and bewildering dreams. She saw glimpses of another life in an office, chatting and laughing with friends, shopping in Waitrose and complaining about the rising cost of living and contemplating regular shops at Lidl. Strangest of all, she dreamt she was riding a cow across a field.

Only, it turned out not to be a dream.

Aaronovitch - the older, balder Aaronovitch - led the beast across a field as Federica walked alongside and steadied Yohanna, who lay slumped forward on the cow's back.

'Am I... am I on a cow?' Yohanna asked, not unreasonably.

'Hey, you're awake.' Federica's face brightened, and she patted Yohanna's hand. 'Yes, you're on a cow.'

'Why am I on a cow?'

'It was the easiest way to get you across this field,' Federica explained. 'You can walk if you like? Are you strong enough to walk?'

Yohanna tried keeping her eyelids open, but it was like lifting gym weights, and her limbs felt boneless. 'Not really,' she said.

'Okay, stay on the cow,' Federica said. 'You'll be fine. We'll be there soon.'

'Where are we going?'

'We're taking you home, my darling.'

'On a cow?'

'On a cow.'

'I'm still not totally sure why I'm on a—'

'Whoa, Daisy,' Aaronovitch said as he brought the beast to a halt, 'Look after her, will you?' He smiled at Federica, before dashing off.

'Hey, where are you going?' Federica called after him. 'You can't just leave me here with a semi-conscious woman on a cow.'

'I won't be long,' Aaronovitch said, half-jogging to where a gate nestled in the hedgerow. 'Just need to open this thing.' Aaronovitch pulled on the gate, but it didn't budge.

The hairs on the nape of Federica's neck stood on end as she became aware of a movement behind her. She turned to find more cows closing in on her, at least a dozen. 'Aaronovitch,' she called, 'I don't like the look of this.'

'Calm yourself, my good woman,' he said, his voice straining as he leaned and pulled on the jammed gate. 'They're perfectly friendly beasts. Nothing to fear.'

'That's easy for you to say.' Federica had grown up in Rome, then London. A city girl who had never been so close to so many cows before. They began to huff at her, sniffing at her legs, and swishing their tails with enthusiasm at making a new friend.

'Bugger off.' Federica began shooing the cows away, but they only licked their nostrils with their long pink tongues. Flies buzzed around their heads. One moved around the rear of Yohanna's cow. 'Go away.'

'Nearly got it,' Aaronovitch's voice called. 'Bloody thing won't... Ah, here we go.' The gate swung open with the kind of metal-on-metal grinding you might expect from one of the gates of hell. This unearthly noise startled the cows, who all took a unanimous vote to run away.

Including the cow with Yohanna on its back.

'No.' Federica chased after Yohanna's runaway cow. 'Stop. Heel! Come back, you stupid cow.'

AARONOVITCH HAD LIVED a long and varied life, travelling the world and enjoying its many cultures, and seen some extraordinary things - including many of the ancient wonders of the world. But he had never seen anything quite as remarkable as when he looked up from opening the gate to see, in the distance, a small Italian woman taking down a cow with a rugby tackle in a field in England.

The creature toppled forward on its front knees, ejecting Yohanna from its back. She landed safely on the grass, rolling like a rag doll, and the cow got to its feet again, leaving a cowpat as a token of gratitude, before strolling away as if nothing had happened.

'Is everything all right?' he called to Federica.

She was such a long way off that he saw her angry gestures before the sound of her voice could travel across the field.

'Aaronovitch, get your bah-luddy backside over here and help me with this girl.'

WINGS OVER AMERICA

Rand came through with tickets for the first flight to Heathrow and soon he, Jo and Aaronovitch were bound for England.

Over Greenland the northern lights put on a spectacular show, but Jo was hunched over a map of Glastonbury with Aaronovitch. He worked with a set of protractors, compasses, pencils and a six-inch ruler from a tin pencil case. He drew lines across the map and made calculations with a slide rule and scribbled notes in the white spaces.

'We have a problem,' he told her.

'You told me this would be as simple as walking through a door, Ronnie. What problem?'

'You've seen what happens if the connection between the two universes is weak,' he said.

'It's like a bad TV signal.'

'Indeed, and incredibly dangerous for crossing,' Aaronovitch said. 'There's no telling where you might end up or what might become of you. So, we need to find a convergence that's strong enough to ensure your safe passage. I've been cross-referencing the map with the notes I made when I was last in Glastonbury, and it's clear to me there's only really one convergence that suits our purposes.' He jabbed a finger on the map where all the lines converged. It was in the middle of a field.

'Okay,' Jo shrugged. 'We knew that, right? It's in the middle of the Glastonbury festival somewhere. Probably some hippy's tent. We ask them if we can play with our prism for a while and all's cool.'

'I'm afraid not.' Aaronovitch took a crumpled sheet of paper from his shoulder bag and laid it over the map of the farm. 'This is the layout of last year's festival. Stages come and go and move around, but one will always stay in the same place.'

'The Pyramid Stage,' Jo said, dreading what was coming next.

'Precisely, the Pyramid Stage is on the exact same spot as the convergence, and that's no accident. The power of the ley lines, the resonance of the pyramid, the energy of the crowd, the level of sun - all these factors come into play and will increase your chances of getting home.'

'You're saying I need to somehow be on the Pyramid Stage to get home?'

'At sunset tomorrow night.'

'Are you mental? That's when Diemond's playing. There's no way I can get on stage then. Can't I hang around backstage and do it there?'

'If my calculations are correct, you will need to be standing front and centre of the Pyramid Stage,' Aaronovitch said. 'And you'll need time to achieve the bardo state, too.'

'You mean I have to do this literally standing on one leg?'

'Not only that, we all need to be with you, too,' Aaronovitch said. 'Rand has the prism, and I need to oversee the procedure and ensure your exchange goes safely.'

Jo fell back in her seat, catching a glimpse of the iridescent glow of the northern lights over Greenland. Something that must have seemed magical to ancient people, but was explained by science now. Who's to say she wasn't experiencing the same thing? Perhaps one day travelling through time and space would be something you could do through your local travel agent? Or was any of this even real? Not for the first time she had to wonder if she was passed out on the kitchen floor, and this was all part of some weird trick of the brain.

Maybe she'd had a stroke? A brain haemorrhage? She was dead and instead of seeing her life flash before her eyes, she was seeing a life that could have been?

But her plane seat felt real, the wine she was drinking was definitely real, and she could smell the body odour of a businessman in a suit from two rows away. If this was a hallucination, it was a bloody good one.

'Let me get this clear in my head,' Jo said. 'We land in three hours, we hire a car, we bomb it to Glastonbury with no tickets, no passes, no contacts, and we not only have to gatecrash the world's biggest festival, we also have to somehow be on stage in the middle of the most coveted slot in music today, one currently taken by my mortal enemy, and it's dark and we're wearing sunglasses.'

'Yes.' Aaronovitch frowned. 'Er, what?'

'Let's do it.'

HUSH

Yohanna could feel the Earth moving beneath her. Her back was to the ground, and she imagined herself clinging on to the planet as it hurtled through the universe.

She'd got into meditation in her late teens. A dance teacher had introduced her to the Alexander technique, Yoga and meditation. Yohanna had got into the habit of finding time every morning and at the end of the day. It was her way of putting the world to one side, if only for a short time. She slept better and her mind was clearer.

It was a habit that she'd let slip these past few days. Not having an actual body, and finding herself inhabiting someone else's, would put a crimp in anyone's weekly routine. But she took the time now. Allowing herself to breathe naturally, she focused on her body's movement, trying to keep her mind in the moment.

'I say, Madame Federica.' Aaronovitch's voice broke the silence. 'I do believe she's still with us.'

Yohanna opened her eyes to find Aaronovitch, Federica and a cow all looking down at her with concern.

'Yohanna, darling, are you okay?' Federica asked, offering her a hand. Yohanna was too exhausted to take it.

'Am I going home?' she asked, her voice dry and cracked.

'Soon,' Federica said. 'We've found the convergence, but...'

'There's a slight problem,' Aaronovitch interrupted, 'but I'm on the case.'

'Then bah-luddy get on with it,' Federica said. 'And take this cow with you.'

The sky was lavender, streaked with pink. The sun was setting. They didn't have much time left.

Aaronovitch had left the gate open when they had gone chasing after Yohanna and the cows, and the remainder of the herd had elected to explore the field next door. They were drawn to the skeletal structure of the Pyramid Stage, now a permanent landmark in the farm's fields, and gathered beneath it like four-legged lactating druids.

'I keep dreaming.' Yohanna's voice was little more than a whisper. 'I keep seeing my Mum.'

Federica gently squeezed Yohanna's hand. 'Your mother?' Then she added, to keep Yohanna talking. 'How much do you remember of her?'

'Not much,' Yohanna said. 'Just bits of memories. I wish...' Her head lolled over to one side, but Federica gently patted her cheek.

'What? What do you wish?'

'Don't... Don't go into the tunnel.'

'Tunnel? What tunnel?'

But Yohanna was unconscious again.

A howl of pain came from across the field. Federica looked for Aaronovitch, but he was lost amongst the cows. Though his voice could be heard loud and clear, 'I think I've broken my bloody foot!' he cried. 'Which one of you dozy cows trod on my foot? Madame Federica. Help!'

THE IMPOSSIBLE DREAM

Jo had forgotten just how much she missed clouds. The bright blue sunshine of California had a lot going for it, but it simply couldn't compete with England's ever-changing canopy. As she drove their hire car down the A303 she took a moment to enjoy the sun dashing between pillows of grey-bottomed nimbus, its bright beam swooping over meadows, showing them the way to Glastonbury.

They had made excellent progress, landing at Heathrow without incident and picking up the cherry red Nissan Micra that Sarah had arranged for them with such ease that the pessimistic part of Jo's mind half-expected it to fall apart like a clown car. But it defied her worst expectations and resolutely stayed in one piece as they bombed down the motorway. Jo didn't dare say it out loud, but they were actually going to get there with time to spare, and it was such a stupid, outlandish, impossible idea that it might just work.

It started to pelt down, the sky darkened and flickered with silent lightning.

'The weather gods are less than pleased with our progress,' Aaronovitch said, peering over a map from the passenger seat.

'It's Glasto' weekend in midsummer,' Jo replied. 'Torrential rain and mudslides are all part of the fun.'

THEY HEARD the Glastonbury festival before they saw it. The muffled *oomph-oomph-oomph* of bass drums combined with the white noise of hundreds of thousands of people who had collectively left planet Earth for an extended weekend to have a good time. The rain took a brief break as they parked, and the sun made a cameo appearance. Jo wore her guitar over her back and they followed the signs to the VIP entrance. As they walked over a rise they found themselves looking into the vast Glastonbury bowl.

Countless tents of every hue were arrayed on the slopes of the rain-drenched basin. Moving between them were ant-like festival-goers. Banners and flags swayed in the breeze, the regimental colours of the gay community, CND, vegetarians, vegans, lovers of peace and music. A city of chaos and harmony that existed only for a brief shining moment, like a rainbow Brigadoon.

'Oh, it's beautiful,' Jo gasped. 'Look at it.'

'That's pretty damn awesome,' Rand said.

'I hope they have a lavvy,' Aaronovitch said, then added by way of explanation, 'I've a bladder the size of a walnut.'

Jo gave him her best withering glare, before turning back to Rand. 'How do we get in?'

'VIP entrance,' Rand grinned. 'My manager got us three VIP passes. We just need to check in at security and we're good. Nothing to worry about.'

'YOUR NAME'S NOT DOWN,' the security guard at the VIP entrance told them. 'Sorry, can't let you in.'

Now it was Rand's turn to be on the receiving end of one of Jo's withering glares.

'Check again,' Rand insisted, reaching for the list. But the security dude snatched it out of reach. The dude had been born in a hi-viz vest, and he hid behind a scruffy beard and misted glasses that sat askew on his nose.

'Check again, you say?' The dude's voice was well-marinated in skepticism, thanks to a long career fending off every kind of chancer, blagger and ligger. He'd heard every excuse, from *my daughter's in the band*, to *I'm having a baby*, to *please let me in, I'm on fire*. He'd turned them all away.

He glanced down at his list again for all of two seconds. 'Nope. Sorry. Goodbye.'

They were so close, Jo could almost scream. They had arrived at the festival's perimeter fence steaming, exhausted and sweating, and now the rain was picking up again.

'Please,' she begged the dude. 'We've come so far.'

'Everyone has,' the dude said. 'This place is a long way from anywhere.'

'You do know this guy's a major Hollywood star?' Jo gestured to Rand.

'At the risk of repeating myself,' the dude said, repeating himself. 'No one gets in unless—'

'Unless they're on your list, yeah, right, thanks,' Jo muttered. 'Bloody jobsworth.'

'Are you familiar with the work of the beat music combo Khufu?' Aaronovitch said, leaning into the conversation.

The dude acknowledged this interloper through his foggy specs. 'Of course.'

'And you know their masterwork, *The Pharaohs of Albion*?'

'What of it?'

'His father was the drummer and writer of *Spiritual Satellite*.'

'Really?' The dude's mask fell and, for a moment, he looked genuinely impressed.

'So,' Aaronovitch ventured. 'How about you—?'

'Don't care, he's not coming in.'

Jo clenched her fists and was pondering whether punching this obnoxious tit right in the schnozz would do more harm than good, when another voice joined the conversation.

'Your Dad was Cygnus Macbeth?' A woman in a hi-viz vest loomed behind her bespectacled colleague, and the dude began to shift nervously.

'Yeah,' Rand said. 'Real name was—'

'Keith McManus. Yes, I'm a bit of a fan, actually.' The woman was a glorious example of what happened to punks when they reached late middle-age. Her hair was pink, though the roots were grey, she had a spectacular tattoo of a dragon climbing up her neck, and more rings on her fingers than a jeweller's window. But her confident stance suggested she took no crap from anyone.

'That album was bloody awful,' she said, making Jo's heart sink. 'But *Spiritual Satellite*... that really opened my third eye.'

'Though it does require a children's choir, a theramin, and a gong to really capture its majesty,' Jo quoted, making Rand smile.

The woman nodded in approval and turned to her colleague. 'They're not on the list?'

'Nope.'

'You got Joseph's update this morning? Did you check that?'

The dude hesitated. 'Joseph's...?'

The woman rolled her eyes and reached into her coat, pulling out a sheet of paper. 'This is what happens when you miss briefings, Paul.'

Paul checked the list. 'Oh... Rand McManus, Yohanna, and Aaronovitch Eades. Yes, uh, here you are.' Meekly, he ticked their names off the list and handed them a bright pink VIP wristband and a map of the site each. 'Sorry.'

The woman watched the trio rush into the festival. 'Turn anyone else away?' she asked Paul.

'One or two.'

'Think they might have been on the list?'

'Might've been.'

'You know this is why you'll never get a girlfriend, don't you?'

Paul shrugged. 'Sorry, Mum.'

. . .

THEY STEPPED INTO ANOTHER WORLD.

The VIP area was a small village hunkered behind the Pyramid Stage. TV satellite trucks spilled heavy cables that snaked through the mud and under plastic duckboards. Catering trucks filled the air with the scent of frying bacon and veggie alternatives. Cabins played host to hair and make-up experts, everyone was wearing colourful boots, and every other person was famous or looked like they should be, and beyond all this was a maze of luxury yurts that made Jo think of an ancient Roman encampment.

The very air tingled with energy. People were either buzzing as they came offstage, or wrestling with pent-up energy before they went on. Technicians scurried about keeping everything running, and journalists wandered the maze with furry microphones and camera operators in tow, looking for people to interview. All this activity was taking place in the ever-present background noise of cheers of the unseen crowd, and the incredible clamour of the bands onstage.

Jo had waited her whole life to be here, and couldn't believe she'd got here with so much time to spare. But at the same time she couldn't allow herself to enjoy it. She was on an impossible mission.

'I think I've just died and gone to heaven,' Rand said as they walked past a purple double-decker bus converted into a dubious looking mobile health spa. The windows were blacked out and Turkish curtains hung down over the door. As they spoke, deep groans of pleasure came from within.

'Knotty Massage?' Aaronovitch squinted as he read a hand-painted sign on the side of the bus.

'Okay, focus. What do we do now?' Jo asked, unfolding the map.

Mmm. Yes.

'I'll see if I can find Michael Eavis,' Rand said. 'He and Dad were buddies. Maybe he can help us? Give you a five minute slot or something?'

That's the spot.

'You think he'd do that?'

Oh, god, that's good.

'Can't hurt to ask,' Rand said.

Oh, that's fantastic.

'Can you keep it down in there?' Jo yelled at the bus. 'We're trying to have a conversation.'

'To begin with, I shall need to find a gents' loo as I am in desperate need of a pee,' Aaronovitch said. 'Then, I shall reconnoitre the stage area.'

'Go now, before you wet yourself,' Jo said. 'Meet us here in thirty minutes. We'll figure out what our plan is and take it from there.'

'Y'know what?' Rand pulled a face. 'I gotta go, too.'

'Fine.' Jo rolled her eyes. 'Go. God, it's like a school field trip with you pair.'

'I spied a row of those portable loos in this direction,' Aaronovitch said, leading the way. 'Little blue boxes, that, in honour of our time-travelling escapades, I've christened the Turdis.'

Rand was blank-faced.

'Tardis? Turdis?' Aaronovitch persisted. *'Doctor Who?'*

'Who?'

'Never mind.'

The two men hurried away, leaving Jo to study the map.

Oh, yeah, that's great...

The masseuse was at it again, so Jo wandered away from the bus, still engrossed in the map.

'Keep it together lads, cool your balls, play like you're playing for your mothers and you'll knock 'em dead.' A familiar voice caused the hair on Jo's arms to stand on end. She peered over the top of the map to see Lawrie shepherding a trio of young men through the mud.

'What stage we on, Lawrie?' one asked, his voice barely broken.

'Told ya,' Lawrie snapped. 'Acoustic. Why don't you listen?'

'You said we'd be on the NME,' another band member protested, his Adam's apple bobbing.

'Yeah, well, you can't always get what you want, can you, sunshine?'

Jo resisted the temptation to call out to him and let him know she'd made it. But, for all she knew, he'd have her thrown out, so she backed into the shadow of a yurt. Then she saw something that sent a cold chill down her spine.

A man in a lime green suit, pink tie and matching Hunter wellies.

Ricardo, Diemond's personal assistant, was carrying a tiny Chihuahua close to his chest, and heading straight in her direction.

Jo ducked inside the yurt.

It took a moment for her eyes to adjust to the gloom, and when they did, she wondered if she'd crossed over into yet another parallel universe. The inside of the yurt was dominated by a four-poster bed with rich purple velvet sheets. It was flanked by yucca plants and vases bursting with brightly coloured orchids. A Persian rug lay at the side of the bed, and a chandelier hung from the domed ceiling. An opened bottle of Moët and Chandon rested in an ice bucket with a single glass awaiting its owner, and there was even a walk-in wardrobe, lined with furs, feathers, leathers and lace.

Jo took her guitar off her back and rested it on the bed. Rotating her arms and flexing her shoulders, she wondered if she could blag a massage herself. She flopped onto a mahogany Ottoman at the foot of the bed and tried to rub her own shoulder blades.

As she sat, something prodded into her buttock. She reached round to her jeans' back pocket and took out a small sachet.

Aaronovitch's colonic cleanse. The one he had given to her on Venice Beach. She smiled, glad to have dodged that particular bullet. She was about to toss it away, when she saw something that made her freeze.

Next to her, draped across the Ottoman like something from a taxidermist's nightmare, was a white peroxide wig. One she'd seen before in a music video. With a creeping sense of horror, Jo knew whose yurt this was. She had to get out of here, and she had to get out of here right now. Tucking the colonic cleanse back in her pocket she got to her feet.

'You!'

Jo jumped at the sound of the voice to find Diemond looming in the yurt's entrance, pointing an accusing finger at her. 'Ah, yes, sorry,'

Jo said. 'Got a bit lost. Is this... is this the ladies' loos? Thought they looked a bit posh.'

'Intruder! Call the police.' Diemond hollered. 'Security!'

'No, no, please. I didn't mean to—'

'Security! Help! Fire!'

Jo looked for somewhere to run, but there was only one way in or out, so she simply tried to barge past Diemond, but Ricardo appeared, wielding the snarling Chihuahua like a weapon. Jo ducked under them, just as a platoon of muscle-bound security guards arrived.

'Saboteur.' Diemond grabbed Jo by the arm and swung her towards the guards who had little choice but to hold her.

'No, let go, you can't do this,' Jo protested. 'This is just a mistake.'

'It's not enough that you sabotaged your own after-party, but you have to sabotage my show, too?'

'No.'

Others arrived, important-looking people in suits, incongruous in their wellies.

'I want this made perfectly clear,' Diemond declared. 'I will not be going on stage so long as that girl is here. She's here to poison me. Have her removed immediately.'

That was it for the suits. Their investment was in Diemond and they would protect it at all costs.

'Get her out of here,' one of the suits said. 'Off-site, and she doesn't get back in again. Understand?'

'Yessir,' the security guards acknowledged, dragging Jo away.

'No, please don't do this, I just want to get home, I just want to see my daughter again, please no.' Jo wriggled free of their grip and fell face first into the mud. One of the guards pinned her down and cold water seeped into her clothes. As she was hauled to her feet, she saw that more people had gathered around her. Famous faces, sneering faces, all glaring in contempt at this interloper. All except one.

'Lawrie. Please, help me. Tell them it was a mistake.' Lawrie, to his credit, broke through the onlookers, but was shoved back by one of the guards. 'Please,' Jo cried as she was dragged with impressive speed past the VIP entrance and an astonished Paul and his punk Mum. 'I'm a guest of Rand McManus, tell Rand, please. Lawrie, tell them.'

Jo was frogmarched away from the festival entrance and hurled to the ground, exiled and alone.

TUNNEL OF LOVE

'Oi, Yohanna. Psst!'

Jo was walking around the perimeter fence of the festival, desperate to get in. It was mostly chain-link with vicious-looking barbed wire, well over eight feet high and in clear view of the patrolling security guards. It was impregnable, unless you were an Olympic high jumper who didn't mind hard landings.

That's when she heard Lawrie calling to her. He had left the VIP area and ventured into the camping area. He beckoned to her from the festival side of the fence, and Jo ran to him.

'Lawrie, please, you've got to tell them it was just a mistake,' Jo pleaded.

'Sorry, girl, you're definitely persona non grata over here. No chance.'

'I have to get in there, I have to get home.'

'Yeah, yeah, look, take this.' Lawrie fed a folded envelope through the chain-link fence.

Jo turned it over. There was a message written in Lawrie's messy handwriting:

.   .   .

YORKIE - I DID you a favour once, now do one for me and let this girl in for a fair price. Lawrie.

'WHAT'S THIS?' Jo asked.

'Head towards the north fence, the furthest point from the main festival, it's bloody miles away, but you'll find a fella called Yorkie, fancies himself as a white Rasta. Can't miss him. Just ask for the cat in the Bob Marley hat. Give him this, and he'll get you in.'

'And if he doesn't?'

'Tell him I'll tell all his hippy mates that his real name is Benjamin Shelley-Yorke and that his Dad's a Tory MP.'

'That should do it,' Jo said, opening the envelope to find five grubby ten pound notes inside, 'Oh, Lawrie, thank you.'

'Oh, shut up. I'm not doing it for you, I'm doing it to get back at her.'

'Diemond?'

'Who else?'

'Any chance you might un-quit and take me back on?'

'Do I get all rights to your music in perpetuity throughout the universe?'

'Definitely not.'

'That's my girl, you're learning. Now go on, get a move on.'

'Lawrie, one more thing.'

'Who are you? Bloody Columbo?'

'My guitar, I left it in Diemond's yurt. I need someone to get it for me and keep it safe.'

'If you think I'm going anywhere near that dragon's lair, you've got another thing coming.'

'Then ask Rand, Aaronovitch, someone, please.'

'I'll see what I can do. Now go.'

JO FOUND herself slogging uphill through sticky mud, passing security who patrolled the outer perimeter fence like extras from *Escape to*

Victory. Sweat crawled down her back and the rain decided to take it up a notch, spraying her from behind and making the backs of her knees so wet she thought they might never get dry again.

Jo stooped and leaned on the tall chain-link fence to catch her breath. She looked through the fence to see the multi-coloured collage of the countless tents, miles away from the main stages, all crammed together in a fug of body odour, mud-stained clothes flapping on makeshift washing lines in the breeze, and trench foot. Although that could be attributed to a pile of abandoned shoes, bundled as tall as a full-grown adult like some pyre worshipping the God Nike. Portable stereos played a cacophonous mixture of rock, rave and rap, and every third tent there was someone with a guitar singing earnestly. It made Jo think of refugee camps, only self-inflicted. Camping no longer held any allure for Jo, camping with a quarter of a million people washing their socks and listening to the Prodigy, even less so.

Something caught her eye. Five people crawled out of a bright orange two-person tent, one after another in single file. Jo squinted as another six people came out in quick succession.

'What the...' Jo started counting, 'Fourteen, fifteen, sixteen, seventeen...?' Her brain started to hurt.

The sickly-sweet smell of marijuana permeating the air hit her nose. She looked down the outer perimeter of the fence. There was no mistaking it. On the outside of the fence sat Yorkie. He wore a purple tie-dye T-shirt with a CND logo, his Afro hair nestled under a tall hat with Jamaican colours. He sat legs akimbo on a sleeping bag and was as white as Bing Crosby.

'Yorkie?' Jo puffed as she approached him.

'Who's asking?' His accent was Mancunian, tinged with a splash of cod-Jamaican, and she knew their conversation would, at some point, inevitably employ the phrase '*Mad for it!*'

'I'm a friend of Lawrie Grant.' She started to hand him the envelope with Lawrie's note, but he recoiled.

'Whoa, back off darlin'. How do I know that's not a summons or summat?'

'Just read the note, please.' Jo deposited the envelope in his lap.

Yorkie pulled away, defiantly not touching it with his hands, 'Are you wearing a wire? This is entrapment. You can't prove nothin'.'

'Don't be ridiculous, I'm not wearing a wire.'

'Take your top off and prove it,' he cackled lecherously.

Jo narrowed her eyes, wondering if a swift kick in the balls was in order. Instead, she played her trump card, and raised her voice to a *Mum-knows-best* threat level. 'Benjamin Shelley-Yorke, read the note and help me out, or Lawrie will tell everyone he knows that your Dad's a Tory MP and you're nothing but a gap year trustafarian narc.'

Yorkie's head darted left and right, desperately hoping no one could hear her. 'Shut up, right. No one calls me that.' The Jamaican evaporated from his accent, replaced with something closer to the home counties.

'Read the note, Benjamin.'

'All right, all right. Fuck's sake.' He snatched up the envelope and read Lawrie's message. 'You're a mate of Lawrie's?'

'We're blood,' she told Yorkie. 'Piss me off and you piss him off.'

'How is the old bastard, he all right?'

'He'll be a lot happier when you tell me how you can get me inside and I tell him how co-operative you've been.'

'Yeah, sure he will.' Yorkie scrunched up the note and tossed it to one side. 'Two hundred.'

'What? Pounds?'

'No, fucking rupees. Yes, pounds.'

'I've got fifty,' Jo said.

'Fifty? You're fuckin' jokin', right?'

'Benjamin,' Jo bellowed.

'All right, all right, Jesus, give it here.' He beckoned to Jo and she handed him the tenners. He licked his thumb, and counted them off, holding them up to the light.

'Don't push your luck,' Jo warned him. 'So, how does this work?'

'You have to go between my legs,' Yorkie grinned.

'What?'

He lifted the sleeping bag he was sitting on, revealing a small hole dug at a steep angle into the ground.

'A tunnel?' Jo turned her head to look into it. 'Where does it come —?' Jo didn't have to finish her question.

'Come out? That tent there.' Yorkie nodded to the bright orange two-person tent inside the fence. In his excitement, the Manc accent returned. 'Got here four days early, one ticket for meself, dug me a hole, and charge desperate wankers two hundred quid a time. I've made ten grand just today. Mad for it!'

And there it was.

Yorkie shuffled to one side and held the sleeping bag entrance open for Jo, 'Keep your elbows tucked in, right? Breathe in and wiggle like a snake. Nowt to it.'

Jo got to her knees and got a better look. It was narrow, dark, muddy and with at least an inch of cold, brown rainwater waiting for her at the bottom. 'In for a penny,' she muttered, before squirming into the darkness.

Immediately, she regretted it. Her belly was wet, her jeans were filling with water, great clumps of damp mud were attaching themselves to her hair, and the air became hot and stifling. At first, she could only move by nudging herself forward on her elbows. When she was about halfway through she could push with her feet, too.

'Keep wiggling,' Yorkie called after her.

Jo wanted to swear back at him, but she could hardly breathe.

'*Don't go into the tunnel,*' a voice said as though it was right next to her, sending the hairs on her neck standing on end. A girl's voice. It sounded a bit like Ellie. Or was it Yohanna?

'Did you say something?' Jo called back, but Yorkie didn't answer. The heat became oppressive, she could hardly breathe, but she kept shuffling forwards. *Don't panic, don't panic.* The tunnel began to rise with a sharp gradient, and she could see weak daylight through the gauze of the orange canvas of a tent. She tried to claw herself up. As she did a clump of earth broke away and rolled down towards her. Jo tried to move forward but was now stuck.

'I've got one. I've got one! North perimeter, section five.' A two-way radio. Jo froze.

'Oh shit,' said Yorkie. Jo tried to listen over her heavy breath. Something was kicking off behind her. She heard yelling, voices getting further away. Jo felt her heart pounding against the tunnel floor as she waited for the commotion to subside.

She had to get out of here. Jo looked up to the light. She was inches from getting herself out of this hellhole. With one last effort she pulled with all her might. Someone grabbed her ankles.

She was yanked backwards through the mud, hands gripping her legs, then grabbing her jeans by the waist. Covered head-to-toe in liquid earth, Jo rolled over on the grass to find half a dozen festival security guards grinning down at her.

'Time to go home, darlin',' one of them said, as the others gripped her by the arms and legs.

As she screamed, swore and thrashed in their grip, she could see Yorkie being handcuffed and bundled into a police van. Another van waited for her, though not a police one.

'Just get her off the site, Barry,' one of the guards said. 'Far away enough, so she can't walk back. Usual drill, all right.'

Jo's yelling was frantic now, nonsensical and hysterical. They hauled her into the back of the van and locked the door shut, taking any hope of her getting home with it.

FADING FAST

Aronovitch hopped on his unbroken foot with a dowsing rod in his hands. It twitched and he moved in little circles as the cows closed in on them. Federica cradled Yohanna in her arms.

'The sun is setting,' Federica said. 'How long will this take?'

'You can't rush this,' Aaronovitch said as he was nudged by one of the cows.

Federica had never been scared of cows before. To her, they had always been docile animals that she rushed by in her car, but now that she was face-to-snout with them she could better appreciate their size and heft. She held Yohanna tighter as the creatures stomped the mud around them.

'Get a move on,' Federica cried. 'I do not want to go by being squashed by a cow.'

'Frighten them off or something,' Aaronovitch said, keeping his eyes on his dowsing rod.

'Have you seen the size of them?' Federica snapped. 'How do you frighten a cow, anyway?' Yohanna mumbled something, and Federica patted her hand. 'It's okay, darling, you'll be home soon.'

Yohanna shook her head and beckoned Federica to lean in closer. 'Google it,' she whispered.

Federica froze for a second. 'Actually, that's not a bad idea.' She shifted around, resting Yohanna's head in her lap, and fished out her phone. 'How... do... you... scare... a... cow?' she typed, then raised an eyebrow. 'Nearly three million results. I'm impressed.'

'What does it say?' Aaronovitch was now boxed-in by a trio of mean-looking heifers.

'Hold on.' Federica thumbed through a series of funny videos about cows and found a blog that she thought might help her. 'It says I should make a lot of noise and make myself big.'

'Do it.'

'I'm a tiny little Italian lady. How am I supposed to make myself big?'

'You scare the willies out of me, woman. I'm sure the cows will have a similar reaction.'

'Cheeky bastard,' Federica muttered, gently laying Yohanna's head on the ground. She stood, made a star shape and yelled, 'RAH!' at the top of her voice.

The cows remained in place, unimpressed and drooling.

'What else does it say?' Aaronovitch was just a voice now, lost in the crowd of cows.

Federica thumbed her phone, 'Oh,' she said.

'What?'

'It says... No, I can't do this.'

'What?'

'It says I should punch them on the nose. That's cruel, surely?'

'Not if it's a life or death situation,' Aaronovitch yelled. 'I can't move my arms. I'm hemmed in. You'll have to... Ow! My other foot!'

Federica rolled up her sleeve, made a fist, gritted her teeth and smacked the nearest cow with a roundhouse right on the snout, accompanying it with a war cry designed to curdle milk.

The punched cow shook its head and retreated, barging the other cows out of the way and running to safety.

'Ha!' Federica clapped her hands, and turned to the other cows. 'Right, anyone else want some?'

The cows, deciding that discretion was the better part of valour, casually dispersed, later telling themselves that they could have taken the old lady, but they abhorred violence and were above that sort of thing.

'Nice work,' Aaronovitch said. Federica turned to help him to his feet with a series of pained hisses. 'My ballroom dancing days are behind me.' He hobbled to a spot underneath the apex of the Pyramid Stage with his dowsing rod. 'Ah.'

'What? You've found it?'

Aaronovitch didn't answer, but fished the prism out of his pocket and put it to his eye. He winced, cried out in pain, and fell back onto the ground.

'You've found it?'

'Yes.' Aaronovitch blinked his eyes shut and opened them again. 'I say, that's rather bright.' He waved Federica over. 'Bring the girl.'

Yohanna lay still, barely breathing. Federica took her arms and dragged her over to where Aaronovitch sat.

'What do we do now?' Federica asked.

'She needs to step through.'

'Step through? She's unconscious.'

'Get her on her feet,' Aaronovitch suggested, while remaining on his backside.

'How about you get off your lazy arse and help me?' Federica suggested.

'I'm walking wounded. Metatarsal fracture.' Aaronovitch tried moving his leg, wincing somewhat theatrically. 'I fear I shall need to be stretchered off this field when we are done.'

'Not if I bury you in it first,' Federica said, ready for another round of fisticuffs. Something caught her eye. A silhouette appearing over a rise against the backdrop of a glowing sunset. Whoever it was, they were running towards Federica, Aaronovitch and Yohanna.

'Stop!' a voice cried. 'That's my Mum!'

THE BENDS

Jo and her fellow festival deportees were deposited on a scrubland roundabout at a motorway service station called Solstice Park. The other vagabonds, druggies, drunks and dead-eyed festival poopers wandered zombie-like through the shining rain and glistening puddles towards the service station. Unsure what to do next, Jo followed, but they were turned away by the security staff who pointed at a sign especially made for the Glastonbury weekend:

PLEASE WAIT TO BE SEATED, *if you have washed in the last four days.*

IT HAD TAKEN an hour to get here, and there were a little more than two hours before she needed to be on stage. She had no money, no phone, no transport and after her scuffle with the guards she was caked with mud.

'Excuse me, can you spare some change for the phone, please? I just need to make a call and...'

The looks of disgust people gave her were not dissimilar to the looks she might have given someone if they approached her covered in filth, arms outstretched, pleading for change with an elaborate sob story. Jo loitered by the services' entrance, intercepting people as they left, but they all took long detours to avoid her, and now the service station security staff were taking a specific interest in her.

'No begging,' one of them said. 'Bugger off, or I call the police.'

'Please, I just need to make one call—'

'Seriously, sod off. Last warning.'

JO FOUND herself staring across the car park wondering if she could steal a car. She soon realised she hadn't the first bloody clue how to do it. She'd seen plenty of movies where people would yank away a section of the car's dashboard, touch a couple of bare wires together, and drive off into the sunset. But she suspected it was a bit more complicated than that.

Screw it. She would have to hitchhike and hope that the good Samaritan/serial killer ratio of drivers on the A303 was in her favour. Gritting her teeth, she crossed the roundabout where she'd first been dumped and headed for the motorway. At that moment, a truck drove by, its tyres digging into a puddle, sending a sine wave of grey water laced with grit slapping into her face.

To say that the language that spewed forth from her mouth was X-rated would be an understatement. There were Quentin Tarantino movies that didn't have this many F-bombs, C-bombs and *muddyfunsters* in their entire running time, let alone the full minute and a half that Jo let rip for. Thankfully, the only creatures in earshot were a pair of pigeons, and a startled rabbit.

Jo was snapped out of her anger by the *ptt-tish* of the truck's airbrakes. The truck had stopped. Maybe he was going to apologise? Offer her a lift? At the very least she could vent her anger at him, though she doubted she had the time.

Wiping away the water from her face, she looked over to the petrol station forecourt to see the driver of the truck clamber down from his cab to start filling his truck with diesel.

A truck that was towing a long trailer loaded with ten familiar-looking blue portable loos. They were the same ones that she'd seen at the festival. What had Ronnie called them? The Turdis?

All thoughts of apologies and vengeance gone, Jo ran, squishing like a wet mop, dashing across the forecourt, leaping up the cab's steps and daring to look inside for any clue that might confirm where the driver was headed. On the passenger seat was a clipboard with delivery paperwork. She framed her hands around her eyes for a closer look and saw a Glastonbury festival site pass. She yelped with delight.

Without a moment's hesitation, she leapt off the cab, ran to the back of the trailer and clambered up among the loos. They were packed tight, but the rearmost loo's door was facing out with just enough room for Jo to wedge the door open and squeeze herself inside.

She cackled at her ingenuity as she sat on the plastic throne. Soon this Trojan Horse would deliver her back to Glastonbury in plenty of time for her to get on stage.

Jo heard the driver open his cabin door. The trailer gently rocked as he got in and started the engine. It lurched forward at great speed. This guy was clearly in a hurry, and she braced herself for a few bumps in the road. But it was the first roundabout, the one that sent her slamming face-first into the side of the plastic loo's wall, making her see stars, that gave her some idea of the intensity of the hellish journey ahead of her.

ALL ALONG THE A303, Jo gripped the loo roll holder, hanging on for dear life as the portable loos rattled around her, their flimsy plastic walls threatening to break apart. The motorway was one thing, the bumpy fields approaching the festival were something else. This was like stepping into the ring with a wrestler as she was slammed against the inner walls again and again and again. There was no time to recover between blows, barely a heartbeat to take a breath or right herself as she was bounced around the inside of the Turdis like salt in a shaker. She had to endure face-plant after face-plant in silence, as screaming for help would only get her ejected once more.

Eventually, mercifully, it stopped.

Jo could hear the driver chatting with someone as the engine kept running. In the distance she could hear the faint thud of a bassline. She was on the outer perimeter of the festival.

'Straight on? Okay, mate. Ta,' the muffled voice of the driver said as he stepped on the gas. They were moving again, much slower now, thank God, allowing Jo to at least compose herself and prepare to jump out before she could be discovered.

She pushed on the door. It wouldn't budge. Jo tried again and again, pushing and pulling, but it remained jammed. She sat on the toilet and inspected it. Something was wrong. Somehow, in her bruising voyage, Jo must have hit it in a way that it was stuck fast. Gripping the door handle with both hands, and pressing her feet against the walls, she pulled harder.

The handle broke off.

'Shit,' she said as she tossed it in the Turdis as the truck came to another standstill.

Jo was distracted by a loud mechanical noise outside, but she did her best to ignore it as she tried to figure out what to do next. There was nothing else for it. She would have to kick the door down. It was only plastic. How hard could it be? She raised her right leg just as the whole loo lurched and tipped over, sending her flying into the door. Jo groaned as she tried to pick herself up, but the loo began to sway.

The mechanical noise was the trailer's loading ramp, the swaying was the loo being lowered onto a trolley.

Jo's momentum sent the trolley and Turdis tumbling off the rear of the trailer, crashing onto the ground. The door broke open, Jo tumbled across the mud, coming to a stop in a pool of blue liquid leaking from a row of faulty portable loos awaiting collection.

She'd landed in a maintenance area somewhere backstage in the festival. In amongst this mud bath and effluent, the thud of the music and roar of the crowd made her heart swell. She was back.

Jo gave a thumbs-up to the astonished truck driver. 'A little sharp on some of the bends, there, but I'm happy to tell you that you've passed your test.'

Before he could reply, Jo ran, disappearing into the maze of cabins, loos and trucks, like a street urchin who had stolen an apple. She now blended in with the other mud-caked revellers. The perfect disguise for now. The sun was low on the horizon and she had to get on stage. But first, and more important than any of that, she had to find a working shower.

BRAIN DAMAGE

Ellie's lungs burned as she ran full-pelt across the field towards the body of her mother.

Oh god, she's dead, she's dead.

Ellie pushed the thought away as she approached her Mum, who was lying under the steel framework of the festival's Pyramid Stage. That peculiar man was sitting down and Federica was standing over her body, all watched by an apprehensive-looking herd of cows nearby.

Please don't be dead, don't let me be too late, I'll never forgive myself.

Federica had told Ellie they were heading for the town, and Dad was driving them there as fast as he could, but when Ellie thought of Glastonbury and ley lines, she thought of the festival and insisted that they try the home of the festival, Worthy Farm, first.

What she hadn't realised was how enormous the place was. Dad had parked miles away and wanted to do everything by the book, calling the police and getting permission from the owners to go onto the land. Ellie just got out of the car and ran. Federica had spoken of ley lines, so Ellie bought a map from an esoteric gift shop and saw that most of the lines converged in this field. They had to be here.

And she was right.

She might also be too late.

Federica backed away as Ellie fell to her knees by her mother. 'Mum, Mum. Wake up.' Ellie shook her mum, leaning close to her mouth and relieved to the point of tears that she could feel a faint breath brush against her skin. Ellie rested her head on her mother's chest. There was a heartbeat. Slow and distant, but it was there. In the hospital, she'd been at death's door, now she was somehow alive. She cradled Mum's head before turning to Federica. 'What have you done to her? How is she even still alive?'

Federica looked lost for words. She turned to the man, who remained sitting and appeared to be in some pain. He got to his feet with a series of groans, and approached Ellie with upraised palms as he hobbled, 'We need to get her on her feet,' he said. 'We have to—'

'Keep away from her,' Ellie said, and Aaronovitch backed away.

'We just need to move her a few feet over this way,' Aaronovitch said. 'And then—'

'Shut up, just shut up.' Ellie wriggled her phone out of her jeans pocket, keeping her eyes on Federica and Aaronovitch as she thumbed the screen and dialled. Something was wrong. She glanced down at the phone. No signal. *Shit*. She bluffed it out anyway. 'Dad? Dad, I've found her. In the field with the Pyramid Stage. Yeah, call the police, but get here as soon as you can. Yeah, I'm okay. Please be quick.'

'Ellie, please understand,' Federica said in a gentle voice. 'You have to believe that we are trying to help your mother.'

'Be quiet, don't say anything, you're all mental.'

A cow mooed and Federica turned on the herd, her fists clenched, 'And you lot can be quiet, unless you want me to thump you again.'

'Mental,' Ellie confirmed in a whisper to herself. How on Earth was she going to get Mum out of here?

'I'm just going to continue my measurements over here,' the man said, hobbling to a spot close, but not too close, to Ellie and her mum. He produced a Y-shaped stick and started twitching it in his hands, then held a prism to his eyes. Ellie caught him glancing at Federica and nodding. They were up to something.

'Come on, Mum.' Ellie got to her feet, taking a grip under her mother's arms and dragging her back in the direction she'd come.

'No, Ellie, please don't,' Federica said, taking a step towards her.

Ellie moved around to avoid her. Mum was bloody heavy, and this would be the slowest rescue of all time.

The sun dipped below the hills around them. The sky near the horizon was still a bright yellow, but it blended into oranges, purples and indigos the higher you looked up. It would be dark soon.

Ellie's detour took her closer to where Aaronovitch stood. That's when, in a day of strange events, something very strange indeed happened.

Ellie could only stare as a rainbow light began to emanate from her Mum's belly. It snaked through the air, piercing the very fabric of the universe and breaking a hole in it. An elliptical split opened up, as bright as day.

'Bloody hell,' the old man gasped. 'I was actually onto something.'

WILD THING

I f there was one thing that marked out an interloper at a festival like Glastonbury, it was the lack of a valid wristband. You could be covered head-to-toe in mud and chemical toilet effluent, and festivalgoers wouldn't give you so much as a second glance, but if you didn't have that day-glow bit of plastic dangling from your arm someone would be hollering for security without a moment's hesitation.

Jo was a bare-wristed fugitive, scurrying between luxury yurts, looking for Lawrie, Aaronovitch or Rand, or anyone who could help her. The clouds above broke, revealing a twilight sky streaked with the cotton candy pink of a summer sunset. She didn't have long now.

Jo headed back to the massage bus. She, Rand and Aaronovitch had promised that they would meet back there about three hours ago, and she had to hope that they would have enough faith in her to wait.

They didn't.

Jo sidled along the edge of the massage bus to peek around the corner. Just the usual bustle of roadies, crew, managers and artistes backstage at a festival. No sign of her friends.

'Oh yeah, that's great, baby.'

Someone in the massage bus was clearly having a good time.

'Man, I haven't been this relaxed since before *The Tonight Show*, y'know? *Oh, yeah, right there.* That was such a tense experience. *Damn, that's good.* I'm not sure I'm cut out for live TV. *Oh, boy.*'

THE CREATURE that burst into the massage bus would later go down in Glastonbury legend. Decades later, stories would be told around campfires of a crazed banshee that turned the masseuse's hair white at the very sight of her. Others claimed it was a woodwose, the wild and hairy beast of ancient myth that roamed the festival, howling in despair to ward off evil spirits. Some claimed it was a woman who travelled across universes to be with her daughter again, but that story was dismissed as crazy. To Rand, who had grown up on a steady diet of comics, it looked like the Swamp Thing. Until it spoke.

'Rand! What the fuck? You were supposed to wait for me.'

The masseuse screamed and jumped back in fright.

'Sorry, poppet, can we have five minutes?' Jo asked the petrified and oily-handed woman, who nodded and ran from the bus.

'Yohanna? Is that you?' Rand asked, sitting up on the massage bed, covering his genitals with a tiny towel. 'Where have you been?'

'Oh, just dragged through hell and back.' Jo was literally steaming as she closed in on Rand. 'While you've been getting a happy ending from Madame Palm, apparently.'

'No, it ain't like that. We figured you had a plan and that you'd tell us sooner or later what you wanted us to do. In the meantime, Rachel, the masseuse there, she offered me a freebie.'

'I bet she did,' Jo said. 'Where's Aaronovitch? And have you seen Lawrie with my guitar?'

'Aaronovitch's still scoping the stage,' Rand said. 'And I ain't seen Lawrie or your guitar. Sorry.'

'That means it can only be in one place,' Jo said, realising with dread what she had to do next. 'I need your help, Rand. I need you to face a dragon for me. Can you do that?'

. . .

IT'S SAID that Glastonbury festivalgoers have as many names for mud as the Inuit people have for snow. Jo had come to know many of them over the past few hours and was currently surrounded by a runny variant with a cobalt tinge known as 'Blue Thunder'. This was found wherever the blue sanitation liquid from the chemical toilets leaked onto the ground. Still caked with filth, Jo hunkered by a row of portable Turdis loos arrayed around the back of Diemond's yurt. These rested on raised pallets, but were succumbing to the pull of gravity as they slowly sank into the mud. Jo absent-mindedly picked at the plastic tape wrapped around one of the loos, the words 'Out Of Service: Do Not Use' printed in red letters repeatedly along its length.

'Ricardo. Where are my feathers?' Diemond barked, her voice cutting through the canvas of the luxury yurt. Ricardo's reply was merely a muffle from here, but clearly unsatisfactory. 'No, no, no! The Congo Peafowl, you dumbass. My god, I've shit turds with more vitality than you.'

One of Diemond's security team rounded the yurt. Jo ducked back. Dressed in black, with Ray-Bans and an earpiece, he moved in a slow orbit, scanning the perimeter like the Terminator. Jo watched him stroll out of sight. She reckoned she had about three minutes before he appeared again.

'Now, Rand, c'mon, *now*,' she whispered to herself.

'Rand. Darling!' Diemond whooped with joy. As planned, Rand was abusing his celebrity status to break through security for a pre-show visit and distract Diemond from Jo's incursion. 'How lovely to see you, but make it quick honey, I'm on in twenty.'

Jo dashed from the loos to the bottom of the yurt, where she encountered a dry, flaky variation of Glastonbury wet earth known as 'mud flaps'. Jo carefully hitched up the bottom of the yurt's canvas, and eased herself inside, letting the mud flake over her as she did. She shuffled into position in the shadows behind the bed. Jo peered over the bedstead and was able to see Rand cowering before Diemond, who wore a glittery, scarlet corset trimmed in gold, black suspenders and fishnet stockings all piled on four-inch heels. She looked like a goth Moulin Rouge dancer, though she was lacking a head-dress and her hair was tied back tight, making her eyebrows look permanently startled.

'I just wanted to wish you the best for the show.' Rand sounded awkward, almost shy. For an actor, he wasn't very good at lying, but all he had to do was keep Diemond occupied while Jo retrieved her guitar. 'I know we've had our differences in the past, but I know how important this is to you.'

'If you can call a pissy field full of mud people *important*? Sure, whatever,' Diemond said. 'Ricardo! Feathers. Head-dress. C'mon.'

The guitar was still on the bed, but Ricardo was scurrying about preparing a head-dress that looked like a high speed collision between Foghorn Leghorn and the NBC peacock. Diemond had her back to Jo and the bed, but Ricardo only had to look up to see her. Jo held her breath. She had to time this perfectly.

Rand's *aw-shucks* routine went up a gear. He was starting to sound like Jimmy Stewart. 'Well, gee, I know you've worked real hard to get here anyways, and I think it's real neat.'

'Neat?' Diemond pulled a face and snorted. 'What are you, Clark Kent? *Ricardo! Feathers. Jesus Wept.*'

Ricardo hurried to Diemond's side with the feathers. His back was to Jo. Her moment had come. A mud-caked ninja, she lunged forward, silently took the guitar, and slipped under the bed in one graceful movement.

Oblivious, Diemond continued to abuse Ricardo. 'Were you repeatedly dropped on your head as a child? These are not the Congo Peafowl. What the fuck am I paying you for? Remind me again? Your charm? Your wit? Do I get a refund?'

Ricardo bowed his head, backed away and returned to the clothes rack, snapping through clothes hangers in search of the elusive Congo Peafowl.

'What do you really want, Rand?' Diemond said and the temperature in the yurt suddenly dropped. 'You're acting all weird.'

'Weird? M-me?'

'Stay for some champagne.' Diemond gestured at the bottle of Moët and Chandon resting in an ice bucket.

As soon as she saw the bottle, gleeful thoughts of revenge blossomed in Jo's mind. She knew exactly what she had to do.

'N-no, thank you,' Rand said.

Jo gently lowered the guitar to the floor under the bed, and reached into her back pocket.

'Just one glass, nothing kinky,' Diemond said. 'If you think I'll take you back you're very much mistaken.'

Jo pulled out the colonic cleanse sachet.

'I know,' Rand said. 'I just wanted you to know that all the bad vibes are behind us. That's all.'

'Whatever, Romeo,' Diemond sneered. 'I never go back, darling. You know that. But for you... I might make an exception.'

Jo quietly tore open a corner of the sachet, fashioning it into a spout.

'Can't we just be friends?' Rand took Diemond's hands. Ricardo was still busy, his head buried in the clothes rack. It was now or never.

'Friends?' Diemond asked. 'With... benefits?'

Jo rolled from under the bed, moved in a crouch to the open champagne bottle, raised the open sachet to empty the contents into the bottle... and she froze.

Ricardo was looking straight at her.

Jo's blood turned ice cold. There was no way she could even begin to explain this away. This was it. Game over.

Without a sound, Ricardo strode straight to her and took the sachet from her frozen hand.

With a twitch of his head, he gestured for her to return under the bed.

Jo did so without hesitation, and she watched as Ricardo poured the entire sachet of colon cleanse into the champagne.

'I don't know, Die,' Rand said, backing away now that Jo's job was done. 'Y'know, I think I should go now.'

'No, no, stay,' Diemond insisted. 'Ricardo. Champagne. Oh, you're there, good,' Diemond said, partly impressed that Ricardo was already by the Champagne. 'What are you waiting for? Pour, fucknut.'

'Yes, ma'am.'

Diemond turned to Rand, 'You're having some, too. I won't take no for an answer.'

Jo couldn't see Rand from her vantage point under the bed, so she could only imagine the look on his face. He knew what was in that champagne now. He knew what would happen if he drank so much as a drop of it.

'There's, uh, only one glass,' Rand said, his voice tremulous.

'That's fine.' There was a clink as Diemond poured the Champagne. 'You have the glass. I'll have the bottle. Bottoms up.'

Jo wasn't a praying person, but she gave thanks to any deity that might be listening for Rand's sacrifice as he sipped the Champagne. Diemond glugged the bottle, downing about a third of it.

'I... I really should go now.' Rand began backing away.

'I won't hear of it.' Diemond gripped his hand. 'I never get nervous before a show, you know that, but sometimes... I need a little something to invigorate me.' She grabbed Rand and hurled him on the bed. 'Ricardo, skidaddle,' Diemond ordered. 'I need a little me and Rand time.'

Ricardo, who had finally found the Congo Peafowl head-dress, hurried from the yurt with it still in his hands. Jo flattened herself on the floor beneath the bed, hoping that it wouldn't collapse on her.

'Remember Lake Como?' Diemond's voice purred. 'I'm gonna milk you dry, little man. You and me are—' The last words were strained as Diemond doubled over.

'Uh, Die?' Rand did his best to make his concern sound genuine. 'You okay?'

'What's happening?' Diemond clutched her belly, her knees gave way. A tragic squeak came from her backside. 'Oh, Jesus, no. *Ricardo!* Ricardo, where the hell are you? I need you!'

'Ma'am?' Ricardo hurried back into the yurt, also feigning concern. 'Ma'am, you okay?'

'I got the Hershey squirts.' Diemond's voice quivered like a weightlifter straining for a world record. 'Gemme to a john, now. I can't hold this in much longer.'

'This way.'

Jo peeked from under the bed as Ricardo bustled Diemond from the yurt. Rand was still prone on the bed as Jo clambered out of her hiding place. 'Rand, I am so sorry.'

'It's okay.' He remained immobile on the bed, his belly gurgling. 'I'm gonna need a little time... lying here... not moving. I... I can't go on, Yohanna. If I do, I... It'll get real messy. I just need to lay here, see this through and afterwards I'll see if there are any clean clothes on that rack that fit me.'

'I'm sorry I have to leave you, Rand.'

'Go, please, go. You don't want to see me like this. Go see your daughter, save Yohanna. Here.' Rand unfastened the prism from its necklace. 'Take this. Tell Aaronovitch I want it back.'

'I will, I promise.'

'A shame,' Rand said. 'I really wanted to see if my Dad was right.'

'You still can.'

Rand shook his head, 'There's no way I'm leaving this yurt with any kind of dignity.'

'I'm sorry, I'm so sorry.' Jo kissed him the forehead. 'Bye, Rand,' and fled the yurt, smiling at the puzzled security guard as he continued his patrol. He had been ordered to look for people sneaking in. No one had said anything about people coming out.

THE NOISE outside of the yurt was incredible. A band was coming to the end of their set on the Pyramid Stage, accompanied by the frenzied appreciation of the hundreds of thousands of music fans in the field. Jo could barely hear her own heartbeat as it pounded in her ears. She knew exactly where to go. There was a row of portable loos behind the luxury yurts and Diemond would be in one of them. She found Ricardo leaning against the last one in the row, fanning himself with the Congo Peafowl head-dress. Diemond's voice wailed wordlessly from inside. He beckoned Jo closer when he saw her. They spoke as low as they could with the onstage racket drowning everything else out.

'Thank you,' Jo said.

'No, thank you,' Ricardo replied, the haunted look of exhaustion in his eyes. 'She never used to be like this, y'know. She was like a mother to me. It was all about the music once. But we created a monster, constantly feeding it with its own shit. I grew up on a farm. You know what happens when you feed animals their own shit? It never ends well.'

'I can't let her out again, not till I'm done on stage,' Jo said, 'You know what I have to do?'

'Do it.'

Jo rushed to the loo that she'd been hiding by earlier, unwrapping the 'Out Of Service: Do Not Use' tape from it, then, running laps around Diemond's loo, she wrapped it tight, tying it in a double knot. The door was sealed shut.

'Think that'll keep her in there for long enough?'

'I can do better than that,' Ricardo winked. 'Oh, boys!' he cried, and two men in hi-viz jackets hopped out of the cabin of a Turdis truck. 'This is John and Joe. Die was rather rude to them earlier today, wasn't she, boys?'

'She called me a dickless eunuch,' John said, pouting like a scolded schoolboy. 'We were trying to help her with a faulty loo. That's no way to talk to people working with effluent.'

'And she told me I must like working with turds, as everyone needs something to aspire to,' Joe said, his head hung low. 'There was no need for that. There are some blockages that just can't be fixed,' he added, enigmatically.

'See? She makes enemies wherever she goes.' Ricardo stood back as John and Joe moved a crane hook into position over Diemond's loo. They attached the hook to the loo. 'Take it away, boys.'

The crane hoisted the loo into the air, Diemond's groans of pain now becoming confused cries of anguish as it swung about.

'What's happening? Oh, god, it's getting everywhere. Oh, my god, oh Jesus Christ!' Diemond's shrill voice became lost in the white noise of the band and the crowd as she was lowered onto the Turdis truck.

'Where will they take her?' Jo asked, unsure if she wanted to know the answer.

'I'll book her into rehab. Six weeks of clean living should bring her back to me.'

'Won't she hate you for this?'

'To start with, yeah,' Ricardo sighed as the truck pulled away, taking Diemond's screams with it. 'I'll bring her round, don't worry. It's always boom and bust with Diana.' He sniffed the air and looked Jo up and down, 'Eww. We need to get you in the shower, honey.'

'There's no time,' Jo said. 'I need to get on stage.'

'Oh, I can get you onstage.' Ricardo stopped fanning himself with Diemond's Congo Peafowl head-dress, and wrapped it around Jo's head. 'Ready to dazzle Glastonbury?'

BLINDED BY THE LIGHT

'What the hell is that?' Ellie backed away from the rainbow light that snaked from her mother into the elliptical hole in the universe. It wasn't easy to look at. Bright as the sun, but shifting like the first flashes of a migraine in the corner of her eye - its edges dark as a blacklight, as if it didn't want to be seen by human eyes.

Aaronovitch was jubilant. 'I believe it's nothing less than a gateway between alternate realities and—'

'It's how you get your mother back.' Federica cut him off. The last thing the girl needed was a lecture on the mysteries of the universe. 'We think that if we can place her body in that opening, then your mother will return. I know it sounds insane, and I thought it was too, but you have to trust us.'

'Get away, you bovine idiot.' Aaronovitch hobbled out of the way of a curious cow as it approached the opening. 'Shoo, shoo!'

Ignoring Aaronovitch, the cow stepped into the light and, with a blinding flash, it was gone. The light remained, but the cow had vanished.

'It worked. It actually worked.' Even Aaronovitch was unable to believe what he was seeing.

'W-what happened?' Ellie's voice trembled. 'What happened to the cow?'

'It's gone through,' Aaronovitch declared.

'To where?'

'No idea,' he shrugged.

Ellie rushed back to her mother, and with every ounce of her strength pulled her further away from the light. 'Mental, completely mental.'

'No, it's fine,' Aaronovitch insisted. 'It's supposed to do that.'

As Aaronovitch chased after Ellie, Federica approached the light. 'What happens if one of us steps through?'

'That would be a monumentally bad idea,' he told her. 'Without a kindred spirit on the other side, there's no telling where you would end up.'

Federica closed her eyes, raised her arms to shoulder height, and breathed deeply. The energy emanating from the light felt remarkably familiar. Whenever Federica held a seance, she would be able to sense the presence of what she'd always thought were the spirits of the departed. Now she began to wonder if they were simply the echoes of people like Jo and Yohanna, where one reality brushed up against another. The energy was uncanny. The same overwhelming feeling of emotion when you suddenly remembered someone you loved. Beyond the light were an infinite number of worlds, that was true, but there was something missing.

'She's not there,' Federica said. 'Aaronovitch, it's just a big hole in the universe. Jo isn't there.'

'How do you know?'

'I knew it was her when she first came to me, and I would know her now. She's not... hold on, wait a second.'

'What?'

'Bah-luddy hell, it's her. She's here. Ellie! Bring that body back.'

SING

'He's who?'

'Said he was an old friend of Michael Eavis.'

'Did you check?'

'He's got a VIP wristband, and he looks like a weirdo, so I figured he was legit.'

'And what's he doing out there?'

'Checking the alignment of the ley lines, or something? Said he'd be five minutes.'

Mike sighed. Getting the Pyramid Stage manager job was supposed to be VIPs, celebs, roadies, and a ring of security to keep the liggers away. It was stressful, especially now they were on live TV, and people only ever seemed to notice when things went wrong. But this was Mike's dream gig after years on the college circuit and the smaller Glastonbury stages. He'd earned this, and the last thing he needed was some corduroy druid prancing around the stage with a dowsing rod, getting in the way of the roadies hooking up the next act's gear. Changeover between sets was chaos at the best of times, even without a rogue hippy.

'Get him off!' Mike told his assistant.

'But, look...' Keith, assistant stage manager, had never worked with Mike before, so he trod carefully. 'Look at the crowd. They love him.'

Keith wasn't wrong. The first fifty rows were mimicking the balding man's head down shimmy and the crafty sod was enjoying the attention, grinning as he shuffled back and forth.

The heavens opened again. Cheers turned to groans, and chants of 'Die, Die, Die!' were accompanied by slow claps. The crowd wanted their superstar, and she was late. Mike had been warned about the diva in great detail at their briefing. She would be demanding, she would be abusive, and she would definitely be late. Five minutes was standard, ten minutes he could tolerate, but she was now over twenty minutes late. Her band was milling about in the wings, her manager was absent, and Mike's blood began to boil.

Someone in the crowd threw a bottle at the balding guy on the stage and it smashed by his feet. That's when Mike noticed that the weirdo was moving the mic stand from its mark to another spot a few inches downstage. Enough was enough.

'Just get him off my bloody stage, will you?' Mike told Keith, then barked into his radio. 'Tony, where the fuck is Diemond? The natives are getting restless, over.'

Just when Mike's day couldn't get any worse, a cow appeared on the stage.

AARONOVITCH HAD JUST GOT the mic stand where he needed it when he felt the universe around him begin to vibrate. He jumped back just as a dazzling flash of rainbow light burst into existence before him, and a black and white dairy cow stepped through from the other side and ambled onto the stage.

It trod on Aaronovitch's foot, and he saw another bright light, but this time it was a flash of excruciating pain as his big toe broke. Wailing in agony, Aaronovitch dropped his dowsing rod and hopped in circles.

The glowing opening in the universe disappeared in a spiral, and the crowd went wild, impressed with what they thought was an incredible light and effects show. The cow loomed large on the jumbotron screens on the side of the stage. She took it all in her stride, staring back at the crowd, chewing cud, raising her tail and leaving a cowpat by the drum riser. Several festival security personnel rushed on to shove the cow off stage left, but she wasn't having any of it, mooing in protest.

'Are you in pain, sir?' A kindly St John's Ambulance nurse took the crook of Aaronovitch's arm and led him away from the chaos. 'Where does it hurt?'

'Right foot, big toe,' Aaronovitch winced. 'Bloody cow. What the hell is a cow doing on stage?'

'This is Glastonbury, sir.' The nurse wrapped Aaronovitch's arm around her shoulders, taking the weight. 'I've seen stuff here that I'll never be able to explain. Come and rest off the stage. What's your name, sir?'

'I... I...' Aaronovitch stammered and looked into the middle distance with a baffled expression.

'Sir, are you okay? Are you with me?'

'Can you see that, too?' Aaronovitch nodded towards the wings. 'Some sort of peacock-human hybrid.'

'I think it's just the next act, sir.'

'Thank Christ, I thought I was hallucinating. The cow I could believe, but this...'

Diemond stood in the wings, wearing glittering wellington boots, an outrageous Moulin Rouge outfit, and a head-dress topped with enough feathers to keep a pillow factory going for a week. They formed a mane around her face, obscuring her features, but it could only be her. Aaronovitch began to wonder where Jo was, but he saw the diva had a familiar three-quarter length Martin guitar. Aaronovitch wriggled free of the nurse's hold. 'A moment, please.'

'Sir, come back.'

Aaronovitch hopped away from the nurse towards the singer in the wings, but the security guards intercepted him, gripping his arms and steering him away.

'Is that you?' he cried as he was dragged away.

The singer raised her hand and beckoned Aaronovitch closer. The guards hesitantly released their grip on Aaronovitch, who hopped over to her and gently brushed aside the feathered mane to find Jo looking meek inside. 'It is you, it *is* you!'

'Shh!' Jo hissed.

'Yes, yes, of course,' he whispered back. 'I've placed the microphone stand exactly where you need to be. That's it, that's the convergence. The sun is setting. You're nearly home.'

'The rainbow light's gone, Ronnie.' Jo gestured at the spot by the mic where the cow had made her spectacular entrance. 'Where's it gone? Will it come back?'

'Err...'

'*Err?*' Jo mimicked with a shake of her head that sent her feathers dancing and rippling. 'You've got to do better than *err*, Ronnie. And how are we supposed to do anything with a cow on the stage?'

'Ah, the cow is a good sign,' Aaronovitch said. 'It suggests that something is coming through.'

Terrified shouts came from the stage. Aaronovitch looked over his shoulder to see the cow beginning to glow like a child's night light. The security team ran from it, shielding their eyes, just as the cow rose into the air to head height, then was vaporised in a blast of rainbow light. The crowd went crazy. They didn't know what any of it meant, but they were loving it.

'Ronnie.' Jo's eyes were fixed on the spot where the cow had just been. 'What the fuck just happened?

Aaronovitch made a noise like a door creaking as he assembled his conclusion, 'I'm sure it's nothing to worry about. Get on the spot by the microphone stand and you should make a connection as the sun sets. Just... just be cautious. Wait until you get some kind of sign before you step through.'

'What sort of sign?'

'Something that connects you with your other you.'

'Thanks, Ronnie. Could you be any vaguer?'

'You have the prism?' Aaronovitch asked, and Jo fished it out of her costume. 'Good. Use it.'

'How?'

'It will show the way. Make a connection.' Aaronovitch brought his hands together in prayer. 'Good luck.'

Mike bellowed over everyone else as he struggled to reclaim control of the situation. 'Right, people, I don't know what the hell just happened, but can we get back on track here? Talent on standby, please. Lights and sound, are we good?'

Jo could only hear the blood rushing in her ears, and her heart threatening to break out of her chest.

This was it.

This was her moment.

She was standing on the edge of the precipice. A moment of pure reality as her skin tingled, her hair stood on end, and her lips trembled.

The band rushed by her and waved to the roaring crowd as they took their positions behind keyboards, guitars and drums. They began to play one of Diemond's hits.

This was it.

Jo took a breath, and strode out onto the stage on legs of jelly.

She hadn't thought the noise from the crowd could get any louder, but it surged like a rocket's engines on lift-off when the fans saw their favourite diva appear in such an incredible outfit. Despite the rain, all of Glastonbury was here chanting, 'Die! Die! Die!' in an escalating frenzy. Jo kept her head down, her face hidden by the mane of feathers. She didn't wave, or acknowledge them in any way. She felt enough of a fraud as it was.

Jo was surprised by how high up the stage was. The heat from the lights brushed her skin like a sunbed. The view was stunning. A sea of soaked, cagoule-wearing, smiling faces. Over a hundred and fifty thousand of them looking at her with high expectations. She couldn't see where it ended, and the reality of her situation hit her with a cold flush down her spine.

This was it.

Her childhood dream come true.

Flushed with adrenaline, everything became hyper-real, and she embraced the energy. Jo felt both invincible and more vulnerable than ever.

The band had played the eight-bar intro to this song three times now, and out of the corner of her eye Jo was aware of them shifting nervously as they went around again. In the front rows of the crowd, Jo could see the confused faces of the fans, 'C'mon, Die!' someone cried. 'Get on with it!' shouted another, followed by the inevitable, 'Get your tits out!'

Some of the crowd were booing now, the band's playing was faltering.

Jo turned to the band and waved them into silence, shaking her head. They shared confused looks. The guitarist approached her to find out what the hell was going on, but Jo kept him away with a raised hand, before turning back to the mic stand and the crowd.

They were more than confused now. The boos were becoming more and more aggressive.

'Make a connection,' she muttered to herself under her breath. 'Make a connection.' She began to idly strum the guitar. It wasn't plugged into an amp, so no one but Jo could hear it, but she knew the song well.

This was it.

The moment she'd always dreamed of.

And it was a complete fucking disaster.

LAWRIE HURRIED to find a vantage spot in the wings. Word had gone round that Diemond had finally lost it. Or had she? There was something familiar about the way the singer stood, something very familiar about the three-quarter sized guitar she had around her neck. A dread realisation set in.

'Oh, shitting Nora.'

'Make room, please, sir,' a St John Ambulance nurse asked Lawrie as she helped a balding man navigate the astonished onlookers in the wings. Lawrie recognised him immediately.

'You mad bastard.' Lawrie grabbed Aaronovitch by the lapels, wrenching him from the grip of the nurse. 'I warned her about you, but she wouldn't listen. You put stupid bloody ideas in her head and this is what happens.'

'I'm trying to help her, sir.' Aaronovitch shoved Lawrie back. 'It's you who has poisoned her mind, sending her fleeing in a double-decker bus and starting this entire episode.'

'Gentlemen, please.' The nurse put herself between the two men, but they continued to flap their hands at each other like kids in a playground scrap.

'You've ruined her.' Lawrie jabbed an accusing finger at Aaronovitch. 'She'll never work again after this.'

'On the contrary, this will be her finest moment,' Aaronovitch cried. 'She just needs a little more time.'

'Hey!' Rand had arrived in a clean pair of trousers, bringing his big California smile with him. 'How's it going?'

Lawrie's pallid face told the American all he needed to know.

'That's it,' the stage manager bellowed. 'I'm pulling the plug. Drop the sound and the lights now.'

'No, you bloody don't.' Lawrie shoved Mike the stage manager aside, and snapped his fingers at Keith. 'Get a mic on her guitar now.'

Keith's head jerked left and right as each man yelled at him.

'Don't you dare,' Mike growled.

'Do it now,' Lawrie ordered.

'Keith, I'm warning you.'

'Pull her off now and the crowd will riot and you'll both be to blame,' Lawrie said.

'I don't know what to do!' Keith yelped.

'Listen to me.' Lawrie gripped both men on the shoulder. 'That isn't Diemond out there. It's a girl who is a better singer and songwriter than anyone I've met in the last ten years. I've put every waking minute of the last year into making her a star. I've re-mortgaged my house, I've called in every favour, I've put my credibility on the line again and again because I reckon she's got something. I reckon she's special, and I am asking you, I am *begging* you, to give her a few minutes to prove herself. Please.'

Mike's face softened.

He looked to Keith.

Then back to Lawrie.

'Sorry. My stage. My rules. Get her off.'

Lawrie shoved Mike to one side and dashed across the stage.

'Stop him!' Mike cried, and a pair of security guards rushed forwards, but found themselves falling flat on their faces.

'I'm most terribly sorry, please allow me to... whoa.' Aaronovitch stooped to help, but accidentally-on-purpose flopped on top of them, pinning them down. Lawrie scurried across the stage, scooping up a cable and microphone, which he attached to the mic stand at the height of her guitar's sound hole. He gave a thumbs-up and the sound of Jo's three-quarter sized Martin acoustic drifted across the festival crowd, who whooped in appreciation, happy to hear something resembling music at last.

'Lawrie?' Jo gasped, her voice booming over the PA. She winced and turned her vocal mic away from her. 'Thank you,' she whispered.

'Do me a favour,' he said. 'Take all that peacock bollocks off. If you're gonna do this, then show them who you are. Be yourself.'

'You reckon?'

'If you don't take it off, then I will.'

Jo smiled. 'What have I told you about dressing me, Lawrie?' She reached up, took the peacock feather head-dress off her head with a flourish, and shook her frizzy hair free.

The shrieks of sheer astonishment from the crowd were louder than any band. Diemond's fans began to boo, but the rest of the crowd knew that something strange and extraordinary was happening. Some busker had somehow blagged her way onto the Pyramid Stage on the last night of the festival.

A trio of burly security men marched across the stage towards the singer, but backed away again when the glowing rainbow light returned, circling above her head. Lawrie scurried to safety, too. The crowd was silenced. They had all seen what happened to the cow.

This was it.

This was Jo's moment. And there was only one song she wanted to sing.

Lawrie and Aaronovitch looked on from the wings as she turned her vocal mic back to face her, and strummed the guitar.

'Come on, girl, you can do it,' Lawrie said, clenching his fists.

Jo came to the first verse, took a breath, stepped up to the mic, 'Huck...'

'Oh, for fuck's sake.' Lawrie buried his head in his hands.

JO STEPPED BACK from the mic, cleared her throat with a drawn-out cough that sounded like a stalled car engine. 'Sorry about this,' she told the crowd. 'I always dreamed of coming here and doing this, but, y'know, not like this. This is bloody ridiculous, and I have this mental block when it comes to this song. But I'm going to do it anyway. I'm going to sing for my beautiful daughter. I'm going to sing for Ellie in the hope that she might hear me, wherever she might be. I love you, Ellie. And, at the risk of sounding all wanky like Bono, don't die with your music still inside you.'

No one in the crowd seemed to be listening, the booing was relentless. Jo took a deep breath and sang it anyway.

The words came. Her voice was croaky and weak, but she was singing, she was actually singing *Ellie's Song*.

The crowd's booing intensified, drowning out her voice.

VOICES IN THE SKY

'Do you hear that?' Federica pulled Ellie towards where the light pulsated in the air under the Pyramid Stage. Ellie resisted. The sun was below the horizon, and she didn't fancy dragging her mother's body across a field in the pitch darkness. 'Listen,' Federica insisted.

'Let me go.' Ellie tried to shake herself free, but Federica's bony hands had an iron grip.

'That song,' Federica said. 'Do you hear it?' Federica inclined her head towards the light.

Ellie did the same.

That song.

That song was Mum's song.

It came drifting through the light, faint like an old radio signal. The voice was flat and wavered like the singer was drunk or something, but Ellie would have known that voice anywhere.

'Mum?'

Federica nodded.

Ellie lunged toward the light, but the little Italian woman put herself between Ellie and the light.

'Not you,' she told Ellie, gesturing to where her mother lay under the darkening sky. 'It has to be her.'

'Let the singer know you're here,' Aaronovitch said. 'If you can hear her, she might be able to hear you.'

'Mum!' Ellie yelled into the light. 'Mum, it's me!'

There was no response. Her Mum just kept singing, her voice getting weaker.

So Ellie joined in.

Feeling silly and self-conscious, Ellie avoided any eye contact with Federica and the old man, and sang the song that her mother had been singing to her since before she was born.

SONGBIRD

In all the years of the Glastonbury festival, no one had ever seen anything like it. It wasn't unusual for a crowd to be muted or express their disappointment, but the torrent of boos and bottles thrown at Jo was unprecedented. No one deserved this.

The pitter-patter of the rain intensified into a torrential down-pour. In moments it was absolutely lashing it down.

But she kept singing.

And a voice was singing the song with her.

Ellie.

It was Ellie.

It was distant and tinny, but it was her girl.

Jo's heart swelled, tears bloomed. She blinked them away and strummed the guitar with renewed vigour, her face blasted by stinging cold rain, singing stronger than ever before. Now that she had someone to sing along with, she'd found her voice again.

The bright light above her grew. As did the sound of Ellie's voice.

Jo's voice soared. This was the dream, this was what she loved. It didn't matter where she was singing - the Pyramid Stage, a karaoke bar, or in the shower at home. This was utter bliss. Jo threw her head back and hit the high notes effortlessly. The booing had stopped. The bottles had stopped. A stunned silence came over the crowd. She thought back to the karaoke night on her birthday, and the feeling she'd experienced then. It wasn't even close to this sensation of pure happiness. Jo's eyes were closed as she sang, so she didn't realise she was floating about a foot above the stage, drifting up towards the light.

She brought the song to its end.

Glastonbury went crazy. The news later reported that the roar could be heard in Dorset. All Jo knew was that it was deafening and overwhelming. She looked out over the ecstatic crowd, thousands of people tripping over themselves in the squelching mud, and, for one moment, every face out there was Ellie's.

THE RAIN SUBSIDED, the clouds parted and the sunset was revealed in a watercolour burst of blood red and indigo. The final beams from the sunset hit the prism and it began to glow around Jo's neck. Jo began to glow, too. A huge shaft of rainbow light burst upwards with an afterburner roar that split the air. It punched through the apex of the Pyramid Stage into the indigo sky. The ground began to rumble. The audience gasped in unison, witness to the most incredible light show ever. The whole stage shook. The fabric of the world peeled apart around Jo, and she stepped forward into the light.

MOTHER AND CHILD REUNION

L ight became darkness.

Jo stepped into a void. Ellie was nowhere to be seen. Jo's heart sank. This wasn't the right place. It couldn't be. Where was Ellie? Ahead of her, nothing but an eternal blackness. Behind her, the scene at Glastonbury was frozen in time, and the portal she'd stepped through was already shrinking.

The prism. The prism would show the way. The peacock feathers, corset and fishnet stockings were gone, as was Ziggy the guitar. She was dressed in her regular work clothes, exactly what she had been wearing when she encountered Yohanna in her kitchen a lifetime ago, but the prism was still around her neck, glowing like a lantern. She took the necklace off, turning in a circle, throwing a weak circle of light into the emptiness.

Nothing. No lights showing the way.

'Buggery-bollocks, Ronnie.' Jo broke the silence, reassured to hear the sound of her own voice. 'You said there would be... Oh, there you are.' Jo caught a glimpse of rainbow light through the prism. It was emanating from her belly once again, and snaked away from her into the darkness. She held up the prism and followed its beam. It rippled like a flag in a breeze and took a sharp turn. And that's when she saw them.

'Oh, god.'

Two figures sat entwined in the distance, the rainbow light casting long shadows behind them. Jo ran to them, and she recognised Yohanna in her crop top and faded jeans. The girl lay asleep in the lap of the other woman who gently stroked Yohanna's hair, toying with her frizzy curls. She was humming a tune, a gentle lullaby with a melody that Jo recognised.

Ellie's Song.

The woman sensed Jo's presence and looked up at her with kind, brown eyes.

'Oh, Mum.' Jo felt the unstoppable sorrow rise from within her. The woman she knew only from painful fragments of memory was here, in this place, with her now. Jo had dreams like this most weeks. Dreams where she longed for just a few minutes with her mother, where she could ask her all those questions that went unsaid. Now she couldn't think of a single thing to say as the overwhelming sensation of grief and happiness had her laughing and crying at the same time.

'Hello, Mummy,' she managed between the tears.

'Hello, sweetie,' her Mum said, reaching out to Jo. 'Come and give your Mum a hug, eh?'

Jo wiped the wetness from her face, and rushed forward to embrace her Mum. She sobbed into her shoulder, never wanting the moment to end. The warmth of her Mum's body, the sweet smell of her clothes, the soft touch of her skin, all unlocked a torrent of childhood memories. The pain of all her years as an orphan was released in one deep sigh.

'My girls,' Mum said. 'My lovely girls.' Mum hadn't aged a day. She was just how Jo remembered her. How Jo would always remember her.

'Come and sit next to us, poppet.' Mum patted a spot next to where Yohanna was lying. They huddled together.

'Where are we, Mum?' Jo asked.

'Does it matter?' Mum smiled. 'We're together and that's all that matters.'

Jo allowed herself to agree. The warmth and joy in just being with her mother was all she needed, and she wallowed in it, holding her Mum, taking in the spring scent of her hair, the soft touch of her hand. It felt so real, and Jo wanted to stay here forever.

Yohanna shifted in her mother's lap, moaning in her sleep.

Confused thoughts began to prick at Jo's conscience. 'Yohanna.' She nudged the younger her who still lay curled up like a cat. 'Hey, Yohanna. You okay?'

'She's tired,' Mum said. 'She needs a rest.'

'Mum?'

'Yes, sweetie?'

'Are you my Mum, or hers?'

Mum smiled. 'I'm yours,' she said, glancing down at Yohanna. 'Hers, too.'

Jo said nothing, but felt a creeping sense of unease. 'Seriously, what is this place, Mum?'

'I don't know,' Mum replied. 'I found myself here one day. I've been so lonely.'

'You've been here all this time?'

'It feels like yesterday.' Her Mum looked confused now, as if this thought hadn't occurred to her before. 'And it feels like a lifetime. But you girls are here with me now and that's all that matters. I've been calling to you since I got here, and you came. You came to me.' She squeezed Jo tightly. As she did, Yohanna shifted in her lap, groaning. Yohanna's face was as pale as candle wax, her breathing ragged.

'I don't think we're supposed to be here, Mum. She's not well.'

'She's fine.'

'Mum, look at me.' Jo took her mother's hands. 'Please, look at me. I'm older than you. Can you see that? That doesn't make sense, does it? I'm older than you when you... Do you remember what happened to you? What's the last thing you remember?'

Mum thought about it. And her face fell as her heart broke with the memory. She looked up into Jo's eyes, and in a half-whisper said, 'Mummy, Mummy, I forgot my dolly.'

Jo's breath left her, and tears came again as the guilt that had been locked away inside her for so long now returned. 'I'm sorry, Mum, I'm so sorry. It was all my fault,' she said over and over as her mother took her in her arms.

'No, no, no, silly Yo-Yo,' Mum said. 'Hush now. It wasn't your fault.'

'It was, Mum.' Jo squeezed her eyes shut, replaying that moment again and again.

Mummy, Mummy, I forgot my dolly.

'If I hadn't been so stupid, so selfish,' she said.

'No,' Mum said, her voice stern. 'I won't have it. You were a child. It was an accident. That's the end of it.'

The words were meant well, but they were just words. Jo's burning guilt still remained.

Jo glanced back over her shoulder. She couldn't be sure if the light she had stepped through had halved in size or was further away. Either way, she didn't have much time left.

'Mum, I have to help Yohanna,' Jo said. 'She's not well. She has to go back.'

'Stop being silly. Just hold me.'

'Sorry, Mum, but we have to go, we can't stay.'

'No.'

Jo gently moved her mother's hand from Yohanna's hair, 'Please, understand.'

'No.' Mum tightened her grip on Yohanna.

'Mum, why are you doing this? You're hurting her.'

'I need her, I need you both here with me.'

Jo was quick and forceful, pulling Yohanna free from her mother's grip.

'No, please don't take her,' Mum pleaded, rooted to the spot, unable to follow, reaching out to her girls.

Jo hefted Yohanna to her feet. 'I'm sorry, Mum.'

'She needs to be here with me.'

'This is hurting her, Mum. It's not fair.'

'I need her.'

Jo wished she could block her ears, but she needed both hands to carry Yohanna. She kept her eyes on the bright portal and kept moving, her heart breaking as she left her wailing mother behind in the dark. The rainbow light moved with Jo and Yohanna.

'Oh... hey.' Yohanna's eyes blinked open and she recognised Jo.

Jo smiled at her younger self. 'Remember me?'

'How could I forget? What happened to us? I... I was like a ghost, and then I was you.'

'And I was you,' Jo said. 'A proper rock star.'

'Was it real?' Yohanna seemed stronger already, still in Jo's embrace, but carrying herself on her own two feet now.

'As real as anything else these days.'

'Please. Don't leave me!' Their mother's voice cried in the darkness.

Jo tensed at the sound that followed, her mother howling in pain. 'Oh, Christ, I can't do this,' Jo said. 'I can't leave her alone.'

'That's not our mother,' Yohanna said. 'Have you spoken to her?'

'Yeah, she's so sad. It's breaking my heart.'

'Did she give you the *I forgot my dolly* bit?'

'Yeah, but—'

'Me too. She makes me feel bad, she takes every opportunity to remind me of what I did,' Yohanna said. 'Our mother would never do that. Think about it. What connects you and me?'

'The song. *Ellie's Song.*'

Yohanna shook her head. 'No, not the song. What connects us is the way we feel about *her*. Our mother. The guilt. That thing out there isn't our mother. It's the guilt that you and me feel about what happened.'

'But she looks like her, she even smells like her.'

'I know, and at first it was so wonderful,' Yohanna said. 'But that's your mind messing with you. Don't go back there.'

Jo hesitated, then nodded. 'Hey, we're here. Look.' Jo turned Yohanna to look at the sea of astonished faces in the fields of Glastonbury. They could hear their cheers playing on a repeating loop just a few seconds long. Time had frozen and was waiting for her to return.

'Holy shit, I'm playing Glastonbury?'

'Yeah, kind of,' Jo said. 'I hijacked Diemond's slot a bit, and she's going to want to kill you, but I'm pretty sure Lawrie will forgive you after what just happened.'

'What? What happened while I was gone?'

'Oh, not much, you'll catch up fast. Call it payback for dumping me in the driving seat of a bus about to go over a cliff.' Jo grinned. 'I've been walking in your shoes for a bit, and it's been... mental. Really crazy. It's fun and scary, but never forget that you're the one in control. It might not feel like it sometimes, but you are. Put Lawrie in his place more often, y'know?'

'Lawrie's a kitten. I can handle him.'

'Sure, just don't let him push you around... or dress you. God, that was weird.'

Yohanna chuckled. 'Yeah, that definitely has to stop.'

'You have the voice, the talent, and it's incredible, and it's going to be hard,' Jo told her. 'But if you want it, take it. Enjoy the ride.'

'Oh, I will,' Yohanna said with a wicked grin. 'I have plans.'

'Cool. Take this, and give it back to Rand.' Jo took the prism from around her neck, handed it to Yohanna, and turned her towards the portal. 'Go. Be amazing.'

'What about you? How do you get home?'

'Easy,' Jo reassured her. 'I'll be right behind you.'

'You're not going back there to that thing, are you?'

'No, no. Now go, hurry.'

Yohanna took a step, then turned to Jo. 'Hey, your kid really loves you, y'know. She's never given up on you. Not for a second.'

Jo's heart swelled. 'I know. Bye, Yohanna.'

'Bye, old lady.'

'Old? You cheeky bitch, I'm not—'

There was a flash of light and Yohanna was gone, leaving Jo in the darkness. She could hear her mother sobbing quietly.

'It's okay, Mum. I'm here now.'

Jo sat by her mother and gently brushed her hair.

ELLIE'S TEARS

Nothing. Ellie's singing had done absolutely nothing.

As the sun set, the light disappeared. No noise, no dramatic light show. It was like someone just flicked a switch.

Ellie wailed and fell to her knees by her mother's still body. Federica rushed to her side, holding her and speaking words of comfort, but all Ellie heard were muffled mumbles.

The knot in Ellie's stomach tightened. It had been eating her from the inside since she found Mum unconscious on the kitchen floor. A guilt worm burrowing through her, every bite telling Ellie she was to blame. She felt nauseous. Detached from the real world. The sound of Federica's voice faded away. Aaronovitch, slumped on the ground nearby, was nothing but a shadow.

The worm fed on one moment. One that Ellie had been reliving over and over.

Fuck you.

Ellie's last words to her mother.

'I'm sorry, I'm so sorry, Mum, this is all my fault.' Ellie's cheeks burned as she spoke. A mess of tears streamed down her face, and she succumbed to uncontrollable sobs as she said, 'I'm sorry,' again and again.

'Don't you dare blame yourself,' Federica's voice was distant. The words lost in Ellie's sorrow. 'This is not your fault.'

How could it not be? Everything started with that argument, and all the bitter words that had come before, each one chipping away at their love.

Federica pressed something into Ellie's palm.

'You dropped this,' the old woman said.

Ellie blinked away the tears to find the photo of her and her Mum at Climping Beach. Happier times. Smiles, sunshine and a simpler life.

Ellie dared to look long and hard at her mother's pale face. She was no longer breathing.

Ellie placed the photo in her mother's hand and kissed her cold forehead.

THERE IS A LIGHT THAT NEVER GOES OUT

'I have a daughter,' Jo told her mother. They were still entwined in a soft pool of light in the abyss, hands held tight.

Jo saw something lying in the darkness. It hadn't been there just a moment ago. She moved forward to pick it up, but her mother's grip tightened.

'It's okay, Mum. I'm not going anywhere.' Jo stretched to pick up a crumpled photo of her and Ellie at Climping Beach. She showed it to her mother.

'Oh, she's lovely,' Mum said. 'She looks just like you. What's she like?'

'She drives me mad,' Jo said with a smile. 'Actually, I drive her mad. We argue all the time. I don't know why. We argue because... I love her. I love her so much it actually causes me pain. And she needs me.'

'Aw, bless her, she's only little.'

'Oh, no, that photo was ages ago. She's eighteen now.'

They sat for a while. Neither one speaking.

'What are your arguments with Ellie about?' Mum eventually asked.

'Doesn't matter.'

'You're right,' Mum said. 'It doesn't matter. Life is too short for petty arguments and grudges.'

'If you let me go, then I'll apologise to her. First thing I'll do.'

'She doesn't want an apology,' Mum said, tipping her head knowingly. 'Does she, hmm? She wants her freedom.'

'How... how can you even know that? Oh, god.' Jo pressed her fingers to her forehead, then looked at her mother. 'You're not her, are you? Yohanna was right. You're not my mother. You're the part of me that hates myself for what happened.'

Jo's mother smiled kindly, 'I don't know what you mean, poppet. Oh, I've missed you so much.'

'And I've missed you, too.'

'We have so much to catch up on. I'm sure you have all sorts of questions for me. I'll answer them all.'

'I do have one question.'

'Go on.'

'Do you blame me for what happened?'

Jo's mother didn't answer.

'Was there a moment...?' Jo's voice began to break. She took a second to compose herself. 'Was there a moment, just before the bus hit, when you thought that stupid little girl just got me killed?'

Jo's mother looked away into the darkness, still smiling as if she hadn't heard the question.

'Okay. That's okay, I understand. I have to accept that. And I do, I really do. But, at the same time, I wasn't driving the bus, Mum. I was just a child. And you keeping me here won't change anything. It won't bring you back, it won't stop the hurt, and I have a daughter who needs me.'

'She's an adult now. You need to let Ellie be her own person, grow up and make her own mistakes.'

'I know,' Jo said. 'But I also want to be there for her when things go wrong.'

'You also want to be with me, don't you, poppet?'

Her question filled the emptiness around them. All her life, Jo had wanted more time with her mother and now she could have it. As much as she wanted.

'No,' Jo said. 'Not any more. We had our time. It was too short, but it was more than some people get, and it was full of love and happiness and I will always cherish it. I'm sorry, Mum, but it's over. We have to accept that.'

Her mother started to wail again.

'Mum, please, stop. It won't work.'

Mum trembled as she wiped her tears away, 'I'll be gone forever, you know?'

'I know.'

'Don't waste a single day,' her mother said. 'Life doesn't wait for your wounds to heal. It's fast and unfair.'

The pain and regret in her mother's eyes was too much to bear, and now Jo began to wonder if this really was her mother after all. Perhaps she would never know. Jo pulled her Mum closer and embraced her. 'I know, Mum. I know.' They held each other for some time. 'Okay, one more hug, and then I go.'

'Yes. Yes, please.' Mum squeezed her tighter.

When Jo opened her eyes, her mother was gone.

BREATHE

E llie felt a slight squeeze of her hand.
Jo's eyes fluttered open.
'Hello, pickle.'

FIRE!

Rand had seen some weird shit in his life, but what happened that day on the Pyramid Stage would stay with him forever.

As Yohanna ascended god-like into the air, there was a dazzling flash of light, all colours of the spectrum refracted, sweeping across the frenzied crowd. She disappeared for ten long seconds in which the world held its breath, and then she was back, landing on one knee like a superhero centre stage.

The beam of rainbow light still shone upwards, lighting the sky like a rainbow of Northern Lights. An intense heat was building. Everyone could feel it.

'Hey, Glastonbury,' Yohanna cried and the festival roared back at her. 'How about one more?'

She scooped up her guitar and began to play. Not *Ellie's Song*, but an up-tempo rocker that had hit written all over it. Festival crowds usually hated anything new, but after a few bars Yohanna had them pogo jumping like punk rockers. It was a song about being scared and running away, it was a song about love and it was a song about being brave and doing it anyway. It was Yohanna's life in three minutes. She ended with a fist raised in the air and the crowd went crazy. 'I am Yohanna and you are awesome!'

The rainbow light in the sky folded up into a single beam and shot back down the apex, and into the prism.

The heat was intense. Stage lights fizzed, sparks billowed onto the curtains in the wings, and flames licked into life, spreading across the backdrop in seconds. The Glastonbury crew leapt into action, some herding people to safety, others fighting the fire with extinguishers.

The watching crowd reached a fever pitch of excitement, still unsure if this was part of the show, but loving it anyway. Yohanna, wobbling on unsteady legs, waved at them, gripping the microphone.

'Thanks everyone,' she cried. 'See you next year!'

Cradling her guitar she dashed under fritzing sparks and bursting bulbs to the relative safety of the wings. Rand, Aaronovitch and Lawrie were still waiting for her, despite the stage manager yelling at them to move away from the spreading fire. She grinned like a drunk, the adrenaline still coursing through her system.

'Hey, the gang's all here. You've no idea of the kind of weird shit I've been through.'

'Don't care.' Lawrie hurried them off a stage that belched black smoke and bloomed with roiling orange flames. 'Move, move.'

They hurried down the stage steps, herded by festival staff to safety. The heavens opened again and began to douse the fire, but even from here the heat was so intense that it tanned their faces. People ran in every direction. Wet mud splashed up the back of Lawrie's shirt, and Aaronovitch squelched in puddles that shimmered with the reflection of the blaze.

Lawrie took off his jacket and covered Yohanna's head to conceal her identity as they dashed through the maze of yurts and backstage pandemonium.

'We need a motor,' he said. 'Mine's miles away. How did you lot get here?'

'Our car is in a sea of vehicles in a parking lot some distance that way,' Aaronovitch said, pointing east, before hesitating and turning west. 'Or perhaps... that way?'

'Hey, I got an idea. Wait there,' Rand said, racing off into the chaos.

'Where's that bloody fake action hero going?'

'So... How you been?' Yohanna asked as nonchalantly as possible as she dragged Lawrie and Aaronovitch between yurts. Their little refuge from the madness unfolding around them.

'I've had less interesting weeks,' Lawrie said. 'You've made some powerful enemies, but also made a Glastonbury debut that will be talked about for the rest of time.'

'And there was a great bit with a cow,' Aaronovitch added.

The ground rumbled again and the purple double-decker massage bus pulled up. Rand stuck his head out of the cab and revved the engine.

'Jump in.'

'What is it with you and buses?' Yohanna asked.

'Half the price of cocaine, and twice the fun,' he yelled over the Routemaster's rattle. 'C'mon, Let's go.'

'ROCK N'ROLL!' Yohanna whooped as the bus hit a final bump and skidded out of the backstage exit onto the dark country lane.

'Where in God's name did you learn to drive like that?' Aaronovitch asked, feeling queasy and desperate to wind down his window, but the high hedges lining the road whipped and scratched against the glass.

'I do all my own stunts.' Rand beamed at them as he accelerated round a sharp corner.

'*Look out!*' Yohanna cried, pointing ahead.

Rand mashed the brakes and wrestled with the wheel, dodging an oncoming Turdis truck as it rounded the bend, honking its horn in anger as it disappeared into the darkness.

'Are you taking the piss?' Yohanna yelled at Rand. 'The last thing I need is another bloody close encounter in a double-decker bus, thank you very much.'

'C'mon Yohanna, live a little.' Rand grinned like a movie star, steering them around a roundabout, accelerating as they sped onto the motorway.

Everyone took this as their cue to breathe easy once more.

'It's good to be back,' Yohanna said, nudging Lawrie. 'Hey, boss, we're gonna be rich.'

'Yo-Yo, after today's debacle I doubt any record company will touch us with a barge pole.'

'Record companies? You're living in the past, grandpa. Don't need 'em. Not when we've got em-pee-threes, digital music, streaming, merchandise rights, and a direct marketing relationship with our fanbase.'

'What the bloody hell are you on about?'

'The future, Lawrie,' Yohanna said. 'Our future.'

HAPPY

'Have you heard of a kind of music called Powerviolence?'

Ellie's question brought Jo back down to earth. She'd been daydreaming. It was over a month since she'd woken up in a field to find Ellie, Aunty Federica and an older Aaronovitch peering down at her - and so much of it felt like an unreal memory. It was only in Jo's daydreams that she was able to recall just how vivid it had all felt.

Ellie, Federica and Aaronovitch had all seen the strange light and the disappearing cow, but Ronnie had asked them to keep it to themselves, promising them all a percentage of the intellectual property rights, just as Nick arrived with the car to take Jo back to the hospital. As far as the real world was concerned, Jo had collapsed into a short, unexplained coma, and made a full recovery. Jo couldn't bring herself to tell anyone, not even Ellie, about her experiences on the other side. As time passed, even Jo was beginning to doubt if any of it had actually happened.

'Power-what?' she replied, pushing her thoughts aside to concentrate on Ellie. They had agreed to find time to be together, just the two of them, over tea and cake in a nice little café by the river.

'Powerviolence,' Ellie grinned.

'Is that the ungodly noise that I hear coming from your room?'

'It's music, mother dearest, music. Anyway, I've met these girls and we're going to reclaim Powerviolence and give it a feminist angle.'

'Okay. Cool.'

'You're sure you're okay with it?'

'Pickle, you're eighteen.' Jo rested her hand on Ellie's. 'I hereby officially stop trying to control your life and you are free to do your thing with your Powerviolence friends. Make wonderful music, reclaim it for feminism, do whatever you want. Just don't hurt anyone or set anything on fire and we're fine.'

'Awesome, thanks Mum.'

'What are you called?'

'The band?'

'Yeah.'

'Anal Beads.'

'That's... lovely.'

'Cos anal beads are—'

'Yes, yes, I know what they are, dear. I've been to Ann Summers parties.'

'Eww, Mum.'

'In my defence, you started it.'

'There's something else.' Ellie toyed with her tea cup, swishing the contents around as she bit her lip.

'What?'

'If we're going to be a band, then...' Ellie hesitated, holding her breath, before blurting, 'I'm moving in with the other girls in the band.'

'Wow,' Jo said. 'Okay, that's news. When?'

'Laura has a flat, and I said if we all live together we can write when we get the muse, y'know? Get material down quicker.'

'It was your idea?'

Ellie bit her lip again, pushing the tea cup away. 'Yeah. That okay?'

'That's brilliant,' Jo smiled.

'Really?'

'Yeah, really.' Jo felt a lump in her throat.

'You're not going to want to make some sarcastic comment about how it's all going to go tits up?'

'Well, obviously I *want* to...' Jo grinned. 'I'm proud of you, pickle.'

'Thanks, Mum.'

'What does Dad think?'

'I haven't told him yet,' Ellie shrugged. 'Thought I'd check with the rock star in the family first.'

'The rock star approves,' Jo smiled. 'But make sure he knows soon, pickle. You don't want him feeling left out.' Her separation from Nick was as amicable and grown up as anyone could ever hope, but she knew that something like this could rock the boat. Nick was settling in with Andy, Jo still had the house - though it looked like she might need to downsize if Ellie left - and everyone was satisfied.

'Mum, there's one more thing, and it's quite a biggie.'

'Yes, pickle.'

'Would you mind if, uh...' Ellie lowered her voice and glanced around. 'Would you mind if you stopped calling me pickle?'

Jo's heart sank a little. 'Actually, I would mind,' she said, choosing her words carefully. 'But... You're not a child anymore and I have to respect that. I can't promise I won't slip the odd 'pickle' into conversation on special occasions like Christmas and birthdays, but I'll do my best. How about that?'

'Thanks, Mum.' Ellie smiled as she took Jo's hand and gave it a little squeeze. 'Ah, yeah, nearly forgot.' She rummaged in her backpack, taking out a neatly wrapped present and handing it to her mother. 'Go on, open it.'

Jo carefully unwrapped the paper and found herself staring at the gift, unable to speak for fear she might cry.

'Is it okay?' Ellie sounded nervous, unsure of her Mum's reaction. 'I picked the frame out myself and asked the guy in the photo shop to remount it. I got the photo duplicated so I could have one to take with me.'

In the photo, Ellie and Jo smiled in a moment of happiness on

Climping Beach. 'It's beautiful.' Jo's voice was a teary whisper. 'Can't wait to see it in your new room.'

'Thought you'd like it.' Ellie smiled again.

'I do. I really do.' Jo wiped her eyes as her phone buzzed an alert. 'Oh, blimey, drink up. I'll be late for my gig.'

'King's Arms?'

'Open mic night, baby.'

'Nervous?'

'Absolutely pissing myself,' Jo laughed and Ellie joined her.

'You'll be fine. Want me to come?'

'No bloody chance. Last thing I need to see is you staring at me,' Jo said, experiencing a brief flashback to the moment on the Pyramid Stage when every face had briefly been Ellie's. The image stopped Jo in her tracks and she stared into space just a little too long for Ellie's comfort.

'Mum? You all right?'

'Hmm? Fine.'

'You're not... You've not had any funny turns since, have you?'

'No,' Jo said. 'Y'know what? I've never been happier.'

'IT'S GOING TO BE HUGE!'

Jo wasn't sure how Aaronovitch got her mobile number, but she was happy to hear from him. He had zero proof of what had happened in a field in Glastonbury that night, and he had completely failed to open the portal between universes again, but it was enough to spur a comeback. He was working on a novel based on their adventures and, from the sound of things, world domination.

'The book is coming along fantastically. My editor loves the outline, it's already fifty thousand words long, and they've sold the rights in three languages already. Oh, and I'm starting a podcast to promote it.'

'You always did love the sound of your own voice,' Jo said. 'I'll subscribe to it, but only if I can leave a snarky review on iTunes.'

'I want you as a special guest on the first episode, my dear.'

'Nice try, but no thanks.'

'I had to ask. Oh, and my agent's sold the film rights on just a two-page proposal,' he said. 'They say Harrison Ford might be interested.'

'Playing you?' Jo asked, trying to rein in her disbelief.

'Of course. Why the cynicism?'

'No. None. No cynicism,' Jo stammered. 'I just had you as more of a... Patrick Stewart, that's all.'

'Ooh, he's good,' Aaronovitch said. 'I'll add him to the 'maybes' list. And you won't change your mind about your anonymity? Fame and fortune await.'

'And that's where it can stay, thanks, Ronnie,' Jo said. He had kindly offered her a cut of the book's advance if she would reveal to the world that it was based on a true story, but the idea held no allure for her whatsoever. 'Listen, I have to go. Good luck with it all, and I'll see you at the Oscars, okay?'

Jo hung up, distracted by something she'd seen.

A familiar guitar in a music shop window. A battered Martin acoustic guitar. Three-quarter sized, with a sun-bleached spruce top, faded maple neck and steel strings. There were dinks and chips all around its poor body, and a scar running the length of its top, but it was beautiful.

And it was hers. It was Ziggy.

'Holy shit,' she whispered to herself. How could this be? This was impossible. Even Jo, whose sense of what was possible had been greatly expanded recently, couldn't figure it out. She had also learned that sometimes it paid not to ask too many questions and just accept a bit of good fortune. It was pricey, but Mayer Marketing had settled out of court for a very tidy sum for the viral video debacle, and Jo decided it was time to treat herself.

'You, baby, are coming with me.'

Jo pushed open the door of the music shop.

THE KING'S Arms had an open mic night every Tuesday. It was hardly the Pyramid Stage, but there was little chance of any cross-dimensional blowback here, and the audience was a friendly one. Michela was here with a few friends from Mayer, and so were Federica and her children. Jo saw Federica every weekend now, teaching the kids music and generally helping about the house. It was good to be part of that family again.

Jo played a short set. A bit of Joni Mitchell, Nick Drake, Cohen's *Hallelujah*, obviously, and a few other crowd-pleasers. But she had to end with one song in particular. *Ellie's Song* would be unknown to the audience, but now that Jo could sing it she was never going to stop. She finished to rapturous applause and a few whoops. Someone bought her a pint, and a few people asked if she was selling CDs. She told them no, but that she planned to be back next Tuesday, and returned to packing away her guitar.

'That was bloody brilliant.'

The voice made the hairs on the back of Jo's neck stand on end. Jo turned to find Lawrie, an older Lawrie wrapped in an ill-fitting suit, approaching her with a look of awe on his face. It was after closing, and the pub had been emptied, but somehow the ever-opportunistic manager had snuck in. 'Seriously, I've heard some amazing voices, darlin', and you've got it.'

'Thank you very much.' Jo clicked the guitar case shut, and noticed him squinting at her.

'Do I... do I know you? Have we met?'

'Not in this universe,' Jo smiled, neglecting to mention that wedding gig all those years ago. More recently though, he had probably seen her viral video.

'You sure?'

'I was in an early series of *Bake Off*,' Jo said, reciting the stock answer that she had concocted to ward off such awkward conversations. 'Voted off in the first round. My gateau collapsed.'

'You ever thought of recording that last song?'

'As a matter of fact,' Jo teased. 'No.'

'You should.' Lawrie puffed after Jo as she headed for the door. 'Look, do me a favour, take my card. Think about it. Give me a call. We could make millions.'

'No thanks.'

'Seriously love, I could make you a star.'

Jo's hand hesitated on the brass door handle. On the other side, Federica and the kids would be waiting for her. On this side was fortune and glory. Jo turned back to Lawrie.

'That's okay,' she said. 'I'm happy as I am, Lawrie. And that's all that matters.'

Jo stepped outside.

THE BESTSELLER EXPERIMENT

In October 2016, Mark Desvaux and Mark Stay began The Bestseller Experiment, a podcast where they set out to discover what makes a bestselling book while trying to write, publish and market one in just year. This novel is the result of that epic quest!

To find out more about the podcast (and for a free eBook) visit;
bestsellerexperiment.com/podcasts/

WANT TO WRITE A BOOK?

DREAMING OF A BESTSELLER?

Get your exclusive copy of the Writer's Vault of Gold, full of tips from the bestselling authors we have interviewed in our podcast - The Bestseller Experiment.

The Vault is packed with indispensable advice from writers who have collectively sold over 100 million books, including Michael Connelly, Joanne Harris and Martina Cole.

As used by The Two Marks to write this book (we are still working on the million sales bit!)

Download it now at bestsellerexperiment.com/vault

GLOSSARY FOR NON-BRITS

As we started to get feedback from our beta team it became clear that some of our overseas readers were perplexed by some of the peculiar British terms and references used by our characters. Here are some helpful pointers for those who want to know more...

Marks & Spencer and the Colin the Caterpillar Cake.

M&S has been on the British high street since 1884 and is a national institution. This chain store sells clothes, gifts and high quality foodstuffs, and is generally considered the best place to buy sensible underwear (Mr. Stay is particularly fond of their socks). The Colin the Caterpillar cake is a delightful birthday confection sold in their food stores. It's a chocolate sponge roll, dotted with chocolate beans, all shaped like a caterpillar featuring the eponymous Colin's smiling face at one end. It's simply too delicious to be confined to children's parties and has become the ironic birthday cake of choice for adult and office birthday celebrations, with such dubious luminaries as former Prime Minister David Cameron and we-hope-he-never-becomes-Prime-Minister Boris Johnson enjoying Colin's delights.

Waitrose

The Bentley of British supermarkets, and part of the John Lewis Partnership, which is renowned for its excellent customer service. Those with high expectations and a few quid to spare shop at Waitrose. James Bond probably gets his groceries at Waitrose.

Yonks

A word that confused a few of our beta readers. It means a very long time. 'That parcel took yonks to arrive.' It probably derives from the Cocky rhyming slang of 'Donkey's Ears' for 'years'.

The Duke of Edinburgh's Award

This is a youth awards programme begun in 1956 by Prince Philip, the Duke of Edinburgh. It's one of those things that looks great on a young person's resumé. The U.S. equivalent might be something like the Peace Corps, but the DofE has more hiking and camping in the pissing rain.

Barnet

A word used by Lawrie when looking aghast at Jo's hair. It's Cockney rhyming slang: Barnet Fair = hair. It's still commonly used amongst a certain kind of Londoner.

Nando's

A restaurant chain specialising in grilled chicken dishes made with piri piri (aka peri peri) sauces of increasing levels of heat. Going for "a cheeky Nando's" is considered the height of sophistication when you're fifteen. The chain started in South Africa, and has locations all over the world. However, there are currently only 40 restaurants in the United States. America, you have no idea what you're missing.

Fascinator

A decorative headpiece attached to the hair with a clip or a band. Diemond is a fan of them and we were inspired by the annual display of silly hats at the Ascot races (Google it).

Blag

Another UK word that confused some of our American readers. To blag is to scrounge or steal, but it's also commonly used in the vernacular when attending corporate events, 'I want to blag a couple of goodie bags!'

We use UK spellings throughout, ie: realise, not realize. We also use single speech marks, as is common in the UK and Commonwealth. From some of the feedback we've received these idiosyncrasies might appear strange to American readers. One day we might be able to release a full American edition, but there simply wasn't time in the run-up to publication to produce two distinct versions. However, the two Marks both grew up reading Stephen King and other great American authors and we enjoyed discovering the mysteries of American speech and culture within the pages of these books. So we suggest you blag yourselves a cheeky Nando's, grab a cuppa, followed by a Colin the Caterpillar cake, pop a fascinator on your barnet and enjoy.

Also, as declared by Ben Aaronovitch in episode 22 of the podcast, we write in the vernacular. If a character says something that's grammatically incorrect, that's because that's how people speak, innit...

ACKNOWLEDGMENTS

We wrote this teetering on the edge of disaster for a year. These people saved us from hurtling over the edge of oblivion in a fiery double-decker bus of doom...

Our editor Dave Nelson is not only a podcast guru and online genius, but also a calm and wise voice in all the chaos.

Our publicist Lisa Shakespeare believed in us before anyone else and never stopped.

Our editor Jenny Parrott made us better writers and our copy editor Sarah Palmer buffed us into shape.

Ricardo Fayet and the gang at Reedsy were a guiding light.

Cover designer Patrick Knowles bore the brunt of our testing tests and produced an incredible cover and many more that may never be seen.

Alisha Moore at Damonza for revamping the cover in 2019.

Thanks to Andy Bowden for the late night, last minute formatting magic.

Thanks to Peter Campling and Tim Hill for helping us with the technicalities of Routemaster Double-Decker buses.

Thanks to Andreza Tonello for putting us in touch with Moira

Murphy at Guy's Hospital who set us straight on what happens to patients in a coma.

And, of course, thank you to David, Julia and everyone at Literature and Latte, our podcast sponsors, for enabling us to stay on air for our first year, and for creating the incredible Scrivener.

A massive thank to each and every one of our guests. Your wisdom has inspired so many writers and will continue to do so...

Annie Stone, Ben Aaronovitch, Bryan Cranston, Callan Macauliffe, Darren Hardy, David Shelley, Deon Meyer, Elaine Egan, Emma Yorke, Erica James, Federica Leonardis, Grant Faulkner, Jennifer McMenemy, Jennifer Niven, Jo Ho, Joanna Penn, Joanne Harris, Joe Abercrombie, Joe Hill, John Connolly, John Yorke, Julianne Labrecque, Julie Cohen, Juliet Ewers, Karen Ball, Kate Harrison, Katherine May, Katie Seaman, Keith Mathieson, Laura Barnett, Lauren Woosey, Liz Fenwick, Lucy Vine, Marcus Gipps, Maria Semple, Mark Dawson, Mark Edwards, Mark Huckerby, Martina Cole, Michael Connelly, Michael R Miller, Michelle Paver, Nick Ostler, Paul Joseph, Robin Stevens, Sam Eades, Samantha King, Sara Mulryan, Sarah Pinborough, Shannon Mayer, Sonya Lalli, Stevie Finnegan, Susan Kaye Quinn, Vics Tranter, Virginia Woolstencroft

And a big thank you to all the publicists who found room for us in their very busy schedules.

To our regular Tweeters, Facebookers and Instagrammers - you've made us smile and inspired us when we were at low ebbs. Thank you!

And, finally, to our BXP team of Beta readers whose passion, forensic feedback and attention to detail have made this book as shiny as new boots!

Mark Stay would like to thank...

Dominic Currie, Chris Stay, Graeme Williams, Ed Wilson and Jon Wright for tea and sympathy.

Everyone at Orion for not making this weird.

And Claire, Emily and George for their eternal patience.

Mark Oliver (aka Mark Desvaux) would like to thank...

Jenni for your constant love and support. You are an angel in disguise.

Juliette, Luke and Sophia for inspiring me (and turning off Netflix when we were recording the podcast).

Shannon Mayer for being a beacon of light and showing me what is possible.

Everyone in my writing group for their guidance and encouragement.

The Arbutus TM crew for helping me speak proper.

All the teachers from primary school to the university of life and beyond.

Everyone who believes in the power of a dream.

ABOUT THE AUTHORS

UK-based author and screenwriter Mark Stay co-wrote the screenplay for Robot Overlords which became a movie with Sir Ben Kingsley and Gillian Anderson, and premiered at the 58th London Film Festival. He has also worked in bookselling and publishing for over twenty years, and now lives in Kent with his family and a trio of retired chickens. His debut fantasy novel The End of Magic is available now. He blogs and humblebrags over at markstaywrites.com

Fellow-Brit Mark Desvaux writes fiction as Mark Oliver. He also authors inspirational non-fiction and online courses, and is a professional speaker in the fields of self-development and spiritual growth. He is chairman and co-founder of the charity Foodshare. As a best-selling recording artist (Urban Myth Club), Mark's two critically-acclaimed albums have led to appearances at festivals such as Glastonbury (which he tries to mention on every podcast). He lives on Vancouver Island with his family, surrounded by the beautiful mountains and seas, with chickens, bees and very tall trees.